THE JESUITS IN NORTH AMERICA IN THE SEVENTEENTH CENTURY

Francis Parkman

THE JESUITS IN NORTH AMERICA IN THE SEVENTEENTH CENTURY

A Series of Historical Narratives.

Part Second

BIBLIOBAZAAR

THE JESUITS IN
NORTH AMERICA IN THE
SEVENTEENTH CENTURY

PREFACE.

Few passages of history are more striking than those which record the efforts of the earlier French Jesuits to convert the Indians. Full as they are of dramatic and philosophic interest, bearing strongly on the political destinies of America, and closely involved with the history of its native population, it is wonderful that they have been left so long in obscurity. While the infant colonies of England still clung feebly to the shores of the Atlantic, events deeply ominous to their future were in progress, unknown to them, in the very heart of the continent. It will be seen, in the sequel of this volume, that civil and religious liberty found strange allies in this Western World.

The sources of information concerning the early Jesuits of New France are very copious. During a period of forty years, the Superior of the Mission sent, every summer, long and detailed reports, embodying or accompanied by the reports of his subordinates, to the Provincial of the Order at Paris, where they were annually published, in duodecimo volumes, forming the remarkable series known as the Jesuit Relations. Though the productions of men of scholastic training, they are simple and often crude in style, as might be expected of narratives hastily written in Indian lodges or rude mission-houses in the forest, amid annoyances and interruptions of all kinds. In respect to the value of their contents, they are exceedingly unequal. Modest records of marvellous adventures and sacrifices, and vivid pictures of forest-life, alternate with prolix and monotonous details of the conversion of individual savages, and the praiseworthy deportment of some exemplary neophyte. With regard to the condition and character of the primitive inhabitants of North America, it is impossible to exaggerate their value as an authority. I should add, that the closest examination has left me no doubt that these missionaries wrote in perfect good faith, and that the Relations hold a high place as authentic and trustworthy historical documents. They are very scarce, and no complete collection of them exists in America. The entire series was, however, republished, in 1858, by the Canadian government, in three large octavo volumes.

[Both editions—the old and the new—are cited in the following pages. Where the reference is to the old edition, it is indicated by the name of the publisher (Cramoisy), appended to the citation, in brackets.

In extracts given in the notes, the antiquated orthography and accentuation are preserved.]

These form but a part of the surviving writings of the French-American Jesuits. Many additional reports, memoirs, journals, and letters, official and private, have come down to us; some of which have recently been printed, while others remain in manuscript. Nearly every prominent actor in the scenes to be described has left his own record of events in which he bore part, in the shape of reports to his Superiors or letters to his friends. I have studied and compared these authorities, as well as a great mass of collateral evidence, with more than usual care, striving to secure the greatest possible accuracy of statement, and to reproduce an image of the past with photographic clearness and truth.

The introductory chapter of the volume is independent of the rest; but a knowledge of the facts set forth in it is essential to the full understanding of the narrative which follows.

In the collection of material, I have received valuable aid from Mr. J. G. Shea, Rev. Felix Martin, S.J., the Abbés Laverdière and H. R. Casgrain, Dr. J. C. Taché, and the late Jacques Viger, Esq.

I propose to devote the next volume of this series to the discovery and occupation by the French of the Valley of the Mississippi.

BOSTON, 1st May, 1867.

CONTENTS

on his Rounds.—Efforts at Conversion.—Priests
and Sorcerers.—The Man-Devil.—The Magician's
Prescription.—Indian Doctors and Patients.—Covert
Baptisms.—Self-Devotion of the Jesuits.

of Saint Michael.—Return to Sainte Marie.—Intrepidity
of the Priests.—Their Mental Exaltation.

Sainte Marie.—Domestic Economy.—Missions.—A
Meeting of Jesuits.—The Dead Missionary.

1648. ANTOINE DANIEL.
Huron Traders.—Battle at Three Rivers.—St. Joseph.—
Onset of the Iroquois.—Death of Daniel.—The Town
destroyed.

1649. RUIN OF THE HURONS.
St. Louis on Fire.—Invasion.—St. Ignace captured.—
Brébeuf and Lalemant.—Battle at St. Louis.—Sainte
Marie threatened.—Renewed Fighting.—Desperate
Conflict.—A Night of Suspense.—Panic among the
Victors.—Burning of St. Ignace.—Retreat of the Iroquois.

1649. THE MARTYRS.
The Ruins of St. Ignace.—The Relics found.—Brébeuf at
the Stake.—His Unconquerable Fortitude.—Lalemant.—
Renegade Hurons.—Iroquois Atrocities.—Death of
Brébeuf.—His Character.—Death of Lalemant.

1649, 1650. THE SANCTUARY.
Dispersion of the Hurons.—Sainte Marie abandoned.—
Isle St. Joseph.—Removal of the Mission.—The New
Fort.—Misery of the Hurons.—Famine.—Epidemic.—
Employments of the Jesuits.

1649. GARNIER.—CHABANEL.
The Tobacco Missions.—St. Jean attacked.—Death of
Garnier.—The Journey of Chabanel.—His Death.—
Garreau and Grelon.

INTRODUCTION.

NATIVE TRIBES.

DIVISIONS.—THE ALGONQUINS.—THE HURONS.—
THEIR HOUSES.—FORTIFICATIONS.—HABITS.—ARTS.—
WOMEN.—TRADE.—FESTIVITIES.—MEDICINE.—
THE TOBACCO NATION.—THE NEUTRALS.—THE
ERIES.—THE ANDASTES.—THE IROQUOIS.—SOCIAL
AND POLITICAL ORGANIZATION.—IROQUOIS
INSTITUTIONS, CUSTOMS, AND CHARACTER.—INDIAN
RELIGION AND SUPERSTITIONS.—THE INDIAN MIND.

America, when it became known to Europeans, was, as
it had long been, a scene of wide-spread revolution. North and
South, tribe was giving place to tribe, language to language; for the
Indian, hopelessly unchanging in respect to individual and social
development, was, as regarded tribal relations and local haunts,
mutable as the wind. In Canada and the northern section of the
United States, the elements of change were especially active. The
Indian population which, in 1535, Cartier found at Montreal and
Quebec, had disappeared at the opening of the next century,
and another race had succeeded, in language and customs widely
different; while, in the region now forming the State of New York,
a power was rising to a ferocious vitality, which, but for the presence
of Europeans, would probably have subjected, absorbed, or
exterminated every other Indian community east of the Mississippi
and north of the Ohio.

The vast tract of wilderness from the Mississippi to the
Atlantic, and from the Carolinas to Hudson's Bay, was divided

between two great families of tribes, distinguished by a radical difference of language. A part of Virginia and of Pennsylvania, New Jersey, Southeastern New York, New England, New Brunswick, Nova Scotia, and Lower Canada were occupied, so far as occupied at all, by tribes speaking various Algonquin languages and dialects. They extended, moreover, along the shores of the Upper Lakes, and into the dreary Northern wastes beyond. They held Wisconsin, Michigan, Illinois, and Indiana, and detached bands ranged the lonely hunting-round of Kentucky.

[The word Algonquin is here used in its broadest signification. It was originally applied to a group of tribes north of the River St. Lawrence. The difference of language between the original Algonquins and the Abenaquis of New England, the Ojibwas of the Great Lakes, or the Illinois of the West, corresponded to the difference between French and Italian, or Italian and Spanish. Each of these languages, again, had its dialects, like those of different provinces of France.]

Like a great island in the midst of the Algonquins lay the country of tribes speaking the generic tongue of the Iroquois. The true Iroquois, or Five Nations, extended through Central New York, from the Hudson to the Genesee. Southward lay the Andastes, on and near the Susquehanna; westward, the Eries, along the southern shore of Lake Erie, and the Neutral Nation, along its northern shore from Niagara towards the Detroit; while the towns of the Hurons lay near the lake to which they have left their name.

[To the above general statements there was, in the first half of the seventeenth century, but one exception worth notice. A detached branch of the Dahcotah stock, the Winnebago, was established south of Green Bay, on Lake Michigan, in the midst of Algonquins; and small Dahcotah bands had also planted themselves on the eastern side of the Mississippi, nearly in the same latitude.

There was another branch of the Iroquois in the Carolinas, consisting of the Tuscaroras and kindred bands. In 1716 they were joined to the Five Nations.]

Of the Algonquin populations, the densest, despite a recent epidemic which had swept them off by thousands, was in New England. Here were Mohicans, Pequots, Narragansetts, Wampanoags, Massachusetts, Penacooks, thorns in the side of the Puritan. On the whole, these savages were favorable specimens of the Algonquin stock, belonging to that section of it which tilled the soil, and was thus in some measure spared the extremes of misery and degradation to which the wandering hunter tribes were often reduced. They owed much, also, to the bounty of the sea, and hence they tended towards the coast; which, before the epidemic, Champlain and Smith had seen at many points studded with wigwams and waving with harvests of maize. Fear, too, drove, them eastward; for the Iroquois pursued them with an inveterate enmity. Some paid yearly tribute to their tyrants, while others were still subject to their inroads, flying in terror at the sound of the Mohawk war-cry. Westward, the population thinned rapidly; northward, it soon disappeared. Northern New Hampshire, the whole of Vermont, and Western Massachusetts had no human tenants but the roving hunter or prowling warrior.

We have said that this group of tribes was relatively very populous; yet it is more than doubtful whether all of them united, had union been possible, could have mustered eight thousand fighting men. To speak further of them is needless, for they were not within the scope of the Jesuit labors. The heresy of heresies had planted itself among them; and it was for the apostle Eliot, not the Jesuit, to essay their conversion.

[These Indians, the Armouchiquois of the old French writers, were in a state of chronic war with the tribes of New Brunswick and Nova Scotia. Champlain, on his voyage of 1603, heard strange accounts of them. The following is literally rendered from the first narrative of that heroic, but credulous explorer.

"They are savages of shape altogether monstrous: for their heads are small, their bodies short, and their arms thin as a skeleton, as are also their thighs; but their legs are stout and long, and all of one size, and, when they are seated on their heels, their knees rise more than half a foot above their heads, which seems a thing strange and against Nature. Nevertheless, they are active and bold, and they have the best country on all the coast towards Acadia."— Des Sauvages, f. 84.

This story may match that of the great city of Norembega, on the Penobscot, with its population of dwarfs, as related by Jean Alphonse.]

Landing at Boston, three years before a solitude, let the traveller push northward, pass the River Piscataqua and the Penacooks, and cross the River Saco. Here, a change of dialect would indicate a different tribe, or group of tribes. These were the Abenaquis, found chiefly along the course of the Kennebec and other rivers, on whose banks they raised their rude harvests, and whose streams they ascended to hunt the moose and bear in the forest desert of Northern Maine, or descended to fish in the neighboring sea.

[The Tarratines of New-England writers were the Abenaquis, or a portion of them.]

Crossing the Penobscot, one found a visible descent in the scale of humanity. Eastern Maine and the whole of New Brunswick were occupied by a race called Etchemins, to whom agriculture was unknown, though the sea, prolific of fish, lobsters, and seals, greatly lightened their miseries. The Souriquois, or Micmacs, of Nova Scotia, closely resembled them in habits and condition. From Nova Scotia to the St. Lawrence, there was no population worthy of the name. From the Gulf of St. Lawrence to Lake Ontario, the southern border of the great river had no tenants but hunters. Northward, between the St. Lawrence and Hudson's Bay, roamed the scattered hordes of the Papinachois, Bersiamites, and others, included by the French under the general name of Montagnais. When, in spring, the French trading-ships arrived and anchored in the port of Tadoussac, they gathered from far and near, toiling painfully through the desolation of forests, mustering by hundreds at the point of traffic, and setting up their bark wigwams along the strand of that wild harbor. They were of the lowest Algonquin type. Their ordinary sustenance was derived from the chase; though often, goaded by deadly famine, they would subsist on roots, the bark and buds of trees, or the foulest offal; and in extremity, even cannibalism was not rare among them.

Ascending the St. Lawrence, it was seldom that the sight of a human form gave relief to the loneliness, until, at Quebec, the roar of Champlain's cannon from the verge of the cliff announced that the savage prologue of the American drama was drawing to a close, and that the civilization of Europe was advancing on the scene. Ascending farther, all was solitude, except at Three Rivers, a noted place of trade, where a few Algonquins of the tribe called Atticamegues might possibly be seen. The fear of the Iroquois was everywhere; and as the voyager passed some wooded point, or thicket-covered island, the whistling of a stone-headed arrow proclaimed, perhaps, the presence of these fierce marauders. At Montreal there was no human life, save during a brief space in early summer, when the shore swarmed with savages, who had come to the yearly trade from the great communities of the interior. To-day there were dances, songs, and feastings; to-morrow all again was solitude, and the Ottawa was covered with the canoes of the returning warriors.

Along this stream, a main route of traffic, the silence of the wilderness was broken only by the splash of the passing paddle. To the north of the river there was indeed a small Algonquin band, called *La Petite Nation*, together with one or two other feeble communities; but they dwelt far from the banks, through fear of the ubiquitous Iroquois. It was nearly three hundred miles, by the windings of the stream, before one reached that Algonquin tribe, *La Nation de l'Isle*, who occupied the great island of the Allumettes. Then, after many a day of lonely travel, the voyager found a savage welcome among the Nipissings, on the lake which bears their name; and then circling west and south for a hundred and fifty miles of solitude, he reached for the first time a people speaking a dialect of the Iroquois tongue. Here all was changed. Populous towns, rude fortifications, and an extensive, though barbarous tillage, indicated a people far in advance of the famished wanderers of the Saguenay, or their less abject kindred of New England. These were the Hurons, of whom the modern Wyandots are a remnant. Both in themselves and as a type of their generic stock they demand more than a passing notice.

[The usual confusion of Indian tribal names prevails in the case of the Hurons. The following are their synonymes:—

Hurons (of French origin); Ochateguins (Champlain); Attigouantans (the name of one of their tribes, used by Champlain for the whole nation); Ouendat (their true name, according to Lalemant); Yendat, Wyandot, Guyandot (corruptions of the preceding); Ouaouakecinatouek (Potier), Quatogies (Colden).]

THE HURONS.

More than two centuries have elapsed since the Hurons vanished from their ancient seats, and the settlers of this rude solitude stand perplexed and wondering over the relics of a lost people. In the damp shadow of what seems a virgin forest, the axe and plough bring strange secrets to light: huge pits, close packed with skeletons and disjointed bones, mixed with weapons, copper kettles, beads, and trinkets. Not even the straggling Algonquins, who linger about the scene of Huron prosperity, can tell their origin. Yet, on ancient worm-eaten pages, between covers of begrimed parchment, the daily life of this ruined community, its firesides, its festivals, its funeral rites, are painted with a minute and vivid fidelity.

The ancient country of the Hurons is now the northern and eastern portion of Simcoe County, Canada West, and is embraced within the peninsula formed by the Nottawassaga and Matchedash Bays of Lake Huron, the River Severn, and Lake Simcoe. Its area was small,—its population comparatively large. In the year 1639 the Jesuits made an enumeration of all its villages, dwellings, and families. The result showed thirty-two villages and hamlets, with seven hundred dwellings, about four thousand families, and twelve thousand adult persons, or a total population of at least twenty thousand.

[Lalemant, Relation des Hurons, 1640, 88 (Cramoisy). His words are, "de feux enuiron deux mille, et enuiron douze mille personnes." There were two families to every fire. That by "personnes" adults only are meant cannot be doubted, as the Relations abound in incidental evidence of a total population far exceeding twelve thousand. A Huron family usually numbered from five to eight persons. The number of the Huron towns changed from year to year. Champlain and Le Caron in 1615, reckoned them at seventeen or eighteen, with a population of about ten thousand, meaning, no doubt, adults. Brébeuf, in 1635, found twenty villages, and, as he thinks, thirty thousand souls. Both Le Mercier and De Quen, as well as Dollier de Casson and the anonymous author of the Relation of 1660, state the population at from thirty to thirty-five thousand. Since the time of Champlain's visit, various kindred tribes or fragments of tribes had been incorporated with the Hurons, thus more than balancing the ravages of a pestilence which had decimated them.]

The region whose boundaries we have given was an alternation of meadows and deep forests, interlaced with footpaths leading from town to town. Of these towns, some were fortified, but the greater number were open and defenceless. They were of a construction common to all tribes of Iroquois lineage, and peculiar to them. Nothing similar exists at the present day. [The permanent bark villages of the Dahcotah of the St. Peter's are the nearest modern approach to the Huron towns. The whole Huron country abounds with evidences of having been occupied by a numerous population. "On a close inspection of the forest," Dr. Taché writes to me, "the greatest part of it seems to have been cleared at former periods, and almost the only places bearing the character of the primitive forest are the low grounds."] They covered a space of from one to ten acres, the dwellings clustering together with little or no pretension to order. In general, these singular structures were about thirty or thirty-five feet in length, breadth, and height; but many were much larger, and a few were of prodigious length. In some of the villages there were dwellings two hundred and forty feet long, though in breadth and height they did not much exceed the others. [Brébeuf, Relation des Hurons, 1635, 31. Champlain says that he saw them, in 1615, more than thirty fathoms long; while Vanderdonck reports the length, from actual measurement, of an Iroquois house, at a hundred and eighty yards, or five hundred and forty feet!] In shape they were much like an arbor overarching a garden-walk. Their frame was of tall and strong saplings, planted in a double row to form the two sides of the house, bent till they met, and lashed together at the top. To these other poles were bound transversely, and the whole was covered with large sheets of the bark of the oak, elm, spruce, or white cedar, overlapping like the shingles of a roof, upon which, for their better security, split poles were made fast with cords of linden bark. At the crown of the arch, along the entire length of the house, an opening a foot wide was left for the admission of light and the escape of smoke. At each end was a close porch of similar construction; and here were stowed casks of bark, filled with smoked fish, Indian corn, and other stores not liable to injury from frost. Within, on both sides, were wide scaffolds, four feet from the floor, and extending the entire length of the house, like the seats of a colossal omnibus. [Often, especially among the Iroquois, the internal arrangement was different. The scaffolds or platforms were raised only a foot from the earthen floor, and were only twelve or thirteen feet long, with intervening spaces, where the occupants stored their family provisions and other articles. Five or six feet above was another platform, often occupied by children. One pair of platforms sufficed for a family, and here during summer they slept pellmell, in the clothes they wore by day, and without pillows.] These were formed of thick sheets of bark, supported by posts and transverse poles, and covered with mats and skins. Here, in summer, was the sleeping place of the inmates, and the space beneath served for storage of their firewood. The fires were on the ground, in a line down the middle of the house. Each sufficed for two families, who, in winter, slept closely packed around them. Above, just under the vaulted roof, were a great number of poles, like the perches of a hen-roost, and here were suspended weapons, clothing, skins, and ornaments. Here, too, in harvest time, the squaws hung the ears of unshelled corn, till the rude abode, through all its length, seemed decked with a golden tapestry. In general, however, its only lining was a thick coating of soot from the smoke of fires with neither draught, chimney, nor window. So pungent was the smoke, that it produced inflammation of the eyes, attended in old age with frequent blindness. Another annoyance was the fleas; and a third, the unbridled and unruly children. Privacy there was none. The house was one chamber, sometimes lodging more than twenty families.

[One of the best descriptions of the Huron and Iroquois houses is that of Sagard, Voyage des Hurons, 118. See also Champlain (1627), 78; Brébeuf, Relation des Hurons, 1635, 31; Vanderdonck, New Netherlands, in N. Y. Hist. Coll., Second Ser., I. 196; Lafitau, Mœurs des Sauvages, II. 10. The account given by Cartier of the houses he saw at Montreal corresponds with the above. He describes them as about fifty yards long. In this case, there were partial partitions for the several families, and a sort of loft above. Many of the Iroquois and Huron houses were of similar construction, the partitions being at the sides only, leaving a wide passage down the middle of the house. Bartram, Observations on a Journey from Pennsylvania to Canada, gives a description and plan of the Iroquois Council-House in 1751, which was of this construction. Indeed, the Iroquois preserved this mode of building, in all essential points, down to a recent period. They usually framed the sides of their houses on rows of upright posts, arched with separate poles for the roof. The Hurons, no doubt, did the same in their larger structures. For a door, there was a sheet of bark hung on wooden hinges, or suspended by cords from above.

On the site of Huron towns which were destroyed by fire, the size, shape, and arrangement of the houses can still, in some instances, be traced by remains in the form of charcoal, as well as by the charred bones and fragments of pottery found among the ashes.

Dr. Taché, after a zealous and minute examination of the Huron country, extended through five years, writes to me as follows. "From the remains I have found, I can vouch for the scrupulous correctness of our ancient writers. With the aid of their indications and descriptions, I have been able to detect the sites of villages in the midst of the forest, and by time study, in situ, of archæological monuments, small as they are, to understand and confirm their many interesting details of the habits, and especially the funeral rites, of these extraordinary tribes."]

He who entered on a winter night beheld a strange spectacle: the vista of fires lighting the smoky concave; the bronzed groups encircling each,—cooking, eating, gambling, or amusing themselves with idle badinage; shrivelled squaws, hideous with threescore years of hardship; grisly old warriors, scarred with Iroquois war-clubs; young aspirants, whose honors were yet to be won; damsels gay with ochre and wampum; restless children pellmell with restless dogs. Now a tongue of resinous flame painted each wild feature in vivid light; now the fitful gleam expired, and the group vanished from sight, as their nation has vanished from history.

The fortified towns of the Hurons were all on the side exposed to Iroquois incursions. The fortifications of all this family of tribes were, like their dwellings, in essential points alike. A situation was chosen favorable to defence,—the bank of a lake, the crown of a difficult hill, or a high point of land in the fork of confluent rivers. A ditch, several feet deep, was dug around the village, and the earth thrown up on the inside. Trees were then felled by an alternate process of burning and hacking the burnt part with stone hatchets, and by similar means were cut into lengths to form palisades. These were planted on the embankment, in one, two, three, or four concentric rows,—those of each row inclining towards those of the other rows until they intersected. The whole was lined within, to the height of a man, with heavy sheets of bark;

and at the top, where the palisades crossed, was a gallery of timber for the defenders, together with wooden gutters, by which streams of water could be poured down on fires kindled by the enemy. Magazines of stones, and rude ladders for mounting the rampart, completed the provision for defence. The forts of the Iroquois were stronger and more elaborate than those of the Hurons; and to this day large districts in New York are marked with frequent remains of their ditches and embankments.

[There is no mathematical regularity in these works. In their form, the builders were guided merely by the nature of the ground. Frequently a precipice or river sufficed for partial defence, and the line of embankment occurs only on one or two sides. In one instance, distinct traces of a double line of palisades are visible along the embankment. (See Squier, Aboriginal Monuments of New York, 38.) It is probable that the palisade was planted first, and the earth heaped around it. Indeed, this is stated by the Tuscarora Indian, Cusick, in his curious History of the Six Nations (Iroquois). Brébeuf says, that as early as 1636 the Jesuits taught the Hurons to build rectangular palisaded works, with bastions. The Iroquois adopted the same practice at an early period, omitting the ditch and embankment; and it is probable, that, even in their primitive defences, the palisades, where the ground was of a nature to yield easily to their rude implements, were planted simply in holes dug for the purpose. Such seems to have been the Iroquois fortress attacked by Champlain in 1615.

The Muscogees, with other Southern tribes, and occasionally the Algonquins, had palisaded towns; but the palisades were usually but a single row, planted upright. The tribes of Virginia occasionally surrounded their dwellings with a triple palisade.—Beverly, History of Virginia, 149.]

Among these tribes there was no individual ownership of land, but each family had for the time exclusive right to as much as it saw fit to cultivate. The clearing process—a most toilsome one—consisted in hacking off branches, piling them together with brushwood around the foot of the standing trunks, and setting fire to the whole. The squaws, working with their hoes of wood and bone among the charred stumps, sowed their corn, beans, pumpkins, tobacco, sunflowers, and Huron hemp. No manure was used; but, at intervals of from ten to thirty years, when the soil was exhausted, and firewood distant, the village was abandoned and a new one built.

There was little game in the Huron country; and here, as among the Iroquois, the staple of food was Indian corn, cooked without salt in a variety of forms, each more odious than the last. Venison was a luxury found only at feasts; dog-flesh was in high esteem; and, in some of the towns captive bears were fattened for festive occasions. These tribes were far less improvident than the roving Algonquins, and stores of provision were laid up against a season of want. Their main stock of corn was buried in *caches*, or deep holes in the earth, either within or without the houses.

In respect to the arts of life, all these stationary tribes were in advance of the wandering hunters of the North. The women made a species of earthen pot for cooking, but these were supplanted by the copper kettles of the French traders. They wove rush mats with no little skill. They spun twine from hemp, by the primitive process of rolling it on their thighs; and of this twine they made nets. They extracted oil from fish and from the seeds of the sunflower,— the latter, apparently, only for the purposes of the toilet. They pounded their maize in huge mortars of wood, hollowed by alternate burnings and scrapings. Their stone axes, spear and arrow heads, and bone fish-hooks, were fast giving place to the iron of the French; but they had not laid aside their shields of raw bison-hide, or of wood overlaid with plaited and twisted thongs of skin. They still used, too, their primitive breastplates and greaves of twigs interwoven with cordage. [Some of the northern tribes of California, at the present day, wear a sort of breastplate "composed of thin parallel battens of very tough wood, woven together with a small cord."] The masterpiece of Huron handiwork, however, was the birch canoe, in the construction of which the Algonquins were no less skilful. The Iroquois, in the absence of the birch, were forced to use the bark of the elm, which was greatly inferior both in lightness and strength. Of pipes, than which nothing was more important in their eyes, the Hurons made a great variety, some of baked clay, others of various kinds of stone, carved by the men, during their long periods of monotonous leisure, often with great skill and ingenuity. But their most mysterious fabric was wampum. This was at once their currency, their ornament, their pen, ink, and parchment; and its use was by no means confined to tribes of the

Iroquois stock. It consisted of elongated beads, white and purple, made from the inner part of certain shells. It is not easy to conceive how, with their rude implements, the Indians contrived to shape and perforate this intractable material. The art soon fell into disuse, however; for wampum better than their own was brought them by the traders, besides abundant imitations in glass and porcelain. Strung into necklaces, or wrought into collars, belts, and bracelets, it was the favorite decoration of the Indian girls at festivals and dances. It served also a graver purpose. No compact, no speech, or clause of a speech, to the representative of another nation, had any force, unless confirmed by the delivery of a string or belt of wampum. [Beaver-skins and other valuable furs were sometimes, on such occasions, used as a substitute.] The belts, on occasions of importance, were wrought into significant devices, suggestive of the substance of the compact or speech, and designed as aids to memory. To one or more old men of the nation was assigned the honorable, but very onerous, charge of keepers of the wampum,— in other words, of the national records; and it was for them to remember and interpret the meaning of the belts. The figures on wampum-belts were, for the most part, simply mnemonic. So also were those carved on wooden tablets, or painted on bark and skin, to preserve in memory the songs of war, hunting, or magic.] Engravings of many specimens of these figured songs are given in the voluminous reports on the condition of the Indians, published by Government, under the editorship of Mr. Schoolcraft. The specimens are chiefly Algonquin.] The Hurons had, however, in common with other tribes, a system of rude pictures and arbitrary signs, by which they could convey to each other, with tolerable precision, information touching the ordinary subjects of Indian interest.

Their dress was chiefly of skins, cured with smoke after the well-known Indian mode. That of the women, according to the Jesuits, was more modest than that "of our most pious ladies of France." The young girls on festal occasions must be excepted from this commendation, as they wore merely a kilt from the waist to the knee, besides the wampum decorations of the breast and arms. Their long black hair, gathered behind the neck, was decorated with disks of native copper, or gay pendants made in France, and now occasionally unearthed in numbers from their graves. The men, in summer, were nearly naked,—those of a kindred tribe wholly so, with the sole exception of their moccasins. In winter they were clad in tunics and leggins of skin, and at all seasons, on occasions of ceremony, were wrapped from head to foot in robes of beaver or otter furs, sometimes of the greatest value. On the inner side, these robes were decorated with painted figures and devices, or embroidered with the dyed quills of the Canada hedgehog. In this art of embroidery, however, the Hurons were equalled or surpassed by some of the Algonquin tribes. They wore their hair after a variety of grotesque and startling fashions. With some, it was loose on one side, and tight braided on the other; with others, close shaved, leaving one or more long and cherished locks; while, with others again, it bristled in a ridge across the crown, like the back of a hyena. [See Le Jeune, Relation, 1638, 35.—"Quelles hures!" exclaimed some astonished Frenchman. Hence the name, Hurons.] When in full dress, they were painted with ochre, white clay, soot, and the red juice of certain berries. They practised tattooing, sometimes covering the whole body with indelible devices. [Bressani, Relation Abrégée, 72.—Champlain has a picture of a warrior thus tattooed.] When of such extent, the process was very severe; and though no murmur escaped the sufferer, he sometimes died from its effects.

Female life among the Hurons had no bright side. It was a youth of license, an age of drudgery. Despite an organization which, while it perhaps made them less sensible of pain, certainly made them less susceptible of passion, than the higher races of men, the Hurons were notoriously dissolute, far exceeding in this respect the wandering and starving Algonquins.[1] Marriage existed among them,

---

1   Among the Iroquois there were more favorable features in the condition of women. The matrons had often a considerable influence on the decisions of the councils. Lafitau, whose book appeared in 1724, says that the nation was corrupt in his time, but that this was a degeneracy from their ancient manners. La Potherie and Charlevoix make a similar statement. Megapolensis, however, in 1644, says that they were then exceedingly debauched; and Greenhalgh, in 1677, gives ample evidence of a shameless license. One of their most earnest advocates of the present day admits that the passion of love among them had no other than an animal existence. (Morgan, League of the Iroquois, 322.) There is clear proof that the tribes of the South were equally corrupt. (See Lawson, Carolina, 34, and other early writers.) On the other hand, chastity in women was recognized as a virtue by many tribes. This was peculiarly the case among the Algonquins of Gaspé, where a lapse in this regard was counted a disgrace. (See Le Clerc, Nouvelle Relation de la Gaspésie, 417, where a contrast is drawn between the modesty of the girls of this

and polygamy was exceptional; but divorce took place at the will or caprice of either party. A practice also prevailed of temporary or experimental marriage, lasting a day, a week, or more. The seal of the compact was merely the acceptance of a gift of wampum made by the suitor to the object of his desire or his whim. These gifts were never returned on the dissolution of the connection; and as an attractive and enterprising damsel might, and often did, make twenty such marriages before her final establishment, she thus collected a wealth of wampum with which to adorn herself for the village dances.[1] This provisional matrimony was no bar to a license boundless and apparently universal, unattended with loss of reputation on either side. Every instinct of native delicacy quickly vanished under the influence of Huron domestic life; eight or ten families, and often more, crowded into one undivided house, where privacy was impossible, and where strangers were free to enter at all hours of the day or night.

Once a mother, and married with a reasonable permanency, the Huron woman from a wanton became a drudge. In March and April she gathered the year's supply of firewood. Then came sowing, tilling, and harvesting, smoking fish, dressing skins, making cordage and clothing, preparing food. On the march it was she who bore the burden; for, in the words of Champlain, "their women were their mules." The natural effect followed. In every Huron town

region and the open prostitution practised among those of other tribes.) Among the Sioux, adultery on the part of a woman is punished by mutilation.

The remarkable forbearance observed by Eastern and Northern tribes towards female captives was probably the result of a superstition. Notwithstanding the prevailing license, the Iroquois and other tribes had among themselves certain conventional rules which excited the admiration of the Jesuit celibates. Some of these had a superstitious origin; others were in accordance with the iron requirements of their savage etiquette. To make the Indian a hero of romance is mere nonsense.

1   "Il s'en trouue telle qui passe ainsi sa ieunesse, qui aura en plus de vingt maris, lesquels vingt maris ne sont pas seuls en la jouyssance de la beste, quelques mariez qu'ils soient: car la nuict venuë, las ieunes femmes courent d'une cabane en une autre, come font les ieunes hommes de leur costé, qui en prennent par ou bon leur semble, toutesfois sans violence aucune, et n'en reçoiuent aucune infamie, ny injure, la coustume du pays estant telle."—Champlain (1627), 90. Compare Sagard, Voyage des Hurons, 176. Both were personal observers.

The ceremony, even of the most serious marriage, consisted merely in the bride's bringing a dish of boiled maize to the bridegroom, together with an armful of fuel. There was often a feast of the relatives, or of the whole village.

were shrivelled hags, hideous and despised, who, in vindictiveness, ferocity, and cruelty, far exceeded the men.

To the men fell the task of building the houses, and making weapons, pipes, and canoes. For the rest, their home-life was a life of leisure and amusement. The summer and autumn were their seasons of serious employment,—of war, hunting, fishing, and trade. There was an established system of traffic between the Hurons and the Algonquins of the Ottawa and Lake Nipissing: the Hurons exchanging wampum, fishing-nets, and corn for fish and furs. [Champlain (1627), 84.] From various relics found in their graves, it may be inferred that they also traded with tribes of the Upper Lakes, as well as with tribes far southward, towards the Gulf of Mexico. Each branch of traffic was the monopoly of the family or clan by whom it was opened. They might, if they could, punish interlopers, by stripping them of all they possessed, unless the latter had succeeded in reaching home with the fruits of their trade,—in which case the outraged monopolists had no further right of redress, and could not attempt it without a breaking of the public peace, and exposure to the authorized vengeance of the other party. [Brébeuf, Relation des Hurons, 1636, 168 (Cramoisy).] Their fisheries, too, were regulated by customs having the force of laws. These pursuits, with their hunting,—in which they were aided by a wolfish breed of dogs unable to bark,—consumed the autumn and early winter; but before the new year the greater part of the men were gathered in their villages.

Now followed their festal season; for it was the season of idleness for the men, and of leisure for the women. Feasts, gambling, smoking, and dancing filled the vacant hours. Like other Indians, the Hurons were desperate gamblers, staking their all,—ornaments, clothing, canoes, pipes, weapons, and wives. One of their principal games was played with plum-stones, or wooden lozenges, black on one side and white on the other. These were tossed up in a wooden bowl, by striking it sharply upon the ground, and the players betted on the black or white. Sometimes a village challenged a neighboring village. The game was played in one of the houses. Strong poles were extended from side to side, and on these sat or perched the company, party facing party, while two players struck the bowl on the ground between. Bets ran high; and Brébeuf relates, that once, in midwinter, with the snow nearly three feet deep, the men of his village returned from a gambling visit, bereft of their leggins, and barefoot, yet in excellent humor. [Brébeuf, Relation des Hurons, 1636, 113.—This game is still a favorite among the Iroquois, some of whom hold to the belief that they will play it after death in the realms of bliss. In all their important games of chance, they employed charms, incantations, and all the resources of their magical art, to gain good luck.] Ludicrous as it may appear, these games were often medical prescriptions, and designed as a cure of the sick.

Their feasts and dances were of various character, social, medical, and mystical or religious. Some of their feasts were on a scale of extravagant profusion. A vain or ambitious host threw all his substance into one entertainment, inviting the whole village, and perhaps several neighboring villages also. In the winter of 1635 there was a feast at the village of Contarrea, where thirty kettles were on the fires, and twenty deer and four bears were served up. [Brébeuf, Relation des Hurons, 1636, 111.] The invitation was simple. The messenger addressed the desired guest with the concise summons, "Come and eat"; and to refuse was a grave offence. He took his dish and spoon, and repaired to the scene of festivity. Each, as he entered, greeted his host with the guttural ejaculation, Ho! and ranged himself with the rest, squatted on the earthen floor or on the platform along the sides of the house. The kettles were slung over the fires in the midst. First, there was a long prelude of lugubrious singing. Then the host, who took no share in the feast, proclaimed in a loud voice the contents of each kettle in turn, and at each announcement the company responded in unison, Ho! The attendant squaws filled with their ladles the bowls of all the guests. There was talking, laughing, jesting, singing, and smoking; and at times the entertainment was protracted through the day.

When the feast had a medical or mystic character, it was indispensable that each guest should devour the whole of the portion given him, however enormous. Should he fail, the host would be outraged, the community shocked, and the spirits roused to vengeance. Disaster would befall the nation,—death, perhaps, the individual. In some cases, the imagined efficacy of the feast was proportioned to the rapidity with which the viands were despatched. Prizes of tobacco were offered to the most rapid feeder; and the spectacle then became truly porcine. [This superstition was not confined to the Hurons, but extended to many other tribes, including, probably, all the Algonquins, with some of which it holds in full force to this day. A feaster, unable to do his full part, might, if he could, hire another to aid him; otherwise, he must remain in his place till the work was done.] These *festins à manger tout* were much dreaded by many of the Hurons, who, however, were never known to decline them.

Invitation to a dance was no less concise than to a feast. Sometimes a crier proclaimed the approaching festivity through the village. The house was crowded. Old men, old women, and children thronged the platforms, or clung to the poles which supported the sides and roof. Fires were raked out, and the earthen floor cleared. Two chiefs sang at the top of their voices, keeping time to their song with tortoise-shell rattles.[1] The men danced with great violence and gesticulation; the women, with a much more measured action. The former were nearly divested of clothing,—in mystical dances, sometimes wholly so; and, from a superstitious motive, this was now and then the case with the women. Both, however, were abundantly decorated with paint, oil, beads, wampum, trinkets, and feathers.

Religious festivals, councils, the entertainment of an envoy, the inauguration of a chief, were all occasions of festivity, in which social pleasure was joined with matter of grave import, and which at times gathered nearly all the nation into one great and harmonious concourse. Warlike expeditions, too, were always preceded by feasting, at which the warriors vaunted the fame of their ancestors, and their own past and prospective exploits. A hideous scene of feasting followed the torture of a prisoner. Like the torture itself, it was, among the Hurons, partly an act of vengeance, and partly a religious rite. If the victim had shown courage, the heart was first

---

1   Sagard gives specimens of their songs. In both dances and feasts there was no little variety. These were sometimes combined. It is impossible, in brief space, to indicate more than their general features. In the famous "war-dance,"—which was frequently danced, as it still is, for amusement,—speeches, exhortations, jests, personal satire, and repartee were commonly introduced as a part of the performance, sometimes by way of patriotic stimulus, sometimes for amusement. The music in this case was the drum and the war-song. Some of the other dances were also interspersed with speeches and sharp witticisms, always taken in good part, though Lafitau says that he has seen the victim so pitilessly bantered that he was forced to hide his head in his blanket.

roasted, cut into small pieces, and given to the young men and boys, who devoured it to increase their own courage. The body was then divided, thrown into the kettles, and eaten by the assembly, the head being the portion of the chief. Many of the Hurons joined in the feast with reluctance and horror, while others took pleasure in it.[1] This was the only form of cannibalism among them, since, unlike the wandering Algonquins, they were rarely under the desperation of extreme famine.

A great knowledge of simples for the cure of disease is popularly ascribed to the Indian. Here, however, as elsewhere, his knowledge is in fact scanty. He rarely reasons from cause to effect, or from effect to cause. Disease, in his belief, is the result of sorcery, the agency of spirits or supernatural influences, undefined and indefinable. The Indian doctor was a conjurer, and his remedies were to the last degree preposterous, ridiculous, or revolting. The well-known Indian sweating- bath is the most prominent of the few means of cure based on agencies simply physical; and this, with all the other natural remedies, was applied, not by the professed doctor, but by the sufferer himself, or his friends.

[The Indians had many simple applications for wounds, said to have been very efficacious; but the purity of their blood, owing to the absence from their diet of condiments and stimulants, as well as to their active habits, aided the remedy. In general, they were remarkably exempt from disease or deformity, though often seriously injured by alternations of hunger and excess. The Hurons sometimes died from the effects of their *festins à manger tout*.]

The Indian doctor beat, shook, and pinched his patient, howled, whooped, rattled a tortoise-shell at his ear to expel the evil spirit, bit him till blood flowed, and then displayed in triumph a small piece of wood, bone, or iron, which he had hidden in his mouth, and which he affirmed was the source of the disease, now

---

1   "Il y en a qui en mangent auec plaisir."—Brébeuf, Relation des Hurons, 1636, 121.—Le Mercier gives a description of one of these scenes, at which he was present. (Ibid., 1637, 118.) The same horrible practice prevailed to a greater extent among the Iroquois. One of the most remarkable instances of Indian cannibalism is that furnished by a Western tribe, the Miamis, among whom there was a clan, or family, whose hereditary duty and privilege it was to devour the bodies of prisoners burned to death. The act had somewhat of a religious character, was attended with ceremonial observances, and was restricted to the family in question.—See Hon. Lewis Cass, in the appendix to Colonel Whiting's poem, "Ontwa."

happily removed.[1] Sometimes he prescribed a dance, feast, or game; and the whole village bestirred themselves to fulfil the injunction to the letter. They gambled away their all; they gorged themselves like vultures; they danced or played ball naked among the snow-drifts from morning till night. At a medical feast, some strange or unusual act was commonly enjoined as vital to the patient's cure: as, for example, the departing guest, in place of the customary monosyllable of thanks, was required to greet his host with an ugly grimace. Sometimes, by prescription, half the village would throng into the house where the patient lay, led by old women disguised with the heads and skins of bears, and beating with sticks on sheets of dry bark. Here the assembly danced and whooped for hours together, with a din to which a civilized patient would promptly have succumbed. Sometimes the doctor wrought himself into a prophetic fury, raving through the length and breadth of the dwelling, snatching firebrands and flinging them about him, to the terror of the squaws, with whom, in their combustible tenements, fire was a constant bugbear.

Among the Hurons and kindred tribes, disease was frequently ascribed to some hidden wish ungratified. Hence the patient was overwhelmed with gifts, in the hope, that, in their multiplicity, the desideratum might be supplied. Kettles, skins, awls, pipes, wampum, fish-hooks, weapons, objects of every conceivable variety, were piled before him by a host of charitable contributors and if, as often happened, a dream, the Indian oracle, had revealed to the sick man the secret of his cure, his demands were never refused, however extravagant, idle, nauseous, or abominable.[2] Hence it is

---

1   The Hurons believed that the chief cause of disease and death was a monstrous serpent, that lived under the earth. By touching a tuft of hair, a feather, or a fragment of bone, with a portion of his flesh or fat, the sorcerer imparted power to it of entering the body of his victim, and gradually killing him. It was an important part of the doctor's function to extract these charms from the vitals of his patient.—Ragueneau, Relation des Hurons, 1648, 75.

2   "Dans le pays de nos Hurons, il se faict aussi des assemblées de toutes les filles d'vn bourg auprés d'vne malade, tant à sa priere, suyuant la resuerie ou le songe qu'elle en aura euë, que par l'ordonnance de Loki (the doctor), pour sa santé et guerison. Les filles ainsi assemblées, on leur demande à toutes, les vnes apres les autres, celuy qu'elles veulent des ieunes hommes du bourg pour dormir auec elles la nuict prochaine: elles en nomment chacune vn, qui sont aussi-tost aduertis par les Maistres de la ceremonie, lesquels viennent tous au soir en la presence de la malade dormir chacun auec celle qui l'a choysi, d'vn bout à l'autre de la Cabane et passent

no matter of wonder that sudden illness and sudden cures were frequent among the Hurons. The patient reaped profit, and the doctor both profit and honor.

THE HURON-IROQUOIS FAMILY.

And now, before entering upon the very curious subject of Indian social and tribal organization, it may be well briefly to observe the position and prominent distinctive features of the various communities speaking dialects of the generic tongue of the Iroquois. In this remarkable family of tribes occur the fullest developments of Indian character, and the most conspicuous examples of Indian intelligence. If the higher traits popularly ascribed to the race are not to be found here, they are to be found nowhere. A palpable proof of the superiority of this stock is afforded in the size of the Iroquois and Huron brains. In average internal capacity of the cranium, they surpass, with few and doubtful exceptions, all other aborigines of North and South America, not excepting the civilized races of Mexico and Peru.

["On comparing five Iroquois heads, I find that they give an average internal capacity of eighty-eight cubic inches, which is within two inches of the Caucasian mean."—Morton, Crania Americana, 195.—It is remarkable that the internal capacity of the skulls of the barbarous American tribes is greater than that of either the Mexicans or the Peruvians. "The difference in volume is chiefly confined to the occipital and basal portions,"—in other words, to the region of the animal propensities; and hence, it is argued, the ferocious, brutal, and uncivilizable character of the

---

ainsi toute la nuict, pendant que deux Capitaines aux deux bouts du logis chantent et sonnent de leur Tortuë du soir au lendemain matin, que la ceremonie cesse. Dieu vueille abolir vne si damnable et malheureuse ceremonie."—Sagard, Voyage des Hurons, 158.—This unique mode of cure, which was called Andacwandet, is also described by Lalemant, who saw it. (Relation des Hurons, 1639, 84.) It was one of the recognized remedies.

For the medical practices of the Hurons, see also Champlain, Brébeuf, Lafitau, Charlevoix, and other early writers. Those of the Algonquins were in some points different. The doctor often consulted the spirits, to learn the cause and cure of the disease, by a method peculiar to that family of tribes. He shut himself in a small conical lodge, and the spirits here visited him, manifesting their presence by a violent shaking of the whole structure. This superstition will be described in another connection.

wild tribes.—See J. S. Phillips, Admeasurements of Crania of the Principal Groups of Indians in the United States.]

In the woody valleys of the Blue Mountains, south of the Nottawassaga Bay of Lake Huron, and two days' journey west of the frontier Huron towns, lay the nine villages of the Tobacco Nation, or Tionnontates. [Synonymes: Tionnontates, Etionontates, Tuinontatek, Dionondadies, Khionontaterrhonons, Petuneux or Nation du Petun (Tobacco).] In manners, as in language, they closely resembled the Hurons. Of old they were their enemies, but were now at peace with them, and about the year 1640 became their close confederates. Indeed, in the ruin which befell that hapless people, the Tionnontates alone retained a tribal organization; and their descendants, with a trifling exception, are to this day the sole inheritors of the Huron or Wyandot name. Expatriated and wandering, they held for generations a paramount influence among the Western tribes. ["L'ame de tous les Conseils."—Charlevoix, Voyage, 199.—In 1763 they were Pontiac's best warriors.] In their original seats among the Blue Mountains, they offered an example extremely rare among Indians, of a tribe raising a crop for the market; for they traded in tobacco largely with other tribes. Their Huron confederates, keen traders, would not suffer them to pass through their country to traffic with the French, preferring to secure for themselves the advantage of bartering with them in French goods at an enormous profit.

[On the Tionnontates, see Le Mercier, Relation, 1637, 163; Lalemant, Relation, 1641, 69; Ragueneau, Relation, 1648, 61. An excellent summary of their character and history, by Mr. Shea, will be found in Hist. Mag., V. 262.]

Journeying southward five days from the Tionnontate towns, the forest traveller reached the border villages of the Attiwandarons, or Neutral Nation. [Attiwandarons, Attiwendaronk, Atirhagenrenrets, Rhagenratka (Jesuit Relations), Attionidarons (Sagard). They, and not the Eries, were the Kahkwas of Seneca tradition.] As early as 1626, they were visited by the Franciscan friar, La Roche Dallion, who reports a numerous population in twenty-eight towns, besides many small hamlets. Their country, about forty leagues in extent, embraced wide and fertile districts on the north shore of Lake Erie, and their frontier extended eastward across the Niagara, where they had three or four outlying towns. [Lalemant, Relation des Hurons,

1641, 71.—The Niagara was then called the River of the Neutrals, or the Onguiaahra. Lalemant estimates the Neutral population, in 1640, at twelve thousand, in forty villages.] Their name of Neutrals was due to their neutrality in the war between the Hurons and the Iroquois proper. The hostile warriors, meeting in a Neutral cabin, were forced to keep the peace, though, once in the open air, the truce was at an end. Yet this people were abundantly ferocious, and, while holding a pacific attitude betwixt their warring kindred, waged deadly strife with the Mascoutins, an Algonquin horde beyond Lake Michigan. Indeed, it was but recently that they had been at blows with seventeen Algonquin tribes. [Lettre du Père La Roche Dallion, 8 Juillet, 1627, in Le Clerc, Établissement de la Foy, I. 346.] They burned female prisoners, a practice unknown to the Hurons. [Women were often burned by the Iroquois: witness the case of Catherine Mercier in 1661, and many cases of Indian women mentioned by the early writers.] Their country was full of game and they were bold and active hunters. In form and stature they surpassed even the Hurons, whom they resembled in their mode of life, and from whose language their own, though radically similar, was dialectically distinct. Their licentiousness was even more open and shameless; and they stood alone in the extravagance of some of their usages. They kept their dead in their houses till they became insupportable; then scraped the flesh from the bones, and displayed them in rows along the walls, there to remain till the periodical Feast of the Dead, or general burial. In summer, the men wore no clothing whatever, but were usually tattooed from head to foot with powdered charcoal.

The sagacious Hurons refused them a passage through their country to the French; and the Neutrals apparently had not sense or reflection enough to take the easy and direct route of Lake Ontario, which was probably open to them, though closed against the Hurons by Iroquois enmity. Thus the former made excellent profit by exchanging French goods at high rates for the valuable furs of the Neutrals.

[The Hurons became very jealous, when La Roche Dallion visited the Neutrals, lest a direct trade should be opened between the latter and the French, against whom they at once put in circulation a variety of slanders: that they were a people who lived on snakes and venom; that they were furnished with tails; and that

French women, though having but one breast, bore six children at a birth. The missionary nearly lost his life in consequence, the Neutrals conceiving the idea that he would infect their country with a pestilence.—La Roche Dallion, in Le Clerc, I. 346.]

Southward and eastward of Lake Erie dwelt a kindred people, the Eries, or Nation of the Cat. Little besides their existence is known of them. They seem to have occupied Southwestern New York as far east as the Genesee, the frontier of the Senecas, and in habits and language to have resembled the Hurons. [Ragueneau, Relation des Hurons, 1648, 46.] They were noted warriors, fought with poisoned arrows, and were long a terror to the neighboring Iroquois.

[Le Mercier, Relation, 1654, 10.—"Nous les appellons la Nation Chat, à cause qu'il y a dans leur pais vne quantité prodigieuse de Chats sauuages."—Ibid.—The Iroquois are said to have given the same name, Jegosasa, Cat Nation, to the Neutrals.—Morgan, League of the Iroquois, 41.

Synonymes: Eriés, Erigas, Eriehronon, Riguehronon. The Jesuits never had a mission among them, though they seem to have been visited by Champlain's adventurous interpreter, Étienne Brulé, in the summer of 1615.—They are probably the Carantoüans of Champlain.]

On the Lower Susquehanna dwelt the formidable tribe called by the French Andastes. Little is known of them, beyond their general resemblance to their kindred, in language, habits, and character. Fierce and resolute warriors, they long made head against the Iroquois of New York, and were vanquished at last more by disease than by the tomahawk.

[Gallatin erroneously places the Andastes on the Alleghany, Bancroft and others adopting the error. The research of Mr. Shea has shown their identity with the Susquehannocks of the English, and the Minquas of the Dutch.—See Hist. Mag., II. 294.

Synonymes: Andastes, Andastracronnons, Andastaeronnons, Andastaguez, Antastoui (French), Susquehannocks (English), Mengwe, Minquas (Dutch), Conestogas, Conessetagoes (English).]

In Central New York, stretching east and west from the Hudson to the Genesee, lay that redoubted people who have lent their name to the tribal family of the Iroquois, and stamped it indelibly on the early pages of American history. Among all the barbarous nations of the continent, the Iroquois of New York stand paramount. Elements which among other tribes were crude, confused, and embryotic, were among them systematized and concreted into an established polity. The Iroquois was the Indian of Indians. A thorough savage, yet a finished and developed savage, he is perhaps an example of the highest elevation which man can reach without emerging from his primitive condition of the hunter. A geographical position, commanding on one hand the portal of the Great Lakes, and on the other the sources of the streams flowing both to the Atlantic and the Mississippi, gave the ambitious and aggressive confederates advantages which they perfectly understood, and by which they profited to the utmost. Patient and politic as they were ferocious, they were not only conquerors of their own race, but the powerful allies and the dreaded foes of the French and English colonies, flattered and caressed by both, yet too sagacious to give themselves without reserve to either. Their organization and their history evince their intrinsic superiority. Even their traditionary lore, amid its wild puerilities, shows at times the stamp of an energy and force in striking contrast with the flimsy creations of Algonquin fancy. That the Iroquois, left under their institutions to work out their destiny undisturbed, would ever have developed a civilization of their own, I do not believe. These institutions, however, are sufficiently characteristic and curious, and we shall soon have occasion to observe them.

[The name Iroquois is French. Charlevoix says: "Il a été formé du terme Hiro, ou Hero, qui signifie J'ai dit, et par lequel ces sauvages finissent tous leur discours, comme les Latins faisoient autrefois par leur Dixi; et de Koué, qui est un cri tantôt de tristesse, lorsqu'on le prononce en traînant, et tantôt de joye, quand on le prononce plus court."—Hist. de la N. F., I. 271.—Their true name is Hodenosaunee, or People of the Long House, because their confederacy of five distinct nations, ranged in a line along Central New York, was likened to one of the long bark houses already described, with five fires and five families. The name Agonnonsionni, or Aquanuscioni, ascribed to them by Lafitau and Charlevoix, who translated it "House-Makers," Faiseurs de Cabannes, may be a conversion of the true name with an erroneous rendering. The following are the true names of the five nations severally, with their

French and English synonymes. For other synonymes, see "History of the Conspiracy of Pontiac," 8, note.

	English.	French.
Ganeagaono,	Mohawk,	Agnier.
Onayotekaono,	Oneida,	Onneyut.
Onundagaono,	Onondaga,	Onnontagué.
Gweugwehono,	Cayuga,	Goyogouin.
Nundawaono,	Seneca,	Tsonnontouans.

The Iroquois termination in ono—or onon, as the French write it—simply means people.]

SOCIAL AND POLITICAL ORGANIZATION.

In Indian social organization, a problem at once suggests itself. In these communities, comparatively populous, how could spirits so fierce, and in many respects so ungoverned, live together in peace, without law and without enforced authority? Yet there were towns where savages lived together in thousands with a harmony which civilization might envy. This was in good measure due to peculiarities of Indian character and habits. This intractable race were, in certain external respects, the most pliant and complaisant of mankind. The early missionaries were charmed by the docile acquiescence with which their dogmas were received; but they soon discovered that their facile auditors neither believed nor understood that to which they had so promptly assented. They assented from a kind of courtesy, which, while it vexed the priests, tended greatly to keep the Indians in mutual accord. That well-known self-control, which, originating in a form of pride, covered the savage nature of the man with a veil, opaque, though thin, contributed not a little to the same end. Though vain, arrogant, boastful, and vindictive, the Indian bore abuse and sarcasm with an astonishing patience. Though greedy and grasping, he was lavish without stint, and would give away his all to soothe the manes of a departed relative, gain influence and applause, or ingratiate himself with his neighbors. In his dread of public opinion, he rivalled some of his civilized successors.

All Indians, and especially these populous and stationary tribes, had their code of courtesy, whose requirements were rigid and exact; nor might any infringe it without the ban of public censure. Indian nature, inflexible and unmalleable, was peculiarly under the control of custom. Established usage took the place of law,—was, in fact, a sort of common law, with no tribunal to expound or enforce it. In these wild democracies,—democracies in spirit, though not in form,—a respect for native superiority, and a willingness to yield to it, were always conspicuous. All were prompt to aid each other in distress, and a neighborly spirit was often exhibited among them. When a young woman was permanently married, the other women of the village supplied her with firewood for the year, each contributing an armful. When one or more families were without shelter, the men of the village joined in building them a house. In return, the recipients of the favor gave a feast, if they could; if not, their thanks were sufficient. [The following testimony concerning Indian charity and hospitality is from Ragueneau: "As often as we have seen tribes broken up, towns destroyed, and their people driven to flight, we have seen them, to the number of seven or eight hundred persons, received with open arms by charitable hosts, who gladly gave them aid, and even distributed among them a part of the lands already planted, that they might have the means of living."—Relation, 1650, 28.] Among the Iroquois and Hurons—and doubtless among the kindred tribes—there were marked distinctions of noble and base, prosperous and poor; yet, while there was food in the village, the meanest and the poorest need not suffer want. He had but to enter the nearest house, and seat himself by the fire, when, without a word on either side, food was placed before him by the women.

[The Jesuit Brébeuf, than whom no one knew the Hurons better, is very emphatic in praise of their harmony and social spirit. Speaking of one of the four nations of which the Hurons were composed, he says: "Ils ont vne douceur et vne affabilité quasi incroyable pour des Sauuages; ils ne se picquent pas aisément . . . Ils se maintiennent dans cette si parfaite intelligence par les frequentes visites, les secours qu'ils se donnent mutuellement dans leurs maladies, par les festins et les alliances . . . Ils sont moins en leurs Cabanes que chez leurs amis . . . S'ils ont vn bon morceau,

ils en font festin à leurs amis, et ne le mangent quasi iamais en leur particulier," etc.—Relation des Hurons, 1636, 118.]

Contrary to the received opinion, these Indians, like others of their race, when living in communities, were of a very social disposition. Besides their incessant dances and feasts, great and small, they were continually visiting, spending most of their time in their neighbors' houses, chatting, joking, bantering one another with witticisms, sharp, broad, and in no sense delicate, yet always taken in good part. Every village had its adepts in these wordy tournaments, while the shrill laugh of young squaws, untaught to blush, echoed each hardy jest or rough sarcasm.

In the organization of the savage communities of the continent, one feature, more or less conspicuous, continually appears. Each nation or tribe—to adopt the names by which these communities are usually known—is subdivided into several clans. These clans are not locally separate, but are mingled throughout the nation. All the members of each clan are, or are assumed to be, intimately joined in consanguinity. Hence it is held an abomination for two persons of the same clan to intermarry; and hence, again, it follows that every family must contain members of at least two clans. Each clan has its name, as the clan of the Hawk, of the Wolf, or of the Tortoise; and each has for its emblem the figure of the beast, bird, reptile, plant, or other object, from which its name is derived. This emblem, called totem by the Algonquins, is often tattooed on the clansman's body, or rudely painted over the entrance of his lodge. The child belongs, in most cases, to the clan, not of the father, but of the mother. In other words, descent, not of the totem alone, but of all rank, titles, and possessions, is through the female. The son of a chief can never be a chief by hereditary title, though he may become so by force of personal influence or achievement. Neither can he inherit from his father so much as a tobacco-pipe. All possessions alike pass of right to the brothers of the chief, or to the sons of his sisters, since these are all sprung from a common mother. This rule of descent was noticed by Champlain among the Hurons in 1615. That excellent observer refers it to an origin which is doubtless its true one. The child may not be the son of his reputed father, but must be the son of his mother,—a consideration of more than ordinary force in an Indian community.

["Les enfans ne succedent iamais aux biens et dignitez de leurs peres, doubtant comme i'ay dit de leur geniteur, mais bien font-ils leurs successeurs et heritiers, les enfans de leurs sœurs, et desquels ils sont asseurez d'estre yssus et sortis."—Champlain (1627), 91.

Captain John Smith had observed the same, several years before, among the tribes of Virginia: "For the Crowne, their heyres inherite not, but the first heyres of the Sisters."—True Relation, 43 (ed. Deane).]

This system of clanship, with the rule of descent usually belonging to it, was of very wide prevalence. Indeed, it is more than probable that close observation would have detected it in every tribe east of the Mississippi; while there is positive evidence of its existence in by far the greater number. It is found also among the Dahcotah and other tribes west of the Mississippi; and there is reason to believe it universally prevalent as far as the Rocky Mountains, and even beyond them. The fact that with most of these hordes there is little property worth transmission, and that the most influential becomes chief, with little regard to inheritance, has blinded casual observers to the existence of this curious system.

It was found in full development among the Creeks, Choctaws, Cherokees, and other Southern tribes, including that remarkable people, the Natchez, who, judged by their religious and political institutions, seem a detached offshoot of the Toltec family. It is no less conspicuous among the roving Algonquins of the extreme North, where the number of totems is almost countless. Everywhere it formed the foundation of the polity of all the tribes, where a polity could be said to exist.

The Franciscans and Jesuits, close students of the languages and superstitions of the Indians, were by no means so zealous to analyze their organization and government. In the middle of the seventeenth century the Hurons as a nation had ceased to exist, and their political portraiture, as handed down to us, is careless and unfinished. Yet some decisive features are plainly shown. The Huron nation was a confederacy of four distinct contiguous nations, afterwards increased to five by the addition of the Tionnontates;—it was divided into clans;—it was governed by chiefs, whose office was hereditary through the female;—the power of these chiefs, though great, was wholly of a persuasive or advisory character;—there were two principal chiefs, one for peace, the other for war;—there were chiefs assigned to special national functions, as the charge of the great Feast of the Dead, the direction of trading voyages to other nations, etc.;—there were numerous other chiefs, equal in rank, but very unequal in influence, since the measure of their influence depended on the measure of their personal ability;—each nation of the confederacy had a separate organization, but at certain periods grand councils of the united nations were held, at which were present, not chiefs only, but also a great concourse of the people; and at these and other councils the chiefs and principal men voted on proposed measures by means of small sticks or reeds, the opinion of the plurality ruling.

[These facts are gathered here and there from Champlain, Sagard, Bressani, and the Jesuit Relations prior to 1650. Of the Jesuits, Brébeuf is the most full and satisfactory. Lafitau and Charlevoix knew the Huron institutions only through others.

The names of the four confederate Huron nations were the Ataronchronons, Attignenonghac, Attignaouentans, and Ahrendarrhonons. There was also a subordinate "nation" called Tohotaenrat, which had but one town. (See the map of the Huron Country.) They all bore the name of some animal or other object: thus the Attignaouentans were the Nation of the Bear. As the clans are usually named after animals, this makes confusion, and may easily lead to error. The Bear Nation was the principal member of the league.]

THE IROQUOIS.

The Iroquois were a people far more conspicuous in history, and their institutions are not yet extinct. In early and recent times, they have been closely studied, and no little light has been cast upon a subject as difficult and obscure as it is curious. By comparing the statements of observers, old and new, the character of their singular organization becomes sufficiently clear.

[Among modern students of Iroquois institutions, a place far in advance of all others is due to Lewis H. Morgan, himself an Iroquois by adoption, and intimate with the race from boyhood. His work, The League of the Iroquois, is a production of most thorough and able research, conducted under peculiar advantages, and with the aid of an efficient co-laborer, Hasanoanda (Ely S. Parker), an educated and highly intelligent Iroquois of the Seneca nation. Though often differing widely from Mr. Morgan's conclusions, I cannot bear a too emphatic testimony to the value of his researches. The Notes on the Iroquois of Mr. H. R. Schoolcraft also contain some interesting facts; but here, as in all Mr. Schoolcraft's productions, the reader must scrupulously reserve his right of private judgment. None of the old writers are so satisfactory as Lafitau. His work, Mœurs des Sauvages Ameriquains comparées aux Mœurs des Premiers Temps, relates chiefly to the Iroquois and Hurons: the basis for his account of the former being his own observations and those of Father Julien Garnier, who was a missionary among them more than sixty years, from his novitiate to his death.]

Both reason and tradition point to the conclusion, that the Iroquois formed originally one undivided people. Sundered, like countless other tribes, by dissension, caprice, or the necessities of the hunter life, they separated into five distinct nations, cantoned from east to west along the centre of New York, in the following order: Mohawks, Oneidas, Onondagas, Cayugas, Senecas. There was discord among them; wars followed, and they lived in mutual fear, each ensconced in its palisaded villages. At length, says tradition, a celestial being, incarnate on earth, counselled them to compose their strife and unite in a league of defence and aggression. Another personage, wholly mortal, yet wonderfully endowed, a renowned warrior and a mighty magician, stands, with his hair of writhing snakes, grotesquely conspicuous through the dim light of tradition at this birth of Iroquois nationality. This was Atotarho, a chief of the Onondagas; and from this honored source has sprung a long line of chieftains, heirs not to the blood alone, but to the name of their great predecessor. A few years since, there lived in Onondaga Hollow a handsome Indian boy on whom the dwindled remnant of the nation looked with pride as their destined Atotarho. With earthly and celestial aid the league was consummated, and through all the land the forests trembled at the name of the Iroquois.

The Iroquois people was divided into eight clans. When the original stock was sundered into five parts, each of these clans was also sundered into five parts; and as, by the principle already indicated, the clans were intimately mingled in every village, hamlet, and cabin, each one of the five nations had its portion of each of the eight clans.[1] When the league was formed, these separate portions readily resumed their ancient tie of fraternity. Thus, of the Turtle clan, all the members became brothers again, nominal members of one family, whether Mohawks, Oneidas, Onondagas, Cayugas, or Senecas; and so, too, of the remaining clans. All the Iroquois, irrespective of nationality, were therefore divided into eight families, each tracing its descent to a common mother, and each designated by its distinctive emblem or totem. This connection of clan or family was exceedingly strong, and by it the five nations of the league were linked together as by an eightfold chain.

The clans were by no means equal in numbers, influence, or honor. So marked were the distinctions among them, that some of the early writers recognize only the three most conspicuous,— those of the Tortoise, the Bear, and the Wolf. To some of the clans, in each nation, belonged the right of giving a chief to the nation and to the league. Others had the right of giving three, or, in one case, four chiefs; while others could give none. As Indian clanship was but an extension of the family relation, these chiefs were, in a certain sense, hereditary; but the law of inheritance,

---

1   With a view to clearness, the above statement is made categorical. It requires, however, to be qualified. It is not quite certain, that, at the formation of the confederacy, there were eight clans, though there is positive proof of the existence of seven. Neither is it certain, that, at the separation, every clan was represented in every nation. Among the Mohawks and Oneidas there is no positive proof of the existence of more than three clans,—the Wolf, Bear, and Tortoise; though there is presumptive evidence of the existence of several others.—See Morgan, 81, note.

The eight clans of the Iroquois were as follows: Wolf, Bear, Beaver, Tortoise, Deer, Snipe, Heron, Hawk. (Morgan, 79.) The clans of the Snipe and the Heron are the same designated in an early French document as La famille du Petit Pluvier and La famille du Grand Pluvier. (New York Colonial Documents, IX. 47.) The anonymous author of this document adds a ninth clan, that of the Potato, meaning the wild Indian potato, Glycine apios. This clan, if it existed, was very inconspicuous, and of little importance.

Remarkable analogies exist between Iroquois clanship and that of other tribes. The eight clans of the Iroquois were separated into two divisions, four in each. Originally, marriage was interdicted between all the members of the same division, but in time the interdict was limited to the members of the individual clans. Another tribe, the Choctaws, remote from the Iroquois, and radically different in language, had also eight clans, similarly divided, with a similar interdict of marriage.—Gallatin, Synopsis, 109.

The Creeks, according to the account given by their old chief, Sekopechi, to Mr. D. W. Eakins, were divided into nine clans, named in most cases from animals: clanship being transmitted, as usual, through the female.

though binding, was extremely elastic, and capable of stretching to the farthest limits of the clan. The chief was almost invariably succeeded by a near relative, always through the female, as a brother by the same mother, or a nephew by the sister's side. But if these were manifestly unfit, they were passed over, and a chief was chosen at a council of the clan from among remoter kindred. In these cases, the successor is said to have been nominated by the matron of the late chief's household. [Lafitau, I. 471.] Be this as it may, the choice was never adverse to the popular inclination. The new chief was "raised up," or installed, by a formal council of the sachems of the league; and on entering upon his office, he dropped his own name, and assumed that which, since the formation of the league, had belonged to this especial chieftainship.

The number of these principal chiefs, or, as they have been called by way of distinction, sachems, varied in the several nations from eight to fourteen. The sachems of the five nations, fifty in all, assembled in council, formed the government of the confederacy. All met as equals, but a peculiar dignity was ever attached to the Atotarho of the Onondagas.

There was a class of subordinate chiefs, in no sense hereditary, but rising to office by address, ability, or valor. Yet the rank was clearly defined, and the new chief installed at a formal council. This class embodied, as might be supposed, the best talent of the nation, and the most prominent warriors and orators of the Iroquois have belonged to it. In its character and functions, however, it was purely civil. Like the sachems, these chiefs held their councils, and exercised an influence proportionate to their number and abilities.

There was another council, between which and that of the subordinate chiefs the line of demarcation seems not to have been very definite. The Jesuit Lafitau calls it "the senate." Familiar with the Iroquois at the height of their prosperity, he describes it as the central and controlling power, so far, at least, as the separate nations were concerned. In its character it was essentially popular, but popular in the best sense, and one which can find its application only in a small community. Any man took part in it whose age and experience qualified him to do so. It was merely the gathered wisdom of the nation. Lafitau compares it to the Roman Senate, in the early and rude age of the Republic, and affirms that it loses nothing by the comparison. He thus describes it: "It is a greasy assemblage, sitting *sur leur derrière*, crouched like apes, their knees as high as their ears, or lying, some on their bellies, some on their backs, each with a pipe in his mouth, discussing affairs of state with as much coolness and gravity as the Spanish Junta or the Grand Council of Venice." [Lafitau, I. 478.]

The young warriors had also their councils; so, too, had the women; and the opinions and wishes of each were represented by means of deputies before the "senate," or council of the old men, as well as before the grand confederate council of the sachems.

The government of this unique republic resided wholly in councils. By councils all questions were settled, all regulations established,—social, political, military, and religious. The war-path, the chase, the council-fire,—in these was the life of the Iroquois; and it is hard to say to which of the three he was most devoted.

The great council of the fifty sachems formed, as we have seen, the government of the league. Whenever a subject arose before any of the nations, of importance enough to demand its assembling, the sachems of that nation might summon their colleagues by means of runners, bearing messages and belts of wampum. The usual place of meeting was the valley of Onondaga, the political as well as geographical centre of the confederacy. Thither, if the matter were one of deep and general interest, not the sachems alone, but the greater part of the population, gathered from east and west, swarming in the hospitable lodges of the town, or bivouacked by thousands in the surrounding fields and forests. While the sachems deliberated in the council-house, the chiefs and old men, the warriors, and often the women, were holding their respective councils apart; and their opinions, laid by their deputies before the council of sachems, were never without influence on its decisions.

The utmost order and deliberation reigned in the council, with rigorous adherence to the Indian notions of parliamentary propriety. The conference opened with an address to the spirits, or the chief of all the spirits. There was no heat in debate. No speaker interrupted another. Each gave his opinion in turn, supporting it with what reason or rhetoric he could command,—but not until he had stated the subject of discussion in full, to prove that he understood it, repeating also the arguments, pro and con, of previous speakers. Thus their debates were excessively prolix; and the consumption of tobacco was immoderate. The result, however, was a thorough sifting of the matter in hand; while the practised astuteness of these savage politicians was a marvel to their civilized contemporaries. "It is by a most subtle policy," says Lafitau, "that they have taken the ascendant over the other nations, divided and overcome the most warlike, made themselves a terror to the most remote, and now hold a peaceful neutrality between the French and English, courted and feared by both."

[Lafitau, I. 480.—Many other French writers speak to the same effect. The following are the words of the soldier historian, La Potherie, after describing the organization of the league: "C'est donc là cette politique qui les unit si bien, à peu près comme tous les ressorts d'une horloge, qui par une liaison admirable de toutes les parties qui les composent, contribuent toutes unanimement au merveilleux effet qui en resulte."—Hist. de l'Amérique Septentrionale, III. 32.—He adds: "Les François ont avoüé eux-mêmes qu'ils étoient nez pour la guerre, & quelques maux qu'ils nous ayent faits nous les avons toujours estimez."—Ibid., 2.—La Potherie's book was published in 1722.]

Unlike the Hurons, they required an entire unanimity in their decisions. The ease and frequency with which a requisition seemingly so difficult was fulfilled afford a striking illustration of Indian nature,—on one side, so stubborn, tenacious, and impracticable; on the other, so pliant and acquiescent. An explanation of this harmony is to be found also in an intense spirit of nationality: for never since the days of Sparta were individual life and national life more completely fused into one.

The sachems of the league were likewise, as we have seen, sachems of their respective nations; yet they rarely spoke in the councils of the subordinate chiefs and old men, except to present subjects of discussion. [Lafitau, I. 479.] Their influence in these councils was, however, great, and even paramount; for they commonly succeeded in securing to their interest some of the most dexterous and influential of the conclave, through whom, while they themselves remained in the background, they managed the debates.

[The following from Lafitau is very characteristic: "Ce que je dis de leur zèle pour le bien public n'est cependant pas si universel, que plusieurs ne pensent à leur interêts particuliers, & que les Chefs (sachems) principalement ne fassent joüer plusieurs ressorts secrets pour venir à bout de leurs intrigues. Il y en a tel, dont l'adresse joüe si bien à coup sûr, qu'il fait déliberer le Conseil plusieurs jours de suite, sur une matière dont la détermination est arrêtée entre lui & les principales têtes avant d'avoir été mise sur le tapis. Cependant comme les Chefs s'entre-regardent, & qu'aucun ne veut paroître se donner une superiorité qui puisse piquer la jalousie, ils se ménagent dans les Conseils plus que les autres; & quoiqu'ils en soient l'ame, leur politique les oblige à y parler peu, & à écouter plûtôt le sentiment d'autrui, qu'à y dire le leur; mais chacun a un homme à sa main, qui est comme une espèce de Brûlot, & qui étant sans consequence pour sa personne hazarde en pleine liberté tout ce qu'il juge à propos, selon qu'il l'a concerté avec le Chef même pour qui il agit."—Mœurs des Sauvages, I. 481.]

There was a class of men among the Iroquois always put forward on public occasions to speak the mind of the nation or defend its interests. Nearly all of them were of the number of the subordinate chiefs. Nature and training had fitted them for public speaking, and they were deeply versed in the history and traditions of the league. They were in fact professed orators, high in honor and influence among the people. To a huge stock of conventional metaphors, the use of which required nothing but practice, they often added an astute intellect, an astonishing memory, and an eloquence which deserved the name.

In one particular, the training of these savage politicians was never surpassed. They had no art of writing to record events, or preserve the stipulations of treaties. Memory, therefore, was tasked to the utmost, and developed to an extraordinary degree. They had various devices for aiding it, such as bundles of sticks, and that system of signs, emblems, and rude pictures, which they shared with other tribes. Their famous wampum-belts were so many mnemonic signs, each standing for some act, speech, treaty, or clause of a treaty. These represented the public archives, and were divided among various custodians, each charged with the memory and interpretation of those assigned to him. The meaning of the belts was from time to time expounded in their councils. In conferences with them, nothing more astonished the French, Dutch, and English officials than the precision with which, before replying to their addresses, the Indian orators repeated them point by point.

It was only in rare cases that crime among the Iroquois or Hurons was punished by public authority. Murder, the most heinous offence, except witchcraft, recognized among them, was rare. If the slayer and the slain were of the same household or clan, the affair was regarded as a family quarrel, to be settled by the immediate kin on both sides. This, under the pressure of public opinion, was commonly effected without bloodshed, by presents given in atonement. But if the murderer and his victim were of different clans or different nations, still more, if the slain was a foreigner, the whole community became interested to prevent the discord or the war which might arise. All directed their efforts, not to bring the murderer to punishment, but to satisfy the injured parties by a vicarious atonement. [Lalemant, while inveighing against a practice which made the public, and not the criminal, answerable for an offence, admits that heinous crimes were more rare than in France, where the guilty party himself was punished.—Lettre au P. Provincial, 15 May, 1645.] To this end, contributions were made and presents collected. Their number and value were determined by established usage. Among the Hurons, thirty presents of very considerable value were the price of a man's life. That of a woman's was fixed at forty, by reason of her weakness, and because on her depended the continuance and increase of the population. This was when the slain belonged to the nation. If of a foreign tribe, his death demanded a higher compensation, since it involved the danger of war. [Ragueneau, Relation des Hurons, 1648, 80.] These presents were offered in solemn council, with prescribed formalities. The relatives of the slain might refuse them, if they chose, and in this case the murderer was given them as a slave; but they might by no means kill him, since, in so doing, they would incur public censure, and be compelled in their turn to make atonement. Besides the principal gifts, there was a great number of less value, all symbolical, and each delivered with a set form of words: as, "By this we wash out the blood of the slain: By this we cleanse his wound: By this we clothe his corpse with a new shirt: By this we place food on his grave": and so, in endless prolixity, through particulars without number.

[Ragueneau, Relation des Hurons, 1648, gives a description of one of these ceremonies at length. Those of the Iroquois on such occasions were similar. Many other tribes had the same custom, but attended with much less form and ceremony. Compare Perrot, 73-76.]

The Hurons were notorious thieves; and perhaps the Iroquois were not much better, though the contrary has been asserted. Among both, the robbed was permitted not only to retake his property by force, if he could, but to strip the robber of all he had. This apparently acted as a restraint in favor only of the strong, leaving the weak a prey to the plunderer; but here the tie of family and clan intervened to aid him. Relatives and clansmen espoused the quarrel of him who could not right himself.

[The proceedings for detecting thieves were regular and methodical, after established customs. According to Bressani, no thief ever inculpated the innocent.]

Witches, with whom the Hurons and Iroquois were grievously infested, were objects of utter abomination to both, and any one might kill them at any time. If any person was guilty of treason, or by his character and conduct made himself dangerous or obnoxious to the public, the council of chiefs and old men held a secret session on his case, condemned him to death, and appointed some young man to kill him. The executioner, watching his opportunity, brained or stabbed him unawares, usually in the dark porch of one of the houses. Acting by authority, he could not be held answerable; and the relatives of the slain had no redress, even if they desired it. The council, however, commonly obviated all difficulty in advance, by charging the culprit with witchcraft, thus alienating his best friends.

The military organization of the Iroquois was exceedingly imperfect and derived all its efficiency from their civil union and their personal prowess. There were two hereditary war-chiefs, both belonging to the Senecas; but, except on occasions of unusual importance, it does not appear that they took a very active part in the conduct of wars. The Iroquois lived in a state of chronic warfare with nearly all the surrounding tribes, except a few from whom they exacted tribute. Any man of sufficient personal credit might raise a war-party when he chose. He proclaimed his purpose through the village, sang his war-songs, struck his hatchet into the war-post, and danced the war-dance. Any who chose joined him; and the party usually took up their march at once, with a little parched-corn-meal and maple-sugar as their sole provision. On great occasions, there was concert of action,—the various parties meeting at a rendezvous, and pursuing the march together. The leaders of war-parties, like the orators, belonged, in nearly all cases, to the class of subordinate chiefs. The Iroquois had a discipline suited to the dark and tangled forests where they fought. Here they were a terrible foe: in an open country, against a trained European force, they were, despite their ferocious valor, far less formidable.

In observing this singular organization, one is struck by the incongruity of its spirit and its form. A body of hereditary oligarchs was the head of the nation, yet the nation was essentially democratic. Not that the Iroquois were levellers. None were more prompt to acknowledge superiority and defer to it, whether established by usage and prescription, or the result of personal endowment. Yet each man, whether of high or low degree, had a voice in the conduct of affairs, and was never for a moment divorced from his wild spirit of independence. Where there was no property worthy the name, authority had no fulcrum and no hold. The constant aim of sachems and chiefs was to exercise it without seeming to do so. They had no insignia of office. They were no richer than others; indeed, they were often poorer, spending their substance in largesses and bribes to strengthen their influence. They hunted and fished for subsistence; they were as foul, greasy, and unsavory as the rest; yet in them, withal, was often seen a native dignity of bearing, which ochre and bear's grease could not hide, and which comported well with their strong, symmetrical, and sometimes majestic proportions.

To the institutions, traditions, rites, usages, and festivals of the league the Iroquois was inseparably wedded. He clung to them with Indian tenacity; and he clings to them still. His political fabric was one of ancient ideas and practices, crystallized into regular and enduring forms. In its component parts it has nothing peculiar to itself. All its elements are found in other tribes: most of them belong to the whole Indian race. Undoubtedly there was a distinct and definite effort of legislation; but Iroquois legislation invented nothing. Like all sound legislation, it built of materials already prepared. It organized the chaotic past, and gave concrete forms to Indian nature itself. The people have dwindled and decayed; but, banded by its ties of clan and kin, the league, in feeble miniature, still subsists, and the degenerate Iroquois looks back with a mournful pride to the glory of the past.

Would the Iroquois, left undisturbed to work out their own destiny, ever have emerged from the savage state? Advanced as they were beyond most other American tribes, there is no indication whatever of a tendency to overpass the confines of a wild hunter and warrior life. They were inveterately attached to it, impracticable conservatists of barbarism, and in ferocity and cruelty they matched the worst of their race. Nor did the power of expansion apparently belonging to their system ever produce much result. Between the years 1712 and 1715, the Tuscaroras, a kindred people, were admitted into the league as a sixth nation; but they were never admitted on equal terms. Long after, in the period of their decline, several other tribes were announced as new members of the league; but these admissions never took effect. The Iroquois were always reluctant to receive other tribes, or parts of tribes, collectively, into the precincts of the "Long House." Yet they constantly practised a system of adoptions, from which, though cruel and savage, they drew great advantages. Their prisoners of war, when they had burned and butchered as many of them as would serve to sate their own ire and that of their women, were divided, man by man, woman by woman, and child by child, adopted into different families and clans, and thus incorporated into the nation. It was by this means, and this alone, that they could offset the losses of their incessant wars. Early in the eighteenth century, and ever-long before, a vast proportion of their population consisted of adopted prisoners.

[Relation, 1660, 7 (anonymous). The Iroquois were at the height of their prosperity about the year 1650. Morgan reckons their number at this time at 25,000 souls; but this is far too high an estimate. The author of the Relation of 1660 makes their whole number of warriors 2,200. Le Mercier, in the Relation of 1665, says 2,350. In the Journal of Greenhalgh, an Englishman who visited them in 1677, their warriors are set down at 2,150. Du Chesneau, in 1681, estimates them at 2,000; De la Barre, in 1684, at 2,600, they having been strengthened by adoptions. A memoir addressed to the Marquis de Seignelay, in 1687, again makes them 2,000. (See

N. Y. Col. Docs., IX. 162, 196, 321.) These estimates imply a total population of ten or twelve thousand.

The anonymous writer of the Relation of 1660 may well remark: "It is marvellous that so few should make so great a havoc, and strike such terror into so many tribes."]

It remains to speak of the religious and superstitious ideas which so deeply influenced Indian life.

RELIGION AND SUPERSTITIONS.

The religious belief of the North-American Indians seems, on a first view, anomalous and contradictory. It certainly is so, if we adopt the popular impression. Romance, Poetry, and Rhetoric point, on the one hand, to the august conception of a one all-ruling Deity, a Great Spirit, omniscient and omnipresent; and we are called to admire the untutored intellect which could conceive a thought too vast for Socrates and Plato. On the other hand, we find a chaos of degrading, ridiculous, and incoherent superstitions. A closer examination will show that the contradiction is more apparent than real. We will begin with the lowest forms of Indian belief, and thence trace it upward to the highest conceptions to which the unassisted mind of the savage attained.

To the Indian, the material world is sentient and intelligent. Birds, beasts, and reptiles have ears for human prayers, and are endowed with an influence on human destiny. A mysterious and inexplicable power resides in inanimate things. They, too, can listen to the voice of man, and influence his life for evil or for good. Lakes, rivers, and waterfalls are sometimes the dwelling-place of spirits; but more frequently they are themselves living beings, to be propitiated by prayers and offerings. The lake has a soul; and so has the river, and the cataract. Each can hear the words of men, and each can be pleased or offended. In the silence of a forest, the gloom of a deep ravine, resides a living mystery, indefinite, but redoubtable. Through all the works of Nature or of man, nothing exists, however seemingly trivial, that may not be endowed with a secret power for blessing or for bane.

Men and animals are closely akin. Each species of animal has its great archetype, its progenitor or king, who is supposed to exist somewhere, prodigious in size, though in shape and nature like his subjects. A belief prevails, vague, but perfectly apparent, that men themselves owe their first parentage to beasts, birds, or reptiles, as bears, wolves, tortoises, or cranes; and the names of the totemic clans, borrowed in nearly every case from animals, are the reflection of this idea.

[This belief occasionally takes a perfectly definite shape. There was a tradition among Northern and Western tribes, that men were created from the carcasses of beasts, birds, and fishes, by Manabozho, a mythical personage, to be described hereafter. The Amikouas, or People of the Beaver, an Algonquin tribe of Lake Huron, claimed descent from the carcass of the great original beaver, or father of the beavers. They believed that the rapids and cataracts on the French River and the Upper Ottawa were caused by dams made by their amphibious ancestor. (See the tradition in Perrot, Mémoire sur les Mœurs, Coustumes et Relligion des Sauvages de l'Amérique Septentrionale, p. 20.) Charlevoix tells the same story. Each Indian was supposed to inherit something of the nature of the animal whence he sprung.]

An Indian hunter was always anxious to propitiate the animals he sought to kill. He has often been known to address a wounded bear in a long harangue of apology. [McKinney, Tour to the Lakes, 284, mentions the discomposure of a party of Indians when shown a stuffed moose. Thinking that its spirit would be offended at the indignity shown to its remains, they surrounded it, making apologetic speeches, and blowing tobacco-smoke at it as a propitiatory offering.] The bones of the beaver were treated with especial tenderness, and carefully kept from the dogs, lest the spirit of the dead beaver, or his surviving brethren, should take offence. [This superstition was very prevalent, and numerous examples of it occur in old and recent writers, from Father Le Jeune to Captain Carver.] This solicitude was not confined to animals, but extended to inanimate things. A remarkable example occurred among the Hurons, a people comparatively advanced, who, to propitiate their fishing-nets, and persuade them to do their office with effect, married them every year to two young girls of the tribe, with a ceremony more formal than that observed in the case of mere human wedlock.[1] The fish, too, no less than the nets, must be propitiated; and to this end they were addressed every evening from the fishing-camp by one of the party chosen for that function, who exhorted them to take courage and be caught, assuring them that the utmost respect should be shown to their bones. The harangue, which took place after the evening meal, was made in solemn form; and while it lasted, the whole party, except the speaker, were required to lie on their backs, silent and motionless, around the fire.[2]

Besides ascribing life and intelligence to the material world, animate and inanimate, the Indian believes in supernatural existences, known among the Algonquins as *Manitous*, and among the Iroquois and Hurons as *Okies* or *Otkons*. These words comprehend all forms of supernatural being, from the highest to the lowest, with the exception, possibly, of certain diminutive fairies or hobgoblins, and certain giants and anomalous monsters, which appear under various forms, grotesque and horrible, in the Indian fireside legends. [Many tribes have tales of diminutive beings, which, in the absence of a better word, may be called fairies. In the Travels of Lewis and Clarke, there is mention of a hill on the Missouri, supposed to be haunted by them. These Western fairies correspond to the *Puck Wudj Ininee* of Ojibwa tradition. As an example of the monsters alluded to, see the Saginaw story of the Weendigoes, in Schoolcraft, Algic Researches, II. 105.] There are local manitous of streams, rocks, mountains, cataracts, and forests. The conception of these beings betrays, for the most part, a striking poverty of imagination. In nearly every case, when they reveal themselves to mortal sight, they bear the semblance of beasts, reptiles, or birds, in shapes unusual or distorted. [The figure of a large bird is perhaps the most common,—as, for example, the

---

1   There are frequent allusions to this ceremony in the early writers. The Algonquins of the Ottawa practised it, as well as the Hurons. Lalemant, in his chapter "Du Regne de Satan en ces Contrées" (Relation des Hurons, 1639), says that it took place yearly, in the middle of March. As it was indispensable that the brides should be virgins, mere children were chosen. The net was held between them; and its spirit, or oki, was harangued by one of the chiefs, who exhorted him to do his part in furnishing the tribe with food. Lalemant was told that the spirit of the net had once appeared in human form to the Algonquins, complaining that he had lost his wife, and warning them, that, unless they could find him another equally immaculate, they would catch no more fish.

2   Sagard, Le Grand Voyage du Pays des Hurons, 257. Other old writers make a similar statement.

good spirit of Rock Island: "He was white, with wings like a swan, but ten times larger."—Autobiography of Blackhawk, 70.] There are other manitous without local habitation, some good, some evil, countless in number and indefinite in attributes. They fill the world, and control the destinies of men,—that is to say, of Indians: for the primitive Indian holds that the white man lives under a spiritual rule distinct from that which governs his own fate. These beings, also, appear for the most part in the shape of animals. Sometimes, however, they assume human proportions; but more frequently they take the form of stones, which, being broken, are found full of living blood and flesh.

Each primitive Indian has his guardian manitou, to whom he looks for counsel, guidance, and protection. These spiritual allies are gained by the following process. At the age of fourteen or fifteen, the Indian boy blackens his face, retires to some solitary place, and remains for days without food. Superstitious expectancy and the exhaustion of abstinence rarely fail of their results. His sleep is haunted by visions, and the form which first or most often appears is that of his guardian manitou,—a beast, a bird, a fish, a serpent, or some other object, animate or inanimate. An eagle or a bear is the vision of a destined warrior; a wolf, of a successful hunter; while a serpent foreshadows the future medicine-man, or, according to others, portends disaster.[1] The young Indian thenceforth wears about his person the object revealed in his dream, or some portion of it,—as a bone, a feather, a snake-skin, or a tuft of hair. This, in the modern language of the forest and prairie, is known as his "medicine." The Indian yields to it a sort of worship, propitiates it with offerings of tobacco, thanks it in prosperity, and upbraids it in disaster.[2] If his medicine fails to bring the desired success,

---

1   Compare Cass, in North-American Review, Second Series, XIII. 100. A turkey-buzzard, according to him, is the vision of a medicine-man. I once knew an old Dahcotah chief, who was greatly respected, but had never been to war, though belonging to a family of peculiarly warlike propensities. The reason was, that, in his initiatory fast, he had dreamed of an antelope,—the peace-spirit of his people.

     Women fast, as well as men,—always at the time of transition from childhood to maturity. In the Narrative of John Tanner, there is an account of an old woman who had fasted, in her youth, for ten days, and throughout her life placed the firmest faith in the visions which had appeared to her at that time. Among the Northern Algonquins, the practice, down to a recent day, was almost universal.

2   The author has seen a Dahcotah warrior open his medicine-bag, talk with an air of affectionate respect to the bone, feather, or horn within, and blow tobacco-smoke

he will sometimes discard it and adopt another. The superstition now becomes mere fetich-worship, since the Indian regards the mysterious object which he carries about him rather as an embodiment than as a representative of a supernatural power.

Indian belief recognizes also another and very different class of beings. Besides the giants and monsters of legendary lore, other conceptions may be discerned, more or less distinct, and of a character partly mythical. Of these the most conspicuous is that remarkable personage of Algonquin tradition, called Manabozho, Messou, Michabou, Nanabush, or the Great Hare. As each species of animal has its archetype or king, so, among the Algonquins, Manabozho is king of all these animal kings. Tradition is diverse as to his origin. According to the most current belief, his father was the West-Wind, and his mother a great-granddaughter of the Moon. His character is worthy of such a parentage. Sometimes he is a wolf, a bird, or a gigantic hare, surrounded by a court of quadrupeds; sometimes he appears in human shape, majestic in stature and wondrous in endowment, a mighty magician, a destroyer of serpents and evil manitous; sometimes he is a vain and treacherous imp, full of childish whims and petty trickery, the butt and victim of men, beasts, and spirits. His powers of transformation are without limit; his curiosity and malice are insatiable; and of the numberless legends of which he is the hero, the greater part are as trivial as they are incoherent.[1] It does not appear that Manabozho was ever an object of worship; yet, despite his absurdity, tradition declares him to be chief among the manitous, in short, the "Great Spirit." ["Presque toutes les Nations Algonquines ont donné le nom de Grand Lièvre au Premier Esprit, quelques-uns l'appellent Michabou (Manabozho)."—Charlevoix, Journal Historique, 344.] It was he who restored the world, submerged by a deluge. He was

---

upon it as an offering. "Medicines" are acquired not only by fasting, but by casual dreams, and otherwise. They are sometimes even bought and sold. For a curious account of medicine-bags and fetich-worship among the Algonquins of Gaspé, see Le Clerc, Nouvelle Relation de la Gaspésie, Chap. XIII.

1   Mr. Schoolcraft has collected many of these tales. See his Algic Researches, Vol. I. Compare the stories of Messou, given by Le Jeune (Relations, 1633, 1634), and the account of Nanabush, by Edwin James, in his notes to Tanner's Narrative of Captivity and Adventures during a Thirty-Years' Residence among the Indians; also the account of the Great Hare, in the Mémoire of Nicolas Perrot, Chaps. I., II.

hunting in company with a certain wolf, who was his brother, or, by other accounts, his grandson, when his quadruped relative fell through the ice of a frozen lake, and was at once devoured by certain serpents lurking in the depths of the waters. Manabozho, intent on revenge, transformed himself into the stump of a tree, and by this artifice surprised and slew the king of the serpents, as he basked with his followers in the noontide sun. The serpents, who were all manitous, caused, in their rage, the waters of the lake to deluge the earth. Manabozho climbed a tree, which, in answer to his entreaties, grew as the flood rose around it, and thus saved him from the vengeance of the evil spirits. Submerged to the neck, he looked abroad on the waste of waters, and at length descried the bird known as the loon, to whom he appealed for aid in the task of restoring the world. The loon dived in search of a little mud, as material for reconstruction, but could not reach the bottom. A musk-rat made the same attempt, but soon reappeared floating on his back, and apparently dead. Manabozho, however, on searching his paws, discovered in one of them a particle of the desired mud, and of this, together with the body of the loon, created the world anew.[1]

There are various forms of this tradition, in some of which Manabozho appears, not as the restorer, but as the creator of the world, forming mankind from the carcasses of beasts, birds, and fishes.[2] Other stories represent him as marrying a female musk-rat, by whom he became the progenitor of the human race.[3]

---

1   This is a form of the story still current among the remoter Algonquins. Compare the story of Messou, in Le Jeune, Relation, 1633, 16. It is substantially the same.

2   In the beginning of all things, Manabozho, in the form of the Great Hare, was on a raft, surrounded by animals who acknowledged him as their chief. No land could be seen. Anxious to create the world, the Great Hare persuaded the beaver to dive for mud but the adventurous diver floated to the surface senseless. The otter next tried, and failed like his predecessor. The musk-rat now offered himself for the desperate task. He plunged, and, after remaining a day and night beneath the surface, reappeared, floating on his back beside the raft, apparently dead, and with all his paws fast closed. On opening them, the other animals found in one of them a grain of sand, and of this the Great Hare created the world.—Perrot, Mémoire, Chap. I.

3   Le Jeune, Relation, 1633, 16.—The musk-rat is always a conspicuous figure in Algonquin cosmogony.

It is said that Messou, or Manabozho, once gave to an Indian the gift of immortality, tied in a bundle, enjoining him never to open it. The Indian's wife,

Searching for some higher conception of supernatural existence, we find, among a portion of the primitive Algonquins, traces of a vague belief in a spirit dimly shadowed forth under the name of Atahocan, to whom it does not appear that any attributes were ascribed or any worship offered, and of whom the Indians professed to know nothing whatever;[1] but there is no evidence that this belief extended beyond certain tribes of the Lower St. Lawrence. Others saw a supreme manitou in the Sun.[2] The Algonquins believed also in a malignant manitou, in whom the early missionaries failed not to recognize the Devil, but who was far less dreaded than his wife. She wore a robe made of the hair of her victims, for she was the cause of death; and she it was whom, by yelling, drumming, and stamping, they sought to drive away from the sick. Sometimes, at night, she was seen by some terrified squaw in the forest, in shape like a flame of fire; and when the vision was announced to the circle crouched around the lodge-fire, they burned a fragment of meat to appease the female fiend.

The East, the West, the North, and the South were vaguely personified as spirits or manitous. Some of the winds, too, were personal existences. The West-Wind, as we have seen, was father of Manabozho. There was a Summer-Maker and a Winter-Maker; and the Indians tried to keep the latter at bay by throwing firebrands into the air.

When we turn from the Algonquin family of tribes to that of the Iroquois, we find another cosmogony, and other conceptions of spiritual existence. While the earth was as yet a waste of waters, there was, according to Iroquois and Huron traditions, a heaven with lakes, streams, plains, and forests, inhabited by animals, by spirits, and, as some affirm, by human beings. Here a certain female spirit, named Ataentsic, was once chasing a bear, which, slipping through a hole,

however, impelled by curiosity, one day cut the string, the precious gift flew out, and Indians have ever since been subject to death. Le Jeune, Relation, 1634, 13.

1   Le Jeune, Relation, 1633, 16; Relation, 1634, 13.

2   Biard, Relation, 1611, Chap. VIII.—This belief was very prevalent. The Ottawas, according to Ragueneau (Relation des Hurons, 1648, 77), were accustomed to invoke the "Maker of Heaven" at their feasts; but they recognized as distinct persons the Maker of the Earth, the Maker of Winter, the God of the Waters, and the Seven Spirits of the Wind. He says, at the same time, "The people of these countries have received from their ancestors no knowledge of a God"; and he adds, that there is no sentiment of religion in this invocation.

fell down to the earth. Ataentsic's dog followed, when she herself, struck with despair, jumped after them. Others declare that she was kicked out of heaven by the spirit, her husband, for an amour with a man; while others, again, hold the belief that she fell in the attempt to gather for her husband the medicinal leaves of a certain tree. Be this as it may, the animals swimming in the watery waste below saw her falling, and hastily met in council to determine what should be done. The case was referred to the beaver. The beaver commended it to the judgment of the tortoise, who thereupon called on the other animals to dive, bring up mud, and place it on his back. Thus was formed a floating island, on which Ataentsic fell; and here, being pregnant, she was soon delivered of a daughter, who in turn bore two boys, whose paternity is unexplained. They were called Taouscaron and Jouskeha, and presently fell to blows, Jouskeha killing his brother with the horn of a stag. The back of the tortoise grew into a world full of verdure and life; and Jouskeha, with his grandmother, Ataentsic, ruled over its destinies.

[The above is the version of the story given by Brébeuf, Relation des Hurons, 1636, 86 (Cramoisy). No two Indians told it precisely alike, though nearly all the Hurons and Iroquois agreed as to its essential points. Compare Vanderdonck, Cusick, Sagard, and other writers. According to Vanderdonck, Ataentsic became mother of a deer, a bear, and a wolf, by whom she afterwards bore all the other animals, mankind included. Brébeuf found also among the Hurons a tradition inconsistent with that of Ataentsic, and bearing a trace of Algonquin origin. It declares, that, in the beginning, a man, a fox, and a skunk found themselves together on an island, and that the man made the world out of mud brought him by the skunk.

The Delawares, an Algonquin tribe, seem to have borrowed somewhat of the Iroquois cosmogony, since they believed that the earth was formed on the back of a tortoise.

According to some, Jouskeha became the father of the human race; but, in the third generation, a deluge destroyed his posterity, so that it was necessary to transform animals into men.—Charlevoix, III. 345.]

He is the Sun; she is the Moon. He is beneficent; but she is malignant, like the female demon of the Algonquins. They have a bark house, made like those of the Iroquois, at the end of the earth, and they often come to feasts and dances in the Indian villages. Jouskeha raises corn for himself, and makes plentiful harvests for mankind. Sometimes he is seen, thin as a skeleton, with a spike of shrivelled corn in his hand, or greedily gnawing a human limb; and then the Indians know that a grievous famine awaits them. He constantly interposes between mankind and the malice of his wicked grandmother, whom, at times, he soundly cudgels. It was he who made lakes and streams: for once the earth was parched and barren, all the water being gathered under the armpit of a colossal frog; but Jouskeha pierced the armpit, and let out the water. No prayers were offered to him, his benevolent nature rendering them superfluous.

[Compare Brébeuf, as before cited, and Sagard, Voyage des Hurons, p. 228.]

The early writers call Jouskeha the creator of the world, and speak of him as corresponding to the vague Algonquin deity, Atahocan. Another deity appears in Iroquois mythology, with equal claims to be regarded as supreme. He is called Areskoui, or Agreskoui, and his most prominent attributes are those of a god of war. He was often invoked, and the flesh of animals and of captive enemies was burned in his honor. [Father Jogues saw a female prisoner burned to Areskoui, and two bears offered to him to atone for the sin of not burning more captives.—Lettre de Jogues, 6 Aug., 1643.] Like Jouskeha, he was identified with the sun; and he is perhaps to be regarded as the same being, under different attributes. Among the Iroquois proper, or Five Nations, there was also a divinity called Tarenyowagon, or Teharonhiawagon,[1] whose place and character it is very difficult to determine. In some traditions he appears as the son of Jouskeha. He had a prodigious influence; for it was he who spoke to men in dreams. The Five Nations recognized still another superhuman personage,—plainly a deified chief or hero. This was Taounyawatha, or Hiawatha, said to be a divinely appointed messenger, who made his abode on earth for the political and social instruction of the chosen race, and

---

1   Le Mercier, Relation, 1670, 66; Dablon, Relation, 1671, 17. Compare Cusick, Megapolensis, and Vanderdonck. Some writers identify Tarenyowagon and Hiawatha. Vanderdonck assumes that Areskoui is the Devil, and Tarenyowagon is God. Thus Indian notions are often interpreted by the light of preconceived ideas.

whose counterpart is to be found in the traditions of the Peruvians, Mexicans, and other primitive nations.[1]

Close examination makes it evident that the primitive Indian's idea of a Supreme Being was a conception no higher than might have been expected. The moment he began to contemplate this object of his faith, and sought to clothe it with attributes, it became finite, and commonly ridiculous. The Creator of the World stood on the level of a barbarous and degraded humanity, while a natural tendency became apparent to look beyond him to other powers sharing his dominion. The Indian belief, if developed, would have developed into a system of polytheism.

[Some of the early writers could discover no trace of belief in a supreme spirit of any kind. Perrot, after a life spent among the Indians, ignores such an idea. Allouez emphatically denies that it existed among the tribes of Lake Superior. (Relation, 1667, 11.) He adds, however, that the Sacs and Foxes believed in a great *génie*, who lived not far from the French settlements.—Ibid., 21.]

In the primitive Indian's conception of a God the idea of moral good has no part. His deity does not dispense justice for this world or the next, but leaves mankind under the power of subordinate spirits, who fill and control the universe. Nor is the good and evil of these inferior beings a moral good and evil. The good spirit is the spirit that gives good luck, and ministers to the necessities and desires of mankind: the evil spirit is simply a malicious agent of disease, death, and mischance.

In no Indian language could the early missionaries find a word to express the idea of God. Manitou and Oki meant anything endowed with supernatural powers, from a snake-skin, or a greasy Indian conjurer, up to Manabozho and Jouskeha. The priests were forced to use a circumlocution,—"The Great Chief of Men," or

---

1   For the tradition of Hiawatha, see Clark, History of Onondaga, I. 21. It will also be found in Schoolcraft's Notes on the Iroquois, and in his History, Condition, and Prospects of Indian Tribes.

The Iroquois name for God is Hawenniio, sometimes written Owayneo; but this use of the word is wholly due to the missionaries. Hawenniio is an Iroquois verb, and means, "he rules, he is master". There is no Iroquois word which, in its primitive meaning, can be interpreted, the Great Spirit, or God. On this subject, see Études Philologiques sur quelques Langues Sauvages (Montreal, 1866), where will also be found a curious exposure of a few of Schoolcraft's ridiculous blunders in this connection.

"He who lives in the Sky." [See "Divers Sentimens," appended to the Relation of 1635, § 27; and also many other passages of early missionaries.] Yet it should seem that the idea of a supreme controlling spirit might naturally arise from the peculiar character of Indian belief. The idea that each race of animals has its archetype or chief would easily suggest the existence of a supreme chief of the spirits or of the human race,—a conception imperfectly shadowed forth in Manabozho. The Jesuit missionaries seized this advantage. "If each sort of animal has its king," they urged, "so, too, have men; and as man is above all the animals, so is the spirit that rules over men the master of all the other spirits." The Indian mind readily accepted the idea, and tribes in no sense Christian quickly rose to the belief in one controlling spirit. The Great Spirit became a distinct existence, a pervading power in the universe, and a dispenser of justice. Many tribes now pray to him, though still clinging obstinately to their ancient superstitions; and with some, as the heathen portion of the modern Iroquois, he is clothed with attributes of moral good.

[In studying the writers of the last and of the present century, it is to be remembered that their observations were made upon savages who had been for generations in contact, immediate or otherwise, with the doctrines of Christianity. Many observers have interpreted the religious ideas of the Indians after preconceived ideas of their own; and it may safely be affirmed that an Indian will respond with a grunt of acquiescence to any question whatever touching his spiritual state. Loskiel and the simple-minded Heckewelder write from a missionary point of view; Adair, to support a theory of descent from the Jews; the worthy theologian, Jarvis, to maintain his dogma, that all religious ideas of the heathen world are perversions of revelation; and so, in a greater or less degree, of many others. By far the most close and accurate observers of Indian superstition were the French and Italian Jesuits of the first half of the seventeenth century. Their opportunities were unrivalled; and they used them in a spirit of faithful inquiry, accumulating facts, and leaving theory to their successors. Of recent American writers, no one has given so much attention to the subject as Mr. Schoolcraft; but, in view of his opportunities and his zeal, his results are most unsatisfactory. The work in six large quarto volumes, History, Condition, and Prospects of Indian

Tribes, published by Government under his editorship, includes the substance of most of his previous writings. It is a singularly crude and illiterate production, stuffed with blunders and contradictions, giving evidence on every page of a striking unfitness either for historical or philosophical inquiry, and taxing to the utmost the patience of those who would extract what is valuable in it from its oceans of pedantic verbiage.]

The primitive Indian believed in the immortality of the soul,[1] but he did not always believe in a state of future reward and punishment. Nor, when such a belief existed, was the good to be rewarded a moral good, or the evil to be punished a moral evil. Skilful hunters, brave warriors, men of influence and consideration, went, after death, to the happy hunting-ground; while the slothful, the cowardly, and the weak were doomed to eat serpents and ashes in dreary regions of mist and darkness. In the general belief, however, there was but one land of shades for all alike. The spirits, in form and feature as they had been in life, wended their way through dark forests to the villages of the dead, subsisting on bark and rotten wood. On arriving, they sat all day in the crouching posture of the sick, and, when night came, hunted the shades of animals, with the shades of bows and arrows, among the shades of trees and rocks: for all things, animate and inanimate, were alike immortal, and all passed together to the gloomy country of the dead.

The belief respecting the land of souls varied greatly in different tribes and different individuals. Among the Hurons there were those who held that departed spirits pursued their journey through the sky, along the Milky Way, while the souls of dogs took another route, by certain constellations, known as the "Way of the Dogs." [Sagard, Voyage des Hurons, 233.]

At intervals of ten or twelve years, the Hurons, the Neutrals, and other kindred tribes, were accustomed to collect the bones of their dead, and deposit them, with great ceremony, in a common place of burial. The whole nation was sometimes assembled at this solemnity; and hundreds of corpses, brought from their temporary resting-places, were inhumed in one capacious pit.

---

1   The exceptions are exceedingly rare. Father Gravier says that a Peoria Indian once told him that there was no future life. It would be difficult to find another instance of the kind.

From this hour the immortality of their souls began. They took wing, as some affirmed, in the shape of pigeons; while the greater number declared that they journeyed on foot, and in their own likeness, to the land of shades, bearing with them the ghosts of the wampum-belts, beaver-skins, bows, arrows, pipes, kettles, beads, and rings buried with them in the common grave. [The practice of burying treasures with the dead is not peculiar to the North American aborigines. Thus, the London Times of Oct. 25, 1885, describing the funeral rites of Lord Palmerston, says: "And as the words, 'Dust to dust, ashes to ashes,' were pronounced, the chief mourner, as a last precious offering to the dead, threw into the grave several diamond and gold rings."] But as the spirits of the old and of children are too feeble for the march, they are forced to stay behind, lingering near their earthly villages, where the living often hear the shutting of their invisible cabin-doors, and the weak voices of the disembodied children driving birds from their corn-fields. [Brébeuf, Relation des Hurons, 1636, 99 (Cramoisy).] An endless variety of incoherent fancies is connected with the Indian idea of a future life. They commonly owe their origin to dreams, often to the dreams of those in extreme sickness, who, on awaking, supposed that they had visited the other world, and related to the wondering bystanders what they had seen.

The Indian land of souls is not always a region of shadows and gloom. The Hurons sometimes represented the souls of their dead—those of their dogs included—as dancing joyously in the presence of Ataentsic and Jouskeha. According to some Algonquin traditions, heaven was a scene of endless festivity, the ghosts dancing to the sound of the rattle and the drum, and greeting with hospitable welcome the occasional visitor from the living world: for the spirit-land was not far off, and roving hunters sometimes passed its confines unawares.

Most of the traditions agree, however, that the spirits, on their journey heavenward, were beset with difficulties and perils. There was a swift river which must be crossed on a log that shook beneath their feet, while a ferocious dog opposed their passage, and drove many into the abyss. This river was full of sturgeon and other fish, which the ghosts speared for their subsistence. Beyond was a narrow path between moving rocks, which each instant crashed together, grinding to atoms the less nimble of the pilgrims who essayed to pass. The Hurons believed that a personage named Oscotarach, or the Head-Piercer, dwelt in a bark house beside the path, and that it was his office to remove the brains from the heads of all who went by, as a necessary preparation for immortality. This singular idea is found also in some Algonquin traditions, according to which, however, the brain is afterwards restored to its owner.

[On Indian ideas of another life, compare Sagard, the Jesuit Relations, Perrot, Charlevoix, and Lafitau, with Tanner, James, Schoolcraft, and the Appendix to Morse's Indian Report.

Le Clerc recounts a singular story, current in his time among the Algonquins of Gaspé and Northern New Brunswick. The favorite son of an old Indian died; whereupon the father, with a party of friends, set out for the land of souls to recover him. It was only necessary to wade through a shallow lake, several days' journey in extent. This they did, sleeping at night on platforms of poles which supported them above the water. At length they arrived, and were met by Papkootparout, the Indian Pluto, who rushed on them in a rage, with his war-club upraised; but, presently relenting, changed his mind, and challenged them to a game of ball. They proved the victors, and won the stakes, consisting of corn, tobacco, and certain fruits, which thus became known to mankind. The bereaved father now begged hard for his son's soul, and Papkootparout at last gave it to him, in the form and size of a nut, which, by pressing it hard between his hands, he forced into a small leather bag. The delighted parent carried it back to earth, with instructions to insert it in the body of his son, who would thereupon return to life. When the adventurers reached home, and reported the happy issue of their journey, there was a dance of rejoicing; and the father, wishing to take part in it, gave his son's soul to the keeping of a squaw who stood by. Being curious to see it, she opened the bag; on which it escaped at once, and took flight for the realms of Papkootparout, preferring them to the abodes of the living.—Le Clerc, Nouvelle Relation de la Gaspésie, 310-328.]

Dreams were to the Indian a universal oracle. They revealed to him his guardian spirit, taught him the cure of his diseases, warned him of the devices of sorcerers, guided him to the lurking-places of his enemy or the haunts of game, and unfolded the secrets of good and evil destiny. The dream was a mysterious and inexorable power, whose least behests must be obeyed to the letter,—a source, in every Indian town, of endless mischief and abomination. There were professed dreamers, and professed interpreters of dreams. One of the most noted festivals among the Hurons and Iroquois was the Dream Feast, a scene of frenzy, where the actors counterfeited madness, and the town was like a bedlam turned loose. Each pretended to have dreamed of something necessary to his welfare, and rushed from house to house, demanding of all he met to guess his secret requirement and satisfy it.

Believing that the whole material world was instinct with powers to influence and control his fate, that good and evil spirits, and existences nameless and indefinable, filled all Nature, that a pervading sorcery was above, below, and around him, and that issues of life and death might be controlled by instruments the most unnoticeable and seemingly the most feeble, the Indian lived in perpetual fear. The turning of a leaf, the crawling of an insect, the cry of a bird, the creaking of a bough, might be to him the mystic signal of weal or woe.

An Indian community swarmed with sorcerers, medicine-men, and diviners, whose functions were often united in the same person. The sorcerer, by charms, magic songs, magic feasts, and the beating of his drum, had power over the spirits and those occult influences inherent in animals and inanimate things. He could call to him the souls of his enemies. They appeared before him in the form of stones. He chopped and bruised them with his hatchet; blood and flesh issued forth; and the intended victim, however distant, languished and died. Like the sorcerer of the Middle Ages, he made images of those he wished to destroy, and, muttering incantations, punctured them with an awl, whereupon the persons represented sickened and pined away.

The Indian doctor relied far more on magic than on natural remedies. Dreams, beating of the drum, songs, magic feasts and dances, and howling to frighten the female demon from his patient, were his ordinary methods of cure.

The prophet, or diviner, had various means of reading the secrets of futurity, such as the flight of birds, and the movements of water and fire. There was a peculiar practice of divination very general in the Algonquin family of tribes, among some of whom it still subsists. A small, conical lodge was made by planting poles in a circle, lashing the tops together at the height of about seven feet from the ground, and closely covering them with hides. The prophet crawled in, and closed the aperture after him. He then beat his drum and sang his magic songs to summon the spirits, whose weak, shrill voices were soon heard, mingled with his lugubrious chanting, while at intervals the juggler paused to interpret their communications to the attentive crowd seated on the ground without. During the whole scene, the lodge swayed to and fro with a violence which has astonished many a civilized beholder, and which some of the Jesuits explain by the ready solution of a genuine diabolic intervention.

[This practice was first observed by Champlain. (See "Pioneers of France in the New World.") From his time to the present, numerous writers have remarked upon it. Le Jeune, in the Relation of 1637, treats it at some length. The lodge was sometimes of a cylindrical, instead of a conical form.]

The sorcerers, medicine-men, and diviners did not usually exercise the function of priests. Each man sacrificed for himself to the powers he wished to propitiate, whether his guardian spirit, the spirits of animals, or the other beings of his belief. The most common offering was tobacco, thrown into the fire or water; scraps of meat were sometimes burned to the manitous; and, on a few rare occasions of public solemnity, a white dog, the mystic animal of many tribes, was tied to the end of an upright pole, as a sacrifice to some superior spirit, or to the sun, with which the superior spirits were constantly confounded by the primitive Indian. In recent times, when Judaism and Christianity have modified his religious ideas, it has been, and still is, the practice to sacrifice dogs to the Great Spirit. On these public occasions, the sacrificial function is discharged by chiefs, or by warriors appointed for the purpose.

[Many of the Indian feasts were feasts of sacrifice,— sometimes to the guardian spirit of the host, sometimes to an animal of which he has dreamed, sometimes to a local or other spirit. The food was first offered in a loud voice to the being to be propitiated, after which the guests proceeded to devour it for him. This unique method of sacrifice was practised at war-feasts and similar solemnities. For an excellent account of Indian religious feasts, see Perrot, Chap. V.

One of the most remarkable of Indian sacrifices was that practised by the Hurons in the case of a person drowned or frozen to death. The flesh of the deceased was cut off; and thrown into a fire made for the purpose, as an offering of propitiation to the spirits of the air or water. What remained of the body was then buried near the fire.—Brébeuf, Relation des Hurons, 1636, 108.

The tribes of Virginia, as described by Beverly and others, not only had priests who offered sacrifice, but idols and houses of worship.]

Among the Hurons and Iroquois, and indeed all the stationary tribes, there was an incredible number of mystic ceremonies, extravagant, puerile, and often disgusting, designed for the cure of the sick or for the general weal of the community. Most of their observances seem originally to have been dictated by dreams, and transmitted as a sacred heritage from generation to generation. They consisted in an endless variety of dances, masqueradings, and nondescript orgies; and a scrupulous adherence to all the traditional forms was held to be of the last moment, as the slightest failure in this respect might entail serious calamities. If children were seen in their play imitating any of these mysteries, they were grimly rebuked and punished. In many tribes secret magical societies existed, and still exist, into which members are initiated with peculiar ceremonies. These associations are greatly respected and feared. They have charms for love, war, and private revenge, and exert a great, and often a very mischievous influence. The societies of the Metai and the Wabeno, among the Northern Algonquins, are conspicuous examples; while other societies of similar character have, for a century, been known to exist among the Dahcotah.

[The Friendly Society of the Spirit, of which the initiatory ceremonies were seen and described by Carver (Travels, 271), preserves to this day its existence and its rites.]

A notice of the superstitious ideas of the Indians would be imperfect without a reference to the traditionary tales through which these ideas are handed down from father to son. Some of these tales can be traced back to the period of the earliest intercourse with Europeans. One at least of those recorded by the first missionaries, on the Lower St. Lawrence, is still current among the tribes of the Upper Lakes. Many of them are curious combinations of beliefs seriously entertained with strokes intended for humor and drollery, which never fail to awaken peals of laughter in the lodge-circle. Giants, dwarfs, cannibals, spirits, beasts, birds, and anomalous monsters, transformations, tricks, and sorcery, form the staple of the story. Some of the Iroquois tales embody conceptions which, however preposterous, are of a bold and striking character; but those of the Algonquins are, to an incredible degree, flimsy, silly, and meaningless; nor are those of the Dahcotah tribes much better. In respect to this wigwam lore, there is a curious superstition of very wide prevalence. The tales must not be told in summer; since at that season, when all Nature is full of life, the spirits are awake, and, hearing what is said of them, may take offence; whereas in winter they are fast sealed up in snow and ice, and no longer capable of listening.

[The prevalence of this fancy among the Algonquins in the remote parts of Canada is well established. The writer found it also among the extreme western bands of the Dahcotah. He tried, in the month of July, to persuade an old chief, a noted story-teller, to tell him some of the tales; but, though abundantly loquacious in respect to his own adventures, and even his dreams, the Indian obstinately refused, saying that winter was the time for the tales, and that it was bad to tell them in summer.

Mr. Schoolcraft has published a collection of Algonquin tales, under the title of Algic Researches. Most of them were translated by his wife, an educated Ojibwa half-breed. This book is perhaps the best of Mr. Schoolcraft's works, though its value is much impaired by the want of a literal rendering, and the introduction of decorations which savor more of a popular monthly magazine than of an Indian wigwam. Mrs. Eastman's interesting Legends of the Sioux (Dahcotah) is not free from the same defect. Other tales are scattered throughout the works of Mr. Schoolcraft and various modern writers. Some are to be found in the works of Lafitau and the other Jesuits. But few of the Iroquois legends have been printed, though a considerable number have been written down. The singular History of the Five Nations, by the old Tuscarora Indian, Cusick, gives the substance of some of them. Others will be found in Clark's History of Onondaga.]

It is obvious that the Indian mind has never seriously occupied itself with any of the higher themes of thought. The beings of its belief are not impersonations of the forces of Nature, the courses of human destiny, or the movements of human intellect, will, and passion. In the midst of Nature; the Indian knew nothing of her laws. His perpetual reference of her phenomena to occult agencies forestalled inquiry and precluded inductive reasoning. If the wind blew with violence, it was because the water-lizard, which makes the wind, had crawled out of his pool; if the lightning was sharp and frequent, it was because the young of the thunder-bird were restless in their nest; if a blight fell upon the corn, it was because the Corn Spirit was angry; and if the beavers were shy and difficult to catch, it was because they had taken offence at seeing the bones of one of their race thrown to a dog. Well, and even highly developed, in a few instances,—I allude especially to the Iroquois,—with respect to certain points of material concernment, the mind of the Indian in other respects was and is almost hopelessly stagnant. The very traits that raise him above the servile races are hostile to the kind and degree of civilization which those races so easily attain. His intractable spirit of independence, and the pride which forbids him to be an imitator, reinforce but too strongly that savage lethargy of mind from which it is so hard to rouse him. No race, perhaps, ever offered greater difficulties to those laboring for its improvement.

To sum up the results of this examination, the primitive Indian was as savage in his religion as in his life. He was divided between fetich-worship and that next degree of religious development which consists in the worship of deities embodied in the human form. His conception of their attributes was such as might have been expected. His gods were no whit better than himself. Even when he borrows from Christianity the idea of a Supreme and Universal Spirit, his tendency is to reduce Him to a local habitation and a bodily shape; and this tendency disappears only in tribes that have been long in contact with civilized white men. The primitive Indian, yielding his untutored homage to One All-pervading and Omnipotent Spirit, is a dream of poets, rhetoricians, and sentimentalists.

THE JESUITS IN NORTH AMERICA.

CHAPTER I.

1634.

NOTRE-DAME DES ANGES.

QUEBEC IN 1634.—FATHER LE JEUNE.—THE MISSION-HOUSE.—ITS DOMESTIC ECONOMY.—THE JESUITS AND THEIR DESIGNS.

Opposite Quebec lies the tongue of land called Point Levi. One who, in the summer of the year 1634, stood on its margin and looked northward, across the St. Lawrence, would have seen, at the distance of a mile or more, a range of lofty cliffs, rising on the left into the bold heights of Cape Diamond, and on the right sinking abruptly to the bed of the tributary river St. Charles. Beneath these cliffs, at the brink of the St. Lawrence, he would have descried a cluster of warehouses, sheds, and wooden tenements. Immediately above, along the verge of the precipice, he could have traced the outlines of a fortified work, with a flagstaff, and a few small cannon to command the river; while, at the only point where Nature had made the heights accessible, a zigzag path connected the warehouses and the fort.

Now, embarked in the canoe of some Montagnais Indian, let him cross the St. Lawrence, land at the pier, and, passing the cluster of buildings, climb the pathway up the cliff. Pausing for rest and breath, he might see, ascending and descending, the tenants of this outpost of the wilderness: a soldier of the fort, or an officer in slouched hat and plume; a factor of the fur company, owner and sovereign lord of all Canada; a party of Indians; a trader from the upper country, one of the precursors of that hardy race of *coureurs de bois*, destined to form a conspicuous and striking feature of the Canadian population: next, perhaps, would appear a figure widely different. The close, black cassock, the rosary hanging from the waist, and the wide, black hat, looped up at the sides, proclaimed the Jesuit,—Father Le Jeune, Superior of the Residence of Quebec.

And now, that we may better know the aspect and condition of the infant colony and incipient mission, we will follow the priest on his way. Mounting the steep path, he reached the top of the cliff, some two hundred feet above the river and the warehouses. On the left lay the fort built by Champlain, covering a part of the ground now forming Durham Terrace and the Place d'Armes. Its ramparts were of logs and earth, and within was a turreted building of stone, used as a barrack, as officers' quarters, and for other purposes. [Compare the various notices in Champlain (1632) with that of Du Creux, Historia Canadensis, 204.] Near the fort stood a small chapel, newly built. The surrounding country was cleared and partially cultivated; yet only one dwelling-house worthy the name appeared. It was a substantial cottage, where lived Madame Hébert, widow of the first settler of Canada, with her daughter, her son-in-law Couillard, and their children, good Catholics all, who, two years before, when Quebec was evacuated by the English,[1] wept for joy at beholding Le Jeune, and his brother Jesuit, De Noué, crossing their threshold to offer beneath their roof the long-forbidden sacrifice of the Mass. There were inclosures with cattle near at hand; and the house, with its surroundings, betokened industry and thrift.

Thence Le Jeune walked on, across the site of the modern market-place, and still onward, near the line of the cliffs which sank abruptly on his right. Beneath lay the mouth of the St. Charles; and, beyond, the wilderness shore of Beauport swept in a wide curve eastward, to where, far in the distance, the Gulf of Montmorenci yawned on the great river. [The settlement of Beauport was begun this year, or the year following, by the Sieur Giffard, to whom a large tract had been granted here—Langevin, Notes sur les Archives de

---

1   See "Pioneers of France in the New World." Hébert's cottage seems to have stood between Ste.-Famille and Couillard Streets, as appears by a contract of 1634, cited by M. Ferland.

N. D. de Beauport, 5.] The priest soon passed the clearings, and entered the woods which covered the site of the present suburb of St. John. Thence he descended to a lower plateau, where now lies the suburb of St. Roch, and, still advancing, reached a pleasant spot at the extremity of the Pointe-aux-Lièvres, a tract of meadow land nearly inclosed by a sudden bend of the St. Charles. Here lay a canoe or skiff; and, paddling across the narrow stream, Le Jeune saw on the meadow, two hundred yards from the bank, a square inclosure formed of palisades, like a modern picket fort of the Indian frontier.[1] Within this inclosure were two buildings, one of which had been half burned by the English, and was not yet repaired. It served as storehouse, stable, workshop, and bakery. Opposite stood the principal building, a structure of planks, plastered with mud, and thatched with long grass from the meadows. It consisted of one story, a garret, and a cellar, and contained four principal rooms, of which one served as chapel, another as refectory, another as kitchen, and the fourth as a lodging for workmen. The furniture of all was plain in the extreme. Until the preceding year, the chapel had had no other ornament than a sheet on which were glued two coarse engravings; but the priests had now decorated their altar with an image of a dove representing the Holy Ghost, an image of Loyola, another of Xavier, and three images of the Virgin. Four cells opened from the refectory, the largest of which was eight feet square. In these lodged six priests, while two lay brothers found shelter in the garret. The house had been hastily built, eight years before, and now leaked in all parts. Such was the Residence of Notre-Dame des Anges. Here was nourished the germ of a vast enterprise, and this was the cradle of the great mission of New France.[2]

---

1   This must have been very near the point where the streamlet called the River Lairet enters the St. Charles. The place has a triple historic interest. The wintering-place of Cartier in 1535-6 (see "Pioneers of France") seems to have been here. Here, too, in 1759, Montcalm's bridge of boats crossed the St. Charles; and in a large intrenchment, which probably included the site of the Jesuit mission-house, the remnants of his shattered army rallied, after their defeat on the Plains of Abraham.—See the very curious Narrative of the Chevalier Johnstone, published by the Historical Society of Quebec.

2   The above particulars are gathered from the Relations of 1626 (Lalemant), and 1632, 1633, 1634, 1635 (Le Jeune), but chiefly from a long letter of the Father Superior to the Provincial of the Jesuits at Paris, containing a curiously minute report of the state of the mission. It was sent from Quebec by the returning

Of the six Jesuits gathered in the refectory for the evening meal, one was conspicuous among the rest,—a tall, strong man, with features that seemed carved by Nature for a soldier, but which the mental habits of years had stamped with the visible impress of the priesthood. This was Jean de Brébeuf, descendant of a noble family of Normandy, and one of the ablest and most devoted zealots whose names stand on the missionary rolls of his Order. His companions were Masse, Daniel, Davost, De Noüe, and the Father Superior, Le Jeune. Masse was the same priest who had been the companion of Father Biard in the abortive mission of Acadia. [See "Pioneers of France in the New World."] By reason of his useful qualities, Le Jeune nicknamed him "le Père Utile." At present, his special function was the care of the pigs and cows, which he kept in the inclosure around the buildings, lest they should ravage the neighboring fields of rye, barley, wheat, and maize.[1] De Noüe had charge of the eight or ten workmen employed by the mission, who gave him at times no little trouble by their repinings and complaints.[2] They were forced to hear mass every morning and prayers every evening, besides an exhortation on Sunday. Some of them were for returning home, while two or three, of a different complexion, wished to be Jesuits themselves. The Fathers, in their intervals of leisure, worked with their men, spade in hand. For the rest, they were busied in preaching, singing vespers, saying mass and hearing confessions at the fort of Quebec, catechizing a few Indians, and striving to master the enormous difficulties of the Huron and Algonquin languages.

Well might Father Le Jeune write to his Superior, "The harvest is plentiful, and the laborers few." These men aimed at the conversion of a continent. From their hovel on the St. Charles they

---

ships in the summer of 1634, and will be found in Carayon, Première Mission des Jésuites au Canada, 122. The original is in the archives of the Order at Rome.

1   "Le P. Masse, que je nomme quelquefois en riant le Père Utile, est bien cognu de V. R. Il a soin des choses domestiques et du bestail que nous avons, en quoy il a très-bien reussy."—Lettre du P. Paul le Jeune au R. P. Provincial, in Carayon, 122.—Le Jeune does not fail to send an inventory of the "bestail" to his Superior, namely: "Deux grosses truies qui nourissent chacune quatre petits cochons, deux vaches, deux petites genisses, et un petit taureau."

2   The methodical Le Jeune sets down the causes of their discontent under six different heads, each duly numbered. Thus:—

        "1. C'est le naturel des artisans de se plaindre et de gronder."

        "2. La diversité des gages les fait murmurer," etc.

surveyed a field of labor whose vastness might tire the wings of thought itself; a scene repellent and appalling, darkened with omens of peril and woe. They were an advance-guard of the great army of Loyola, strong in a discipline that controlled not alone the body and the will, but the intellect, the heart, the soul, and the inmost consciousness. The lives of these early Canadian Jesuits attest the earnestness of their faith and the intensity of their zeal; but it was a zeal bridled, curbed, and ruled by a guiding hand. Their marvellous training in equal measure kindled enthusiasm and controlled it, roused into action a mighty power, and made it as subservient as those great material forces which modern science has learned to awaken and to govern. They were drilled to a factitious humility, prone to find utterance in expressions of self-depreciation and self-scorn, which one may often judge unwisely, when he condemns them as insincere. They were devoted believers, not only in the fundamental dogmas of Rome, but in those lesser matters of faith which heresy despises as idle and puerile superstitions. One great aim engrossed their lives. "For the greater glory of God"—ad majorem Dei gloriam—they would act or wait, dare, suffer, or die, yet all in unquestioning subjection to the authority of the Superiors, in whom they recognized the agents of Divine authority itself.

CHAPTER II.

LOYOLA AND THE JESUITS.

CONVERSION OF LOYOLA.—FOUNDATION OF THE SOCIETY OF JESUS.—PREPARATION OF THE NOVICE.—CHARACTERISTICS OF THE ORDER.—THE CANADIAN JESUITS.

It was an evil day for new-born Protestantism, when a French artilleryman fired the shot that struck down Ignatius Loyola in the breach of Pampeluna. A proud noble, an aspiring soldier, a graceful courtier, an ardent and daring gallant was metamorphosed by that stroke into the zealot whose brain engendered and brought forth the mighty Society of Jesus. His story is a familiar one: how, in the solitude of his sick-room, a change came over him, upheaving, like an earthquake, all the forces of his nature; how, in the cave of Manresa, the mysteries of Heaven were revealed to him; how he passed from agonies to transports, from transports to the calm of a determined purpose. The soldier gave himself to a new warfare. In the forge of his great intellect, heated, but not disturbed by the intense fires of his zeal, was wrought the prodigious enginery whose power has been felt to the uttermost confines of the world.

Loyola's training had been in courts and camps: of books he knew little or nothing. He had lived in the unquestioning faith of one born and bred in the very focus of Romanism; and thus, at the age of about thirty, his conversion found him. It was a change of life and purpose, not of belief. He presumed not to inquire into the doctrines of the Church. It was for him to enforce those doctrines; and to this end he turned all the faculties of his potent intellect, and all his deep knowledge of mankind. He did not aim to build up barren communities of secluded monks, aspiring to heaven through prayer, penance, and meditation, but to subdue the world to the dominion of the dogmas which had subdued him; to organize and discipline a mighty host, controlled by one purpose and one mind, fired by a quenchless zeal or nerved by a fixed resolve, yet impelled, restrained, and directed by a single master hand. The Jesuit is no dreamer: he is emphatically a man of action; action is the end of his existence.

It was an arduous problem which Loyola undertook to solve,—to rob a man of volition, yet to preserve in him, nay, to stimulate, those energies which would make him the most efficient instrument of a great design. To this end the Jesuit novitiate and the constitutions of the Order are directed. The enthusiasm of the novice is urged to its intensest pitch; then, in the name of religion, he is summoned to the utter abnegation of intellect and will in favor of the Superior, in whom he is commanded to recognize the representative of God on earth. Thus the young zealot makes no slavish sacrifice of intellect and will; at least, so he is taught: for he sacrifices them, not to man, but to his Maker. No limit is set to his submission: if the Superior pronounces black to be white, he is bound in conscience to acquiesce.

[Those who wish to know the nature of the Jesuit virtue of obedience will find it set forth in the famous Letter on Obedience of Loyola.]

Loyola's book of Spiritual Exercises is well known. In these exercises lies the hard and narrow path which is the only entrance to the Society of Jesus. The book is, to all appearance, a dry and superstitious formulary; but, in the hands of a skilful director of consciences, it has proved of terrible efficacy. The novice, in solitude and darkness, day after day and night after night, ponders its images of perdition and despair. He is taught to hear, in imagination, the howlings of the damned, to see their convulsive agonies, to feel the flames that burn without consuming, to smell the corruption of the tomb and the fumes of the infernal pit. He must picture to himself an array of adverse armies, one commanded by Satan on the plains of Babylon, one encamped under Christ about the walls of Jerusalem; and the perturbed mind, humbled by long contemplation of its own vileness, is ordered to enroll itself under one or the other banner. Then, the choice made, it is led to a region of serenity and celestial peace, and soothed with images of divine benignity and grace. These meditations last, without intermission, about a month, and, under an astute and experienced directorship, they have been found of such power, that the Manual of Spiritual Exercises boasts to have saved souls more in number than the letters it contains.

To this succeed two years of discipline and preparation, directed, above all things else, to perfecting the virtues of humility and obedience. The novice is obliged to perform the lowest menial offices, and the most repulsive duties of the sick-room and the hospital; and he is sent forth, for weeks together, to beg his bread like a common mendicant. He is required to reveal to his confessor, not only his sins, but all those hidden tendencies, instincts, and impulses which form the distinctive traits of character. He is set to watch his comrades, and his comrades are set to watch him. Each must report what he observes of the acts and dispositions of the others; and this mutual espionage does not end with the novitiate, but extends to the close of life. The characteristics of every member of the Order are minutely analyzed, and methodically put on record.

This horrible violence to the noblest qualities of manhood, joined to that equivocal system of morality which eminent casuists of the Order have inculcated, must, it may be thought, produce deplorable effects upon the characters of those under its influence. Whether this has been actually the case, the reader of history may determine. It is certain, however, that the Society of Jesus has numbered among its members men whose fervent and exalted natures have been intensified, without being abased, by the pressure to which they have been subjected.

It is not for nothing that the Society studies the character of its members so intently, and by methods so startling. It not only uses its knowledge to thrust into obscurity or cast out altogether those whom it discovers to be dull, feeble, or unwilling instruments of its purposes, but it assigns to every one the task to which his talents or his disposition may best adapt him: to one, the care of a royal conscience, whereby, unseen, his whispered word may guide the destiny of nations; to another, the instruction of children; to another, a career of letters or science; and to the fervent and the self-sacrificing, sometimes also to the restless and uncompliant, the distant missions to the heathen.

The Jesuit was, and is, everywhere,—in the school-room, in the library, in the cabinets of princes and ministers, in the huts of savages, in the tropics, in the frozen North, in India, in China, in Japan, in Africa, in America; now as a Christian priest, now as a soldier, a mathematician, an astrologer, a Brahmin, a mandarin, under countless disguises, by a thousand arts, luring, persuading, or compelling souls into the fold of Rome.

Of this vast mechanism for guiding and governing the minds of men, this mighty enginery for subduing the earth to the dominion of an idea, this harmony of contradictions, this moral Proteus, the faintest sketch must now suffice. A disquisition on the Society of Jesus would be without end. No religious order has ever united in itself so much to be admired and so much to be detested. Unmixed praise has been poured on its Canadian members. It is not for me to eulogize them, but to portray them as they were.

CHAPTER III.

1632, 1633.

PAUL LE JEUNE.

LE JEUNE'S VOYAGE.—HIS FIRST PUPILS.—HIS STUDIES.—HIS INDIAN TEACHER.—WINTER AT THE MISSION-HOUSE.—LE JEUNE'S SCHOOL.—REINFORCEMENTS.

In another narrative, we have seen how the Jesuits, supplanting the Récollet friars, their predecessors, had adopted as their own the rugged task of Christianizing New France. We have seen, too, how a descent of the English, or rather of Huguenots fighting under English colors, had overthrown for a time the miserable little colony, with the mission to which it was wedded; and how Quebec was at length restored to France, and the broken thread of the Jesuit enterprise resumed. ["Pioneers of France."]

It was then that Le Jeune had embarked for the New World. He was in his convent at Dieppe when he received the order to depart; and he set forth in haste for Havre, filled, he assures us, with inexpressible joy at the prospect of a living or a dying martyrdom. At Rouen he was joined by De Nouë, with a lay brother named Gilbert; and the three sailed together on the eighteenth of April, 1632. The sea treated them roughly; Le Jeune was wretchedly sea-sick; and the ship nearly foundered in a gale. At length they came in sight of "that miserable country," as the missionary calls the scene of his future labors. It was in the harbor of Tadoussac that he first encountered the objects of his apostolic cares; for, as he sat in the ship's cabin with the master, it was suddenly invaded by ten or twelve Indians, whom he compares to a party of maskers at the Carnival. Some had their cheeks painted black, their noses blue, and the rest of their faces red. Others were decorated with a broad band of black across the eyes; and others, again, with diverging rays of black, red, and blue on both cheeks. Their attire was no less uncouth. Some of them wore shaggy bear skins, reminding the priest of the pictures of St. John the Baptist.

After a vain attempt to save a number of Iroquois prisoners whom they were preparing to burn alive on shore, Le Jeune and his companions again set sail, and reached Quebec on the fifth of July. Having said mass, as already mentioned, under the roof of Madame Hébert and her delighted family, the Jesuits made their way to the two hovels built by their predecessors on the St. Charles, which had suffered woful dilapidation at the hands of the English. Here they made their abode, and applied themselves, with such skill as they could command, to repair the shattered tenements and cultivate the waste meadows around.

The beginning of Le Jeune's missionary labors was neither imposing nor promising. He describes himself seated with a small Indian boy on one side and a small negro on the other, the latter of whom had been left by the English as a gift to Madame Hébert. As neither of the three understood the language of the others, the pupils made little progress in spiritual knowledge. The missionaries, it was clear, must learn Algonquin at any cost; and, to this end, Le Jeune resolved to visit the Indian encampments. Hearing that a band of Montagnais were fishing for eels on the St. Lawrence, between Cape Diamond and the cove which now bears the name of Wolfe, he set forth for the spot on a morning in October. As, with toil and trepidation, he scrambled around the foot of the cape,—whose precipices, with a chaos of loose rocks, thrust themselves at that day into the deep tidewater,—he dragged down upon himself the trunk of a fallen tree, which, in its descent, well nigh swept him into the river. The peril past, he presently reached his destination. Here, among the lodges of bark, were stretched innumerable strings of hide, from which hung to dry an incredible multitude of eels. A boy invited him into the lodge of a withered squaw, his grandmother, who hastened to offer him four smoked eels on a piece of birch bark, while other squaws of the household instructed him how to roast them on a forked stick over the embers. All shared the feast together, his entertainers using as napkins their own hair or that of their dogs; while Le Jeune, intent on increasing his knowledge of Algonquin, maintained an active discourse of broken words and pantomime. [Le Jeune, Relation, 1633, 2.]

The lesson, however, was too laborious, and of too little profit, to be often repeated, and the missionary sought anxiously for more stable instruction. To find such was not easy. The interpreters— Frenchmen, who, in the interest of the fur company, had spent years among the Indians—were averse to Jesuits, and refused their aid. There was one resource, however, of which Le Jeune would fain avail himself. An Indian, called Pierre by the French, had been carried to France by the Récollet friars, instructed, converted, and baptized. He had lately returned to Canada, where, to the scandal of the Jesuits, he had relapsed into his old ways, retaining of his French education little besides a few new vices. He still haunted the fort at Quebec, lured by the hope of an occasional gift of wine or tobacco, but shunned the Jesuits, of whose rigid way of life he stood in horror. As he spoke good French and good Indian, he would have been invaluable to the embarrassed priests at the mission. Le Jeune invoked the aid of the Saints. The effect of his prayers soon appeared, he tells us, in a direct interposition of Providence, which so disposed the heart of Pierre that he quarrelled with the French commandant, who thereupon closed the fort against him. He then repaired to his friends and relatives in the woods, but only to encounter a rebuff from a young squaw to whom he made his addresses. On this, he turned his steps towards the mission-house, and, being unfitted by his French education for supporting himself by hunting, begged food and shelter from the priests. Le Jeune gratefully accepted him as a gift vouchsafed by Heaven to his prayers, persuaded a lackey at the fort to give him a cast-off suit of clothes, promised him maintenance, and installed him as his teacher.

Seated on wooden stools by the rough table in the refectory, the priest and the Indian pursued their studies. "How thankful I am," writes Le Jeune, "to those who gave me tobacco last year! At every difficulty I give my master a piece of it, to make him more attentive."

[Relation, 1633, 7. He continues: "Ie ne sçaurois assez rendre graces à Nostre Seigneur de cet heureux rencontre . . . Que Dieu soit beny pour vn iamais, sa prouidence est adorable, et sa bonté n'a point de limites."]

Meanwhile, winter closed in with a severity rare even in Canada. The St. Lawrence and the St. Charles were hard frozen; rivers, forests, and rocks were mantled alike in dazzling sheets of snow. The humble mission-house of Notre-Dame des Anges was half buried in the drifts, which, heaped up in front where a path had been dug through them, rose two feet above the low eaves. The priests, sitting at night before the blazing logs of their wide-throated chimney, heard the trees in the neighboring forest cracking with frost, with a sound like the report of a pistol. Le Jeune's ink froze, and his fingers were benumbed, as he toiled at his declensions and conjugations, or translated the Pater Noster into blundering Algonquin. The water in the cask beside the fire froze nightly, and the ice was broken every morning with hatchets. The blankets of the two priests were fringed with the icicles of their congealed breath, and the frost lay in a thick coating on the lozenge-shaped glass of their cells. [Le Jeune, Relation, 1633, 14, 15.]

By day, Le Jeune and his companion practised with snow-shoes, with all the mishaps which attend beginners,—the trippings, the falls, and headlong dives into the soft drifts, amid the laughter of the Indians. Their seclusion was by no means a solitude. Bands of Montagnais, with their sledges and dogs, often passed the mission-house on their way to hunt the moose. They once invited De Noüe to go with them; and he, scarcely less eager than Le Jeune to learn their language, readily consented. In two or three weeks he appeared, sick, famished, and half dead with exhaustion. "Not ten priests in a hundred," writes Le Jeune to his Superior, "could bear this winter life with the savages." But what of that? It was not for them to falter. They were but instruments in the hands of God, to be used, broken, and thrown aside, if such should be His will.

["Voila, mon Reuerend Pere, vn eschantillon de ce qu'il faut souffrir courant apres les Sauuages . . . Il faut prendre sa vie, et tout ce qu'on a, et le ietter à l'abandon, pour ainsi dire, se contentant d'vne croix bien grosse et bien pesante pour toute richesse. Il est bien vray que Dieu ne se laisse point vaincre, et que plus on quitte, plus on trouue: plus on perd, plus on gaigne: mais Dieu se cache

par fois, et alors le Calice est bien amer."—Le Jeune, Relation 1633, 19.]

An Indian made Le Jeune a present of two small children, greatly to the delight of the missionary, who at once set himself to teaching them to pray in Latin. As the season grew milder, the number of his scholars increased; for, when parties of Indians encamped in the neighborhood, he would take his stand at the door, and, like Xavier at Goa, ring a bell. At this, a score of children would gather around him; and he, leading them into the refectory, which served as his school-room, taught them to repeat after him the Pater, Aye, and Credo, expounded the mystery of the Trinity, showed them the sign of the cross, and made them repeat an Indian prayer, the joint composition of Pierre and himself; then followed the catechism, the lesson closing with singing the Pater Noster, translated by the missionary into Algonquin rhymes; and when all was over, he rewarded each of his pupils with a porringer of peas, to insure their attendance at his next bell-ringing.

["I'ay commencé à appeller quelques enfans auec vne petite clochette. La premiere fois i'en auois six, puis douze, puis quinze, puis vingt et davantage; ie leur fais dire le Pater, Aue, et Credo, etc . . . . Nous finissons par le Pater Noster, que i'ay composé quasi en rimes en leur langue, que ie leur fais chanter: et pour derniere conclusion, ie leur fais donner chacun vne escuellée de pois, qu'ils mangent de bon appetit," etc.—Le Jeune, Relation, 1633, 23.]

It was the end of May, when the priests one morning heard the sound of cannon from the fort, and were gladdened by the tidings that Samuel de Champlain had arrived to resume command at Quebec, bringing with him four more Jesuits,—Brébeuf, Masse, Daniel, and Davost. [See "Pioneers of France."] Brébeuf, from the first, turned his eyes towards the distant land of the Hurons,—a field of labor full of peril, but rich in hope and promise. Le Jeune's duties as Superior restrained him from wanderings so remote. His apostleship must be limited, for a time, to the vagabond hordes of Algonquins, who roamed the forests of the lower St. Lawrence, and of whose language he had been so sedulous a student. His difficulties had of late been increased by the absence of Pierre, who had run off as Lent drew near, standing in dread of that season of fasting. Masse brought tidings of him from Tadoussac, whither he had gone, and where a party of English had given him liquor, destroying the last trace of Le Jeune's late exhortations. "God forgive those," writes the Father, "who introduced heresy into this country! If this savage, corrupted as he is by these miserable heretics, had any wit, he would be a great hindrance to the spread of the Faith. It is plain that he was given us, not for the good of his soul, but only that we might extract from him the principles of his language." [Relation, 1633, 29.]

Pierre had two brothers. One, well known as a hunter, was named Mestigoit; the other was the most noted "medicine-man," or, as the Jesuits called him, sorcerer, in the tribe of the Montagnais. Like the rest of their people, they were accustomed to set out for their winter hunt in the autumn, after the close of their eel-fishery. Le Jeune, despite the experience of De Noüe, had long had a mind to accompany one of these roving bands, partly in the hope, that, in some hour of distress, he might touch their hearts, or, by a timely drop of baptismal water, dismiss some dying child to paradise, but chiefly with the object of mastering their language. Pierre had rejoined his brothers; and, as the hunting season drew near, they all begged the missionary to make one of their party,— not, as he thought, out of any love for him, but solely with a view to the provisions with which they doubted not he would be well supplied. Le Jeune, distrustful of the sorcerer, demurred, but at length resolved to go.

CHAPTER IV.

1633, 1634.

LE JEUNE AND THE HUNTERS.

LE JEUNE JOINS THE INDIANS.—THE FIRST ENCAMPMENT.—THE APOSTATE.—FOREST LIFE IN WINTER.—THE INDIAN HUT.—THE SORCERER.—HIS PERSECUTION OF THE PRIEST.—EVIL COMPANY.— MAGIC. — INCANTATIONS. — CHRISTMAS. — STARVATION.—HOPES OF CONVERSION.— BACKSLIDING.—PERIL AND ESCAPE OF LE JEUNE.—HIS RETURN.

On a morning in the latter part of October, Le Jeune embarked with the Indians, twenty in all, men, women, and children. No other Frenchman was of the party. Champlain bade him an anxious farewell, and commended him to the care of his red associates, who had taken charge of his store of biscuit, flour, corn, prunes, and turnips, to which, in an evil hour, his friends had persuaded him to add a small keg of wine. The canoes glided along the wooded shore of the Island of Orleans, and the party landed, towards evening, on the small island immediately below. Le Jeune was delighted with the spot, and the wild beauties of the autumnal sunset.

His reflections, however, were soon interrupted. While the squaws were setting up their bark lodges, and Mestigoit was shooting wild-fowl for supper, Pierre returned to the canoes, tapped the keg of wine, and soon fell into the mud, helplessly drunk. Revived by the immersion, he next appeared at the camp, foaming at the mouth, threw down the lodges, overset the kettle, and chased the shrieking squaws into the woods. His brother Mestigoit rekindled the fire, and slung the kettle anew; when Pierre, who meanwhile had been raving like a madman along the shore, reeled in a fury to the spot to repeat his former exploit. Mestigoit anticipated him, snatched the kettle from the fire, and threw the scalding contents in his face. "He was never so well washed before in his life," says Le Jeune; "he lost all the skin of his face and breast. Would to God his heart had changed also!"[1] He roared in his frenzy for a hatchet to kill the missionary, who therefore thought it prudent to spend the night in the neighboring woods. Here he stretched himself on the earth, while a charitable squaw covered him with a sheet of birch-bark. "Though my bed," he writes, "had not been made up since the creation of the world, it was not hard enough to prevent me from sleeping."

Such was his initiation into Indian winter life. Passing over numerous adventures by water and land, we find the party, on the twelfth of November, leaving their canoes on an island, and wading ashore at low tide over the flats to the southern bank of the St. Lawrence. As two other bands had joined them, their number was increased to forty-five persons. Now, leaving the river behind, they entered those savage highlands whence issue the springs of the St. John,—a wilderness of rugged mountain-ranges, clad in dense, continuous forests, with no human tenant but this troop of miserable rovers, and here and there some kindred band, as miserable as they. Winter had set in, and already dead Nature was sheeted in funereal white. Lakes and ponds were frozen, rivulets sealed up, torrents encased with stalactites of ice; the black rocks and the black trunks of the pine-trees were beplastered with snow, and its heavy masses crushed the dull green boughs into the drifts beneath. The forest was silent as the grave.

Through this desolation the long file of Indians made its way, all on snow-shoes, each man, woman, and child bending under a heavy load, or dragging a sledge, narrow, but of prodigious length.

---

1   "Iamais il ne fut si bien laué, il changea de peau en la face et en tout l'estomach: pleust à Dieu que son ame eust changé aussi bien que son corps!"—Relation, 1634, 59.

They carried their whole wealth with them, on their backs or on their sledges,—kettles, axes, hides of meat, if such they had, and huge rolls of birch-bark for covering their wigwams. The Jesuit was loaded like the rest. The dogs alone floundered through the drifts unburdened. There was neither path nor level ground. Descending, climbing, stooping beneath half-fallen trees, clambering over piles of prostrate trunks, struggling through matted cedar-swamps, threading chill ravines, and crossing streams no longer visible, they toiled on till the day began to decline, then stopped to encamp.[1] Burdens were thrown down, and sledges unladen. The squaws, with knives and hatchets, cut long poles of birch and spruce saplings; while the men, with snow-shoes for shovels, cleared a round or square space in the snow, which formed an upright wall three or four feet high, inclosing the area of the wigwam. On one side, a passage was cut for an entrance, and the poles were planted around the top of the wall of snow, sloping and converging. On these poles were spread the sheets of birch-bark; a bear-skin was hung in the passage-way for a door; the bare ground within and the surrounding snow were covered with spruce boughs; and the work was done.

This usually occupied about three hours, during which Le Jeune, spent with travel, and weakened by precarious and unaccustomed fare, had the choice of shivering in idleness, or taking part in a labor which fatigued, without warming, his exhausted frame. The sorcerer's wife was in far worse case. Though in the extremity of a mortal sickness, they left her lying in the snow till the wigwam was made,—without a word, on her part, of remonstrance or complaint. Le Jeune, to the great ire of her husband, sometimes spent the interval in trying to convert her; but she proved intractable, and soon died unbaptized.

---

1   "S'il arriuoit quelque dégel, ô Dieu quelle peine! Il me sembloit que ie marchois sur vn chemin de verre qui se cassoit à tous coups soubs mes pieds: la neige congelée venant à s'amollir, tomboit et s'enfonçoit par esquarres ou grandes pieces, et nous en auions bien souuent iusques aux genoux, quelquefois iusqu'à la ceinture. Que s'il y auoit de la peine à tomber, il y en auoit encor plus à se retirer: car nos raquettes se chargeoient de neiges et se rendoient si pesantes, que quand vous veniez à les retirer il vous sembloit qu'on vous tiroit les iambes pour vous démembrer. I'en ay veu qui glissoient tellement soubs des souches enseuelies soubs la neige, qu'ils ne pouuoient tirer ny iambes ny raquettes sans secours: or figurez vous maintenant vne personne chargée comme vn mulet, et iugez si la vie des Sauuages est douce."— Relation, 1634, 67.

Thus lodged, they remained so long as game could be found within a circuit of ten or twelve miles, and then, subsistence failing, removed to another spot. Early in the winter, they hunted the beaver and the Canada porcupine; and, later, in the season of deep snows, chased the moose and the caribou.

Put aside the bear-skin, and enter the hut. Here, in a space some thirteen feet square, were packed nineteen savages, men, women, and children, with their dogs, crouched, squatted, coiled like hedgehogs, or lying on their backs, with knees drawn up perpendicularly to keep their feet out of the fire. Le Jeune, always methodical, arranges the grievances inseparable from these rough quarters under four chief heads,—Cold, Heat, Smoke, and Dogs. The bark covering was full of crevices, through which the icy blasts streamed in upon him from all sides; and the hole above, at once window and chimney, was so large, that, as he lay, he could watch the stars as well as in the open air. While the fire in the midst, fed with fat pine-knots, scorched him on one side, on the other he had much ado to keep himself from freezing. At times, however, the crowded hut seemed heated to the temperature of an oven. But these evils were light, when compared to the intolerable plague of smoke. During a snow-storm, and often at other times, the wigwam was filled with fumes so dense, stifling, and acrid, that all its inmates were forced to lie flat on their faces, breathing through mouths in contact with the cold earth. Their throats and nostrils felt as if on fire; their scorched eyes streamed with tears; and when Le Jeune tried to read, the letters of his breviary seemed printed in blood. The dogs were not an unmixed evil, for, by sleeping on and around him, they kept him warm at night; but, as an offset to this good service, they walked, ran, and jumped over him as he lay, snatched the food from his birchen dish, or, in a mad rush at some bone or discarded morsel, now and then overset both dish and missionary.

Sometimes of an evening he would leave the filthy den, to read his breviary in peace by the light of the moon. In the forest around sounded the sharp crack of frost-riven trees; and from the horizon to the zenith shot up the silent meteors of the northern lights, in whose fitful flashings the awe-struck Indians beheld the dancing of the spirits of the dead. The cold gnawed him to the bone; and, his devotions over, he turned back shivering. The illumined hut, from many a chink and crevice, shot forth into the gloom long streams of light athwart the twisted boughs. He stooped and entered. All within glowed red and fiery around the blazing pine-knots where, like brutes in their kennel, were gathered the savage crew. He stepped to his place, over recumbent bodies and leggined and moccasined limbs, and seated himself on the carpet of spruce boughs. Here a tribulation awaited him, the crowning misery of his winter-quarters,—worse, as he declares, than cold, heat, and dogs.

Of the three brothers who had invited him to join the party, one, we have seen, was the hunter, Mestigoit; another, the sorcerer; and the third, Pierre, whom, by reason of his falling away from the Faith, Le Jeune always mentions as the Apostate. He was a weak-minded young Indian, wholly under the influence of his brother, the sorcerer, who, if not more vicious, was far more resolute and wily. From the antagonism of their respective professions, the sorcerer hated the priest, who lost no opportunity of denouncing his incantations, and who ridiculed his perpetual singing and drumming as puerility and folly. The former, being an indifferent hunter, and disabled by a disease which he had contracted, depended for subsistence on his credit as a magician; and, in undermining it, Le Jeune not only outraged his pride, but threatened his daily bread.[1] He used every device to retort ridicule on his rival. At the outset, he had proffered his aid to Le Jeune in his study of the Algonquin; and, like the Indian practical jokers of Acadia in the case of Father Biard, [See "Pioneers of France," 268.] palmed off upon him the foulest words in the language as the equivalent of things spiritual. Thus it happened, that, while the missionary sought to explain to the assembled wigwam some point of Christian doctrine, he was interrupted by peals of laughter from men, children, and squaws. And now, as Le Jeune took his place in the circle, the sorcerer bent upon him his malignant eyes, and began that course of rude bantering which filled to overflowing the cup of the Jesuit's woes. All took their cue from him, and made their afflicted guest the butt of their inane witticisms. "Look at

---

1   "Ie ne laissois perdre aucune occasion de le conuaincre de niaiserie et de puerilité, mettant au iour l'impertinence de ses superstitions: or c'estoit luy arracher l'ame du corps par violence: car comme il ne sçauroit plus chasser, il fait plus que iamais du Prophete et du Magicien pour conseruer son credit, et pour auoir les bons morceaux; si bien qu'esbranlant son authorité qui se va perdant tous les iours, ie le touchois à la prunelle de l'œil."—Relation, 1634, 56.

him! His face is like a dog's!"—"His head is like a pumpkin!"—"He has a beard like a rabbit's!" The missionary bore in silence these and countless similar attacks; indeed, so sorely was he harassed, that, lest he should exasperate his tormentor, he sometimes passed whole days without uttering a word.[1]

Le Jeune, a man of excellent observation, already knew his red associates well enough to understand that their rudeness did not of necessity imply ill-will. The rest of the party, in their turn fared no better. They rallied and bantered each other incessantly, with as little forbearance, and as little malice, as a troop of unbridled schoolboys.[2] No one took offence. To have done so would have been to bring upon one's self genuine contumely. This motley household was a model of harmony. True, they showed no tenderness or consideration towards the sick and disabled; but for the rest, each shared with all in weal or woe: the famine of one was the famine of the whole, and the smallest portion of food was distributed in fair and equal partition. Upbraidings and complaints were unheard; they bore each other's foibles with wondrous equanimity; and while persecuting Le Jeune with constant importunity for tobacco, and for everything else he had, they never begged among themselves.

When the fire burned well and food was abundant, their conversation, such as it was, was incessant. They used no oaths, for their language supplied none,—doubtless because their mythology had no beings sufficiently distinct to swear by. Their expletives were foul words, of which they had a superabundance, and which men,

---

1   Relation, 1634, 207 (Cramoisy). "Ils me chargeoient incessament de mille brocards & de mille injures; je me suis veu en tel estat, que pour ne les aigrir, je passois les jours entiers sans ouvrir la bouche." Here follows the abuse, in the original Indian, with French translations. Le Jeune's account of his experiences is singularly graphic. The following is his summary of his annoyances:—

"Or ce miserable homme" (the sorcerer), "& la fumée m'ont esté les deux plus grands tourmens que i'aye enduré parmy ces Barbares: ny le froid, ny le chaud, ny l'incommodité des chiens, ny coucher à l'air, ny dormir sur un lict de terre, ny la posture qu'il faut tousiours tenir dans leurs cabanes, se ramassans en peloton, ou se couchans, ou s'asseans sans siege & sans mattelas, ny la faim, ny la soif, ny la pauureté & saleté de leur boucan, ny la maladie, tout cela ne m'a semblé que ieu à comparaison de la fumée & de la malice du Sorcier."—Relation, 1634, 201 (Cramoisy).

2   "Leur vie se passe à manger, à ire, et à railler les vns des autres, et de tous les peuples qu'ils cognoissent; ils n'ont rien de serieux, sinon par fois l'exterieur, faisans parmy nous les graues et les retenus, mais entr'eux sont de vrais badins, de vrais enfans, qui ne demandent qu'à rire."—Relation, 1634, 30.

women, and children alike used with a frequency and hardihood that amazed and scandalized the priest.[1] Nor was he better pleased with their postures, in which they consulted nothing but their ease. Thus, of an evening when the wigwam was heated to suffocation, the sorcerer, in the closest possible approach to nudity, lay on his back, with his right knee planted upright and his left leg crossed on it, discoursing volubly to the company, who, on their part, listened in postures scarcely less remote from decency.

There was one point touching which Le Jeune and his Jesuit brethren had as yet been unable to solve their doubts. Were the Indian sorcerers mere impostors, or were they in actual league with the Devil? That the fiends who possess this land of darkness make their power felt by action direct and potential upon the persons of its wretched inhabitants there is, argues Le Jeune, good reason to conclude; since it is a matter of grave notoriety, that the fiends who infest Brazil are accustomed cruelly to beat and otherwise torment the natives of that country, as many travellers attest. "A Frenchman worthy of credit," pursues the Father, "has told me that he has heard with his own ears the voice of the Demon and the sound of the blows which he discharges upon these his miserable slaves; and in reference to this a very remarkable fact has been reported to me, namely, that, when a Catholic approaches, the Devil takes flight and beats these wretches no longer, but that in presence of a Huguenot he does not stop beating them."

["Surquoy on me rapporte vne chose tres remarquable, c'est que le Diable s'enfuit, et ne frappe point ou cesse de frapper ces miserables, quand vn Catholique entre en leur compagnie, et qu'il ne laisse point de les battre en la presence d'vn Huguenot: d'où vient qu'vn iour se voyans battus en la compagnie d'vn certain François, ils luy dirent: Nous nous estonnons qua le diable nous batte, toy estant auec nous, veu qu'il n'oseroit le faire quand tes compagnons sont presents. Luy se douta incontinent que cela pouuoit prouenir de sa religion (car il estoit Caluiniste); s'addressant donc à Dieu,

---

1   "Aussi leur disois-je par fois, que si les pourceaux et les chiens sçauoient parler, ils tiendroient leur langage … Les filles et les ieunes femmes sont à l'exterieur tres honnestement couuertes, mais entre elles leurs discours sont puants, comme des cloaques."—Relation, 1634, 32.—The social manners of remote tribes of the present time correspond perfectly with Le Jeune's account of those of the Montagnais.

il luy promit de se faire Catholique si le diable cessoit de battre ces pauures peuples en sa presence. Le vœu fait, iamais plus aucun Demon ne molesta Ameriquain en sa compagnie, d'où vient qu'il se fit Catholique, selon la promesse qu'il en auoit faicte. Mais retournons à nostre discours."—Relation, 1634, 22.]

Thus prone to believe in the immediate presence of the nether powers, Le Jeune watched the sorcerer with an eye prepared to discover in his conjurations the signs of a genuine diabolic agency. His observations, however, led him to a different result; and he could detect in his rival nothing but a vile compound of impostor and dupe. The sorcerer believed in the efficacy of his own magic, and was continually singing and beating his drum to cure the disease from which he was suffering. Towards the close of the winter, Le Jeune fell sick, and, in his pain and weakness, nearly succumbed under the nocturnal uproar of the sorcerer, who, hour after hour, sang and drummed without mercy,—sometimes yelling at the top of his throat, then hissing like a serpent, then striking his drum on the ground as if in a frenzy, then leaping up, raving about the wigwam, and calling on the women and children to join him in singing. Now ensued a hideous din; for every throat was strained to the utmost, and all were beating with sticks or fists on the bark of the hut to increase the noise, with the charitable object of aiding the sorcerer to conjure down his malady, or drive away the evil spirit that caused it.

He had an enemy, a rival sorcerer, whom he charged with having caused by charms the disease that afflicted him. He therefore announced that he should kill him. As the rival dwelt at Gaspé, a hundred leagues off, the present execution of the threat might appear difficult; but distance was no bar to the vengeance of the sorcerer. Ordering all the children and all but one of the women to leave the wigwam, he seated himself, with the woman who remained, on the ground in the centre, while the men of the party, together with those from other wigwams in the neighborhood, sat in a ring around. Mestigoit, the sorcerer's brother, then brought in the charm, consisting of a few small pieces of wood, some arrow-heads, a broken knife, and an iron hook, which he wrapped in a piece of hide. The woman next rose, and walked around the hut, behind the company. Mestigoit and the sorcerer now dug a large hole with two pointed stakes, the whole assembly singing, drumming, and howling meanwhile with a deafening uproar. The hole made, the charm, wrapped in the hide, was thrown into it. Pierre, the Apostate, then brought a sword and a knife to the sorcerer, who, seizing them, leaped into the hole, and, with furious gesticulation, hacked and stabbed at the charm, yelling with the whole force of his lungs. At length he ceased, displayed the knife and sword stained with blood, proclaimed that he had mortally wounded his enemy, and demanded if none present had heard his death-cry. The assembly, more occupied in making noises than in listening for them, gave no reply, till at length two young men declared that they had heard a faint scream, as if from a great distance; whereat a shout of gratulation and triumph rose from all the company.

["Le magicien tout glorieux dit que son homme est frappé, qu'il mourra bien tost, demande si on n'a point entendu ses cris: tout le monde dit que non, horsmis deux ieunes hommes ses parens, qui disent auoir ouy des plaintes fort sourdes, et comme de loing. O qu'ils le firent aise! Se tournant vers moy, il se mit à rire, disant: Voyez cette robe noire, qui nous vient dire qu'il ne faut tuer personne. Comme ie regardois attentiuement l'espée et le poignard, il me les fit presenter: Regarde, dit-il, qu'est cela? C'est du sang, repartis-ie. De qui? De quelque Orignac ou d'autre animal. Ils se mocquerent de moy, disants que c'estoit du sang de ce Sorcier de Gaspé. Comment, dis-je, il est à plus de cent lieuës d'icy? Il est vray, font-ils, mais c'est le Manitou, c'est à dire le Diable, qui apporte son sang pardessous la terre."—Relation, 1634, 21.]

There was a young prophet, or diviner, in one of the neighboring huts, of whom the sorcerer took counsel as to the prospect of his restoration to health. The divining-lodge was formed, in this instance, of five or six upright posts planted in a circle and covered with a blanket. The prophet ensconced himself within; and after a long interval of singing, the spirits declared their presence by their usual squeaking utterances from the recesses of the mystic tabernacle. Their responses were not unfavorable; and the sorcerer drew much consolation from the invocations of his brother impostor. [See Introduction. Also, "Pioneers of France," 315.]

Besides his incessant endeavors to annoy Le Jeune, the sorcerer now and then tried to frighten him. On one occasion, when a period of starvation had been followed by a successful hunt, the whole party assembled for one of the gluttonous feasts usual with them at such times. While the guests sat expectant, and the squaws were about to ladle out the banquet, the sorcerer suddenly leaped up, exclaiming, that he had lost his senses, and that knives and hatchets must be kept out of his way, as he had a mind to kill somebody. Then, rolling his eyes towards Le Jeune, he began a series of frantic gestures and outcries,—then stopped abruptly and stared into vacancy, silent and motionless,—then resumed his former clamor, raged in and out of the hut, and, seizing some of its supporting poles, broke them, as if in an uncontrollable frenzy. The missionary, though alarmed, sat reading his breviary as before. When, however, on the next morning, the sorcerer began again to play the maniac, the thought occurred to him, that some stroke of fever might in truth have touched his brain. Accordingly, he approached him and felt his pulse, which he found, in his own words, "as cool as a fish." The pretended madman looked at him with astonishment, and, giving over the attempt to frighten him, presently returned to his senses.

[The Indians, it is well known, ascribe mysterious and supernatural powers to the insane, and respect them accordingly. The Neutral Nation (see Introduction, "The Huron-Iroquois Family" (p. xliv)) was full of pretended madmen, who raved about the villages, throwing firebrands, and making other displays of frenzy.]

Le Jeune, robbed of his sleep by the ceaseless thumping of the sorcerer's drum and the monotonous cadence of his medicine-songs, improved the time in attempts to convert him. "I began," he says, "by evincing a great love for him, and by praises, which I threw to him as a bait whereby I might catch him in the net of truth."[1] But the Indian, though pleased with the Father's flatteries, was neither caught nor conciliated.

Nowhere was his magic in more requisition than in procuring a successful chase to the hunters,—a point of vital interest, since on it hung the lives of the whole party. They often, however,

---

1 "Ie commençay par vn témoignage de grand amour en son endroit, et par des loüanges que ie luy iettay comme vne amorce pour le prendre dans les filets de la verité. Ie luy fis entendre que si vn esprit, capable des choses grandes comme le sien, cognoissoit Dieu, que tous les Sauuages induis par son exemple le voudroient aussi cognoistre."—Relation, 1634, 71.

returned empty-handed; and, for one, two, or three successive days, no other food could be had than the bark of trees or scraps of leather. So long as tobacco lasted, they found solace in their pipes, which seldom left their lips. "Unhappy infidels," writes Le Jeune, "who spend their lives in smoke, and their eternity in flames!"

As Christmas approached, their condition grew desperate. Beavers and porcupines were scarce, and the snow was not deep enough for hunting the moose. Night and day the medicine-drums and medicine-songs resounded from the wigwams, mingled with the wail of starving children. The hunters grew weak and emaciated; and, as after a forlorn march the wanderers encamped once more in the lifeless forest, the priest remembered that it was the eve of Christmas. "The Lord gave us for our supper a porcupine, large as a sucking pig, and also a rabbit. It was not much, it is true, for eighteen or nineteen persons; but the Holy Virgin and St. Joseph, her glorious spouse, were not so well treated, on this very day, in the stable of Bethlehem."

["Pour nostre souper, N. S. nous donna vn Porc-espic gros comme vn cochon de lait, et vn liéure; c'estoit peu pour dix-huit ou vingt personnes que nous estions, il est vray, mais la saincte Vierge et son glorieux Espoux sainct Ioseph ne furent pas si bien traictez à mesme iour dans l'estable de Bethleem."—Relation, 1634, 74.]

On Christmas Day, the despairing hunters, again unsuccessful, came to pray succor from Le Jeune. Even the Apostate had become tractable, and the famished sorcerer was ready to try the efficacy of an appeal to the deity of his rival. A bright hope possessed the missionary. He composed two prayers, which, with the aid of the repentant Pierre, he translated into Algonquin. Then he hung against the side of the hut a napkin which he had brought with him, and against the napkin a crucifix and a reliquary, and, this done, caused all the Indians to kneel before them, with hands raised and clasped. He now read one of the prayers, and required the Indians to repeat the other after him, promising to renounce their superstitions, and obey Christ, whose image they saw before them, if he would give them food and save them from perishing. The pledge given, he dismissed the hunters with a benediction. At night they returned with game enough to relieve the immediate necessity. All was hilarity. The kettles were slung, and the feasters assembled. Le Jeune rose to speak, when Pierre, who, having killed nothing, was in ill humor, said, with a laugh, that the crucifix and the prayer had nothing to do with their good luck; while the sorcerer, his jealousy reviving as he saw his hunger about to be appeased, called out to the missionary, "Hold your tongue! You have no sense!" As usual, all took their cue from him. They fell to their repast with ravenous jubilation, and the disappointed priest sat dejected and silent.

Repeatedly, before the spring, they were thus threatened with starvation. Nor was their case exceptional. It was the ordinary winter life of all those Northern tribes who did not till the soil, but lived by hunting and fishing alone. The desertion or the killing of the aged, sick, and disabled, occasional cannibalism, and frequent death from famine, were natural incidents of an existence which, during half the year, was but a desperate pursuit of the mere necessaries of life under the worst conditions of hardship, suffering, and debasement.

At the beginning of April, after roaming for five months among forests and mountains, the party made their last march, regained the bank of the St. Lawrence, and waded to the island where they had hidden their canoes. Le Jeune was exhausted and sick, and Mestigoit offered to carry him in his canoe to Quebec. This Indian was by far the best of the three brothers, and both Pierre and the sorcerer looked to him for support. He was strong, active, and daring, a skilful hunter, and a dexterous canoeman. Le Jeune gladly accepted his offer; embarked with him and Pierre on the dreary and tempestuous river; and, after a voyage full of hardship, during which the canoe narrowly escaped being ground to atoms among the floating ice, landed on the Island of Orleans, six miles from Quebec. The afternoon was stormy and dark, and the river was covered with ice, sweeping by with the tide. They were forced to encamp. At midnight, the moon had risen, the river was comparatively unencumbered, and they embarked once more. The wind increased, and the waves tossed furiously. Nothing saved them but the skill and courage of Mestigoit. At length they could see the rock of Quebec towering through the gloom, but piles of ice lined the shore, while floating masses were drifting down on the angry current. The Indian watched his moment, shot his canoe through them, gained the fixed ice, leaped out, and shouted to his companions to follow. Pierre scrambled up, but the ice was six feet out of the water, and Le Jeune's agility failed him. He saved himself by clutching the ankle of Mestigoit, by whose aid he gained a firm foothold at the top, and, for a moment, the three voyagers, aghast at the narrowness of their escape, stood gazing at each other in silence.

It was three o'clock in the morning when Le Jeune knocked at the door of his rude little convent on the St. Charles; and the Fathers, springing in joyful haste from their slumbers, embraced their long absent Superior with ejaculations of praise and benediction.

CHAPTER V.

1633, 1634.

THE HURON MISSION.

PLANS OF CONVERSION.—AIMS AND MOTIVES.—
INDIAN DIPLOMACY.—HURONS AT QUEBEC.—
COUNCILS.—THE JESUIT CHAPEL.—LE BORGNE.—THE
JESUITS THWARTED.—THEIR PERSEVERANCE.—THE
JOURNEY TO THE HURONS.—JEAN DE BRÉBEUF.—THE
MISSION BEGUN.

Le Jeune had learned the difficulties of the Algonquin mission.
To imagine that he recoiled or faltered would be an injustice to his
Order; but on two points he had gained convictions: first, that little
progress could be made in converting these wandering hordes till
they could be settled in fixed abodes; and, secondly, that their scanty
numbers, their geographical position, and their slight influence in
the politics of the wilderness offered no flattering promise that their
conversion would be fruitful in further triumphs of the Faith. It
was to another quarter that the Jesuits looked most earnestly. By the
vast lakes of the West dwelt numerous stationary populations, and
particularly the Hurons, on the lake which bears their name. Here
was a hopeful basis of indefinite conquests; for, the Hurons won
over, the Faith would spread in wider and wider circles, embracing,
one by one, the kindred tribes,—the Tobacco Nation, the Neutrals,
the Eries, and the Andastes. Nay, in His own time, God might lead
into His fold even the potent and ferocious Iroquois.

The way was pathless and long, by rock and torrent and the gloom of savage forests. The goal was more dreary yet. Toil, hardship, famine, filth, sickness, solitude, insult,—all that is most revolting to men nurtured among arts and letters, all that is most terrific to monastic credulity: such were the promise and the reality of the Huron mission. In the eyes of the Jesuits, the Huron country was the innermost stronghold of Satan, his castle and his donjon-keep. ["Une des principales forteresses & comme un donjon des Demons."—Lalemant, Relation des Hurons, 1639, 100 (Cramoisy).] All the weapons of his malice were prepared against the bold invader who should assail him in this, the heart of his ancient domain. Far from shrinking, the priest's zeal rose to tenfold ardor. He signed the cross, invoked St. Ignatius, St. Francis Xavier, or St. Francis Borgia, kissed his reliquary, said nine masses to the Virgin, and stood prompt to battle with all the hosts of Hell.

A life sequestered from social intercourse, and remote from every prize which ambition holds worth the pursuit, or a lonely death, under forms, perhaps, the most appalling,—these were the missionaries' alternatives. Their maligners may taunt them, if they will, with credulity, superstition, or a blind enthusiasm; but slander itself cannot accuse them of hypocrisy or ambition. Doubtless, in their propagandism, they were acting in concurrence with a mundane policy; but, for the present at least, this policy was rational and humane. They were promoting the ends of commerce and national expansion. The foundations of French dominion were to be laid deep in the heart and conscience of the savage. His stubborn neck was to be subdued to the "yoke of the Faith." The power of the priest established, that of the temporal ruler was secure. These sanguinary hordes, weaned from intestine strife, were to unite in a common allegiance to God and the King. Mingled with French traders and French settlers, softened by French manners, guided by French priests, ruled by French officers, their now divided bands would become the constituents of a vast wilderness empire, which in time might span the continent. Spanish civilization crushed the Indian; English civilization scorned and neglected him; French civilization embraced and cherished him.

Policy and commerce, then, built their hopes on the priests. These commissioned interpreters of the Divine Will, accredited with letters patent from Heaven, and affiliated to God's anointed on earth, would have pushed to its most unqualified application the Scripture metaphor of the shepherd and the sheep. They would have tamed the wild man of the woods to a condition of obedience, unquestioning, passive, and absolute,—repugnant to manhood, and adverse to the invigorating and expansive spirit of modern civilization. Yet, full of error and full of danger as was their system, they embraced its serene and smiling falsehoods with the sincerity of martyrs and the self-devotion of saints.

We have spoken already of the Hurons, of their populous villages on the borders of the great "Fresh Sea," their trade, their rude agriculture, their social life, their wild and incongruous superstitions, and the sorcerers, diviners, and medicine-men who lived on their credulity. [See Introduction.] Iroquois hostility left open but one avenue to their country, the long and circuitous route which, eighteen years before, had been explored by Champlain, ["Pioneers of France," 364.]—up the river Ottawa, across Lake Nipissing, down French River, and along the shores of the great Georgian Bay of Lake Huron,—a route as difficult as it was tedious. Midway, on Allumette Island, in the Ottawa, dwelt the Algonquin tribe visited by Champlain in 1613, and who, amazed at the apparition of the white stranger, thought that he had fallen from the clouds. ["Pioneers of France," 348.] Like other tribes of this region, they were keen traders, and would gladly have secured for themselves the benefits of an intermediate traffic between the Hurons and the French, receiving the furs of the former in barter at a low rate, and exchanging them with the latter at their full value. From their position, they could at any time close the passage of the Ottawa; but, as this would have been a perilous exercise of their rights,[1] they were forced to act with discretion. An opportunity for the practice

---

1   Nevertheless, the Hurons always passed this way as a matter of favor, and gave yearly presents to the Algonquins of the island, in acknowledgment of the privilege—Le Jeune, Relation, 1636, 70.—By the unwritten laws of the Hurons and Algonquins, every tribe had the right, even in full peace, of prohibiting the passage of every other tribe across its territory. In ordinary cases, such prohibitions were quietly submitted to.

"Ces Insulaires voudraient bien que les Hurons ne vinssent point aux François & que les François n'allassent point aux Hurons, afin d'emporter eux seuls tout le trafic," etc.—Relation, 1633, 205 (Cramoisy),—"desirans eux-mesmes aller recueiller les marchandises des peuples circonvoisins pour les apporter aux François." This "Nation de l'Isle" has been erroneously located at Montreal. Its true position is indicated on the map of Du Creux, and on an ancient MS. map in

of their diplomacy had lately occurred. On or near the Ottawa, at some distance below them, dwelt a small Algonquin tribe, called *La Petite Nation*. One of this people had lately killed a Frenchman, and the murderer was now in the hands of Champlain, a prisoner at the fort of Quebec. The savage politicians of Allumette Island contrived, as will soon be seen, to turn this incident to profit.

In the July that preceded Le Jeune's wintering with the Montagnais, a Huron Indian, well known to the French, came to Quebec with the tidings, that the annual canoe-fleet of his countrymen was descending the St. Lawrence. On the twenty-eighth, the river was alive with them. A hundred and forty canoes, with six or seven hundred savages, landed at the warehouses beneath the fortified rock of Quebec, and set up their huts and camp-sheds on the strand now covered by the lower town. The greater number brought furs and tobacco for the trade; others came as sight-seers; others to gamble, and others to steal, [1]—accomplishments in which the Hurons were proficient: their gambling skill being exercised chiefly against each other, and their thieving talents against those of other nations.

The routine of these annual visits was nearly uniform. On the first day, the Indians built their huts; on the second, they held their council with the French officers at the fort; on the third and fourth, they bartered their furs and tobacco for kettles, hatchets, knives, cloth, beads, iron arrow-heads, coats, shirts, and other commodities; on the fifth, they were feasted by the French; and at daybreak of the next morning, they embarked and vanished like a flight of birds.

["Comme une volée d'oiseaux."—Le Jeune, Relation, 1633, 190 (Cramoisy).—The tobacco brought to the French by the Hurons may have been raised by the adjacent tribe of the Tionnontates, who cultivated it largely for sale. See Introduction.]

On the second day, then, the long file of chiefs and warriors mounted the pathway to the fort,—tall, well-moulded figures, robed in the skins of the beaver and the bear, each wild visage

---

the Dépôt des Cartes, of which a fac-simile is before me. See also "Pioneers of France," 347.

1   "Quelques vns d'entre eux ne viennent à la traite auec les François que pour iouër, d'autres pour voir, quelques vns pour dérober, et les plus sages et les plus riches pour trafiquer."—Le Jeune, Relation, 1633, 34.

glowing with paint and glistening with the oil which the Hurons extracted from the seeds of the sunflower. The lank black hair of one streamed loose upon his shoulders; that of another was close shaven, except an upright ridge, which, bristling like the crest of a dragoon's helmet, crossed the crown from the forehead to the neck; while that of a third hung, long and flowing from one side, but on the other was cut short. Sixty chiefs and principal men, with a crowd of younger warriors, formed their council-circle in the fort, those of each village grouped together, and all seated on the ground with a gravity of bearing sufficiently curious to those who had seen the same men in the domestic circle of their lodge-fires. Here, too, were the Jesuits, robed in black, anxious and intent; and here was Champlain, who, as he surveyed the throng, recognized among the elder warriors not a few of those who, eighteen years before, had been his companions in arms on his hapless foray against the Iroquois. [See "Pioneers of France," 370.]

Their harangues of compliment being made and answered, and the inevitable presents given and received, Champlain introduced to the silent conclave the three missionaries, Brébeuf, Daniel, and Davost. To their lot had fallen the honors, dangers, and woes of the Huron mission. "These are our fathers," he said. "We love them more than we love ourselves. The whole French nation honors them. They do not go among you for your furs. They have left their friends and their country to show you the way to heaven. If you love the French, as you say you love them, then love and honor these our fathers." [Le Jeune, Relation, 1633, 274 (Cramoisy); Mercure Français, 1634. 845.]

Two chiefs rose to reply, and each lavished all his rhetoric in praises of Champlain and of the French. Brébeuf rose next, and spoke in broken Huron,—the assembly jerking in unison, from the bottom of their throats, repeated ejaculations of applause. Then they surrounded him, and vied with each other for the honor of carrying him in their canoes. In short, the mission was accepted; and the chiefs of the different villages disputed among themselves the privilege of receiving and entertaining the three priests.

On the last of July, the day of the feast of St. Ignatius, Champlain and several masters of trading vessels went to the house of the Jesuits in quest of indulgences; and here they were soon beset by a crowd of curious Indians, who had finished their traffic, and were making a tour of observation. Being excluded from the house, they looked in at the windows of the room which served as a chapel; and Champlain, amused at their exclamations of wonder, gave one of them a piece of citron. The Huron tasted it, and, enraptured, demanded what it was. Champlain replied, laughing, that it was the rind of a French pumpkin. The fame of this delectable production was instantly spread abroad; and, at every window, eager voices and outstretched hands petitioned for a share of the marvellous vegetable. They were at length allowed to enter the chapel, which had lately been decorated with a few hangings, images, and pieces of plate. These unwonted splendors filled them with admiration. They asked if the dove over the altar was the bird that makes the thunder; and, pointing to the images of Loyola and Xavier, inquired if they were *okies*, or spirits: nor was their perplexity much diminished by Brébeuf's explanation of their true character. Three images of the Virgin next engaged their attention; and, in answer to their questions, they were told that they were the mother of Him who made the world. This greatly amused them, and they demanded if he had three mothers. "Oh!" exclaims the Father Superior, "had we but images of all the holy mysteries of our faith! They are a great assistance, for they speak their own lesson." [Relation, 1633, 38.] The mission was not doomed long to suffer from a dearth of these inestimable auxiliaries.

The eve of departure came. The three priests packed their baggage, and Champlain paid their passage, or, in other words, made presents to the Indians who were to carry them in their canoes. They lodged that night in the storehouse of the fur company, around which the Hurons were encamped; and Le Jeune and De Noue stayed with them to bid them farewell in the morning. At eleven at night, they were roused by a loud voice in the Indian camp, and saw Le Borgne, the one-eyed chief of Allumette Island, walking round among the huts, haranguing as he went. Brébeuf, listening, caught the import of his words. "We have begged the French captain to spare the life of the Algonquin of the Petite Nation whom he keeps in prison; but he will not listen to us. The prisoner will die. Then his people will revenge him. They will try to kill the three black-robes whom you are about to carry to your country. If you do not defend them, the French will be angry, and charge you with their death. But if you do, then the Algonquins will make war on you, and the river will be closed. If the French captain will not let the prisoner go, then leave the three black-robes where they are; for, if you take them with you, they will bring you to trouble."

Such was the substance of Le Borgne's harangue. The anxious priests hastened up to the fort, gained admittance, and roused Champlain from his slumbers. He sent his interpreter with a message to the Hurons, that he wished to speak to them before their departure; and, accordingly, in the morning an Indian crier proclaimed through their camp that none should embark till the next day. Champlain convoked the chiefs, and tried persuasion, promises, and threats; but Le Borgne had been busy among them with his intrigues, and now he declared in the council, that, unless the prisoner were released, the missionaries would be murdered on their way, and war would ensue. The politic savage had two objects in view. On the one hand, he wished to interrupt the direct intercourse between the French and the Hurons; and, on the other, he thought to gain credit and influence with the nation of the prisoner by effecting his release. His first point was won. Champlain would not give up the murderer, knowing those with whom he was dealing too well to take a course which would have proclaimed the killing of a Frenchman a venial offence. The Hurons thereupon refused to carry the missionaries to their country; coupling the refusal with many regrets and many protestations of love, partly, no doubt, sincere,—for the Jesuits had contrived to gain no little favor in their eyes. The council broke up, the Hurons embarked, and the priests returned to their convent.

Here, under the guidance of Brébeuf, they employed themselves, amid their other avocations, in studying the Huron tongue. A year passed, and again the Indian traders descended from their villages. In the meanwhile, grievous calamities had befallen the nation. They had suffered deplorable reverses at the hands of the Iroquois; while a pestilence, similar to that which a few years before had swept off the native populations of New England, had begun its ravages among them. They appeared at Three Rivers—this year the place of trade—in small numbers, and in a miserable state of dejection and alarm. Du Plessis Bochart, commander of the French fleet, called them to a council, harangued them, feasted them, and made them presents; but they refused to take the Jesuits. In private, however, some of them were gained over; then again refused;

then, at the eleventh hour, a second time consented. On the eve of embarkation, they once more wavered. All was confusion, doubt, and uncertainty, when Brébeuf bethought him of a vow to St. Joseph. The vow was made. At once, he says, the Indians became tractable; the Fathers embarked, and, amid salvos of cannon from the ships, set forth for the wild scene of their apostleship.

They reckoned the distance at nine hundred miles; but distance was the least repellent feature of this most arduous journey. Barefoot, lest their shoes should injure the frail vessel, each crouched in his canoe, toiling with unpractised hands to propel it. Before him, week after week, he saw the same lank, unkempt hair, the same tawny shoulders, and long, naked arms ceaselessly plying the paddle. The canoes were soon separated; and, for more than a month, the Frenchmen rarely or never met. Brébeuf spoke a little Huron, and could converse with his escort; but Daniel and Davost were doomed to a silence unbroken save by the occasional unintelligible complaints and menaces of the Indians, of whom many were sick with the epidemic, and all were terrified, desponding, and sullen. Their only food was a pittance of Indian corn, crushed between two stones and mixed with water. The toil was extreme. Brébeuf counted thirty-five portages, where the canoes were lifted from the water, and carried on the shoulders of the voyagers around rapids or cataracts. More than fifty times, besides, they were forced to wade in the raging current, pushing up their empty barks, or dragging them with ropes. Brébeuf tried to do his part; but the boulders and sharp rocks wounded his naked feet, and compelled him to desist. He and his companions bore their share of the baggage across the portages, sometimes a distance of several miles. Four trips, at the least, were required to convey the whole. The way was through the dense forest, incumbered with rocks and logs, tangled with roots and underbrush, damp with perpetual shade, and redolent of decayed leaves and mouldering wood.[1] The Indians themselves were often spent with fatigue. Brébeuf, a man of iron

---

1   "Adioustez à ces difficultez, qu'il faut coucher sur la terre nue, ou sur quelque dure roche, faute de trouuer dix ou douze pieds de terre en quarré pour placer vne chetiue cabane; qu'il faut sentir incessamment la puanteur des Sauuages recreus, marcher dans les eaux, dans les fanges, dans l'obscurité et l'embarras des forest, où les piqueures d'vne multitude infinie de mousquilles et cousins vous importunent fort."—Brébeuf, Relation des Hurons, 1635, 25, 26.

frame and a nature unconquerably resolute, doubted if his strength would sustain him to the journey's end. He complains that he had no moment to read his breviary, except by the moonlight or the fire, when stretched out to sleep on a bare rock by some savage cataract of the Ottawa, or in a damp nook of the adjacent forest.

All the Jesuits, as well as several of their countrymen who accompanied them, suffered more or less at the hands of their ill-humored conductors.[1] Davost's Indian robbed him of a part of his baggage, threw a part into the river, including most of the books and writing-materials of the three priests, and then left him behind, among the Algonquins of Allumette Island. He found means to continue the journey, and at length reached the Huron towns in a lamentable state of bodily prostration. Daniel, too, was deserted, but fortunately found another party who received him into their canoe. A young Frenchman, named Martin, was abandoned among the Nipissings; another, named Baron, on reaching the Huron country, was robbed by his conductors of all he had, except the

---

1   "En ce voyage, il nous a fallu tous commencer par ces experiences a porter la Croix que Nostre Seigneur nous presente pour son honneur, et pour le salut de ces pauures Barbares. Certes ie me suis trouué quelquesfois si las, que le corps n'en pouuoit plus. Mais d'ailleurs mon âme ressentoit de tres-grands contentemens, considerant que ie souffrois pour Dieu: nul ne le sçait, s'il ne l'experimente. Tous n'en ont pas esté quittes à si bon marché."—Brébeuf, Relation des Hurons, 1635, 26.

    Three years afterwards, a paper was printed by the Jesuits of Paris, called Instruction pour les Pères de nostre Compagnie qui seront enuoiez aux Hurons, and containing directions for their conduct on this route by the Ottawa. It is highly characteristic, both of the missionaries and of the Indians. Some of the points are, in substance, as follows.—You should love the Indians like brothers, with whom you are to spend the rest of your life.—Never make them wait for you in embarking.—Take a flint and steel to light their pipes and kindle their fire at night; for these little services win their hearts.—Try to eat their sagamite as they cook it, bad and dirty as it is.—Fasten up the skirts of your cassock, that you may not carry water or sand into the canoe.—Wear no shoes or stockings in the canoe; but you may put them on in crossing the portages.—Do not make yourself troublesome, even to a single Indian.—Do not ask them too many questions.—Bear their faults in silence, and appear always cheerful.—Buy fish for them from the tribes you will pass; and for this purpose take with you some awls, beads, knives, and fish-hooks.—Be not ceremonious with the Indians; take at once what they offer you: ceremony offends them.—Be very careful, when in the canoe, that the brim of your hat does not annoy them. Perhaps it would be better to wear your night-cap. There is no such thing as impropriety among Indians.—Remember that it is Christ and his cross that you are seeking; and if you aim at anything else, you will get nothing but affliction for body and mind.

weapons in his hands. Of these he made good use, compelling the robbers to restore a part of their plunder.

Descending French River, and following the lonely shores of the great Georgian Bay, the canoe which carried Brébeuf at length neared its destination, thirty days after leaving Three Rivers. Before him, stretched in savage slumber, lay the forest shore of the Hurons. Did his spirit sink as he approached his dreary home, oppressed with a dark foreboding of what the future should bring forth? There is some reason to think so. Yet it was but the shadow of a moment; for his masculine heart had lost the sense of fear, and his intrepid nature was fired with a zeal before which doubts and uncertainties fled like the mists of the morning. Not the grim enthusiasm of negation, tearing up the weeds of rooted falsehood, or with bold hand felling to the earth the baneful growth of overshadowing abuses: his was the ancient faith uncurtailed, redeemed from the decay of centuries, kindled with a new life, and stimulated to a preternatural growth and fruitfulness.

Brébeuf and his Huron companions having landed, the Indians, throwing the missionary's baggage on the ground, left him to his own resources; and, without heeding his remonstrances, set forth for their respective villages, some twenty miles distant. Thus abandoned, the priest kneeled, not to implore succor in his perplexity, but to offer thanks to the Providence which had shielded him thus far. Then, rising, he pondered as to what course he should take. He knew the spot well. It was on the borders of the small inlet called Thunder Bay. In the neighboring Huron town of Toanché he had lived three years, preaching and baptizing;[1] but Toanché had now ceased to exist. Here, Étienne Brulé, Champlain's adventurous interpreter, had recently been murdered by the inhabitants, who, in excitement and alarm, dreading the consequences of their deed, had deserted the spot, and built, at the distance of a few miles, a new town, called Ihonatiria. [Concerning Brulé, see "Pioneers of France," 377-380.] Brébeuf hid his baggage in the woods, including the vessels for the Mass, more precious than all the rest, and began his search for this new abode. He passed the burnt remains of

---

1   From 1626 to 1629. There is no record of the events of this first mission, which was ended with the English occupation of Quebec. Brébeuf had previously spent the winter of 1625-26 among the Algonquins, like Le Jeune in 1633-34.—Lettre du P. Charles Lalemant au T. R. P. Mutio Vitelleschi, 1 Aug., 1626, in Carayon.

Toanché, saw the charred poles that had formed the frame of his little chapel of bark, and found, as he thought, the spot where Brulé had fallen.[1] Evening was near, when, after following, bewildered and anxious, a gloomy forest path, he issued upon a wild clearing, and saw before him the bark roofs of Ihonatiria.

A crowd ran out to meet him. "Echom has come again! Echom has come again!" they cried, recognizing in the distance the stately figure, robed in black, that advanced from the border of the forest. They led him to the town, and the whole population swarmed about him. After a short rest, he set out with a number of young Indians in quest of his baggage, returning with it at one o'clock in the morning. There was a certain Awandoay in the village, noted as one of the richest and most hospitable of the Hurons,—a distinction not easily won where hospitality was universal. His house was large, and amply stored with beans and corn; and though his prosperity had excited the jealousy of the villagers, he had recovered their good-will by his generosity. With him Brébeuf made his abode, anxiously waiting, week after week, the arrival of his companions. One by one, they appeared: Daniel, weary and worn; Davost, half dead with famine and fatigue; and their French attendants, each with his tale of hardship and indignity. At length, all were assembled under the roof of the hospitable Indian, and once more the Huron mission was begun.

---

1   "Ie vis pareillement l'endroit où le pauure Estienne Brulé auoit esté barbarement et traitreusement assommé; ce qui me fit penser que quelque iour on nous pourroit bien traitter de la sorte, et desirer au moins que ce fust en pourchassant la gloire de N. Seigneur."—Brébeuf, Relation des Hurons, 1635, 28, 29.—The missionary's prognostics were but too well founded.

CHAPTER VI.

1634, 1635.

BRÉBEUF AND HIS ASSOCIATES.

THE HURON MISSION-HOUSE.—ITS INMATES.—
ITS FURNITURE.—ITS GUESTS.—THE JESUIT AS A
TEACHER.—AS AN ENGINEER.—BAPTISMS.—HURON
VILLAGE LIFE.—FESTIVITIES AND SORCERIES.—THE
DREAM FEAST.—THE PRIESTS ACCUSED OF MAGIC.—
THE DROUGHT AND THE RED CROSS.

Where should the Fathers make their abode? Their first
thought had been to establish themselves at a place called by the
French Rochelle, the largest and most important town of the Huron
confederacy; but Brébeuf now resolved to remain at Ihonatiria.
Here he was well known; and here, too, he flattered himself, seeds
of the Faith had been planted, which, with good nurture, would in
time yield fruit.

By the ancient Huron custom, when a man or a family wanted
a house, the whole village joined in building one. In the present
case, not Ihonatiria only, but the neighboring town of Wenrio also,
took part in the work,—though not without the expectation of
such gifts as the priests had to bestow. Before October, the task
was finished. The house was constructed after the Huron model.
[See Introduction.] It was thirty-six feet long and about twenty feet
wide, framed with strong sapling poles planted in the earth to form
the sides, with the ends bent into an arch for the roof,—the whole

lashed firmly together, braced with cross-poles, and closely covered with overlapping sheets of bark. Without, the structure was strictly Indian; but within, the priests, with the aid of their tools, made innovations which were the astonishment of all the country. They divided their dwelling by transverse partitions into three apartments, each with its wooden door,—a wondrous novelty in the eyes of their visitors. The first served as a hall, an anteroom, and a place of storage for corn, beans, and dried fish. The second—the largest of the three—was at once kitchen, workshop, dining-room, drawing-room, school-room, and bed-chamber. The third was the chapel. Here they made their altar, and here were their images, pictures, and sacred vessels. Their fire was on the ground, in the middle of the second apartment, the smoke escaping by a hole in the roof. At the sides were placed two wide platforms, after the Huron fashion, four feet from the earthen floor. On these were chests in which they kept their clothing and vestments, and beneath them they slept, reclining on sheets of bark, and covered with skins and the garments they wore by day. Rude stools, a hand-mill, a large Indian mortar of wood for crushing corn, and a clock, completed the furniture of the room.

There was no lack of visitors, for the house of the black-robes contained marvels[1] the fame of which was noised abroad to the uttermost confines of the Huron nation. Chief among them was the clock. The guests would sit in expectant silence by the hour, squatted on the ground, waiting to hear it strike. They thought it was alive, and asked what it ate. As the last stroke sounded, one of the Frenchmen would cry "Stop!"—and, to the admiration of the company, the obedient clock was silent. The mill was another wonder, and they were never tired of turning it. Besides these, there was a prism and a magnet; also a magnifying-glass, wherein a flea was transformed to a frightful monster, and a multiplying lens, which showed them the same object eleven times repeated. "All

---

[1] "Ils ont pensé qu'elle entendoit, principalement quand, pour rire, quelqu'vn de nos François s'escrioit au dernier coup de marteau, c'est assez sonné, et que tout aussi tost elle se taisoit. Ils l'appellent le Capitaine du iour. Quand elle sonne, ils disent qu'elle parle, et demandent quand ils nous viennent veoir, combien de fois le Capitaine a desia parlé. Ils nous interrogent de son manger. Ils demeurent les heures entieres, et quelquesfois plusieurs, afin de la pouuoir ouyr parler."—Brébeuf, Relation des Hurons, 1635, 33.

this," says Brébeuf, "serves to gain their affection, and make them more docile in respect to the admirable and incomprehensible mysteries of our Faith; for the opinion they have of our genius and capacity makes them believe whatever we tell them." [Brébeuf, Relation des Hurons, 1636, 33.]

"What does the Captain say?" was the frequent question; for by this title of honor they designated the clock.

"When he strikes twelve times, he says, 'Hang on the kettle'; and when he strikes four times, he says, 'Get up, and go home.'"

Both interpretations were well remembered. At noon, visitors were never wanting, to share the Fathers' sagamite; but at the stroke of four, all rose and departed, leaving the missionaries for a time in peace. Now the door was barred, and, gathering around the fire, they discussed the prospects of the mission, compared their several experiences, and took counsel for the future. But the standing topic of their evening talk was the Huron language. Concerning this each had some new discovery to relate, some new suggestion to offer; and in the task of analyzing its construction and deducing its hidden laws, these intelligent and highly cultivated minds found a congenial employment. [Lalemant, Relation des Hurons, 1639, 17 (Cramoisy).]

But while zealously laboring to perfect their knowledge of the language, they spared no pains to turn their present acquirements to account. Was man, woman, or child sick or suffering, they were always at hand with assistance and relief,—adding, as they saw opportunity, explanations of Christian doctrine, pictures of Heaven and Hell, and exhortations to embrace the Faith. Their friendly offices did not cease here, but included matters widely different. The Hurons lived in constant fear of the Iroquois. At times the whole village population would fly to the woods for concealment, or take refuge in one of the neighboring fortified towns, on the rumor of an approaching war-party. The Jesuits promised them the aid of the four Frenchmen armed with arquebuses, who had come with them from Three Rivers. They advised the Hurons to make their palisade forts, not, as hitherto, in a circular form, but rectangular, with small flanking towers at the corners for the arquebuse-men. The Indians at once saw the value of the advice, and soon after began to act on it in the case of their great town of Ossossané, or Rochelle. [Brébeuf, Relation des Hurons, 1636, 86.]

At every opportunity, the missionaries gathered together the children of the village at their house. On these occasions, Brébeuf, for greater solemnity, put on a surplice, and the close, angular cap worn by Jesuits in their convents. First he chanted the Pater Noster, translated by Father Daniel into Huron rhymes,—the children chanting in their turn. Next he taught them the sign of the cross; made them repeat the Ave, the Credo, and the Commandments; questioned them as to past instructions; gave them briefly a few new ones; and dismissed them with a present of two or three beads, raisins, or prunes. A great emulation was kindled among this small fry of heathendom. The priests, with amusement and delight, saw them gathered in groups about the village, vying with each other in making the sign of the cross, or in repeating the rhymes they had learned.

At times, the elders of the people, the repositories of its ancient traditions, were induced to assemble at the house of the Jesuits, who explained to them the principal points of their doctrine, and invited them to a discussion. The auditors proved pliant to a fault, responding, "Good," or "That is true," to every proposition; but, when urged to adopt the faith which so readily met their approval, they had always the same reply: "It is good for the French; but we are another people, with different customs." On one occasion, Brébeuf appeared before the chiefs and elders at a solemn national council, described Heaven and Hell with images suited to their comprehension, asked to which they preferred to go after death, and then, in accordance with the invariable Huron custom in affairs of importance, presented a large and valuable belt of wampum, as an invitation to take the path to Paradise. [Brébeuf, Relation des Hurons, 1636, 81. For the use of wampum belts, see Introduction.]

Notwithstanding all their exhortations, the Jesuits, for the present, baptized but few. Indeed, during the first year or more, they baptized no adults except those apparently at the point of death; for, with excellent reason, they feared backsliding and recantation. They found especial pleasure in the baptism of dying infants, rescuing them from the flames of perdition, and changing them, to borrow Le Jeune's phrase, "from little Indians into little angels."

["Le seiziesme du mesme mois, deux petits Sauvages furent changes en deux petits Anges."—Relation, 1636, 89 (Cramoisy).

"O mon cher frère, vous pourrois-je expliquer quelle consolation ce m'etoit quand je voyois un pauure baptisé mourir deux heures, une demi journée, une ou deux journées, après son baptesme, particulièrement quand c'etoit un petit enfant!"—Lettre du Père Garnier à son Frère, MS.—This form of benevolence is beyond heretic appreciation.

"La joye qu'on a quand on a baptisé un Sauvage qui se meurt peu apres, & qui s'envole droit au Ciel, pour devenir un Ange, certainement c'est un joye qui surpasse tout ce qu'on se peut imaginer."—Le Jeune, Relation, 1635, 221 (Cramoisy).]

The Fathers' slumbers were brief and broken. Winter was the season of Huron festivity; and, as they lay stretched on their hard couch, suffocating with smoke and tormented by an inevitable multitude of fleas, the thumping of the drum resounded all night long from a neighboring house, mingled with the sound of the tortoise-shell rattle, the stamping of moccasined feet, and the cadence of voices keeping time with the dancers. Again, some ambitious villager would give a feast, and invite all the warriors of the neighboring towns; or some grand wager of gambling, with its attendant drumming, singing, and outcries, filled the night with discord.

But these were light annoyances, compared with the insane rites to cure the sick, prescribed by the "medicine-men," or ordained by the eccentric inspiration of dreams. In one case, a young sorcerer, by alternate gorging and fasting,—both in the interest of his profession,—joined with excessive exertion in singing to the spirits, contracted a disorder of the brain, which caused him, in mid-winter, to run naked about the village, howling like a wolf. The whole population bestirred itself to effect a cure. The patient had, or pretended to have, a dream, in which the conditions of his recovery were revealed to him. These were equally ridiculous and difficult; but the elders met in council, and all the villagers lent their aid, till every requisition was fulfilled, and the incongruous mass of gifts which the madman's dream had demanded were all bestowed upon him. This cure failing, a "medicine-feast" was tried; then several dances in succession. As the patient remained as crazy as before, preparations were begun for a grand dance, more potent than all the rest. Brébeuf says, that, except the masquerades of the Carnival among Christians, he never saw a folly equal to it.

"Some," he adds, "had sacks over their heads, with two holes for the eyes. Some were as naked as your hand, with horns or feathers on their heads, their bodies painted white, and their faces black as devils. Others were daubed with red, black, and white. In short, every one decked himself as extravagantly as he could, to dance in this ballet, and contribute something towards the health of the sick man." [Relation des Hurons, 1636, 116.] This remedy also failing, a crowning effort of the medical art was essayed. Brébeuf does not describe it, for fear, as he says, of being tedious; but, for the time, the village was a pandemonium.[1] This, with other ceremonies, was supposed to be ordered by a certain image like a doll, which a sorcerer placed in his tobacco-pouch, whence it uttered its oracles, at the same time moving as if alive. "Truly," writes Brébeuf, "here is nonsense enough: but I greatly fear there is something more dark and mysterious in it."

But all these ceremonies were outdone by the grand festival of the *Ononhara*, or Dream Feast,—esteemed the most powerful remedy in cases of sickness, or when a village was infested with evil spirits. The time and manner of holding it were determined at a solemn council. This scene of madness began at night. Men, women, and children, all pretending to have lost their senses, rushed shrieking and howling from house to house, upsetting everything in their way, throwing firebrands, beating those they met or drenching them with water, and availing themselves of this time of license to take a safe revenge on any who had ever offended them. This scene of frenzy continued till daybreak. No corner of the village was secure from the maniac crew. In the morning there was a change. They ran from house to house, accosting the inmates by name, and demanding of each the satisfaction of some secret want, revealed to the pretended madman in a dream, but of the nature of which he gave no hint whatever. The person addressed thereupon threw to him at random any article at hand, as a hatchet, a kettle, or a pipe;

---

1   "Suffit pour le present de dire en general, que iamais les Bacchantes forcenées du temps passé ne firent rien de plus furieux en leurs orgyes. C'est icy à s'entretuer, disent-ils, par des sorts qu'ils s'entreiettent, dont la composition est d'ongles d'Ours, de dents de Loup, d'ergots d'Aigles, de certaines pierres et de nerfs de Chien; c'est à rendre du sang par la bouche et par les narines, ou plustost d'vne poudre rouge qu'ils prennent subtilement, estans tombez sous le sort, et blessez; et dix mille autres sottises que ie laisse volontiers."—Brébeuf, Relation des Hurons, 1636, 117.

and the applicant continued his rounds till the desired gift was hit upon, when he gave an outcry of delight, echoed by gratulatory cries from all present. If, after all his efforts, he failed in obtaining the object of his dream, he fell into a deep dejection, convinced that some disaster was in store for him.

[Brébeuf's account of the Dream Feast is brief. The above particulars are drawn chiefly from Charlevoix, Journal Historique, 356, and Sagard, Voyage du Pays des Hurons, 280. See also Lafitau, and other early writers. This ceremony was not confined to the Hurons, but prevailed also among the Iroquois, and doubtless other kindred tribes. The Jesuit Dablon saw it in perfection at Onondaga. It usually took place in February, occupying about three days, and was often attended with great indecencies. The word ononhara means turning of the brain.]

The approach of summer brought with it a comparative peace. Many of the villagers dispersed,—some to their fishing, some to expeditions of trade, and some to distant lodges by their detached corn-fields. The priests availed themselves of the respite to engage in those exercises of private devotion which the rule of St. Ignatius enjoins. About midsummer, however, their quiet was suddenly broken. The crops were withering under a severe drought, a calamity which the sandy nature of the soil made doubly serious. The sorcerers put forth their utmost power, and, from the tops of the houses, yelled incessant invocations to the spirits. All was in vain; the pitiless sky was cloudless. There was thunder in the east and thunder in the west; but over Ihonatiria all was serene. A renowned "rain-maker," seeing his reputation tottering under his repeated failures, bethought him of accusing the Jesuits, and gave out that the red color of the cross which stood before their house scared the bird of thunder, and caused him to fly another way.[1] On

---

1   The following is the account of the nature of thunder, given to Brébeuf on a former occasion by another sorcerer.

    "It is a man in the form of a turkey-cock. The sky is his palace, and he remains in it when the air is clear. When the clouds begin to grumble, he descends to the earth to gather up snakes, and other objects which the Indians call *okies*. The lightning flashes whenever he opens or closes his wings. If the storm is more violent than usual, it is because his young are with him, and aiding in the noise as well as they can."—Relation des Hurons, 1636, 114.

    The word oki is here used to denote any object endued with supernatural power. A belief similar to the above exists to this day among the Dacotahs. Some

this a clamor arose. The popular ire turned against the priests, and the obnoxious cross was condemned to be hewn down. Aghast at the threatened sacrilege, they attempted to reason away the storm, assuring the crowd that the lightning was not a bird, but certain hot and fiery exhalations, which, being imprisoned, darted this way and that, trying to escape. As this philosophy failed to convince the hearers, the missionaries changed their line of defence.

"You say that the red color of the cross frightens the bird of thunder. Then paint the cross white, and see if the thunder will come."

This was accordingly done; but the clouds still kept aloof. The Jesuits followed up their advantage.

"Your spirits cannot help you, and your sorcerers have deceived you with lies. Now ask the aid of Him who made the world, and perhaps He will listen to your prayers." And they added, that, if the Indians would renounce their sins and obey the true God, they would make a procession daily to implore his favor towards them.

There was no want of promises. The processions were begun, as were also nine masses to St. Joseph; and, as heavy rains occurred soon after, the Indians conceived a high idea of the efficacy of the French "medicine."

["Nous deuons aussi beaucoup au glorieux sainct Ioseph, espoux de Nostre Dame, et protecteur des Hurons, dont nous auons touché au doigt l'assistance plusieurs fois. Ce fut vne chose remarquable, que le iour de sa feste et durant l'Octaue, les commoditez nous venoient de toutes parts."—Brébeuf, Relation des Hurons, 1635, 41.

The above extract is given as one out of many illustrations of the confidence with which the priests rested on the actual and direct aid of their celestial guardians. To St. Joseph, in particular, they find no words for their gratitude.]

In spite of the hostility of the sorcerers, and the transient commotion raised by the red cross, the Jesuits had gained the confidence and good-will of the Huron population. Their patience, their kindness, their intrepidity, their manifest disinterestedness,

---

of the Hurons and Iroquois, however, held that the thunder was a giant in human form. According to one story, he vomited from time to time a number of snakes, which, falling to the earth, caused the appearance of lightning.

the blamelessness of their lives, and the tact which, in the utmost fervors of their zeal, never failed them, had won the hearts of these wayward savages; and chiefs of distant villages came to urge that they would make their abode with them. [Brébeuf preserves a speech made to him by one of these chiefs, as a specimen of Huron eloquence.—Relation des Hurons, 1636, 123.] As yet, the results of the mission had been faint and few; but the priests toiled on courageously, high in hope that an abundant harvest of souls would one day reward their labors.

CHAPTER VII.

1636, 1637.

THE FEAST OF THE DEAD.

HURON GRAVES.—PREPARATION FOR THE CEREMONY.—DISINTERMENT.—THE MOURNING.—THE FUNERAL MARCH.—THE GREAT SEPULCHRE.—FUNERAL GAMES.—ENCAMPMENT OF THE MOURNERS.—GIFTS.—HARANGUES.—FRENZY OF THE CROWD.—THE CLOSING SCENE.—ANOTHER RITE.—THE CAPTIVE IROQUOIS.—THE SACRIFICE.

Mention has been made of those great depositories of human bones found at the present day in the ancient country of the Hurons. [See Introduction.] They have been a theme of abundant speculation;[1] yet their origin is a subject, not of conjecture, but of historic certainty. The peculiar rites to which they owe their existence were first described at length by Brébeuf, who, in the summer of the year 1636, saw them at the town of Ossossané.

The Jesuits had long been familiar with the ordinary rites of sepulture among the Hurons; the corpse placed in a crouching posture in the midst of the circle of friends and relatives; the long, measured wail of the mourners; the speeches in praise of the dead, and consolation to the living; the funeral feast; the gifts at the place

---

1 Among those who have wondered and speculated over these remains is Mr. Schoolcraft. A slight acquaintance with the early writers would have solved his doubts.

of burial; the funeral games, where the young men of the village contended for prizes; and the long period of mourning to those next of kin. The body was usually laid on a scaffold, or, more rarely, in the earth. This, however, was not its final resting-place. At intervals of ten or twelve years, each of the four nations which composed the Huron Confederacy gathered together its dead, and conveyed them all to a common place of sepulture. Here was celebrated the great "Feast of the Dead,"—in the eyes of the Hurons, their most solemn and important ceremonial.

In the spring of 1636, the chiefs and elders of the Nation of the Bear—the principal nation of the Confederacy, and that to which Ihonatiria belonged—assembled in a general council, to prepare for the great solemnity. There was an unwonted spirit of dissension. Some causes of jealousy had arisen, and three or four of the Bear villages announced their intention of holding their Feast of the Dead apart from the rest. As such a procedure was thought abhorrent to every sense of propriety and duty, the announcement excited an intense feeling; yet Brébeuf, who was present, describes the debate which ensued as perfectly calm, and wholly free from personal abuse or recrimination. The secession, however, took place, and each party withdrew to its villages to gather and prepare its dead.

The corpses were lowered from their scaffolds, and lifted from their graves. Their coverings were removed by certain functionaries appointed for the office, and the hideous relics arranged in a row, surrounded by the weeping, shrieking, howling concourse. The spectacle was frightful. Here were all the village dead of the last twelve years. The priests, connoisseurs in such matters, regarded it as a display of mortality so edifying, that they hastened to summon their French attendants to contemplate and profit by it. Each family reclaimed its own, and immediately addressed itself to removing what remained of flesh from the bones. These, after being tenderly caressed, with tears and lamentations, were wrapped in skins and adorned with pendent robes of fur. In the belief of the mourners, they were sentient and conscious. A soul was thought still to reside in them;[1] and to this notion, very general among Indians, is in no

---

1   In the general belief, the soul took flight after the great ceremony was ended. Many
     thought that there were two souls, one remaining with the bones, while the other

small degree due that extravagant attachment to the remains of their dead, which may be said to mark the race.

These relics of mortality, together with the recent corpses,—which were allowed to remain entire, but which were also wrapped carefully in furs,—were now carried to one of the largest houses, and hung to the numerous cross-poles, which, like rafters, supported the roof. Here the concourse of mourners seated themselves at a funeral feast; and, as the squaws of the household distributed the food, a chief harangued the assembly, lamenting the loss of the deceased, and extolling their virtues. This solemnity over, the mourners began their march for Ossossané, the scene of the final rite. The bodies remaining entire were borne on a kind of litter, while the bundles of bones were slung at the shoulders of the relatives, like fagots. Thus the procession slowly defiled along the forest pathways, with which the country of the Hurons was everywhere intersected; and as they passed beneath the dull shadow of the pines, they uttered at intervals, in unison, a dreary, wailing cry, designed to imitate the voices of disembodied souls winging their way to the land of spirits, and believed to have an effect peculiarly soothing to the conscious relics which each man bore. When, at night, they stopped to rest at some village on the way, the inhabitants came forth to welcome them with a grave and mournful hospitality.

From every town of the Nation of the Bear,—except the rebellious few that had seceded,—processions like this were converging towards Ossossané. This chief town of the Hurons stood on the eastern margin of Nottawassaga Bay, encompassed with a gloomy wilderness of fir and pine. Thither, on the urgent invitation of the chiefs, the Jesuits repaired. The capacious bark houses were filled to overflowing, and the surrounding woods gleamed with camp-fires: for the processions of mourners were fast arriving, and the throng was swelled by invited guests of other tribes. Funeral games were in progress, the young men and women practising archery and other exercises, for prizes offered by the mourners in the name of their dead relatives. [Funeral games were not confined to the Hurons and Iroquois: Perrot mentions having seen them among the Ottawas. An illustrated description of them

---

went to the land of spirits.

will be found in Lafitau.] Some of the chiefs conducted Brébeuf and his companions to the place prepared for the ceremony. It was a cleared area in the forest, many acres in extent. In the midst was a pit, about ten feet deep and thirty feet wide. Around it was reared a high and strong scaffolding; and on this were planted numerous upright poles, with cross-poles extended between, for hanging the funeral gifts and the remains of the dead.

Meanwhile there was a long delay. The Jesuits were lodged in a house where more than a hundred of these bundles of mortality were hanging from the rafters. Some were mere shapeless rolls; others were made up into clumsy effigies, adorned with feathers, beads, and belts of dyed porcupine-quills. Amidst this throng of the living and the dead, the priests spent a night which the imagination and the senses conspired to render almost insupportable.

At length the officiating chiefs gave the word to prepare for the ceremony. The relics were taken down, opened for the last time, and the bones caressed and fondled by the women amid paroxysms of lamentation.[1] Then all the processions were formed anew, and, each bearing its dead, moved towards the area prepared for the last solemn rites. As they reached the ground, they defiled in order, each to a spot assigned to it, on the outer limits of the clearing. Here the bearers of the dead laid their bundles on the ground, while those who carried the funeral gifts outspread and displayed them for the admiration of the beholders. Their number was immense, and their value relatively very great. Among them were many robes of beaver and other rich furs, collected and preserved for years, with a view to this festival. Fires were now lighted, kettles slung, and, around the entire circle of the clearing, the scene was like a fair or caravansary. This continued till three o'clock in the afternoon, when the gifts were repacked, and the bones shouldered afresh. Suddenly, at a signal from the chiefs, the crowd ran forward from every side towards the

---

1   "I'admiray la tendresse d'vne femme enuers son pere et ses enfans; elle est fille d'vn Capitaine, qui est mort fort âgé, et a esté autrefois fort considerable dans le Païs: elle luy peignoit sa cheuelure, elle manioit ses os les vns apres les autres, auec la mesme affection que si elle luy eust voulu rendre la vie; elle luy mit aupres de luy son Atsatone8ai, c'est à dire son pacquet de buchettes de Conseil, qui sont tous les liures et papiers du Païs. Pour ses petits enfans, elle leur mit des brasselets de Pourcelaine et de rassade aux bras, et baigna leurs os de ses larmes; on ne l'en pouuoit quasi separer, mais on pressoit, et il fallut incontinent partir."—Brébeuf, Relation des Hurons, 1636, 134.

scaffold, like soldiers to the assault of a town, scaled it by rude ladders with which it was furnished, and hung their relics and their gifts to the forest of poles which surmounted it. Then the ladders were removed; and a number of chiefs, standing on the scaffold, harangued the crowd below, praising the dead, and extolling the gifts, which the relatives of the departed now bestowed, in their names, upon their surviving friends.

During these harangues, other functionaries were lining the grave throughout with rich robes of beaver-skin. Three large copper kettles were next placed in the middle,[1] and then ensued a scene of hideous confusion. The bodies which had been left entire were brought to the edge of the grave, flung in, and arranged in order at the bottom by ten or twelve Indians stationed there for the purpose, amid the wildest excitement and the uproar of many hundred mingled voices.[2] When this part of the work was done, night was fast closing in. The concourse bivouacked around the clearing, and lighted their camp-fires under the brows of the forest which hedged in the scene of the dismal solemnity. Brébeuf and his companions withdrew to the village, where, an hour before dawn, they were roused by a clamor which might have wakened the dead. One of the bundles of bones, tied to a pole on the scaffold, had chanced to fall into the grave. This accident had precipitated the closing act, and perhaps increased its frenzy. Guided by the unearthly din, and the broad glare of flames fed with heaps of fat pine logs, the priests soon reached the spot, and saw what seemed, in their eyes, an image of Hell. All around blazed countless fires, and the air resounded with discordant outcries.[3] The naked multitude, on, under, and around the scaffold, were flinging the remains of their dead, discharged from their envelopments of

---

1   In some of these graves, recently discovered, five or six large copper kettles have been found, in a position corresponding with the account of Brébeuf. In one, there were no less than twenty-six kettles.

2   "Iamais rien ce m'a mieux figuré la confusion qui est parmy les damnez. Vous eussiez veu décharger de tous costez des corps à demy pourris, et de tous costez on entendoit vn horrible tintamarre de voix confuses de personnes qui parloient et ne s'entendoient pas."—Brébeuf, Relation des Hurons, 1636, 135.

3   "Approchans, nous vismes tout à fait une image de l'Enfer: cette grande place estoit toute remplie de feux & de flammes, & l'air retentissoit de toutes parts des voix confuses de ces Barbares," etc.—Brébeuf, Relation des Hurons, 1636, 209 (Cramoisy).

skins, pell-mell into the pit, where Brébeuf discerned men who, as the ghastly shower fell around them, arranged the bones in their places with long poles. All was soon over; earth, logs, and stones were cast upon the grave, and the clamor subsided into a funereal chant,—so dreary and lugubrious, that it seemed to the Jesuits the wail of despairing souls from the abyss of perdition.[1]

---

1   "Se mirent à chanter, mais d'un ton si lamentable & si lugubre, qu'il nous representoit l'horrible tristesse & l'abysme du desespoir dans lequel sont plongées pour iamais ces âmes malheureuses."—Ibid., 210.

    For other descriptions of these rites, see Charlevoix, Bressani, Du Creux, and especially Lafitau, in whose work they are illustrated with engravings. In one form or another, they were widely prevalent. Bartram found them among the Floridian tribes. Traces of a similar practice have been observed in recent times among the Dacotahs. Remains of places of sepulture, evidently of kindred origin, have been found in Tennessee, Missouri, Kentucky, and Ohio. Many have been discovered in several parts of New York, especially near the River Niagara. (See Squier, Aboriginal Monuments of New York.) This was the eastern extremity of the ancient territory of the Neuters. One of these deposits is said to have contained the bones of several thousand individuals. There is a large mound on Tonawanda Island, said by the modern Senecas to be a Neuter burial-place. (See Marshall, Historical Sketches of the Niagara Frontier, 8.) In Canada West, they are found throughout the region once occupied by the Neuters, and are frequent in the Huron district.

    Dr. Taché writes to me,—"I have inspected sixteen bone-pits," (in the Huron country,) "the situation of which is indicated on the little pencil map I send you. They contain from six hundred to twelve hundred skeletons each, of both sexes and all ages, all mixed together purposely. With one exception, these pits also contain pipes of stone or clay, small earthen pots, shells, and wampum wrought of these shells, copper ornaments, beads of glass, and other trinkets. Some pits contained articles of copper of aboriginal Mexican fabric."

    This remarkable fact, together with the frequent occurrence in these graves of large conch-shells, of which wampum was made, and which could have been procured only from the Gulf of Mexico, or some part of the southern coast of the United States, proves the extent of the relations of traffic by which certain articles were passed from tribe to tribe over a vast region. The transmission of pipes from the famous Red Pipe-Stone Quarry of the St. Peter's to tribes more than a thousand miles distant is an analogous modern instance, though much less remarkable.

    The Taché Museum, at the Laval University of Quebec, contains a large collection of remains from these graves. In one instance, the human bones are of a size that may be called gigantic.

    In nearly every case, the Huron graves contain articles of use or ornament of European workmanship. From this it may be inferred, that the nation itself, or its practice of inhumation, does not date back to a period long before the arrival of the French.

    The Northern Algonquins had also a solemn Feast of the Dead; but it was widely different from that of the Hurons.—See the very curious account of it by Lalemant, Relation des Hurons, 1642, 94, 95.

Such was the origin of one of those strange sepulchres which are the wonder and perplexity of the modern settler in the abandoned forests of the Hurons.

The priests were soon to witness another and a more terrible rite, yet one in which they found a consolation, since it signalized the saving of a soul,—the snatching from perdition of one of that dreaded race, into whose very midst they hoped, with devoted daring, to bear hereafter the cross of salvation. A band of Huron warriors had surprised a small party of Iroquois, killed several, and captured the rest. One of the prisoners was led in triumph to a village where the priests then were. He had suffered greatly; his hands, especially, were frightfully lacerated. Now, however, he was received with every mark of kindness. "Take courage," said a chief, addressing him; "you are among friends." The best food was prepared for him, and his captors vied with each other in offices of good-will. [This pretended kindness in the treatment of a prisoner destined to the torture was not exceptional. The Hurons sometimes even supplied their intended victim with a temporary wife.] He had been given, according to Indian custom, to a warrior who had lost a near relative in battle, and the captive was supposed to be adopted in place of the slain. His actual doom was, however, not for a moment in doubt. The Huron received him affectionately, and, having seated him in his lodge, addressed him in a tone of extreme kindness. "My nephew, when I heard that you were coming, I was very glad, thinking that you would remain with me to take the place of him I have lost. But now that I see your condition, and your hands crushed and torn so that you will never use them, I change my mind. Therefore take courage, and prepare to die tonight like a brave man."

The prisoner coolly asked what should be the manner of his death.

"By fire," was the reply.

"It is well," returned the Iroquois.

Meanwhile, the sister of the slain Huron, in whose place the prisoner was to have been adopted, brought him a dish of food, and, her eyes flowing with tears, placed it before him with an air of the utmost tenderness; while, at the same time, the warrior brought him a pipe, wiped the sweat from his brow, and fanned him with a fan of feathers.

About noon he gave his farewell feast, after the custom of those who knew themselves to be at the point of death. All were welcome to this strange banquet; and when the company were gathered, the host addressed them in a loud, firm voice: "My brothers, I am about to die. Do your worst to me. I do not fear torture or death." Some of those present seemed to have visitings of real compassion; and a woman asked the priests if it would be wrong to kill him, and thus save him from the fire.

The Jesuits had from the first lost no opportunity of accosting him; while he, grateful for a genuine kindness amid the cruel hypocrisy that surrounded him, gave them an attentive ear, till at length, satisfied with his answers, they baptized him. His eternal bliss secure, all else was as nothing; and they awaited the issue with some degree of composure.

A crowd had gathered from all the surrounding towns, and after nightfall the presiding chief harangued them, exhorting them to act their parts well in the approaching sacrifice, since they would be looked upon by the Sun and the God of War. [Areskoui (see Introduction). He was often regarded as identical with the Sun. The semi-sacrificial character of the torture in this case is also shown by the injunction, "que pour ceste nuict on n'allast point folastrer dans les bois."—Le Mercier, Relation des Hurons, 1637, 114.] It is needless to dwell on the scene that ensued. It took place in the lodge of the great war chief, Atsan. Eleven fires blazed on the ground, along the middle of this capacious dwelling. The platforms on each side were closely packed with spectators; and, betwixt these and the fires, the younger warriors stood in lines, each bearing lighted pine-knots or rolls of birch-bark. The heat, the smoke, the glare of flames, the wild yells, contorted visages, and furious gestures of these human devils, as their victim, goaded by their torches, bounded through the fires again and again, from end to end of the house, transfixed the priests with horror. But when, as day dawned, the last spark of life had fled, they consoled themselves with the faith that the tortured wretch had found his rest at last in Paradise.

[Le Mercier's long and minute account of the torture of this prisoner is too revolting to be dwelt upon. One of the most atrocious features of the scene was the alternation of raillery and ironical compliment which attended it throughout, as well as the pains taken to preserve life and consciousness in the victim as long as possible. Portions of his flesh were afterwards devoured.]

CHAPTER VIII.

1636, 1637.

THE HURON AND THE JESUIT.

ENTHUSIASM FOR THE MISSION.—SICKNESS OF THE PRIESTS. THE PEST AMONG THE HURONS.—THE JESUIT ON HIS ROUNDS.—EFFORTS AT CONVERSION.— PRIESTS AND SORCERERS.—THE MAN-DEVIL.—THE MAGICIAN'S PRESCRIPTION.—INDIAN DOCTORS AND PATIENTS.—COVERT BAPTISMS.—SELF-DEVOTION OF THE JESUITS.

Meanwhile from Old France to New came succors and reinforcements to the missions of the forest. More Jesuits crossed the sea to urge on the work of conversion. These were no stern exiles, seeking on barbarous shores an asylum for a persecuted faith. Rank, wealth, power, and royalty itself, smiled on their enterprise, and bade them God-speed. Yet, withal, a fervor more intense, a self-abnegation more complete, a self-devotion more constant and enduring, will scarcely find its record on the page of human history.

Holy Mother Church, linked in sordid wedlock to governments and thrones, numbered among her servants a host of the worldly and the proud, whose service of God was but the service of themselves,—and many, too, who, in the sophistry of the human heart, thought themselves true soldiers of Heaven, while earthly pride, interest, and passion were the life-springs of their zeal. This mighty Church of Rome, in her imposing march along the high road of history, heralded as infallible and divine, astounds the gazing world with prodigies of contradiction: now the protector of the oppressed, now the right arm of tyrants; now breathing charity and love, now dark with the passions of Hell; now beaming with celestial truth, now masked in hypocrisy and lies; now a virgin, now a harlot; an imperial queen, and a tinselled actress. Clearly, she is of earth, not of heaven; and her transcendently dramatic life is a type of the good and ill, the baseness and nobleness, the foulness and purity, the love and hate, the pride, passion, truth, falsehood, fierceness, and tenderness, that battle in the restless heart of man.

It was her nobler and purer part that gave life to the early missions of New France. That gloomy wilderness, those hordes of savages, had nothing to tempt the ambitious, the proud, the grasping, or the indolent. Obscure toil, solitude, privation, hardship, and death were to be the missionary's portion. He who set sail for the country of the Hurons left behind him the world and all its prizes. True, he acted under orders,—obedient, like a soldier, to the word of command: but the astute Society of Jesus knew its members, weighed each in the balance, gave each his fitting task; and when the word was passed to embark for New France, it was but the response to a secret longing of the fervent heart. The letters of these priests, departing for the scene of their labors, breathe a spirit of enthusiastic exaltation, which, to a colder nature and a colder faith, may sometimes seem overstrained, but which is in no way disproportionate to the vastness of the effort and the sacrifice demanded of them.

[The following are passages from letters of missionaries at this time. See "Divers Sentimens," appended to the Relation of 1635.

"On dit que les premiers qui fondent les Eglises d'ordinaire sont saincts: cette pensée m'attendrit si fort le cœur, que quoy que ie me voye icy fort inutile dans ceste fortunée Nouuelle France, si faut-il que i'auoüe que ie ne me sçaurois defendre d'vne pensée qui me presse le cœur: Cupio impendi, et superimpendi pro vobis, Pauure Nouuelle France, ie desire me sacrifier pour ton bien, et quand il me deuroit couster mille vies, moyennant que ie puisse aider à sauuer vne seule âme, ie seray trop heureux, et ma vie tres bien employée."

"Ma consolation parmy les Hurons, c'est que tous les iours ie me confesse, et puis ie dis la Messe, comme si ie deuois prendre le Viatique et mourir ce iour là, et ie ne crois pas qu'on puisse mieux viure, ny auec plus de satisfaction et de courage, et mesme de merites, que viure en un lieu, où on pense pouuoir mourir tous les iours, et auoir la deuise de S. Paul, Quotidie morior, fratres, etc. mes freres, ie fais estat de mourir tous les iours."

"Qui ne void la Nouuelle France que par les yeux de chair et de nature, il n'y void que des bois et des croix; mais qui les considere auec les yeux de la grace et d'vne bonne vocation, il n'y void que Dieu, les vertus et les graces, et on y trouue tant et de si solides consolations, que si ie pouuois acheter la Nouuelle France, en donnant tout le Paradis Terrestre, certainement ie l'acheterois. Mon Dieu, qu'il fait bon estre au lieu où Dieu nous a mis de sa grace! veritablement i'ay trouué icy ce que i'auois esperé, vn cœur selon le cœur de Dieu, qui ne cherche que Dieu."]

All turned with longing eyes towards the mission of the Hurons; for here the largest harvest promised to repay their labor, and here hardships and dangers most abounded. Two Jesuits, Pijart and Le Mercier, had been sent thither in 1635; and in midsummer of the next year three more arrived,—Jogues, Chatelain, and Garnier. When, after their long and lonely journey, they reached Ihonatiria one by one, they were received by their brethren with scanty fare indeed, but with a fervor of affectionate welcome which more than made amends; for among these priests, united in a community of faith and enthusiasm, there was far more than the genial comradeship of men joined in a common enterprise of self-devotion and peril.[1] On their way, they had met Daniel and Davost descending to Quebec, to establish there a seminary of Huron children,—a project long cherished by Brébeuf and his companions.

---

[1] "Ie luy preparay de ce que nous auions, pour le receuoir, mais quel festin! vne poignée de petit poisson sec auec vn peu de farine; i'enuoyay chercher quelques nouueaux espics, que nous luy fismes rostir à la façon du pays; mais il est vray que dans son cœur et à l'entendre, il ne fit iamais meilleure chere. La ioye qui se ressent à ces entreueuës semble estre quelque image du contentement des bien-heureux à leur arriuée dans le Ciel, tant elle est pleine de suauité."—Le Mercier, Relation des Hurons, 1637, 106.

Scarcely had the new-comers arrived, when they were attacked by a contagious fever, which turned their mission-house into a hospital. Jogues, Garnier, and Chatelain fell ill in turn; and two of their domestics also were soon prostrated, though the only one of the number who could hunt fortunately escaped. Those who remained in health attended the sick, and the sufferers vied with each other in efforts often beyond their strength to relieve their companions in misfortune. [Lettre de Brébeuf au T. R. P. Mutio Vitelleschi, 20 Mai, 1637, in Carayon, 157. Le Mercier, Relation des Hurons, 1637, 120, 123.] The disease in no case proved fatal; but scarcely had health begun to return to their household, when an unforeseen calamity demanded the exertion of all their energies.

The pestilence, which for two years past had from time to time visited the Huron towns, now returned with tenfold violence, and with it soon appeared a new and fearful scourge,—the small-pox. Terror was universal. The contagion increased as autumn advanced; and when winter came, far from ceasing, as the priests had hoped, its ravages were appalling. The season of Huron festivity was turned to a season of mourning; and such was the despondency and dismay, that suicide became frequent. The Jesuits, singly or in pairs, journeyed in the depth of winter from village to village, ministering to the sick, and seeking to commend their religious teachings by their efforts to relieve bodily distress. Happily, perhaps, for their patients, they had no medicine but a little senna. A few raisins were left, however; and one or two of these, with a spoonful of sweetened water, were always eagerly accepted by the sufferers, who thought them endowed with some mysterious and sovereign efficacy. No house was left unvisited. As the missionary, physician at once to body and soul, entered one of these smoky dens, he saw the inmates, their heads muffled in their robes of skins, seated around the fires in silent dejection. Everywhere was heard the wail of sick and dying children; and on or under the platforms at the sides of the house crouched squalid men and women, in all the stages of the distemper. The Father approached, made inquiries, spoke words of kindness, administered his harmless remedies, or offered a bowl of broth made from game brought in by the Frenchman who hunted for the mission. [Game was so scarce in the Huron country, that it was greatly prized as a luxury. Le Mercier speaks of an Indian, sixty years of age, who walked twelve miles to taste the wild-fowl killed by the French hunter. The ordinary food was corn, beans, pumpkins, and fish.] The body cared for, he next addressed himself to the soul. "This life is short, and very miserable. It matters little whether we live or die." The patient remained silent, or grumbled his dissent. The Jesuit, after enlarging for a time, in broken Huron, on the brevity and nothingness of mortal weal or woe, passed next to the joys of Heaven and the pains of Hell, which he set forth with his best rhetoric. His pictures of infernal fires and torturing devils were readily comprehended, if the listener had consciousness enough to comprehend anything; but with respect to the advantages of the French Paradise, he was slow of conviction. "I wish to go where my relations and ancestors have gone," was a common reply. "Heaven is a good place for Frenchmen," said another; "but I wish to be among Indians, for the French will give me nothing to eat when I get there." [It was scarcely possible to convince the Indians, that there was but one God for themselves and the whites. The proposition was met by such arguments as this: "If we had been of one father, we should know how to make knives and coats as well as you."—Le Mercier, Relation des Hurons, 1637, 147.] Often the patient was stolidly silent; sometimes he was hopelessly perverse and contradictory. Again, Nature triumphed over Grace. "Which will you choose," demanded the priest of a dying woman, "Heaven or Hell?" "Hell, if my children are there, as you say," returned the mother. "Do they hunt in Heaven, or make war, or go to feasts?" asked an anxious inquirer. "Oh, no!" replied the Father. "Then," returned the querist, "I will not go. It is not good to be lazy." But above all other obstacles was the dread of starvation in the regions of the blest. Nor, when the dying Indian had been induced at last to express a desire for Paradise, was it an easy matter to bring him to a due contrition for his sins; for he would deny with indignation that he had ever committed any. When at length, as sometimes happened, all these difficulties gave way, and the patient had been brought to what seemed to his instructor a fitting frame for baptism, the priest, with contentment at his heart, brought water in a cup or in the hollow of his hand, touched his forehead with the mystic drop, and snatched him from an eternity of woe. But the convert, even after his baptism, did not always manifest a satisfactory spiritual condition. "Why did you baptize that Iroquois?" asked one of the dying neophytes, speaking of the prisoner recently tortured; "he will get to Heaven before us, and, when he sees us coming, he will drive us out." [Most of the above traits are drawn from Le Mercier's report of 1637. The rest are from Brébeuf.]

Thus did these worthy priests, too conscientious to let these unfortunates die in peace, follow them with benevolent persecutions to the hour of their death.

It was clear to the Fathers, that their ministrations were valued solely because their religion was supposed by many to be a "medicine," or charm, efficacious against famine, disease, and death. They themselves, indeed, firmly believed that saints and angels were always at hand with temporal succors for the faithful. At their intercession, St. Joseph had interposed to procure a happy delivery to a squaw in protracted pains of childbirth; [Brébeuf, Relation des Hurons, 1636, 89. Another woman was delivered on touching a relic of St. Ignatius. Ibid., 90.] and they never doubted, that, in the hour of need, the celestial powers would confound the unbeliever with intervention direct and manifest. At the town of Wenrio, the people, after trying in vain all the feasts, dances, and preposterous ceremonies by which their medicine-men sought to stop the pest, resolved to essay the "medicine" of the French, and, to that end, called the priests to a council. "What must we do, that your God may take pity on us?" Brébeuf's answer was uncompromising:—

"Believe in Him; keep His commandments; abjure your faith in dreams; take but one wife, and be true to her; give up your superstitious feasts; renounce your assemblies of debauchery; eat no human flesh; never give feasts to demons; and make a vow, that, if God will deliver you from this pest, you will build a chapel to offer Him thanksgiving and praise." [Le Mercier, Relation des Hurons, 1637, 114, 116 (Cramoisy).]

The terms were too hard. They would fain bargain to be let off with building the chapel alone; but Brébeuf would bate them nothing, and the council broke up in despair.

At Ossossané, a few miles distant, the people, in a frenzy of terror, accepted the conditions, and promised to renounce their superstitions and reform their manners. It was a labor of Hercules, a cleansing of Augean stables; but the scared savages were ready to make any promise that might stay the pestilence. One of their principal sorcerers proclaimed in a loud voice through the streets of the town, that the God of the French was their master, and that thenceforth all must live according to His will. "What consolation," exclaims Le Mercier, "to see God glorified by the lips of an imp of Satan!" [Le Mercier, Relation des Hurons, 1637, 127, 128 (Cramoisy).]

Their joy was short. The proclamation was on the twelfth of December. On the twenty-first, a noted sorcerer came to Ossossané. He was of a dwarfish, hump-backed figure,—most rare among this symmetrical people,—with a vicious face, and a dress consisting of a torn and shabby robe of beaver-skin. Scarcely had he arrived, when, with ten or twelve other savages, he ensconced himself in a kennel of bark made for the occasion. In the midst were placed several stones, heated red-hot. On these the sorcerer threw tobacco, producing a stifling fumigation; in the midst of which, for a full half-hour, he sang, at the top of his throat, those boastful, yet meaningless, rhapsodies of which Indian magical songs are composed. Then came a grand "medicine-feast"; and the disappointed Jesuits saw plainly that the objects of their spiritual care, unwilling to throw away any chance of cure, were bent on invoking aid from God and the Devil at once.

The hump-backed sorcerer became a thorn in the side of the Fathers, who more than half believed his own account of his origin. He was, he said, not a man, but an *oki*,—a spirit, or, as the priests rendered it, a demon,—and had dwelt with other *okies* under the earth, when the whim seized him to become a man. Therefore he ascended to the upper world, in company with a female spirit. They hid beside a path, and, when they saw a woman passing, they entered her womb. After a time they were born, but not until the male oki had quarrelled with and strangled his female companion, who came dead into the world. [Le Mercier, Relation des Hurons, 1637, 72 (Cramoisy). This "petit sorcier" is often mentioned elsewhere.] The character of the sorcerer seems to have comported reasonably well with this story of his origin. He pretended to have an absolute control over the pestilence, and his prescriptions were scrupulously followed.

He had several conspicuous rivals, besides a host of humbler competitors. One of these magician-doctors, who was nearly blind, made for himself a kennel at the end of his house, where he fasted for seven days. [See Introduction.] On the sixth day the spirits appeared, and, among other revelations, told him that the disease could be frightened away by means of images of straw, like scarecrows, placed on the tops of the houses. Within forty-eight hours after this announcement, the roofs of Onnentisati and the neighboring villages were covered with an army of these effigies. The Indians tried to persuade the Jesuits to put them on the mission-house; but the priests replied, that the cross before their door was a better protector; and, for further security, they set another on their roof, declaring that they would rely on it to save them from infection. ["Qu'en vertu de ce signe nous ne redoutions point les demons, et esperions que Dieu preserueroit nostre petite maison de cette maladie contagieuse."—Le Mercier, Relation des Hurons, 1637, 150.] The Indians, on their part, anxious that their scarecrows should do their office well, addressed them in loud harangues and burned offerings of tobacco to them. [Ibid., 157.]

There was another sorcerer, whose medical practice was so extensive, that, unable to attend to all his patients, he sent substitutes to the surrounding towns, first imparting to them his own mysterious power. One of these deputies came to Ossossané while the priests were there. The principal house was thronged with expectant savages, anxiously waiting his arrival. A chief carried before him a kettle of mystic water, with which the envoy sprinkled the company,[1] at the same time fanning them with the wing of a wild turkey. Then came a grand medicine-feast, followed by a medicine-dance of women.

Opinion was divided as to the nature of the pest; but the greater number were agreed that it was a malignant oki, who came from Lake Huron.[2] As it was of the last moment to conciliate or frighten him, no means to these ends were neglected. Feasts were held for him, at which, to do him honor, each guest gorged himself

---

1   The idea seems to have been taken from the holy water of the French. Le Mercier says that a Huron who had been to Quebec once asked him the use of the vase of water at the door of the chapel. The priest told him that it was "to frighten away the devils". On this, he begged earnestly to have some of it.

2   Many believed that the country was bewitched by wicked sorcerers, one of whom, it was said, had been seen at night roaming around the villages, vomiting fire. (Le Mercier, Relation des Hurons, 1637, 134.) This superstition of sorcerers vomiting fire was common among the Iroquois of New York.—Others held that a sister of Étienne Brulé caused the evil, in revenge for the death of her brother, murdered some years before. She was said to have been seen flying over the country, breathing forth pestilence.

like a vulture. A mystic fraternity danced with firebrands in their mouths; while other dancers wore masks, and pretended to be hump-backed. Tobacco was burned to the Demon of the Pest, no less than to the scarecrows which were to frighten him. A chief climbed to the roof of a house, and shouted to the invisible monster, "If you want flesh, go to our enemies, go to the Iroquois!"—while, to add terror to persuasion, the crowd in the dwelling below yelled with all the force of their lungs, and beat furiously with sticks on the walls of bark.

Besides these public efforts to stay the pestilence, the sufferers, each for himself, had their own methods of cure, dictated by dreams or prescribed by established usage. Thus two of the priests, entering a house, saw a sick man crouched in a corner, while near him sat three friends. Before each of these was placed a huge portion of food,—enough, the witness declares, for four,—and though all were gorged to suffocation, with starting eyeballs and distended veins, they still held staunchly to their task, resolved at all costs to devour the whole, in order to cure the patient, who meanwhile ceased not in feeble tones, to praise their exertions, and implore them to persevere.

["En fin il leur fallut rendre gorge, ce qu'ils firent à diuerses reprises, ne laissants pas pour cela de continuer à vuider leur plat."—Le Mercier, Relation des Hurons, 1637, 142.—This beastly superstition exists in some tribes at the present day. A kindred superstition once fell under the writer's notice, in the case of a wounded Indian, who begged of every one he met to drink a large bowl of water, in order that he, the Indian, might be cured.]

Turning from these eccentricities of the "noble savage"[1] to the zealots who were toiling, according to their light, to snatch him from the clutch of Satan, we see the irrepressible Jesuits roaming from town to town in restless quest of subjects for baptism. In the case of adults, they thought some little preparation essential; but their efforts to this end, even with the aid of St. Joseph,

---

1   In the midst of these absurdities we find recorded one of the best traits of the Indian character. At Ihonatiria, a house occupied by a family of orphan children was burned to the ground, leaving the inmates destitute. The villagers united to aid them. Each contributed something, and they were soon better provided for than before.

whom they constantly invoked,[1] were not always successful; and, cheaply as they offered salvation, they sometimes failed to find a purchaser. With infants, however, a simple drop of water sufficed for the transfer from a prospective Hell to an assured Paradise. The Indians, who at first had sought baptism as a cure, now began to regard it as a cause of death; and when the priest entered a lodge where a sick child lay in extremity, the scowling parents watched him with jealous distrust, lest unawares the deadly drop should be applied. The Jesuits were equal to the emergency. Father Le Mercier will best tell his own story.

"On the third of May, Father Pierre Pijart baptized at Anonatea a little child two months old, in manifest danger of death, without being seen by the parents, who would not their consent. This is the device which he used. Our sugar does wonders for us. He pretended to make the child drink a little sugared water, and at the same time dipped a finger in it. As the father of the infant began to suspect something, and called out to him not to baptize it, he gave the spoon to a woman who was near, and said to her, 'Give it to him yourself.' She approached and found the child asleep; and at the same time Father Pijart, under pretence of seeing if he was really asleep touched his face with his wet finger, and baptized him. At the end of forty-eight hours he went to Heaven.

"Some days before, the missionary had used the same device *(industrie)* for baptizing a little boy six or seven years old. His father, who was very sick, had several times refused to receive baptism; and when asked if he would not be glad to have his son baptized, he had answered, No. 'At least,' said Father Pijart, 'you will not object to my giving him a little sugar.' 'No; but you must not baptize him.' The missionary gave it to him once; then again; and at the third spoonful, before he had put the sugar into the water, he let a drop of it fall on the child, at the same time pronouncing the sacramental words. A little girl, who was looking at him, cried out,

---

[1]   "C'est nostre refuge ordinaire en semblables necessitez, et d'ordinaire auec tels succez, que nous auons sujet d'en benir Dieu à iamais, qui nous fait cognoistre en cette barbarie le credit de ce S. Patriarche aupres de son infinie misericorde."—Le Mercier, Relation des Hurons, 1637, 153.—In the case of a woman at Onnentisati, "Dieu nous inspira de luy vouër quelques Messes en l'honneur de S. Joseph." The effect was prompt. In half an hour the woman was ready for baptism. On the same page we have another subject secured to Heaven, "sans doute par les merites du glorieux Patriarche S. Joseph."

'Father, he is baptizing him!' The child's father was much disturbed; but the missionary said to him, 'Did you not see that I was giving him sugar?' The child died soon after; but God showed His grace to the father, who is now in perfect health."

[Le Mercier, Relation des Hurons, 1637, 165. Various other cases of the kind are mentioned in the Relations.]

That equivocal morality, lashed by the withering satire of Pascal,—a morality built on the doctrine that all means are permissible for saving souls from perdition, and that sin itself is no sin when its object is the "greater glory of God,"—found far less scope in the rude wilderness of the Hurons than among the interests, ambitions, and passions of civilized life. Nor were these men, chosen from the purest of their Order, personally well fitted to illustrate the capabilities of this elastic system. Yet now and then, by the light of their own writings, we may observe that the teachings of the school of Loyola had not been wholly without effect in the formation of their ethics.

But when we see them, in the gloomy February of 1637, and the gloomier months that followed, toiling on foot from one infected town to another, wading through the sodden snow, under the bare and dripping forests, drenched with incessant rains, till they descried at length through the storm the clustered dwellings of some barbarous hamlet,—when we see them entering, one after another, these wretched abodes of misery and darkness, and all for one sole end, the baptism of the sick and dying, we may smile at the futility of the object, but we must needs admire the self-sacrificing zeal with which it was pursued.

CHAPTER IX.

1637.

CHARACTER OF THE CANADIAN JESUITS.

JEAN DE BRÉBEUF.—CHARLES GARNIER.—JOSEPH MARIE CHAUMONOT.—NOËL CHABANEL.—ISAAC JOGUES.—OTHER JESUITS.—NATURE OF THEIR FAITH.—SUPERNATURALISM.—VISIONS.—MIRACLES.

Before pursuing farther these obscure, but noteworthy, scenes in the drama of human history, it will be well to indicate, so far as there are means of doing so, the distinctive traits of some of the chief actors. Mention has often been made of Brébeuf,—that masculine apostle of the Faith,—the Ajax of the mission. Nature had given him all the passions of a vigorous manhood, and religion had crushed them, curbed them, or tamed them to do her work,—like a dammed-up torrent, sluiced and guided to grind and saw and weave for the good of man. Beside him, in strange contrast, stands his co-laborer, Charles Garnier. Both were of noble birth and gentle nurture; but here the parallel ends. Garnier's face was beardless, though he was above thirty years old. For this he was laughed at by his friends in Paris, but admired by the Indians, who thought him handsome. ["C'est pourquoi j'ai bien gagne quitter la France, où vous me fesiez la guerre de n'avoir point de barbe; car c'est ce qui me fait estimes beau des Sauvages."— Lettres de Garnier, MSS.] His constitution, bodily or mental, was by no means robust. From boyhood, he had shown a delicate and sensitive nature, a tender conscience, and a proneness to religious emotion. He had never gone with his schoolmates to inns and other places of amusement, but kept his pocket-money to give to beggars. One of his brothers relates of him, that, seeing an obscene book, he bought and destroyed it, lest other boys should be injured by it. He had always wished to be a Jesuit, and, after a novitiate which is described as most edifying, he became a professed member of the Order. The Church, indeed, absorbed the greater part, if not the whole, of this pious family,—one brother being a Carmelite, another a Capuchin, and a third a Jesuit, while there seems also to have been a fourth under vows. Of Charles Garnier there remain twenty-four letters, written at various times to his father and two of his brothers, chiefly during his missionary life among the Hurons. They breathe the deepest and most intense Roman Catholic piety, and a spirit enthusiastic, yet sad, as of one renouncing all the hopes and prizes of the world, and living for Heaven alone. The affections of his sensitive nature, severed from earthly objects, found relief in an ardent adoration of the Virgin Mary. With none of the bone and sinew of rugged manhood, he entered, not only without hesitation, but with eagerness, on a life which would have tried the boldest; and, sustained by the spirit within him, he was more than equal to it. His fellow-missionaries thought him a saint; and had he lived a century or two earlier, he would perhaps have been canonized: yet, while all his life was a willing martyrdom, one can discern, amid his admirable virtues, some slight lingerings of mortal vanity. Thus, in three several letters, he speaks of his great success in baptizing, and plainly intimates that he had sent more souls to Heaven than the other Jesuits.

[The above sketch of Garnier is drawn from various sources. Observations du P. Henri de St. Joseph, Carme, sur son Frère le P. Charles Garnier, MS.—Abrégé de la Vie du R. Père Charles Garnier, MS. This unpublished sketch bears the signature of the Jesuit Ragueneau, with the date 1652. For the opportunity of consulting it I am indebted to Rev. Felix Martin, S. J.—Lettres du P. Charles Garnier, MSS. These embrace his correspondence from the Huron country, and are exceedingly characteristic and striking. There is another letter in Carayon, Première Mission.—Garnier's family was wealthy, as well as noble. Its members seem to have been strongly attached to each other, and the young priest's father was greatly distressed at his departure for Canada.]

Next appears a young man of about twenty-seven years, Joseph Marie Chaumonot. Unlike Brébeuf and Garnier, he was of humble origin,—his father being a vine-dresser, and his mother the daughter of a poor village schoolmaster. At an early age they sent him to Châtillon on the Seine, where he lived with his uncle, a priest, who taught him to speak Latin, and awakened his religious susceptibilities, which were naturally strong. This did not prevent him from yielding to the persuasions of one of his companions to run off to Beaune, a town of Burgundy, where the fugitives proposed to study music under the Fathers of the Oratory. To provide funds for the journey, he stole a sum of about the value of a dollar from his uncle, the priest. This act, which seems to have been a mere peccadillo of boyish levity, determined his future career. Finding himself in total destitution at Beaune, he wrote to his mother for money, and received in reply an order from his father to come home. Stung with the thought of being posted as a thief in his native village, he resolved not to do so, but to set out forthwith on a pilgrimage to Rome; and accordingly, tattered and penniless, he took the road for the sacred city. Soon a conflict began within him between his misery and the pride which forbade him to beg. The pride was forced to succumb. He begged from door to door; slept under sheds by the wayside, or in haystacks; and now and then found lodging and a meal at a convent. Thus, sometimes alone, sometimes with vagabonds whom he met on the road, he made his way through Savoy and Lombardy in a pitiable condition of destitution, filth, and disease. At length he reached Ancona, when the thought occured to him of visiting the Holy House of Loretto, and imploring the succor of the Virgin Mary. Nor were his hopes disappointed. He had reached that renowned shrine, knelt, paid his devotions, and offered his prayer, when, as he issued from the door of the chapel, he was accosted by a young man, whom he conjectures to have been an angel descended to his relief, and who was probably some penitent or devotee bent on works of charity or self-mortification. With a voice of the greatest kindness, he proffered his aid to the wretched boy, whose appearance was alike fitted to awaken pity and disgust. The conquering of a natural repugnance to filth, in the interest of charity and humility, is a conspicuous virtue in most of the Roman Catholic saints; and whatever merit may attach to it was acquired in an extraordinary degree by the young man in question. Apparently, he was a physician; for he not only restored the miserable wanderer to a condition of comparative decency, but cured him of a grievous malady, the result of neglect. Chaumonot went on his way, thankful to his benefactor, and overflowing with an enthusiasm of gratitude to Our Lady of Loretto.

["Si la moindre dame m'avoit fait rendre ce service par le dernier de ses valets, n'aurois-je pas dus lui en rendre toutes les reconnoissances possibles? Et si après une telle charité elle s'étoit offerte à me servir toujours de mesme, comment aurois-je dû l'honorer, lui obéir, l'aimer toute ma vie! Pardon, Reine des Anges et des hommes! pardon de ce qu'après avoir reçu de vous tant de marques, par lesquelles vous m'avez convaincu que vous m'avez adopté pour votre fils, j'ai eu l'ingratitude pendant des années entières de me comporter encore plutôt en esclave de Satan qu'en enfant d'une Mère Vierge. O que vous êtes bonne et charitable! puisque quelques obstacles que mes péchés ayent pu mettre à vos graces, vous n'avez jamais cessé de m'attirer au bien; jusque là que vous m'avez fait admettre dans la Sainte Compagnie de Jésus, votre fils."—Chaumonot, Vie, 20. The above is from the very curious autobiography written by Chaumonot, at the command of his Superior, in 1688. The original manuscript is at the Hôtel Dieu of Quebec. Mr. Shea has printed it.]

As he journeyed towards Rome, an old burgher, at whose door he had begged, employed him as a servant. He soon became known to a Jesuit, to whom he had confessed himself in Latin; and as his acquirements were considerable for his years, he was eventually employed as teacher of a low class in one of the Jesuit schools. Nature had inclined him to a life of devotion. He would fain be a hermit, and, to that end, practised eating green ears of wheat; but, finding he could not swallow them, conceived that he had mistaken his vocation. Then a strong desire grew up within him to become a Récollet, a Capuchin, or, above all, a Jesuit; and at length the wish of his heart was answered. At the age of twenty-one, he was admitted to the Jesuit novitiate.[1] Soon after its close, a

---

1   His age, when he left his uncle, the priest, is not mentioned. But he must have been a mere child; for, at the end of his novitiate, he had forgotten his native language, and was forced to learn it a second time.

small duodecimo volume was placed in his hands. It was a Relation of the Canadian mission, and contained one of those narratives of Brébeuf which have been often cited in the preceding pages. Its effect was immediate. Burning to share those glorious toils, the young priest asked to be sent to Canada; and his request was granted.

Before embarking, he set out with the Jesuit Poncet, who was also destined for Canada, on a pilgrimage from Rome to the shrine of Our Lady of Loretto. They journeyed on foot, begging alms by the way. Chaumonot was soon seized with a pain in the knee, so violent that it seemed impossible to proceed. At San Severino, where they lodged with the Barnabites, he bethought him of asking the intercession of a certain poor woman of that place, who had died some time before with the reputation of sanctity. Accordingly he addressed to her his prayer, promising to publish her fame on every possible occasion, if she would obtain his cure from God. ["Je me recommandai à elle en lui promettant de la faire connoître dans toutes les occasions que j'en aurois jamais, si elle vn'obtenoit de Dieu ma guérison."—Chaumonot, Vie, 46.] The intercession was accepted; the offending limb became sound again, and the two pilgrims pursued their journey. They reached Loretto, and, kneeling before the Queen of Heaven, implored her favor and aid; while Chaumonot, overflowing with devotion to this celestial mistress of his heart, conceived the purpose of building in Canada a chapel to her honor, after the exact model of the Holy House of Loretto. They soon afterwards embarked together, and arrived among the Hurons early in the autumn of 1639.

Noël Chabanel came later to the mission; for he did not reach the Huron country until 1643. He detested the Indian life,—the smoke, the

---

"Jamais y eut-il homme sur terre plus obligé que moi à la Sainte Famille de Jésus, de Marie et de Joseph! Marie en me guérissant de ma vilaine galle ou teigne, me délivra d'une infinité de peines et d'incommodités corporelles, que cette hideuse maladie qui me rongeoit m'avoit causé. Joseph m'ayant obtenu la grace d'être incorporé à un corps aussi saint qu'est celui des Jésuites, m'a preservé d'une infinité de misères spirituelles, de tentations très dangereuses et de péchés très énormes. Jésus n'ayant pas permis que j'entrasse dans aucun autre ordre qu'en celui qu'il honore tout à la fois de son beau nom, de sa douce présence et de sa protection spéciale. O Jésus! O Marie! O Joseph! qui méritoit moins que moi vos divines faveurs, et envers qui avez vous été plus prodigue?"—Chaumonot, Vie, 37.

vermin, the filthy food, the impossibility of privacy. He could not study by the smoky lodge-fire, among the noisy crowd of men and squaws, with their dogs, and their restless, screeching children. He had a natural inaptitude to learning the language, and labored at it for five years with scarcely a sign of progress. The Devil whispered a suggestion into his ear: Let him procure his release from these barren and revolting toils, and return to France, where congenial and useful employments awaited him. Chabanel refused to listen; and when the temptation still beset him, he bound himself by a solemn vow to remain in Canada to the day of his death. [Abrégé de la Vie du Père Noël Chabanel, MS. This anonymous paper bears the signature of Ragueneau, in attestation of its truth. See also Ragueneau, Relation, 1650, 17, 18. Chabanel's vow is here given verbatim.]

Isaac Jogues was of a character not unlike Garnier. Nature had given him no especial force of intellect or constitutional energy, yet the man was indomitable and irrepressible, as his history will show. We have but few means of characterizing the remaining priests of the mission otherwise than as their traits appear on the field of their labors. Theirs was no faith of abstractions and generalities. For them, heaven was very near to earth, touching and mingling with it at many points. On high, God the Father sat enthroned: and, nearer to human sympathies, Divinity incarnate in the Son, with the benign form of his immaculate mother, and her spouse, St. Joseph, the chosen patron of New France. Interceding saints and departed friends bore to the throne of grace the petitions of those yet lingering in mortal bondage, and formed an ascending chain from earth to heaven.

These priests lived in an atmosphere of supernaturalism. Every day had its miracle. Divine power declared itself in action immediate and direct, controlling, guiding, or reversing the laws of Nature. The missionaries did not reject the ordinary cures for disease or wounds; but they relied far more on a prayer to the Virgin, a vow to St. Joseph, or the promise of a *neuvaine*, or nine days' devotion, to some other celestial personage; while the touch of a fragment of a tooth or bone of some departed saint was of sovereign efficacy to cure sickness, solace pain, or relieve a suffering squaw in the throes of childbirth. Once, Chaumonot, having a headache, remembered to have heard of a sick man who regained his health by commending his case to St. Ignatius, and at the same time putting a medal stamped with his image into his mouth. Accordingly he tried a similar experiment, putting into his mouth a medal bearing a representation of the Holy Family, which was the object of his especial devotion. The next morning found him cured. [Chaumonot, Vie, 73.]

The relation between this world and the next was sometimes of a nature curiously intimate. Thus, when Chaumonot heard of Garnier's death, he immediately addressed his departed colleague, and promised him the benefit of all the good works which he, Chaumonot, might perform during the next week, provided the defunct missionary would make him heir to his knowledge of the Huron tongue.[1] And he ascribed to the deceased Garnier's influence the mastery of that language which he afterwards acquired.

The efforts of the missionaries for the conversion of the savages were powerfully seconded from the other world, and the refractory subject who was deaf to human persuasions softened before the superhuman agencies which the priest invoked to his aid.

[As these may be supposed to be exploded ideas of the past, the writer may recall an incident of his youth, while spending a few days in the convent of the Passionists, near the Coliseum at Rome. These worthy monks, after using a variety of arguments for his conversion, expressed the hope that a miraculous interposition would be vouchsafed to that end, and that the Virgin would manifest herself to him in a nocturnal vision. To this end they gave him a small brass medal, stamped with her image, to be worn at his neck, while they were to repeat a certain number of Aves and Paters, in which he was urgently invited to join; as the result of which, it was hoped the Virgin would appear on the same night. No vision, however, occurred.]

It is scarcely necessary to add, that signs and voices from another world, visitations from Hell and visions from Heaven, were incidents of no rare occurrence in the lives of these ardent apostles. To Brébeuf, whose deep nature, like a furnace white hot, glowed with the still intensity of his enthusiasm, they were especially frequent. Demons in troops appeared before him, sometimes in the guise of men, sometimes as bears, wolves, or wildcats. He called on God, and the apparitions

---

1   "Je n'eus pas plutôt appris sa glorieuse mort, que je lui promis tout ce que je ferois de bien pendant huit jours, à condition qu'il me feroit son héritier dans la connoissance parfaite qu'il avoit du Huron."—Chaumonot, Vie, 61.

vanished. Death, like a skeleton, sometimes menaced him, and once, as he faced it with an unquailing eye, it fell powerless at his feet. A demon, in the form of a woman, assailed him with the temptation which beset St. Benedict among the rocks of Subiaco; but Brébeuf signed the cross, and the infernal siren melted into air. He saw the vision of a vast and gorgeous palace; and a miraculous voice assured him that such was to be the reward of those who dwelt in savage hovels for the cause of God. Angels appeared to him; and, more than once, St. Joseph and the Virgin were visibly present before his sight. Once, when he was among the Neutral Nation, in the winter of 1640, he beheld the ominous apparition of a great cross slowly approaching from the quarter where lay the country of the Iroquois. He told the vision to his comrades. "What was it like? How large was it?" they eagerly demanded. "Large enough," replied the priest, "to crucify us all."[1] To explain such phenomena is the province of psychology, and not of history. Their occurrence is no matter of surprise, and it would be superfluous to doubt that they were recounted in good faith, and with a full belief in their reality.

In these enthusiasts we shall find striking examples of one of the morbid forces of human nature; yet in candor let us do honor to what was genuine in them,—that principle of self-abnegation which is the life of true religion, and which is vital no less to the highest forms of heroism.

---

[1] Quelques Remarques sur la Vie du Père Jean de Brébeuf, MS. On the margin of this paper, opposite several of the statements repeated above, are the words, signed by Ragueneau, "Ex ipsius autographo," indicating that the statements were made in writing by Brébeuf himself.

Still other visions are recorded by Chaumonot as occurring to Brébeuf, when they were together in the Neutral country. See also the long notice of Brébeuf, written by his colleague, Ragueneau, in the Relation of 1649; and Tanner, Societas Jesu Militans, 533.

CHAPTER X.

1637-1640.

PERSECUTION.

OSSOSSANÉ.—THE NEW CHAPEL.—A TRIUMPH OF THE FAITH.—THE NETHER POWERS.—SIGNS OF A TEMPEST.—SLANDERS.—RAGE AGAINST THE JESUITS.—THEIR BOLDNESS AND PERSISTENCY.—NOCTURNAL COUNCIL.—DANGER OF THE PRIESTS.—BRÉBEUF'S LETTER.—NARROW ESCAPES.—WOES AND CONSOLATIONS.

The town of Ossossané, or Rochelle, stood, as we have seen, on the borders of Lake Huron, at the skirts of a gloomy wilderness of pine. Thither, in May, 1637, repaired Father Pijart, to found, in this, one of the largest of the Huron towns, the new mission of the Immaculate Conception. [The doctrine of the immaculate conception of the Virgin, recently sanctioned by the Pope, has long been a favorite tenet of the Jesuits.] The Indians had promised Brébeuf to build a house for the black-robes, and Pijart found the work in progress. There were at this time about fifty dwellings in the town, each containing eight or ten families. The quadrangular fort already alluded to had now been completed by the Indians, under the instruction of the priests. [Lettres de Garnier, MSS. It was of upright pickets, ten feet high with flanking towers at two angles.]

The new mission-house was about seventy feet in length. No sooner had the savage workmen secured the bark covering on its top and sides than the priests took possession, and began their preparations for a notable ceremony. At the farther end they made an altar, and hung such decorations as they had on the rough walls of bark throughout half the length of the structure. This formed their chapel. On the altar was a crucifix, with vessels and ornaments of shining metal; while above hung several pictures,—among them a painting of Christ, and another of the Virgin, both of life-size. There was also a representation of the Last Judgment, wherein dragons and serpents might be seen feasting on the entrails of the wicked, while demons scourged them into the flames of Hell. The entrance was adorned with a quantity of tinsel, together with green boughs skilfully disposed.

["Nostre Chapelle estoit extraordinairement bien ornée, .. nous auions dressé vn portique entortillé de feüillage, meslé d'oripeau, en vn mot nous auions estallé tout ce que vostre R. nous a enuoié de beau," etc., etc.—Le Mercier, Relation des Hurons, 1637, 175, 176.—In his Relation of the next year he recurs to the subject, and describes the pictures displayed on this memorable occasion.—Relation des Hurons, 1638, 33.]

Never before were such splendors seen in the land of the Hurons. Crowds gathered from afar, and gazed in awe and admiration at the marvels of the sanctuary. A woman came from a distant town to behold it, and, tremulous between curiosity and fear, thrust her head into the mysterious recess, declaring that she would see it, though the look should cost her life. [Ibid., 1637, 176.]

One is forced to wonder at, if not to admire, the energy with which these priests and their scarcely less zealous attendants[1] toiled to carry their pictures and ornaments through the most arduous of journeys, where the traveller was often famished from the sheer difficulty of transporting provisions.

---

1   The Jesuits on these distant missions were usually attended by followers who had taken no vows, and could leave their service at will, but whose motives were religious, and not mercenary. Probably this was the character of their attendants in the present case. They were known as *donnés*, or "given men." It appears from a letter of the Jesuit Du Peron, that twelve hired laborers were soon after sent up to the mission.

A great event had called forth all this preparation. Of the many baptisms achieved by the Fathers in the course of their indefatigable ministry, the subjects had all been infants, or adults at the point of death; but at length a Huron, in full health and manhood, respected and influential in his tribe, had been won over to the Faith, and was now to be baptized with solemn ceremonial, in the chapel thus gorgeously adorned. It was a strange scene. Indians were there in throngs, and the house was closely packed: warriors, old and young, glistening in grease and sunflower-oil, with uncouth locks, a trifle less coarse than a horse's mane, and faces perhaps smeared with paint in honor of the occasion; wenches in gay attire; hags muffled in a filthy discarded deer-skin, their leathery visages corrugated with age and malice, and their hard, glittering eyes riveted on the spectacle before them. The priests, no longer in their daily garb of black, but radiant in their surplices, the genuflections, the tinkling of the bell, the swinging of the censer, the sweet odors so unlike the fumes of the smoky lodge-fires, the mysterious elevation of the Host, (for a mass followed the baptism,) and the agitation of the neophyte, whose Indian imperturbability fairly deserted him,—all these combined to produce on the minds of the savage beholders an impression that seemed to promise a rich harvest for the Faith. To the Jesuits it was a day of triumph and of hope. The ice had been broken; the wedge had entered; light had dawned at last on the long night of heathendom. But there was one feature of the situation which in their rejoicing they overlooked.

The Devil had taken alarm. He had borne with reasonable composure the loss of individual souls snatched from him by former baptisms; but here was a convert whose example and influence threatened to shake his Huron empire to its very foundation. In fury and fear, he rose to the conflict, and put forth all his malice and all his hellish ingenuity. Such, at least, is the explanation given by the Jesuits of the scenes that followed.[1] Whether accepting it or not, let us examine the circumstances which gave rise to it.

1   Several of the Jesuits allude to this supposed excitement among the tenants of the nether world. Thus, Le Mercier says, "Le Diable se sentoit pressé de prés, il ne pouuoit supporter le Baptesme solennel de quelques Sauuages des plus signalez."—Relation des Hurons, 1638, 33.—Several other baptisms of less note followed that above described. Garnier, writing to his brother, repeatedly alludes to the alarm excited in Hell by the recent successes of the mission, and adds,—"Vous

The mysterious strangers, garbed in black, who of late years had made their abode among them, from motives past finding out, marvellous in knowledge, careless of life, had awakened in the breasts of the Hurons mingled emotions of wonder, perplexity, fear, respect, and awe. From the first, they had held them answerable for the changes of the weather, commending them when the crops were abundant, and upbraiding them in times of scarcity. They thought them mighty magicians, masters of life and death; and they came to them for spells, sometimes to destroy their enemies, and sometimes to kill grasshoppers. And now it was whispered abroad that it was they who had bewitched the nation, and caused the pest which threatened to exterminate it.

It was Isaac Jogues who first heard this ominous rumor, at the town of Onnentisati, and it proceeded from the dwarfish sorcerer already mentioned, who boasted himself a devil incarnate. The slander spread fast and far. Their friends looked at them askance; their enemies clamored for their lives. Some said that they concealed in their houses a corpse, which infected the country,—a perverted notion, derived from some half-instructed neophyte, concerning the body of Christ in the Eucharist. Others ascribed the evil to a serpent, others to a spotted frog, others to a demon which the priests were supposed to carry in the barrel of a gun. Others again gave out that they had pricked an infant to death with awls in the forest, in order to kill the Huron children by magic. "Perhaps," observes Father Le Mercier, "the Devil was enraged because we had placed a great many of these little innocents in Heaven."

["Le diable enrageoit peutestre de ce que nous avions placé dans le ciel quantité de ces petits innocens."—Le Mercier, Relation des Hurons, 1638, 12 (Cramoisy).]

The picture of the Last Judgment became an object of the utmost terror. It was regarded as a charm. The dragons and serpents were supposed to be the demons of the pest, and the sinners whom they were so busily devouring to represent its victims. On the top of a spruce-tree, near their house at Ihonatiria, the priests had fastened a small streamer, to show the direction of the wind.

---

pouvez juger quelle consolation nous étoit-ce de voir le diable s'armer contre nous et se servir de ses esclaves pour nous attaquer et tâcher de nous perdre en haine de J. C."

This, too, was taken for a charm, throwing off disease and death to all quarters. The clock, once an object of harmless wonder, now excited the wildest alarm; and the Jesuits were forced to stop it, since, when it struck, it was supposed to sound the signal of death. At sunset, one would have seen knots of Indians, their faces dark with dejection and terror, listening to the measured sounds which issued from within the neighboring house of the mission, where, with bolted doors, the priests were singing litanies, mistaken for incantations by the awe-struck savages.

Had the objects of these charges been Indians, their term of life would have been very short. The blow of a hatchet, stealthily struck in the dusky entrance of a lodge, would have promptly avenged the victims of their sorcery, and delivered the country from peril. But the priests inspired a strange awe. Nocturnal councils were held; their death was decreed; and, as they walked their rounds, whispering groups of children gazed after them as men doomed to die. But who should be the executioner? They were reviled and upbraided. The Indian boys threw sticks at them as they passed, and then ran behind the houses. When they entered one of these pestiferous dens, this impish crew clambered on the roof, to pelt them with snowballs through the smoke-holes. The old squaw who crouched by the fire scowled on them with mingled anger and fear, and cried out, "Begone! there are no sick ones here." The invalids wrapped their heads in their blankets; and when the priest accosted some dejected warrior, the savage looked gloomily on the ground, and answered not a word.

Yet nothing could divert the Jesuits from their ceaseless quest of dying subjects for baptism, and above all of dying children. They penetrated every house in turn. When, through the thin walls of bark, they heard the wail of a sick infant, no menace and no insult could repel them from the threshold. They pushed boldly in, asked to buy some trifle, spoke of late news of Iroquois forays,— of anything, in short, except the pestilence and the sick child; conversed for a while till suspicion was partially lulled to sleep, and then, pretending to observe the sufferer for the first time, approached it, felt its pulse, and asked of its health. Now, while apparently fanning the heated brow, the dexterous visitor touched it with a corner of his handkerchief, which he had previously dipped in water, murmured the baptismal words with motionless lips, and snatched another soul from the fangs of the "Infernal Wolf."[1] Thus, with the patience of saints, the courage of heroes, and an intent truly charitable, did the Fathers put forth a nimble-fingered adroitness that would have done credit to the profession of which the function is less to dispense the treasures of another world than to grasp those which pertain to this.

The Huron chiefs were summoned to a great council, to discuss the state of the nation. The crisis demanded all their wisdom; for, while the continued ravages of disease threatened them with annihilation, the Iroquois scalping-parties infested the outskirts of their towns, and murdered them in their fields and forests. The assembly met in August, 1637; and the Jesuits, knowing their deep stake in its deliberations, failed not to be present, with a liberal gift of wampum, to show their sympathy in the public calamities. In private, they sought to gain the good-will of the deputies, one by one; but though they were successful in some cases, the result on the whole was far from hopeful.

In the intervals of the council, Brébeuf discoursed to the crowd of chiefs on the wonders of the visible heavens,—the sun, the moon, the stars, and the planets. They were inclined to believe what he told them; for he had lately, to their great amazement, accurately predicted an eclipse. From the fires above he passed to the fires beneath, till the listeners stood aghast at his hideous pictures of the flames of perdition,—the only species of Christian instruction which produced any perceptible effect on this unpromising auditory.

The council opened on the evening of the fourth of August, with all the usual ceremonies; and the night was spent in discussing questions of treaties and alliances, with a deliberation and good sense which the Jesuits could not help admiring. [Le Mercier, Relation des Hurons, 1638, 38.] A few days after, the assembly took up the more exciting question of the epidemic and its causes.

---

1   *Ce loup infernal* is a title often bestowed in the Relations on the Devil. The above details are gathered from the narratives of Brébeuf, Le Mercier, and Lalemant, and letters, published and unpublished, of several other Jesuits.

    In another case, an Indian girl was carrying on her back a sick child, two months old. Two Jesuits approached, and while one of them amused the girl with his rosary, "l'autre le baptise lestement; le pauure petit n'attendoit que ceste faueur du Ciel pour s'y enuoler."

Deputies from three of the four Huron nations were present, each deputation sitting apart. The Jesuits were seated with the Nation of the Bear, in whose towns their missions were established. Like all important councils, the session was held at night. It was a strange scene. The light of the fires flickered aloft into the smoky vault and among the soot-begrimed rafters of the great council-house,[1] and cast an uncertain gleam on the wild and dejected throng that filled the platforms and the floor. "I think I never saw anything more lugubrious," writes Le Mercier: "they looked at each other like so many corpses, or like men who already feel the terror of death. When they spoke, it was only with sighs, each reckoning up the sick and dead of his own family. All this was to excite each other to vomit poison against us."

A grisly old chief, named Ontitarac, withered with age and stone-blind, but renowned in past years for eloquence and counsel, opened the debate in a loud, though tremulous voice. First he saluted each of the three nations present, then each of the chiefs in turn,— congratulated them that all were there assembled to deliberate on a subject of the last importance to the public welfare, and exhorted them to give it a mature and calm consideration. Next rose the chief whose office it was to preside over the Feast of the Dead. He painted in dismal colors the woful condition of the country, and ended with charging it all upon the sorceries of the Jesuits. Another old chief followed him. "My brothers," he said, "you know well that I am a war-chief, and very rarely speak except in councils of war; but I am compelled to speak now, since nearly all the other chiefs are dead, and I must utter what is in my heart before I follow them to the grave. Only two of my family are left alive, and perhaps even these will not long escape the fury of the pest. I have seen other diseases ravaging the country, but nothing that could compare with this. In two or three moons we saw their end: but now we have suffered for a year and more, and yet the evil does not abate. And what is worst of all, we have not yet discovered its source." Then, with words of studied moderation, alternating with bursts of angry invective, he proceeded to accuse the Jesuits of causing, by their sorceries, the unparalleled calamities that afflicted them; and in

---

1   It must have been the house of a chief. The Hurons, unlike some other tribes, had no houses set apart for public occasions.

support of his charge he adduced a prodigious mass of evidence. When he had spent his eloquence, Brébeuf rose to reply, and in a few words exposed the absurdities of his statements; whereupon another accuser brought a new array of charges. A clamor soon arose from the whole assembly, and they called upon Brébeuf with one voice to give up a certain charmed cloth which was the cause of their miseries. In vain the missionary protested that he had no such cloth. The clamor increased.

"If you will not believe me," said Brébeuf, "go to our house; search everywhere; and if you are not sure which is the charm, take all our clothing and all our cloth, and throw them into the lake."

"Sorcerers always talk in that way," was the reply.

"Then what will you have me say?" demanded Brébeuf.

"Tell us the cause of the pest."

Brébeuf replied to the best of his power, mingling his explanations with instructions in Christian doctrine and exhortations to embrace the Faith. He was continually interrupted; and the old chief, Ontitarac, still called upon him to produce the charmed cloth. Thus the debate continued till after midnight, when several of the assembly, seeing no prospect of a termination, fell asleep, and others went away. One old chief, as he passed out said to Brébeuf, "If some young man should split your head, we should have nothing to say." The priest still continued to harangue the diminished conclave on the necessity of obeying God and the danger of offending Him, when the chief of Ossossané called out impatiently, "What sort of men are these? They are always saying the same thing, and repeating the same words a hundred times. They are never done with telling us about their *Oki*, and what he demands and what he forbids, and Paradise and Hell." [The above account of the council is drawn from Le Mercier, Relation des Hurons, 1638, Chap. II. See also Bressani, Relation Abrégée, 163.]

"Here was the end of this miserable council," writes Le Mercier; . . ."and if less evil came of it than was designed, we owe it, after God, to the Most Holy Virgin, to whom we had made a vow of nine masses in honor of her immaculate conception."

The Fathers had escaped for the time; but they were still in deadly peril. They had taken pains to secure friends in private, and there were those who were attached to their interests; yet none dared openly take their part. The few converts they had lately made came to them in secret, and warned them that their death was determined upon. Their house was set on fire; in public, every face was averted from them; and a new council was called to pronounce the decree of death. They appeared before it with a front of such unflinching assurance, that their judges, Indian-like, postponed the sentence. Yet it seemed impossible that they should much longer escape. Brébeuf, therefore, wrote a letter of farewell to his Superior, Le Jeune, at Quebec, and confided it to some converts whom he could trust, to be carried by them to its destination.

"We are perhaps," he says, "about to give our blood and our lives in the cause of our Master, Jesus Christ. It seems that His goodness will accept this sacrifice, as regards me, in expiation of my great and numberless sins, and that He will thus crown the past services and ardent desires of all our Fathers here . . . Blessed be His name forever, that He has chosen us, among so many better than we, to aid him to bear His cross in this land! In all things, His holy will be done!" He then acquaints Le Jeune that he has directed the sacred vessels, and all else belonging to the service of the altar, to be placed, in case of his death, in the hands of Pierre, the convert whose baptism has been described, and that especial care will be taken to preserve the dictionary and other writings on the Huron language. The letter closes with a request for masses and prayers.

[The following is the conclusion of the letter (Le Mercier, Relation des Hurons, 1638, 43.)

"En tout, sa sainte volonté soit faite; s'il veut que dés ceste heure nous mourions, ô la bonne heure pour nous! s'il veut nous reseruer à d'autres trauaux, qu'il soit beny; si vous entendez que Dieu ait couronné nos petits trauaux, ou plustost nos desirs, benissez-le: car c'est pour luy que nous desirons viure et mourir, et c'est luy qui nous en donne la grace. Au reste si quelques-vns suruiuent, i'ay donné ordre de tout ce qu'ils doiuent faire. I'ay esté d'aduis que nos Peres et nos domestiques se retirent chez ceux qu'ils croyront estre leurs mei'leurs amis; i'ay donné charge qu'on porte chez Pierre nostre premier Chrestien tout ce qui est de la Sacristie, sur tout qu'on ait vn soin particulier de mettre en lieu d'asseurance le Dictionnaire et tout ce que nous auons de la langue. Pour moy, si Dieu me fait la grace d'aller au Ciel, ie prieray Dieu pour eux, pour les pauures Hurons, et n'oublieray pas Vostre Reuerence.

"Apres tout, nous supplions V. R. et tous nos Peres de ne nous oublier en leurs saincts Sacrifices et prieres, afin qu'en la vie et apres la mort, il nous fasse misericorde; nous sommes tous en la vie et à l'Eternité,

"De vostre Reuerence tres-humbles et tres-affectionnez seruiteurs en Nostre Seigneur,

> "IEAN DE BREBEVF.
> FRANÇOIS IOSEPH LE MERCIER.
> PIERRE CHASTELLAIN.
> CHARLES GARNIER.
> PAVL RAGVENEAV.

> "En la Residence de la Conception, à Ossossané,
> ce 28 Octobre.

"I'ay laissé en la Residence de sainct Ioseph les Peres Pierre Pijart et Isaac Iogves, dans les mesmes sentimens."]

The imperilled Jesuits now took a singular, but certainly a very wise step. They gave one of those farewell feasts—festins d'adieu—which Huron custom enjoined on those about to die, whether in the course of Nature or by public execution. Being interpreted, it was a declaration that the priests knew their danger, and did not shrink from it. It might have the effect of changing overawed friends into open advocates, and even of awakening a certain sympathy in the breasts of an assembly on whom a bold bearing could rarely fail of influence. The house was packed with feasters, and Brébeuf addressed them as usual on his unfailing themes of God, Paradise, and Hell. The throng listened in gloomy silence; and each, when he had emptied his bowl, rose and departed, leaving his entertainers in utter doubt as to his feelings and intentions. From this time forth, however, the clouds that overhung the Fathers became less dark and threatening. Voices were heard in their defence, and looks were less constantly averted. They ascribed the change to the intercession of St. Joseph, to whom they had vowed a nine days' devotion. By whatever cause produced, the lapse of a week wrought a hopeful improvement in their prospects; and when they went out of doors in the morning, it was no longer with the expectation of having a hatchet struck into their brains as they crossed the threshold.

["Tant y a que depuis le 6. de Nouembre que nous acheuasmes nos Messes votiues son honneur, nous auons iouy d'vn repos incroyable, nons nous en emerueillons nous-mesmes de iour en iour, quand nous considerons en quel estat estoient nos affaires il n'y a que huict iours."—Le Mercier, Relation des Hurons, 1638, 44.]

The persecution of the Jesuits as sorcerers continued, in an intermittent form, for years; and several of them escaped very narrowly. In a house at Ossossané, a young Indian rushed suddenly upon François Du Peron, and lifted his tomahawk to brain him, when a squaw caught his hand. Paul Ragueneau wore a crucifix, from which hung the image of a skull. An Indian, thinking it a charm, snatched it from him. The priest tried to recover it, when the savage, his eyes glittering with murder, brandished his hatchet to strike. Ragueneau stood motionless, waiting the blow. His assailant forbore, and withdrew, muttering. Pierre Chaumonot was emerging from a house at the Huron town called by the Jesuits St. Michel, where he had just baptized a dying girl, when her brother, standing hidden in the doorway, struck him on the head with a stone. Chaumonot, severely wounded, staggered without falling, when the Indian sprang upon him with his tomahawk. The bystanders arrested the blow. François Le Mercier, in the midst of a crowd of Indians in a house at the town called St. Louis, was assailed by a noted chief, who rushed in, raving like a madman, and, in a torrent of words, charged upon him all the miseries of the nation. Then, snatching a brand from the fire, he shook it in the Jesuit's face, and told him that he should be burned alive. Le Mercier met him with looks as determined as his own, till, abashed at his undaunted front and bold denunciations, the Indian stood confounded.

[The above incidents are from Le Mercier, Lalemant, Bressani, the autobiography of Chaumonot, the unpublished writings of Garnier, and the ancient manuscript volume of memoirs of the early Canadian missionaries, at St. Mary's College, Montreal.]

The belief that their persecutions were owing to the fury of the Devil, driven to desperation by the home-thrusts he had received at their hands, was an unfailing consolation to the priests. "Truly," writes Le Mercier, "it is an unspeakable happiness for us, in the midst of this barbarism, to hear the roaring of the demons, and to see Earth and Hell raging against a handful of men who will not even defend themselves."[1] In all the copious records of this dark period, not a line gives occasion to suspect that one of this loyal band flinched or hesitated. The iron Brébeuf, the gentle Garnier, the all-enduring Jogues, the enthusiastic Chaumonot, Lalemant, Le Mercier, Chatelain, Daniel, Pijart, Ragueneau, Du Peron, Poncet, Le Moyne,—one and all bore themselves with a tranquil boldness, which amazed the Indians and enforced their respect.

Father Jerome Lalemant, in his journal of 1639, is disposed to draw an evil augury for the mission from the fact that as yet no priest had been put to death, inasmuch as it is a received maxim that the blood of the martyrs is the seed of the Church.[2] He consoles himself with the hope that the daily life of the missionaries may be accepted as a living martyrdom; since abuse and threats without end, the smoke, fleas, filth, and dogs of the Indian lodges,—which are, he says, little images of Hell,—cold, hunger, and ceaseless anxiety, and all these continued for years, are a portion to which many might prefer the stroke of a tomahawk. Reasonable as the Father's hope may be, its expression proved needless in the sequel; for the Huron church was not destined to suffer from a lack of martyrdom in any form.

---

1   "C'est veritablement un bonheur indicible pour nous, au milieu de cette barbarie, d'entendre les rugissemens des demons, & de voir tout l'Enfer & quasi tous les hommes animez & remplis de fureur contre une petite poignée de gens qui ne voudroient pas se defendre."—Relation des Hurons, 1640, 31 (Cramoisy).

2   "Nous auons quelque fois douté, sçauoir si on pouuoit esperer la conuersion de ce païs sans qu'il y eust effusion de sang: le principe reçeu ce semble dans l'Eglise de Dieu, que le sang des Martyrs est la semence des Chrestiens, me faisoit conclure pour lors, que cela n'estoit pas à esperer, voire mesme qu'il n'étoit pas à souhaiter, consideré la gloire qui reuient à Dieu de la constance des Martyrs, du sang desquels tout le reste de la terre ayant tantost esté abreuué, ce seroit vne espece de malediction, que ce quartier du monde ne participast point au bonheur d'auoir contribué à l'esclat de ceste gloire."—Lalemant, Relation des Hurons, 1639, 56, 57.

CHAPTER XI

1638-1640.

PRIEST AND PAGAN.

DU PERON'S JOURNEY.—DAILY LIFE OF THE JESUITS.—
THEIR MISSIONARY EXCURSIONS.—CONVERTS AT
OSSOSSANÉ.—MACHINERY OF CONVERSION.—
CONDITIONS OF BAPTISM.—BACKSLIDERS.—THE
CONVERTS AND THEIR COUNTRYMEN.—THE
CANNIBALS AT ST. JOSEPH.

We have already touched on the domestic life of the Jesuits.
That we may the better know them, we will follow one of their
number on his journey towards the scene of his labors, and observe
what awaited him on his arrival.

Father François Pu Peron came up the Ottawa in a Huron
canoe in September, 1638, and was well treated by the Indian
owner of the vessel. Lalemant and Le Moyne, who had set out
from Three Rivers before him, did not fare so well. The former was
assailed by an Algonquin of Allumette Island, who tried to strangle
him in revenge for the death of a child, which a Frenchman in the
employ of the Jesuits had lately bled, but had failed to restore to
health by the operation. Le Moyne was abandoned by his Huron
conductors, and remained for a fortnight by the bank of the river,
with a French attendant who supported him by hunting. Another
Huron, belonging to the flotilla that carried Du Peron, then took
him into his canoe; but, becoming tired of him, was about to leave

him on a rock in the river, when his brother priest bribed the savage with a blanket to carry him to his journey's end.

It was midnight, on the twenty-ninth of September, when Du Peron landed on the shore of Thunder Bay, after paddling without rest since one o'clock of the preceding morning. The night was rainy, and Ossossané was about fifteen miles distant. His Indian companions were impatient to reach their towns; the rain prevented the kindling of a fire; while the priest, who for a long time had not heard mass, was eager to renew his communion as soon as possible. Hence, tired and hungry as he was, he shouldered his sack, and took the path for Ossossané without breaking his fast. He toiled on, half-spent, amid the ceaseless pattering, trickling, and whispering of innumerable drops among innumerable leaves, till, as day dawned, he reached a clearing, and descried through the mists a cluster of Huron houses. Faint and bedrenched, he entered the principal one, and was greeted with the monosyllable "Shay!"— "Welcome!" A squaw spread a mat for him by the fire, roasted four ears of Indian corn before the coals, baked two squashes in the embers, ladled from her kettle a dish of sagamite, and offered them to her famished guest. Missionaries seem to have been a novelty at this place; for, while the Father breakfasted, a crowd, chiefly of children, gathered about him, and stared at him in silence. One examined the texture of his cassock; another put on his hat; a third took the shoes from his feet, and tried them on her own. Du Peron requited his entertainers with a few trinkets, and begged, by signs, a guide to Ossossané. An Indian accordingly set out with him, and conducted him to the mission-house, which he reached at six o'clock in the evening.

Here he found a warm welcome, and little other refreshment. In respect to the commodities of life, the Jesuits were but a step in advance of the Indians. Their house, though well ventilated by numberless crevices in its bark walls, always smelt of smoke, and, when the wind was in certain quarters, was filled with it to suffocation. At their meals, the Fathers sat on logs around the fire, over which their kettle was slung in the Indian fashion. Each had his wooden platter, which, from the difficulty of transportation, was valued, in the Huron country, at the price of a robe of beaver-skin, or a hundred francs. ["Nos plats, quoyque de bois, nous coûtent plus cher que Les vôtres; ils sont de la valeur d'une robe de castor, c'est à dire cent francs."—Lettre du P. Du Peron à son Frère, 27 Avril, 1639.—The Father's appraisement seems a little questionable.] Their food consisted of sagamite, or "mush," made of pounded Indian-corn, boiled with scraps of smoked fish. Chaumonot compares it to the paste used for papering the walls of houses. The repast was occasionally varied by a pumpkin or squash baked in the ashes, or, in the season, by Indian corn roasted in the ear. They used no salt whatever. They could bring their cumbrous pictures, ornaments and vestments through the savage journey of the Ottawa; but they could not bring the common necessaries of life. By day, they read and studied by the light that streamed in through the large smoke-holes in the roof,—at night, by the blaze of the fire. Their only candles were a few of wax, for the altar. They cultivated a patch of ground, but raised nothing on it except wheat for making the sacramental bread. Their food was supplied by the Indians, to whom they gave, in return, cloth, knives, awls, needles, and various trinkets. Their supply of wine for the Eucharist was so scanty, that they limited themselves to four or five drops for each mass.

[The above particulars are drawn from a long letter of François Du Peron to his brother, Joseph-Imbert Du Peron, dated at La Conception (Ossossané), April 27, 1639, and from a letter, equally long, of Chaumonot to Father Philippe Nappi, dated Du Pays des Hurons, May 26, 1640. Both are in Carayon. These private letters of the Jesuits, of which many are extant, in some cases written on birch-bark, are invaluable as illustrations of the subject.

The Jesuits soon learned to make wine from wild grapes. Those in Maine and Acadia, at a later period, made good candles from the waxy fruit of the shrub known locally as the "bayberry."]

Their life was regulated with a conventual strictness. At four in the morning, a bell roused them from the sheets of bark on which they slept. Masses, private devotions, reading religious books, and breakfasting, filled the time until eight, when they opened their door and admitted the Indians. As many of these proved intolerable nuisances, they took what Lalemant calls the *honnête* liberty of turning out the most intrusive and impracticable,—an act performed with all tact and courtesy, and rarely taken in dudgeon. Having thus winnowed their company, they catechized those that remained, as opportunity offered. In the intervals, the guests squatted by the fire and smoked their pipes.

As among the Spartan virtues of the Hurons that of thieving was especially conspicuous, it was necessary that one or more of the Fathers should remain on guard at the house all day. The rest went forth on their missionary labors, baptizing and instructing, as we have seen. To each priest who could speak Huron[1] was assigned a certain number of houses,—in some instances, as many as forty; and as these often had five or six fires, with two families to each, his spiritual flock was as numerous as it was intractable. It was his care to see that none of the number died without baptism, and by every means in his power to commend the doctrines of his faith to the acceptance of those in health.

At dinner, which was at two o'clock, grace was said in Huron,—for the benefit of the Indians present,—and a chapter of the Bible was read aloud during the meal. At four or five, according to the season, the Indians were dismissed, the door closed, and the evening spent in writing, reading, studying the language, devotion, and conversation on the affairs of the mission.

The local missions here referred to embraced Ossossané and the villages of the neighborhood; but the priests by no means confined themselves within these limits. They made distant excursions, two in company, until every house in every Huron town had heard the annunciation of the new doctrine. On these journeys, they carried blankets or large mantles at their backs, for sleeping in at night, besides a supply of needles, awls, beads, and other small articles, to pay for their lodging and entertainment: for the Hurons, hospitable without stint to each other, expected full compensation from the Jesuits.

At Ossossané, the house of the Jesuits no longer served the double purpose of dwelling and chapel. In 1638, they had in their pay twelve artisans and laborers, sent up from Quebec, [Du Peron in Carayon, 173.] who had built, before the close of the year, a chapel of wood. ["La chapelle est faite d'une charpente bien jolie, semblable presque en façon et grandeur, à notre chapelle de St. Julien."—Ibid., 183.] Hither they removed their pictures and

---

1   At the end of the year 1638, there were seven priests who spoke Huron, and three who had begun to learn it.

ornaments; and here, in winter, several fires were kept burning, for the comfort of the half-naked converts. [Lalemant, Relation des Hurons, 1639, 62.] Of these they now had at Ossossané about sixty,—a large, though evidently not a very solid nucleus for the Huron church,—and they labored hard and anxiously to confirm and multiply them. Of a Sunday morning in winter, one could have seen them coming to mass, often from a considerable distance, "as naked," says Lalemant, "as your hand, except a skin over their backs like a mantle, and, in the coldest weather, a few skins around their feet and legs." They knelt, mingled with the French mechanics, before the altar,—very awkwardly at first, for the posture was new to them,—and all received the sacrament together: a spectacle which, as the missionary chronicler declares, repaid a hundred times all the labor of their conversion. [Lalemant, Relation des Hurons, 1639, 62.]

Some of the principal methods of conversion are curiously illustrated in a letter written by Garnier to a friend in France. "Send me," he says, "a picture of Christ without a beard." Several Virgins are also requested, together with a variety of souls in perdition—âmes damnées—most of them to be mounted in a portable form. Particular directions are given with respect to the demons, dragons, flames, and other essentials of these works of art. Of souls in bliss—âmes bienheureuses—he thinks that one will be enough. All the pictures must be in full face, not in profile; and they must look directly at the beholder, with open eyes. The colors should be bright; and there must be no flowers or animals, as these distract the attention of the Indians.

[Garnier, Lettre 17me, MS. These directions show an excellent knowledge of Indian peculiarities. The Indian dislike of a beard is well known. Catlin, the painter, once caused a fatal quarrel among a party of Sioux, by representing one of them in profile, whereupon he was jibed by a rival as being but half a man.]

The first point with the priests was of course to bring the objects of their zeal to an acceptance of the fundamental doctrines of the Roman Church; but, as the mind of the savage was by no means that beautiful blank which some have represented it, there was much to be erased as well as to be written. They must renounce a host of superstitions, to which they were attached with a strange tenacity, or which may rather be said to have been ingrained in their very natures. Certain points of Christian morality were also strongly urged by the missionaries, who insisted that the convert should take but one wife, and not cast her off without grave cause, and that he should renounce the gross license almost universal among the Hurons. Murder, cannibalism, and several other offences, were also forbidden. Yet, while laboring at the work of conversion with an energy never surpassed, and battling against the powers of darkness with the mettle of paladins, the Jesuits never had the folly to assume towards the Indians a dictatorial or overbearing tone. Gentleness, kindness, and patience were the rule of their intercourse.[1] They studied the nature of the savage, and conformed themselves to it with an admirable tact. Far from treating the Indian as an alien and barbarian, they would fain have adopted him as a countryman; and they proposed to the Hurons that a number of young Frenchmen should settle among them, and marry their daughters in solemn form. The listeners were gratified at an overture so flattering. "But what is the use," they demanded, "of so much ceremony? If the Frenchmen want our women, they are welcome to come and take them whenever they please, as they always used to do." [Le Mercier, Relation des Hurons, 1637, 160.]

The Fathers are well agreed that their difficulties did not arise from any natural defect of understanding on the part of the Indians, who, according to Chaumonot, were more intelligent than the French peasantry, and who, in some instances, showed in their way a marked capacity. It was the inert mass of pride, sensuality, indolence, and superstition that opposed the march of the Faith, and in which the Devil lay intrenched as behind impregnable breastworks.

---

1   The following passage from the "Divers Sentimens," before cited, will illustrate this point. "Pour conuertir les Sauuages, il n'y faut pas tant de science que de bonté et vertu bien solide. Les quatre Elemens d'vn homme Apostolique en la Nouuelle France sont l'Affabilité, l'Humilité, la Patience et vne Charité genereuse. Le zele trop ardent brusle plus qu'il n'eschauffe, et gaste tout; il faut vne grande magnanimité et condescendance, pour attirer peu à peu ces Sauuages. Ils n'entendent pas bien nostre Theologie, mais ils entendent parfaictement bien nostre humilité et nostre affabilité, et se laissent gaigner."

So too Brébeuf, in a letter to Vitelleschi, General of the Jesuits (see Carayon, 163): "Ce qu'il faut demander, avant tout, des ouvriers destinés à cette mission, c'est une douceur inaltérable et une patience à toute épreuve."

[In this connection, the following specimen of Indian reasoning is worth noting. At the height of the pestilence, a Huron said to one of the priests, "I see plainly that your God is angry with us because we will not believe and obey him. Ihonatiria, where you first taught his word, is entirely ruined. Then you came here to Ossossané, and we would not listen; so Ossossané is ruined too. This year you have been all through our country, and found scarcely any who would do what God commands; therefore the pestilence is everywhere." After premises so hopeful, the Fathers looked for a satisfactory conclusion; but the Indian proceeded—"My opinion is, that we ought to shut you out from all the houses, and stop our ears when you speak of God, so that we cannot hear. Then we shall not be so guilty of rejecting the truth, and he will not punish us so cruelly."—Lalemant, Relation des Hurons, 1640, 80.]

It soon became evident that it was easier to make a convert than to keep him. Many of the Indians clung to the idea that baptism was a safeguard against pestilence and misfortune; and when the fallacy of this notion was made apparent, their zeal cooled. Their only amusements consisted of feasts, dances, and games, many of which were, to a greater or less degree, of a superstitious character; and as the Fathers could rarely prove to their own satisfaction the absence of the diabolic element in any one of them, they proscribed the whole indiscriminately, to the extreme disgust of the neophyte. His countrymen, too, beset him with dismal prognostics: as, "You will kill no more game,"—"All your hair will come out before spring," and so forth. Various doubts also assailed him with regard to the substantial advantages of his new profession; and several converts were filled with anxiety in view of the probable want of tobacco in Heaven, saying that they could not do without it. [Lalemant, Relation des Hurons, 1639, 80.] Nor was it pleasant to these incipient Christians, as they sat in class listening to the instructions of their teacher, to find themselves and him suddenly made the targets of a shower of sticks, snowballs, corn-cobs, and other rubbish, flung at them by a screeching rabble of vagabond boys. [Ibid., 78.]

Yet, while most of the neophytes demanded an anxious and diligent cultivation, there were a few of excellent promise; and of one or two especially, the Fathers, in the fulness of their satisfaction, assure us again and again "that they were savage only in name."

[From June, 1639, to June, 1640, about a thousand persons were baptized. Of these, two hundred and sixty were infants, and many more were children. Very many died soon after baptism. Of the whole number, less than twenty were baptized in health,—a number much below that of the preceding year.

The following is a curious case of precocious piety. It is that of a child at St. Joseph. "Elle n'a que deux ans, et fait joliment le signe de la croix, et prend elle-même de l'eau bénite; et une fois se mit à crier, sortant de la Chapelle, à cause que sa mère qui la portoit ne lui avoit donné le loisir d'en prendre. Il l'a fallu reporter en prendre."—Lettres de Garnier, MSS.]

As the town of Ihonatiria, where the Jesuits had made their first abode, was ruined by the pestilence, the mission established there, and known by the name of St. Joseph, was removed, in the summer of 1638, to Teanaustayé, a large town at the foot of a range of hills near the southern borders of the Huron territory. The Hurons, this year, had had unwonted successes in their war with the Iroquois, and had taken, at various times, nearly a hundred prisoners. Many of these were brought to the seat of the new mission of St. Joseph, and put to death with frightful tortures, though not before several had been converted and baptized. The torture was followed, in spite of the remonstrances of the priests, by those cannibal feasts customary with the Hurons on such occasions. Once, when the Fathers had been strenuous in their denunciations, a hand of the victim, duly prepared, was flung in at their door, as an invitation to join in the festivity. As the owner of the severed member had been baptized, they dug a hole in their chapel, and buried it with solemn rites of sepulture. [Lalemant, Relation des Hurons, 1639, 70.]

CHAPTER XII.

1639, 1640.

THE TOBACCO NATION.—
THE NEUTRALS.

A CHANGE OF PLAN.—SAINTE MARIE.—MISSION OF THE TOBACCO NATION.—WINTER JOURNEYING.— RECEPTION OF THE MISSIONARIES.—SUPERSTITIOUS TERRORS.—PERIL OF GARNIER AND JOGUES.— MISSION OF THE NEUTRALS.—HURON INTRIGUES.— MIRACLES.—FURY OF THE INDIANS.—INTERVENTION OF SAINT MICHAEL.—RETURN TO SAINTE MARIE.— INTREPIDITY OF THE PRIESTS.—THEIR MENTAL EXALTATION.

It had been the first purpose of the Jesuits to form permanent missions in each of the principal Huron towns; but, before the close of the year 1639, the difficulties and risks of this scheme had become fully apparent. They resolved, therefore, to establish one central station, to be a base of operations, and, as it were, a focus, whence the light of the Faith should radiate through all the wilderness around. It was to serve at once as residence, fort, magazine, hospital, and convent. Hence the priests would set forth on missionary expeditions far and near; and hither they might retire, as to an asylum, in times of sickness or extreme peril. Here the neophytes could be gathered together, safe from perverting influences; and here in time a Christian settlement, Hurons mingled with Frenchmen, might spring up and thrive under the shadow of the cross.

The site of the new station was admirably chosen. The little river Wye flows from the southward into the Matchedash Bay of Lake Huron, and, at about a mile from its mouth, passes through a small lake. The Jesuits made choice of the right bank of the Wye, where it issues from this lake,—gained permission to build from the Indians, though not without difficulty,—and began their labors with an abundant energy, and a very deficient supply of workmen and tools. The new establishment was called Sainte Marie. The house at Teanaustayé, and the house and chapel at Ossossané, were abandoned, and all was concentrated at this spot. On one hand, it had a short water communication with Lake Huron; and on the other, its central position gave the readiest access to every part of the Huron territory.

During the summer before, the priests had made a survey of their field of action, visited all the Huron towns, and christened each of them with the name of a saint. This heavy draft on the calendar was followed by another, for the designation of the nine towns of the neighboring and kindred people of the Tobacco Nation. [See Introduction.] The Huron towns were portioned into four districts, while those of the Tobacco Nation formed a fifth, and each district was assigned to the charge of two or more priests. In November and December, they began their missionary excursions,—for the Indians were now gathered in their settlements,—and journeyed on foot through the denuded forests, in mud and snow, bearing on their backs the vessels and utensils necessary for the service of the altar.

The new and perilous mission of the Tobacco Nation fell to Garnier and Jogues. They were well chosen; and yet neither of them was robust by nature, in body or mind, though Jogues was noted for personal activity. The Tobacco Nation lay at the distance of a two days' journey from the Huron towns, among the mountains at the head of Nottawassaga Bay. The two missionaries tried to find a guide at Ossossané; but none would go with them, and they set forth on their wild and unknown pilgrimage alone.

The forests were full of snow; and the soft, moist flakes were still falling thickly, obscuring the air, beplastering the gray trunks, weighing to the earth the boughs of spruce and pine, and hiding every footprint of the narrow path. The Fathers missed their way, and toiled on till night, shaking down at every step from the burdened branches a shower of fleecy white on their black cassocks. Night overtook them in a spruce swamp. Here they made a fire with great difficulty, cut the evergreen boughs, piled them for a bed, and lay down. The storm presently ceased; and, "praised be God," writes one of the travellers, "we passed a very good night." [Jogues and Garnier in Lalemant, Relation des Hurons, 1640, 95.]

In the morning they breakfasted on a morsel of corn bread, and, resuming their journey, fell in with a small party of Indians, whom they followed all day without food. At eight in the evening they reached the first Tobacco town, a miserable cluster of bark cabins, hidden among forests and half buried in snow-drifts, where the savage children, seeing the two black apparitions, screamed that Famine and the Pest were coming. Their evil fame had gone before them. They were unwelcome guests; nevertheless, shivering and famished as they were, in the cold and darkness, they boldly pushed their way into one of these dens of barbarism. It was precisely like a Huron house. Five or six fires blazed on the earthen floor, and around them were huddled twice that number of families, sitting, crouching, standing, or flat on the ground; old and young, women and men, children and dogs, mingled pell-mell. The scene would have been a strange one by daylight: it was doubly strange by the flicker and glare of the lodge-fires. Scowling brows, sidelong looks of distrust and fear, the screams of scared children, the scolding of squaws, the growling of wolfish dogs,—this was the greeting of the strangers. The chief man of the household treated them at first with the decencies of Indian hospitality; but when he saw them kneeling in the litter and ashes at their devotions, his suppressed fears found vent, and he began a loud harangue, addressed half to them and half to the Indians. "Now, what are these *okies* doing? They are making charms to kill us, and destroy all that the pest has spared in this house. I heard that they were sorcerers; and now, when it is too late, I believe it." [Lalemant, Relation des Hurons, 1640, 96.] It is wonderful that the priests escaped the tomahawk. Nowhere is the power of courage, faith, and an unflinching purpose more strikingly displayed than in the record of these missions.

In other Tobacco towns their reception was much the same; but at the largest, called by them St. Peter and St. Paul, they fared worse. They reached it on a winter afternoon. Every door of its capacious bark houses was closed against them; and they heard the squaws within calling on the young men to go out and split their heads, while children screamed abuse at the black-robed sorcerers. As night approached, they left the town, when a band of young men followed them, hatchet in hand, to put them to death. Darkness, the forest, and the mountain favored them; and, eluding their pursuers, they escaped. Thus began the mission of the Tobacco Nation.

In the following November, a yet more distant and perilous mission was begun. Brébeuf and Chaumonot set out for the Neutral Nation. This fierce people, as we have already seen, occupied that part of Canada which lies immediately north of Lake Erie, while a wing of their territory extended across the Niagara into Western New York.[1] In their athletic proportions, the ferocity of their manners, and the extravagance of their superstitions, no American tribe has ever exceeded them. They carried to a preposterous excess the Indian notion, that insanity is endowed with a mysterious and superhuman power. Their country was full of pretended maniacs, who, to propitiate their guardian spirits, or *okies*, and acquire the mystic virtue which pertained to madness, raved stark naked through the villages, scattering the brands of the lodge-fires, and upsetting everything in their way.

The two priests left Sainte Marie on the second of November, found a Huron guide at St. Joseph, and, after a dreary march of five days through the forest, reached the first Neutral town. Advancing

---

1 Introduction.—The river Niagara was at this time, 1640, well known to the Jesuits, though none of them had visited it. Lalemant speaks of it as the "famous river of this nation" (the Neutrals). The following translation, from his Relation of 1641, shows that both Lake Ontario and Lake Erie had already taken their present names.

"This river" (the Niagara) "is the same by which our great lake of the Hurons, or Fresh Sea, discharges itself, in the first place, into Lake Erie (le lac d'Erié), or the Lake of the Cat Nation. Then it enters the territories of the Neutral Nation, and takes the name of Onguiaahra (Niagara), until it discharges itself into Ontario, or the Lake of St. Louis; whence at last issues the river which passes before Quebec, and is called the St. Lawrence." He makes no allusion to the cataract, which is first mentioned as follows by Ragueneau, in the Relation of 1648.

"Nearly south of this same Neutral Nation there is a great lake, about two hundred leagues in circuit, named Erie (Erié), which is formed by the discharge of the Fresh Sea, and which precipitates itself by a cataract of frightful height into a third lake, named Ontario, which we call Lake St. Louis."—Relation des Hurons, 1648, 46.

thence, they visited in turn eighteen others; and their progress was a storm of maledictions. Brébeuf especially was accounted the most pestilent of sorcerers. The Hurons, restrained by a superstitious awe, and unwilling to kill the priests, lest they should embroil themselves with the French at Quebec, conceived that their object might be safely gained by stirring up the Neutrals to become their executioners. To that end, they sent two emissaries to the Neutral towns, who, calling the chiefs and young warriors to a council, denounced the Jesuits as destroyers of the human race, and made their auditors a gift of nine French hatchets on condition that they would put them to death. It was now that Brébeuf, fully conscious of the danger, half starved and half frozen, driven with revilings from every door, struck and spit upon by pretended maniacs, beheld in a vision that great cross, which as we have seen, moved onward through the air, above the wintry forests that stretched towards the land of the Iroquois. [See ante, chapter 9 second last paragraph (page 109).]

Chaumonot records yet another miracle. "One evening, when all the chief men of the town were deliberating in council whether to put us to death, Father Brébeuf, while making his examination of conscience, as we were together at prayers, saw the vision of a spectre, full of fury, menacing us both with three javelins which he held in his hands. Then he hurled one of them at us; but a more powerful hand caught it as it flew: and this took place a second and a third time, as he hurled his two remaining javelins . . . Late at night our host came back from the council, where the two Huron emissaries had made their gift of hatchets to have us killed. He wakened us to say that three times we had been at the point of death; for the young men had offered three times to strike the blow, and three times the old men had dissuaded them. This explained the meaning of Father Brébeuf's vision." [Chaumonot, Vie, 55.]

They had escaped for the time; but the Indians agreed among themselves, that thenceforth no one should give them shelter. At night, pierced with cold and faint with hunger, they found every door closed against them. They stood and watched, saw an Indian issue from a house, and, by a quick movement, pushed through the half-open door into this abode of smoke and filth. The inmates, aghast at their boldness, stared in silence. Then a messenger ran out to carry the tidings, and an angry crowd collected.

"Go out, and leave our country," said an old chief, "or we will put you into the kettle, and make a feast of you."

"I have had enough of the dark-colored flesh of our enemies," said a young brave; "I wish to know the taste of white meat, and I will eat yours."

A warrior rushed in like a madman, drew his bow, and aimed the arrow at Chaumonot. "I looked at him fixedly," writes the Jesuit, "and commended myself in full confidence to St. Michael. Without doubt, this great archangel saved us; for almost immediately the fury of the warrior was appeased, and the rest of our enemies soon began to listen to the explanation we gave them of our visit to their country." [Ibid., 57.]

The mission was barren of any other fruit than hardship and danger, and after a stay of four months the two priests resolved to return. On the way, they met a genuine act of kindness. A heavy snow-storm arresting their progress, a Neutral woman took them into her lodge, entertained them for two weeks with her best fare, persuaded her father and relatives to befriend them, and aided them to make a vocabulary of the dialect. Bidding their generous hostess farewell, they journeyed northward, through the melting snows of spring, and reached Sainte Marie in safety.

[Lalemant, in his Relation of 1641, gives the narrative of this mission at length. His account coincides perfectly with the briefer notice of Chaumonot in his Autobiography. Chaumonot describes the difficulties of the journey very graphically in a letter to his friend, Father Nappi, dated Aug. 3, 1640, preserved in Carayon. See also the next letter, Brébeuf au T. R. P. Mutio Vitelleschi, 20 Août, 1641.

The Récollet La Roche Dallion had visited the Neutrals fourteen years before, (see Introduction, note,) and, like his two successors, had been seriously endangered by Huron intrigues.]

The Jesuits had borne all that the human frame seems capable of bearing. They had escaped as by miracle from torture and death. Did their zeal flag or their courage fail? A fervor intense and unquenchable urged them on to more distant and more deadly ventures. The beings, so near to mortal sympathies, so human, yet so divine, in whom their faith impersonated and dramatized the great principles of Christian truth,—virgins, saints, and angels,— hovered over them, and held before their raptured sight crowns of glory and garlands of immortal bliss. They burned to do, to suffer, and to die; and now, from out a living martyrdom, they turned their heroic gaze towards an horizon dark with perils yet more appalling, and saw in hope the day when they should bear the cross into the blood-stained dens of the Iroquois. [This zeal was in no degree due to success; for in 1641, after seven years of toil, the mission counted only about fifty living converts,—a falling off from former years.]

But, in this exaltation and tension of the powers, was there no moment when the recoil of Nature claimed a temporary sway? When, an exile from his kind, alone, beneath the desolate rock and the gloomy pine-trees, the priest gazed forth on the pitiless wilderness and the hovels of its dark and ruthless tenants, his thoughts, it may be, flew longingly beyond those wastes of forest and sea that lay between him and the home of his boyhood. Or rather, led by a deeper attraction, they revisited the ancient centre of his faith, and he seemed to stand once more in that gorgeous temple, where, shrined in lazuli and gold, rest the hallowed bones of Loyola. Column and arch and dome rise upon his vision, radiant in painted light, and trembling with celestial music. Again he kneels before the altar, from whose tablature beams upon him that loveliest of shapes in which the imagination of man has embodied the spirit of Christianity. The illusion overpowers him. A thrill shakes his frame, and he bows in reverential rapture. No longer a memory, no longer a dream, but a visioned presence, distinct and luminous in the forest shades, the Virgin stands before him. Prostrate on the rocky earth, he adores the benign angel of his ecstatic faith, then turns with rekindled fervors to his stern apostleship.

Now, by the shores of Thunder Bay, the Huron traders freight their birch vessels for their yearly voyage; and, embarked with them, let us, too, revisit the rock of Quebec.

CHAPTER XIII.

1636-1646.

QUEBEC AND ITS TENANTS.

THE NEW GOVERNOR.—EDIFYING EXAMPLES.—
LE JEUNE'S CORRESPONDENTS.—RANK AND
DEVOTION.—NUNS.—PRIESTLY AUTHORITY.—
CONDITION OF QUEBEC.—THE HUNDRED
ASSOCIATES.—CHURCH DISCIPLINE.—PLAYS.—
FIREWORKS.—PROCESSIONS.—CATECHIZING.—
TERRORISM.—PICTURES.—THE CONVERTS.—THE
SOCIETY OF JESUS.—THE FORESTERS.

I have traced, in another volume, the life and death of the
noble founder of New France, Samuel de Champlain. It was on
Christmas Day, 1635, that his heroic spirit bade farewell to the
frame it had animated, and to the rugged cliff where he had toiled
so long to lay the corner-stone of a Christian empire.

Quebec was without a governor. Who should succeed
Champlain and would his successor be found equally zealous for
the Faith, and friendly to the mission? These doubts, as he himself
tells us, agitated the mind of the Father Superior, Le Jeune; but
they were happily set at rest, when, on a morning in June, he
saw a ship anchoring in the basin below, and, hastening with his
brethren to the landing-place, was there met by Charles Huault
de Montmagny, a Knight of Malta, followed by a train of officers
and gentlemen. As they all climbed the rock together, Montmagny

saw a crucifix planted by the path. He instantly fell on his knees before it; and nobles, soldiers, sailors, and priests imitated his example. The Jesuits sang Te Deum at the church, and the cannon roared from the adjacent fort. Here the new governor was scarcely installed, when a Jesuit came in to ask if he would be godfather to an Indian about to be baptized. "Most gladly," replied the pious Montmagny. He repaired on the instant to the convert's hut, with a company of gayly apparelled gentlemen; and while the inmates stared in amazement at the scarlet and embroidery, he bestowed on the dying savage the name of Joseph, in honor of the spouse of the Virgin and the patron of New France. [Le Jeune, Relation, 1636, 5 (Cramoisy). "Monsieur le Gouverneur se transporte aux Cabanes de ces pauures barbares, suivy d'une leste Noblesse. Je vous laisse à penser quel estonnement à ces Peuples de voir tant d'écarlate, tant de personnes bien faites sous leurs toits d'écorce!"] Three days after, he was told that a dead proselyte was to be buried; on which, leaving the lines of the new fortification he was tracing, he took in hand a torch, De Lisle, his lieutenant, took another, Repentigny and St. Jean, gentlemen of his suite, with a band of soldiers followed, two priests bore the corpse, and thus all moved together in procession to the place of burial. The Jesuits were comforted. Champlain himself had not displayed a zeal so edifying. [Ibid., 83 (Cramoisy).]

A considerable reinforcement came out with Montmagny, and among the rest several men of birth and substance, with their families and dependants. "It was a sight to thank God for," exclaims Father Le Jeune, "to behold these delicate young ladies and these tender infants issuing from their wooden prison, like day from the shades of night." The Father, it will be remembered, had for some years past seen nothing but squaws, with papooses swathed like mummies and strapped to a board.

He was even more pleased with the contents of a huge packet of letters that was placed in his hands, bearing the signatures of nuns, priests, soldiers, courtiers, and princesses. A great interest in the mission had been kindled in France. Le Jeune's printed Relations had been read with avidity; and his Jesuit brethren, who, as teachers, preachers, and confessors, had spread themselves through the nation, had successfully fanned the rising flame. The Father Superior finds no words for his joy. "Heaven," he exclaims, "is the conductor of this enterprise. Nature's arms are not long enough to touch so many hearts." ["C'est Dieu qui conduit cette entreprise. La Nature n'a pas les bras assez longs," etc.—Relation, 1636, 3.] He reads how in a single convent, thirteen nuns have devoted themselves by a vow to the work of converting the Indian women and children; how, in the church of Montmartre, a nun lies prostrate day and night before the altar, praying for the mission; [Brébeuf, Relation des Hurons, 1636, 76.] how "the Carmelites are all on fire, the Ursulines full of zeal, the sisters of the Visitation have no words to speak their ardor"; [Le Jeune, Relation, 1636, 6. Compare "Divers Sentimens," appended to the Relation of 1635.] how some person unknown, but blessed of Heaven, means to found a school for Huron children; how the Duchesse d'Aiguillon has sent out six workmen to build a hospital for the Indians; how, in every house of the Jesuits, young priests turn eager eyes towards Canada; and how, on the voyage thither, the devils raised a tempest, endeavoring, in vain fury, to drown the invaders of their American domain.

["L'Enfer enrageant de nous veoir aller en la Nouuelle France pour conuertir les infidelles et diminuer sa puissance, par dépit il sousleuoit tous les Elemens contre nous, et vouloit abysmer la flotte."—Divers Sentimens.]

Great was Le Jeune's delight at the exalted rank of some of those who gave their patronage to the mission; and again and again his satisfaction flows from his pen in mysterious allusions to these eminent persons. [Among his correspondents was the young Duc d'Enghien, afterwards the Great Condé, at this time fifteen years old. "Dieu soit loüé! tout le ciel de nostre chere Patrie nous promet de fauorables influences, iusques à ce nouuel astre, qui commence à paroistre parmy ceux de la premiere grandeur."—Le Jeune, Relation, 1636, 3, 4.] In his eyes, the vicious imbecile who sat on the throne of France was the anointed champion of the Faith, and the cruel and ambitious priest who ruled king and nation alike was the chosen instrument of Heaven. Church and State, linked in alliance close and potential, played faithfully into each other's hands; and that enthusiasm, in which the Jesuit saw the direct inspiration of God, was fostered by all the prestige of royalty and all the patronage of power. And, as often happens where the interests of a hierarchy are identified with the interests of a ruling class, religion was become a fashion, as graceful and as comforting as the courtier's embroidered mantle or the court lady's robe of fur.

Such, we may well believe, was the complexion of the enthusiasm which animated some of Le Jeune's noble and princely correspondents. But there were deeper fervors, glowing in the still depths of convent cells, and kindling the breasts of their inmates with quenchless longings. Yet we hear of no zeal for the mission among religious communities of men. The Jesuits regarded the field as their own, and desired no rivals. They looked forward to the day when Canada should be another Paraguay. ["Que si celuy qui a escrit cette lettre a leu la Relation de ce qui se passe au Paraguais, qu'il a veu ce qui se fera un jour en la Nouuelle France."—Le Jeune, Relation, 1637, 304 (Cramoisy).] It was to the combustible hearts of female recluses that the torch was most busily applied; and here, accordingly, blazed forth a prodigious and amazing flame. "If all had their pious will," writes Le Jeune, "Quebec would soon be flooded with nuns." [Chaulmer. Le Nouveau Monde Chrestien, 41, is eloquent on this theme.]

Both Montmagny and De Lisle were half churchmen, for both were Knights of Malta. More and more the powers spiritual engrossed the colony. As nearly as might be, the sword itself was in priestly hands. The Jesuits were all in all. Authority, absolute and without appeal, was vested in a council composed of the governor, Le Jeune, and the syndic, an official supposed to represent the interests of the inhabitants. [Le Clerc, Établissement de la Foy, Chap. XV.] There was no tribunal of justice, and the governor pronounced summarily on all complaints. The church adjoined the fort; and before it was planted a stake bearing a placard with a prohibition against blasphemy, drunkenness, or neglect of mass and other religious rites. To the stake was also attached a chain and iron collar; and hard by was a wooden horse, whereon a culprit was now and then mounted by way of example and warning. [Le Jeune, Relation, 1636, 153, 154 (Cramoisy).] In a community so absolutely priest-governed, overt offences were, however, rare; and, except on the annual arrival of the ships from France, when the rock swarmed with godless sailors, Quebec was a model of decorum, and wore, as its chroniclers tell us, an aspect unspeakably edifying.

In the year 1640, various new establishments of religion and charity might have been seen at Quebec. There was the beginning of a college and a seminary for Huron children, an embryo Ursuline convent, an incipient hospital, and a new Algonquin mission at a place called Sillery, four miles distant. Champlain's fort had been enlarged and partly rebuilt in stone by Montmagny, who had also laid out streets on the site of the future city, though as yet the streets had no houses. Behind the fort, and very near it, stood the church and a house for the Jesuits. Both were of pine wood: and this year, 1640, both were burned to the ground, to be afterwards rebuilt in stone. The Jesuits, however, continued to occupy their rude mission-house of Notre-Dame des Anges, on the St. Charles, where we first found them.

The country around Quebec was still an unbroken wilderness, with the exception of a small clearing made by the Sieur Giffard on his seigniory of Beauport, another made by M. de Puiseaux between Quebec and Sillery, and possibly one or two feeble attempts in other quarters.[1] The total population did not much exceed two hundred, including women and children. Of this number, by far the greater part were agents of the fur company known as the Hundred Associates, and men in their employ. Some of these had brought over their families. The remaining inhabitants were priests, nuns, and a very few colonists.

The Company of the Hundred Associates was bound by its charter to send to Canada four thousand colonists before the year 1643. [See "Pioneers of France," 399.] It had neither the means nor the will to fulfil this engagement. Some of its members were willing to make personal sacrifices for promoting the missions, and building up a colony purely Catholic. Others thought only of the profits of trade; and the practical affairs of the company had passed entirely into the hands of this portion of its members. They sought to evade obligations the fulfilment of which would have ruined them. Instead of sending out colonists, they granted lands with the condition that the grantees should furnish a certain number of settlers to clear and till them, and these were to be credited

---

1   For Giffard, Puiseaux, and other colonists, compare Langevin, Notes sur les Archives de Notre-Dame de Beauport, 5, 6, 7; Ferland, Notes sur les Archives de N. D. de Québec, 22, 24 (1863); Ibid., Cours d'Histoire du Canada, I. 266; Le Jeune, Relation, 1636, 45; Faillon, Histoire de la Colonie Française, I. c. iv., v.

to the Company.[1] The grantees took the land, but rarely fulfilled the condition. Some of these grants were corrupt and iniquitous. Thus, a son of Lauson, president of the Company, received, in the name of a third person, a tract of land on the south side of the St. Lawrence of sixty leagues front. To this were added all the islands in that river, excepting those of Montreal and Orleans, together with the exclusive right of fishing in it through its whole extent.[2] Lauson sent out not a single colonist to these vast concessions.

There was no real motive for emigration. No persecution expelled the colonist from his home; for none but good Catholics were tolerated in New France. The settler could not trade with the Indians, except on condition of selling again to the Company at a fixed price. He might hunt, but he could not fish; and he was forced to beg or buy food for years before he could obtain it from that rude soil in sufficient quantity for the wants of his family. The Company imported provisions every year for those in its employ; and of these supplies a portion was needed for the relief of starving settlers. Giffard and his seven men on his seigniory of Beauport were for some time the only settlers—excepting, perhaps, the Hébert family—who could support themselves throughout the year. The rigor of the climate repelled the emigrant; nor were the attractions which Father Le Jeune held forth—"piety, freedom, and independence"—of a nature to entice him across the sea, when it is remembered that this freedom consisted in subjection to the arbitrary will of a priest and a soldier, and in the liability, should he forget to go to mass, of being made fast to a post with a collar and chain, like a dog.

Aside from the fur trade of the Company, the whole life of the colony was in missions, convents, religious schools, and hospitals. Here on the rock of Quebec were the appendages, useful and otherwise, of an old-established civilization. While as yet there were no inhabitants, and no immediate hope of any, there were

---

1   This appears in many early grants of the Company. Thus, in a grant to Simon Le Maitre, Jan. 15, 1636, "que les hommes que le dit . . . fera passer en la N. F. tourneront à la décharge de la dite Compagnie," etc., etc.—See Pièces sur la Tenure Seigneuriale, published by the Canadian government, passim.

2   Archives du Séminaire de Villemarie, cited by Faillon, I. 350. Lauson's father owned Montreal. The son's grant extended from the River St. Francis to a point far above Montreal.—La Fontaine, Mémoire sur la Famille de Lauson.

institutions for the care of children, the sick, and the decrepit. All these were supported by a charity in most cases precarious. The Jesuits relied chiefly on the Company, who, by the terms of their patent, were obliged to maintain religious worship.[1] Of the origin of the convent, hospital, and seminary I shall soon have occasion to speak.

Quebec wore an aspect half military, half monastic. At sunrise and sunset, a squad of soldiers in the pay of the Company paraded in the fort; and, as in Champlain's time, the bells of the church rang morning, noon, and night. Confessions, masses, and penances were punctiliously observed; and, from the governor to the meanest laborer, the Jesuit watched and guided all. The social atmosphere of New England itself was not more suffocating. By day and by night, at home, at church, or at his daily work, the colonist lived under the eyes of busy and over-zealous priests. At times, the denizens of Quebec grew restless. In 1639, deputies were covertly sent to beg relief in France, and "to represent the hell in which the consciences of the colony were kept by the union of the temporal and spiritual authority in the same hands." ["Pour leur representer la gehenne où estoient les consciences de la Colonie, de se voir gouverné par les mesmes personnes pour le spirituel et pour le temporel."—Le Clerc, I. 478.] In 1642, partial and ineffective measures were taken, with the countenance of Richelieu, for introducing into New France an Order less greedy of seigniories and endowments than the Jesuits, and less prone to political encroachment.[2] No favorable result followed; and the colony remained as before, in a pitiful state of cramping and dwarfing vassalage.

---

1   It is a principle of the Jesuits, that each of its establishments shall find a support of its own, and not be a burden on the general funds of the Society. The Relations are full of appeals to the charity of devout persons in behalf of the missions.

"Of what use to the country at this period could have been two communities of cloistered nuns?" asks the modern historian of the Ursulines of Quebec. And he answers by citing the words of Pope Gregory the Great, who, when Rome was ravaged by famine, pestilence, and the barbarians, declared that his only hope was in the prayers of the three thousand nuns then assembled in the holy city.—Les Ursulines de Québec. Introd., XI.

2   Declaration de Pierre Breant, par devant les Notaires du Roy, MS. The Order was that of the Capuchins, who, like the Récollets, are a branch of the Franciscans. Their introduction into Canada was prevented; but they established themselves in Maine.

This is the view of a heretic. It was the aim of the founders of New France to build on a foundation purely and supremely Catholic. What this involved is plain; for no degree of personal virtue is a guaranty against the evils which attach to the temporal rule of ecclesiastics. Burning with love and devotion to Christ and his immaculate Mother, the fervent and conscientious priest regards with mixed pity and indignation those who fail in this supreme allegiance. Piety and charity alike demand that he should bring back the rash wanderer to the fold of his divine Master, and snatch him from the perdition into which his guilt must otherwise plunge him. And while he, the priest, himself yields reverence and obedience to the Superior, in whom he sees the representative of Deity, it behooves him, in his degree, to require obedience from those whom he imagines that God has confided to his guidance. His conscience, then, acts in perfect accord with the love of power innate in the human heart. These allied forces mingle with a perplexing subtlety; pride, disguised even from itself, walks in the likeness of love and duty; and a thousand times on the pages of history we find Hell beguiling the virtues of Heaven to do its work. The instinct of domination is a weed that grows rank in the shadow of the temple, climbs over it, possesses it, covers its ruin, and feeds on its decay. The unchecked sway of priests has always been the most mischievous of tyrannies; and even were they all well-meaning and sincere, it would be so still.

To the Jesuits, the atmosphere of Quebec was well-nigh celestial. "In the climate of New France," they write, "one learns perfectly to seek only God, to have no desire but God, no purpose but for God." And again: "To live in New France is in truth to live in the bosom of God." "If," adds Le Jeune, "any one of those who die in this country goes to perdition, I think he will be doubly guilty."

["La Nouuelle France est vn vray climat où on apprend parfaictement bien à ne chercher que Dieu, ne desirer que Dieu seul, auoir l'intention purement à Dieu, etc . . . Viure en la Nouuelle France, c'est à vray dire viure dans le sein de Dieu, et ne respirer que l'air de sa Diuine conduite."—Divers Sentimens. "Si quelqu'un de ceux qui meurent en ces contrées se damne, je croy qu'il sera doublement coupable."—Relation, 1640, 5 (Cramoisy).]

The very amusements of this pious community were acts of religion. Thus, on the fête-day of St. Joseph, the patron of New France, there was a show of fireworks to do him honor. In the forty volumes of the Jesuit Relations there is but one pictorial illustration; and this represents the pyrotechnic contrivance in question, together with a figure of the Governor in the act of touching it off. [Relation, 1637, 8. The Relations, as originally published, comprised about forty volumes.] But, what is more curious, a Catholic writer of the present day, the Abbé Faillon, in an elaborate and learned work, dilates at length on the details of the display; and this, too, with a gravity which evinces his conviction that squibs, rockets, blue-lights, and serpents are important instruments for the saving of souls. [Histoire de la Colonie Française, I. 291, 292.] On May-Day of the same year, 1637, Montmagny planted before the church a May-pole surmounted by a triple crown, beneath which were three symbolical circles decorated with wreaths, and bearing severally the names, Iesus, Maria, Ioseph; the soldiers drew up before it, and saluted it with a volley of musketry. [Relation, 1637, 82.]

On the anniversary of the Dauphin's birth there was a dramatic performance, in which an unbeliever, speaking Algonquin for the profit of the Indians present, was hunted into Hell by fiends. [Vimont, Relation, 1640, 6.] Religious processions were frequent. In one of them, the Governor in a court dress and a baptized Indian in beaver-skins were joint supporters of the canopy which covered the Host. [Le Jeune, Relation, 1638, 6.] In another, six Indians led the van, arrayed each in a velvet coat of scarlet and gold sent them by the King. Then came other Indian converts, two and two; then the foundress of the Ursuline convent, with Indian children in French gowns; then all the Indian girls and women, dressed after their own way; then the priests; then the Governor; and finally the whole French population, male and female, except the artillery-men at the fort, who saluted with their cannon the cross and banner borne at the head of the procession. When all was over, the Governor and the Jesuits rewarded the Indians with a feast. [Le Jeune, Relation, 1639, 3.]

Now let the stranger enter the church of Notre-Dame de La Recouvrance, after vespers. It is full, to the very porch: officers in slouched hats and plumes, musketeers, pikemen, mechanics, and laborers. Here is Montmagny himself; Repentigny and Poterie, gentlemen of good birth; damsels of nurture ill fitted to the Canadian woods; and, mingled with these, the motionless Indians, wrapped to the throat in embroidered moose-hides. Le Jeune, not in priestly vestments, but in the common black dress of his Order, is before the altar; and on either side is a row of small red-skinned children listening with exemplary decorum, while, with a cheerful, smiling face, he teaches them to kneel, clasp their hands, and sign the cross. All the principal members of this zealous community are present, at once amused and edified at the grave deportment, and the prompt, shrill replies of the infant catechumens; while their parents in the crowd grin delight at the gifts of beads and trinkets with which Le Jeune rewards his most proficient pupils. [Le Jeune, Relation, 1637, 122 (Cramoisy).]

We have seen the methods of conversion practised among the Hurons. They were much the same at Quebec. The principal appeal was to fear. [Ibid., 1636, 119, and 1637, 32 (Cramoisy). "La crainte est l'auan couriere de la foy dans ces esprits barbares."] "You do good to your friends," said Le Jeune to an Algonquin chief, "and you burn your enemies. God does the same." And he painted Hell to the startled neophyte as a place where, when he was hungry, he would get nothing to eat but frogs and snakes, and, when thirsty, nothing to drink but flames. [Le Jeune, Relation, 1637, 80-82 (Cramoisy). "Avoir faim et ne manger que des serpens et des crapaux, avoir soif et ne boire que des flammes."] Pictures were found invaluable. "These holy representations," pursues the Father Superior, "are half the instruction that can be given to the Indians. I wanted some pictures of Hell and souls in perdition, and a few were sent us on paper; but they are too confused. The devils and the men are so mixed up, that one can make out nothing without particular attention. If three, four, or five devils were painted tormenting a soul with different punishments,—one applying fire, another serpents, another tearing him with pincers, and another holding him fast with a chain,—this would have a good effect, especially if everything were made distinct, and misery, rage, and desperation appeared plainly in his face."

["Les heretiques sont grandement blasmables, de condamner et de briser les images qui ont de si bons effets. Ces sainctes figures sont la moitié de l'instruction qu'on peut donner aux Sauuages. I'auois desiré quelques portraits de l'enfer et de l'âme damnée; on nous en a enuoyé quelques vns en papier, mais cela est trop confus. Les diables sont tellement meslez auec les hommes, qu'on n'y peut rien recognoistre, qu'auec vne particuliere attention. Qui depeindroit trois ou quatre ou cinq demons, tourmentans vne âme de diuers supplices, l'vn luy appliquant des feux, l'autre des serpens, l'autre la tenaillant, l'autre la tenant liée auec des chaisnes, cela auroit vn bon effet, notamment si tout estoit bien distingué, et que la rage et la tristesse parussent bien en la face de cette âme desesperée"—Relation, 1637, 32 (Cramoisy).]

The preparation of the convert for baptism was often very slight. A dying Algonquin, who, though meagre as a skeleton, had thrown himself, with a last effort of expiring ferocity, on an Iroquois prisoner, and torn off his ear with his teeth, was baptized almost immediately.[1] In the case of converts in health there was far more preparation; yet these often apostatized. The various objects of instruction may all be included in one comprehensive word, submission,—an abdication of will and judgment in favor of the spiritual director, who was the interpreter and vicegerent of God. The director's function consisted in the enforcement of dogmas by which he had himself been subdued, in which he believed profoundly, and to which he often clung with an absorbing enthusiasm. The Jesuits, an Order thoroughly and vehemently reactive, had revived in Europe the mediæval type of Christianity, with all its attendant superstitions. Of these the Canadian missions bear abundant marks. Yet, on the whole, the labors of the missionaries tended greatly to the benefit of the Indians. Reclaimed, as the Jesuits tried to reclaim them, from their wandering life, settled in habits of peaceful industry, and reduced to a passive and childlike obedience, they would have gained more than enough to compensate them for the loss of their ferocious and miserable independence. At least,

---

1   "Ce seroit vne estrange cruauté de voir descendre vne âme toute viuante dans les enfers, par le refus d'vn bien que Iesus Christ luy a acquis au prix de son sang."— Relation, 1637, 66 (Cramoisy).

"Considerez d'autre coté la grande appréhension que nous avions sujet de redouter la guérison; pour autant que bien souvent étant guéris il ne leur reste du St. Baptême que le caractère."—Lettres de Garnier, MSS.

It was not very easy to make an Indian comprehend the nature of baptism. An Iroquois at Montreal, hearing a missionary speaking of the water which cleansed the soul from sin, said that he was well acquainted with it, as the Dutch had once given him so much that they were forced to tie him, hand and foot, to prevent him from doing mischief.—Faillon II. 43.

they would have escaped annihilation. The Society of Jesus aspired to the mastery of all New France; but the methods of its ambition were consistent with a Christian benevolence. Had this been otherwise, it would have employed other instruments. It would not have chosen a Jogues or a Garnier. The Society had men for every work, and it used them wisely. It utilized the apostolic virtues of its Canadian missionaries, fanned their enthusiasm, and decorated itself with their martyr crowns. With joy and gratulation, it saw them rival in another hemisphere the noble memory of its saint and hero, Francis Xavier. [Enemies of the Jesuits, while denouncing them in unmeasured terms, speak in strong eulogy of many of the Canadian missionaries. See, for example, Steinmetz, History of the Jesuits, II. 415.]

I have spoken of the colonists as living in a state of temporal and spiritual vassalage. To this there was one exception,—a small class of men whose home was the forest, and their companions savages. They followed the Indians in their roamings, lived with them, grew familiar with their language, allied themselves with their women, and often became oracles in the camp and leaders on the war-path. Champlain's bold interpreter, Étienne Brulé, whose adventures I have recounted elsewhere, ["Pioneers of France," 377.] may be taken as a type of this class. Of the rest, the most conspicuous were Jean Nicollet, Jacques Hertel, François Marguerie, and Nicolas Marsolet.[1] Doubtless, when they returned from their rovings, they often had pressing need of penance and absolution; yet, for the most part, they were good Catholics, and some of them were zealous for the missions. Nicollet and others were at times settled as interpreters at Three Rivers and Quebec. Several of them were men of great intelligence and an invincible courage. From hatred of restraint, and love of a wild and adventurous independence, they encountered privations and dangers scarcely less than those to which the Jesuit exposed himself from motives widely different,—he from religious zeal, charity, and the hope of Paradise; they simply because they liked it. Some of the best families of Canada claim descent from this vigorous and hardy stock.

---

1   See Ferland, Notes sur les Registres de N. D. de Québec, 30.

      Nicollet, especially, was a remarkable man. As early as 1639, he ascended the Green Bay of Lake Michigan, and crossed to the waters of the Mississippi. This was first shown by the researches of Mr. Shea. See his Discovery and Exploration of the Mississippi Valley, XX.

CHAPTER XIV.

1636-1652.

DEVOTEES AND NUNS.

THE HURON SEMINARY.—MADAME DE LA PELTRIE.—
HER PIOUS SCHEMES.—HER SHAM MARRIAGE.—
SHE VISITS THE URSULINES OF TOURS.—MARIE DE
SAINT BERNARD.—MARIE DE L'INCARNATION.—
HER ENTHUSIASM.—HER MYSTICAL MARRIAGE.—
HER DEJECTION.—HER MENTAL CONFLICTS.—HER
VISION.—MADE SUPERIOR OF THE URSULINES.—THE
HÔTEL-DIEU.—THE VOYAGE TO CANADA.—SILLERY.—
LABORS AND SUFFERINGS OF THE NUNS.—CHARACTER
OF MARIE DE L'INCARNATION.—OF MADAME DE LA
PELTRIE.

Quebec, as we have seen, had a seminary, a hospital, and a convent, before it had a population. It will be well to observe the origin of these institutions.

The Jesuits from the first had cherished the plan of a seminary for Huron boys at Quebec. The Governor and the Company favored the design; since not only would it be an efficient means of spreading the Faith and attaching the tribe to the French interest, but the children would be pledges for the good behavior of the parents, and hostages for the safety of missionaries and traders in the Indian towns. ["M. de Montmagny cognoit bien l'importance de ce Seminaire pour la gloire de Nostre Seigneur, et pour le commerce de ces Messieurs"—Relation, 1637, 209 (Cramoisy).] In the summer of 1636, Father Daniel, descending from the Huron country, worn, emaciated, his cassock patched and tattered, and his shirt in rags, brought with him a boy, to whom two others were soon added; and through the influence of the interpreter, Nicollet, the number was afterwards increased by several more. One of them ran away, two ate themselves to death, a fourth was carried home by his father, while three of those remaining stole a canoe, loaded it with all they could lay their hands upon, and escaped in triumph with their plunder. [Le Jeune, Relation, 1637, 55-59. Ibid., Relation, 1638, 23.]

The beginning was not hopeful; but the Jesuits persevered, and at length established their seminary on a firm basis. The Marquis de Gamache had given the Society six thousand crowns for founding a college at Quebec. In 1637, a year before the building of Harvard College, the Jesuits began a wooden structure in the rear of the fort; and here, within one inclosure, was the Huron seminary and the college for French boys.

Meanwhile the female children of both races were without instructors; but a remedy was at hand. At Alençon, in 1603, was born Marie Madeleine de Chauvigny, a scion of the *haute noblesse* of Normandy. Seventeen years later she was a young lady, abundantly wilful and superabundantly enthusiastic,—one who, in other circumstances, might perhaps have made a romantic elopement and a *mésalliance*.[1] But her impressible and ardent nature was absorbed in other objects. Religion and its ministers possessed her wholly, and all her enthusiasm was spent on works of charity and devotion. Her father, passionately fond of her, resisted her inclination for the cloister, and sought to wean her back to the world; but she escaped from the chateau to a neighboring convent, where she resolved to remain. Her father followed, carried her home, and engaged her in a round of fêtes and hunting parties, in the midst of which she found herself surprised into a betrothal to M. de la Peltrie, a young gentleman of rank and character. The marriage proved a happy

---

1   There is a portrait of her, taken at a later period, of which a photograph is before me. She has a semi-religious dress, hands clasped in prayer, large dark eyes, a smiling and mischievous mouth, and a face somewhat pretty and very coquettish. An engraving from the portrait is prefixed to the "Notice Biographique de Madame de la Peltrie" in Les Ursulines de Québec, I. 348.

one, and Madame de la Peltrie, with an excellent grace, bore her part in the world she had wished to renounce. After a union of five years, her husband died, and she was left a widow and childless at the age of twenty-two. She returned to the religious ardors of her girlhood, again gave all her thoughts to devotion and charity, and again resolved to be a nun. She had heard of Canada; and when Le Jeune's first Relations appeared, she read them with avidity. "Alas!" wrote the Father, "is there no charitable and virtuous lady who will come to this country to gather up the blood of Christ, by teaching His word to the little Indian girls?" His appeal found a prompt and vehement response from the breast of Madame de la Peltrie. Thenceforth she thought of nothing but Canada. In the midst of her zeal, a fever seized her. The physicians despaired; but, at the height of the disease, the patient made a vow to St. Joseph, that, should God restore her to health, she would build a house in honor of Him in Canada, and give her life and her wealth to the instruction of Indian girls. On the following morning, say her biographers, the fever had left her.

Meanwhile her relatives, or those of her husband, had confirmed her pious purposes by attempting to thwart them. They pronounced her a romantic visionary, incompetent to the charge of her property. Her father, too, whose fondness for her increased with his advancing age, entreated her to remain with him while he lived, and to defer the execution of her plans till he should be laid in his grave. From entreaties he passed to commands, and at length threatened to disinherit her, if she persisted. The virtue of obedience, for which she is extolled by her clerical biographers, however abundantly exhibited in respect to those who held charge of her conscience, was singularly wanting towards the parent who, in the way of Nature, had the best claim to its exercise; and Madame de la Peltrie was more than ever resolved to go to Canada. Her father, on his part, was urgent that she should marry again. On this she took counsel of a Jesuit,[1] who, "having seriously reflected

---

1   "Partagée ainsi entre l'amour filial et la religion, en proie aux plus poignantes angoisses, elle s'adressa à un religieux de la Compagnie de Jésus, dont elle connaissait la prudence consommée, et le supplia de l'éclairer de ses lumières. Ce religieux, après y avoir sérieusement réfléchi devant Dieu, lui répondit qu'il croyait avoir trouvé un moyen de tout concilier."—Casgrain, Vie de Marie de l'Incarnation, 243.

before God," suggested a device, which to the heretical mind is a little startling, but which commended itself to Madame de la Peltrie as fitted at once to soothe the troubled spirit of her father, and to save her from the sin involved in the abandonment of her pious designs.

Among her acquaintance was M. de Bernières, a gentleman of high rank, great wealth, and zealous devotion. She wrote to him, explained the situation, and requested him to feign a marriage with her. His sense of honor recoiled: moreover, in the fulness of his zeal, he had made a vow of chastity, and an apparent breach of it would cause scandal. He consulted his spiritual director and a few intimate friends. All agreed that the glory of God was concerned, and that it behooved him to accept the somewhat singular overtures of the young widow,[1] and request her hand from her father. M. de Chauvigny, who greatly esteemed Bernières, was delighted; and his delight was raised to transport at the dutiful and modest acquiescence of his daughter.[2] A betrothal took place; all was harmony, and for a time no more was said of disinheriting Madame de la Peltrie, or putting her in wardship.

Bernières's scruples returned. Divided between honor and conscience, he postponed the marriage, until at length M. de Chauvigny conceived misgivings, and again began to speak of disinheriting his daughter, unless the engagement was fulfilled.[3] Bernières yielded, and went with Madame de la Peltrie to consult "the most eminent divines."[4] A sham marriage took place, and

---

[1] "Enfin après avoir longtemps imploré les lumières du ciel, il remit toute l'affaire entre les mains de son directeur et de quelques amis intimes. Tous, d'un commun accord, lui déclarèrent que la gloire de Dieu y était interessée, et qu'il devait accepter."—Ibid., 244.

[2] "The prudent young widow answered him with much respect and modesty, that, as she knew M. de Bernières to be a favorite with him, she also preferred him to all others."

The above is from a letter of Marie de l'Incarnation, translated by Mother St. Thomas, of the Ursuline convent of Quebec, in her Life of Madame de la Peltrie, 41. Compare Les Ursulines de Québec, 10, and the "Notice Biographique" in the same volume.

[3] "Our virtuous widow did not lose courage. As she had given her confidence to M. de Bernières, she informed him of all that passed, while she flattered her father each day, telling him that this nobleman was too honorable to fail in keeping his word."—St. Thomas, Life of Madame de la Peltrie, 42.

[4] "He" (Bernières) "went to stay at the house of a mutual friend, where they had frequent opportunities of seeing each other, and consulting the most eminent

she and her accomplice appeared in public as man and wife. Her relatives, however, had already renewed their attempts to deprive her of the control of her property. A suit, of what nature does not appear, had been decided against her at Caen, and she had appealed to the Parliament of Normandy. Her lawyers were in despair; but, as her biographer justly observes, "the saints have resources which others have not." A vow to St. Joseph secured his intercession and gained her case. Another thought now filled her with agitation. Her plans were laid, and the time of action drew near. How could she endure the distress of her father, when he learned that she had deluded him with a false marriage, and that she and all that was hers were bound for the wilderness of Canada? Happily for him, he fell ill, and died in ignorance of the deceit that had been practised upon him.[1]

Whatever may be thought of the quality of Madame de la Peltrie's devotion, there can be no reasonable doubt of its sincerity or its ardor; and yet one can hardly fail to see in her the signs of that restless longing for *éclat*, which, with some women, is a ruling passion. When, in company with Bernières, she passed from Alençon to Tours, and from Tours to Paris, an object of attention to nuns, priests, and prelates,—when the Queen herself summoned her to an interview,—it may be that the profound contentment of soul ascribed to her had its origin in sources not exclusively of the spirit. At Tours, she repaired to the Ursuline convent. The Superior

---

divines on the means of effecting this pretended marriage."—Ibid., 43.

1   It will be of interest to observe the view taken of this pretended marriage by Madame de la Peltrie's Catholic biographers. Charlevoix tells the story without comment, but with apparent approval. Sainte-Foi, in his Premières Ursulines de France, says, that, as God had taken her under His guidance, we should not venture to criticize her. Casgrain, in his Vie de Marie de l'Incarnation, remarks:—

"Une telle conduite peut encore aujourd'hui paraître étrange à bien des personnes; mais outre que l'avenir fit bien voir que c'était une inspiration du ciel, nous pouvons répondre, avec un savant et pieux auteur, que nous ne devons point juger ceux que Dieu se charge lui-même de conduire."—p. 247.

Mother St. Thomas highly approves the proceeding, and says:—

"Thus ended the pretended engagement of this virtuous lady and gentleman, which caused, at the time, so much inquiry and excitement among the nobility in France, and which, after a lapse of two hundred years, cannot fail exciting feelings of admiration in the heart of every virtuous woman!"

Surprising as it may appear, the book from which the above is taken was written a few years since, in so-called English, for the instruction of the pupils in the Ursuline Convent at Quebec.

and all the nuns met her at the entrance of the cloister, and, separating into two rows as she appeared, sang the *Veni Creator*, while the bell of the monastery sounded its loudest peal. Then they led her in triumph to their church, sang *Te Deum*, and, while the honored guest knelt before the altar, all the sisterhood knelt around her in a semicircle. Their hearts beat high within them. That day they were to know who of their number were chosen for the new convent of Quebec, of which Madame de la Peltrie was to be the foundress; and when their devotions were over, they flung themselves at her feet, each begging with tears that the lot might fall on her. Aloof from this throng of enthusiastic suppliants stood a young nun, Marie de St. Bernard, too timid and too modest to ask the boon for which her fervent heart was longing. It was granted without asking. This delicate girl was chosen, and chosen wisely. [Casgrain, Vie de Marie de l'Incarnation, 271-273. There is a long account of Marie de St. Bernard, by Ragueneau, in the Relation of 1652. Here it is said that she showed an unaccountable indifference as to whether she went to Canada or not, which, however, was followed by an ardent desire to go.]

There was another nun who stood apart, silent and motionless,—a stately figure, with features strongly marked and perhaps somewhat masculine;[1] but, if so, they belied her, for Marie de l'Incarnation was a woman to the core. For her there was no need of entreaties; for she knew that the Jesuits had made her their choice, as Superior of the new convent. She was born, forty years before, at Tours, of a good *bourgeois* family. As she grew up towards maturity, her qualities soon declared themselves. She had uncommon talents and strong religious susceptibilities, joined to a vivid imagination,—an alliance not always desirable under a form of faith where both are excited by stimulants so many and so powerful. Like Madame de la Peltrie, she married, at the desire of her parents, in her eighteenth year. The marriage was not happy. Her biographers say that there was no fault on either side. Apparently, it was a severe case of "incompatibility." She sought her consolation in the churches; and, kneeling in dim chapels, held

---

1   There is an engraved portrait of her, taken some years later, of which a photograph is before me. When she was "in the world," her stately proportions are said to have attracted general attention. Her family name was Marie Guyard. She was born on the eighteenth of October, 1599.

communings with Christ and the angels. At the end of two years her husband died, leaving her with an infant son. She gave him to the charge of her sister, abandoned herself to solitude and meditation, and became a mystic of the intense and passional school. Yet a strong maternal instinct battled painfully in her breast with a sense of religious vocation. Dreams, visions, interior voices, ecstasies, revulsions, periods of rapture and periods of deep dejection, made up the agitated tissue of her life. She fasted, wore hair-cloth, scourged herself, washed dishes among the servants, and did their most menial work. She heard, in a trance, a miraculous voice. It was that of Christ, promising to become her spouse. Months and years passed, full of troubled hopes and fears, when again the voice sounded in her ear, with assurance that the promise was fulfilled, and that she was indeed his bride. Now ensued phenomena which are not infrequent among Roman Catholic female devotees, when unmarried, or married unhappily, and which have their source in the necessities of a woman's nature. To her excited thought, her divine spouse became a living presence; and her language to him, as recorded by herself, is that of the most intense passion. She went to prayer, agitated and tremulous, as if to a meeting with an earthly lover. "O my Love!" she exclaimed, "when shall I embrace you? Have you no pity on me in the torments that I suffer? Alas! alas! my Love, my Beauty, my Life! instead of healing my pain, you take pleasure in it. Come, let me embrace you, and die in your sacred arms!" And again she writes: "Then, as I was spent with fatigue, I was forced to say, 'My divine Love, since you wish me to live, I pray you let me rest a little, that I may the better serve you'; and I promised him that afterward I would suffer myself to consume in his chaste and divine embraces."[1]

---

1   "Allant à l'oraison, je tressaillois en moi-même, et disois: Allons dans la solitude, mon cher amour, afin que je vous embrasse à mon aise, et que, respirant mon âme en vous, elle ne soit plus que vous-même par union d'amour . . . Puis, mon corps étant brisé de fatigues, j'étois contrainte de dire: Mon divin amour, je vous prie de me laisser prendre un peu de repos, afin que je puisse mieux vous servir, puisque vous voulez que je vive . . . Je le priois de me laisser agir; lui promettant de me laisser après cela consumer dans ses chastes et divins embrassemens . . . O amour! quand vous embrasserai-je? N'avez-vous point pitié de moi dans le tourment que je souffre? helas! helas! mon amour, ma beauté, ma vie! au lieu de me guérir, vous vous plaisez à mes maux. Venez donc que je vous embrasse, et que je meure entre vos bras sacréz!"

Clearly, here is a case for the physiologist as well as the theologian; and the "holy widow," as her biographers call her, becomes an example, and a lamentable one, of the tendency of the erotic principle to ally itself with high religious excitement.

But the wings of imagination will tire and droop, the brightest dream-land of contemplative fancy grow dim, and an abnormal tension of the faculties find its inevitable reaction at last. From a condition of highest exaltation, a mystical heaven of light and glory, the unhappy dreamer fell back to a dreary earth, or rather to an abyss of darkness and misery. Her biographers tell us that she became a prey to dejection, and thoughts of infidelity, despair, estrangement from God, aversion to mankind, pride, vanity, impurity, and a supreme disgust at the rites of religion. Exhaustion produced common-sense, and the dreams which had been her life now seemed a tissue of illusions. Her confessor became a weariness to her, and his words fell dead on her ear. Indeed, she conceived a repugnance to the holy man. Her old and favorite confessor, her oracle, guide, and comforter, had lately been taken from her by promotion in the Church,—which may serve to explain her dejection; and the new one, jealous of his predecessor, told her that all his counsels had been visionary and dangerous to her soul. Having overwhelmed her with this announcement, he left her, apparently out of patience with her refractory and gloomy mood; and she remained for several months deprived of spiritual guidance. [Casgrain, 195-197.] Two years elapsed before her mind recovered its tone, when she soared once more in the seventh heaven of imaginative devotion.

Marie de l'Incarnation, we have seen, was unrelenting in every practice of humiliation; dressed in mean attire, did the servants' work, nursed sick beggars, and, in her meditations, taxed her brain

---

The above passages, from various pages of her journal, will suffice though they give but an inadequate idea of these strange extravagances. What is most astonishing is, that a man of sense like Charlevoix; in his Life of Marie de l'Incarnation, should extract them in full, as matter of edification and evidence of saintship. Her recent biographer, the Abbé Casgrain, refrains from quoting them, though he mentions them approvingly as evincing fervor. The Abbé Racine, in his Discours à l'Occasion du 192ème Anniversaire de l'heureuse Mort de la Vén. Mère de l'Incarnation, delivered at Quebec in 1864, speaks of them as transcendent proofs of the supreme favor of Heaven.—Some of the pupils of Marie de l'Incarnation also had mystical marriages with Christ; and the impassioned rhapsodies of one of them being overheard, she nearly lost her character, as it was thought that she was apostrophsizing an earthly lover.

with metaphysical processes of self-annihilation. And yet, when one reads her "Spiritual Letters," the conviction of an enormous spiritual pride in the writer can hardly be repressed. She aspired to that inner circle of the faithful, that aristocracy of devotion, which, while the common herd of Christians are busied with the duties of life, eschews the visible and the present, and claims to live only for God. In her strong maternal affection she saw a lure to divert her from the path of perfect saintship. Love for her child long withheld her from becoming a nun; but at last, fortified by her confessor, she left him to his fate, took the vows, and immured herself with the Ursulines of Tours. The boy, frenzied by his desertion, and urged on by indignant relatives, watched his opportunity, and made his way into the refectory of the convent, screaming to the horrified nuns to give him back his mother. As he grew older, her anxiety increased; and at length she heard in her seclusion that he had fallen into bad company, had left the relative who had sheltered him, and run off, no one knew whither. The wretched mother, torn with anguish, hastened for consolation to her confessor, who met her with stern upbraidings. Yet, even in this her intensest ordeal, her enthusiasm and her native fortitude enabled her to maintain a semblance of calmness, till she learned that the boy had been found and brought back.

Strange as it may seem, this woman, whose habitual state was one of mystical abstraction, was gifted to a rare degree with the faculties most useful in the practical affairs of life. She had spent several years in the house of her brother-in-law. Here, on the one hand, her vigils, visions, and penances set utterly at nought the order of a well-governed family; while, on the other, she made amends to her impatient relative by able and efficient aid in the conduct of his public and private affairs. Her biographers say, and doubtless with truth, that her heart was far away from these mundane interests; yet her talent for business was not the less displayed. Her spiritual guides were aware of it, and saw clearly that gifts so useful to the world might be made equally useful to the Church. Hence it was that she was chosen Superior of the convent which Madame de la Peltrie was about to endow at Quebec. [The combination of religious enthusiasm, however extravagant and visionary, with a talent for business, is not very rare. Nearly all the founders of monastic Orders are examples of it.]

Yet it was from heaven itself that Marie de l'Incarnation received her first "vocation" to Canada. The miracle was in this wise.

In a dream she beheld a lady unknown to her. She took her hand; and the two journeyed together westward, towards the sea. They soon met one of the Apostles, clothed all in white, who, with a wave of his hand, directed them on their way. They now entered on a scene of surpassing magnificence. Beneath their feet was a pavement of squares of white marble, spotted with vermilion, and intersected with lines of vivid scarlet; and all around stood monasteries of matchless architecture. But the two travellers, without stopping to admire, moved swiftly on till they beheld the Virgin seated with her Infant Son on a small temple of white marble, which served her as a throne. She seemed about fifteen years of age, and was of a "ravishing beauty." Her head was turned aside; she was gazing fixedly on a wild waste of mountains and valleys, half concealed in mist. Marie de l'Incarnation approached with outstretched arms, adoring. The vision bent towards her, and, smiling, kissed her three times; whereupon, in a rapture, the dreamer awoke. [Marie de l'Incarnation recounts this dream at great length in her letters; and Casgrain copies the whole, verbatim, as a revelation from God.]

She told the vision to Father Dinet, a Jesuit of Tours. He was at no loss for an interpretation. The land of mists and mountains was Canada, and thither the Virgin called her. Yet one mystery remained unsolved. Who was the unknown companion of her dream? Several years had passed, and signs from heaven and inward voices had raised to an intense fervor her zeal for her new vocation, when, for the first time, she saw Madame de la Peltrie on her visit to the convent at Tours, and recognized, on the instant, the lady of her nocturnal vision. No one can be surprised at this who has considered with the slightest attention the phenomena of religious enthusiasm.

On the fourth of May, 1639, Madame de la Peltrie, Marie de l'Incarnation, Marie de St. Bernard, and another Ursuline, embarked at Dieppe for Canada. In the ship were also three young hospital nuns, sent out to found at Quebec a Hôtel Dieu, endowed by the famous niece of Richelieu, the Duchesse d'Aiguillon. [Juchereau, Histoire de l'Hôtel-Dieu ae Québec, 4.] Here, too, were the Jesuits

Chaumonot and Poncet, on the way to their mission, together with Father Vimont, who was to succeed Le Jeune in his post of Superior. To the nuns, pale from their cloistered seclusion, there was a strange and startling novelty in this new world of life and action,—the ship, the sailors, the shouts of command, the flapping of sails, the salt wind, and the boisterous sea. The voyage was long and tedious. Sometimes they lay in their berths, sea-sick and woe-begone; sometimes they sang in choir on deck, or heard mass in the cabin. Once, on a misty morning, a wild cry of alarm startled crew and passengers alike. A huge iceberg was drifting close upon them. The peril was extreme. Madame de la Peltrie clung to Marie de l'Incarnation, who stood perfectly calm, and gathered her gown about her feet that she might drown with decency. It is scarcely necessary to say that they were saved by a vow to the Virgin and St. Joseph. Vimont offered it in behalf of all the company, and the ship glided into the open sea unharmed.

They arrived at Tadoussac on the fifteenth of July; and the nuns ascended to Quebec in a small craft deeply laden with salted codfish, on which, uncooked, they subsisted until the first of August, when they reached their destination. Cannon roared welcome from the fort and batteries; all labor ceased; the storehouses were closed; and the zealous Montmagny, with a train of priests and soldiers, met the new-comers at the landing. All the nuns fell prostrate, and kissed the sacred soil of Canada.[1] They heard mass at the church, dined at the fort, and presently set forth to visit the new settlement of Sillery, four miles above Quebec.

Noel Brulart de Sillery, a Knight of Malta, who had once filled the highest offices under the Queen Marie de Médicis, had now severed his connection with his Order, renounced the world, and become a priest. He devoted his vast revenues—for a dispensation of the Pope had freed him from his vow of poverty—to the founding of religious establishments.[2] Among other endowments, he had placed an ample fund in the hands of the Jesuits for the

---

1   Juchereau, 14; Le Clerc, II. 33; Ragueneau, Vie de Catherine de St. Augustin, "Epistre dédicatoire;" Le Jeune, Relation, 1639, Chap. II.; Charlevoix, Vie de Marie de l'Incarnation, 264; "Acte de Reception," in Les Ursulines de Québec, I. 21.

2   See Vie de l'Illustre Serviteur de Dieu Noel Brulart de Sillery; also Études et Recherches Bioqraphiques sur le Chevalier Noel Brulart de Sillery, and several documents in Martin's translation of Bressani, Appendix IV.

formation of a settlement of Christian Indians at the spot which still bears his name. On the strand of Sillery, between the river and the woody heights behind, were clustered the small log-cabins of a number of Algonquin converts, together with a church, a mission-house, and an infirmary,—the whole surrounded by a palisade. It was to this place that the six nuns were now conducted by the Jesuits. The scene delighted and edified them; and, in the transports of their zeal, they seized and kissed every female Indian child on whom they could lay hands, "without minding," says Father Le Jeune, "whether they were dirty or not." "Love and charity," he adds, "triumphed over every human consideration."[1]

The nuns of the Hôtel-Dieu soon after took up their abode at Sillery, whence they removed to a house built for them at Quebec by their foundress, the Duchesse d'Aiguillon. The Ursulines, in the absence of better quarters, were lodged at first in a small wooden tenement under the rock of Quebec, at the brink of the river. Here they were soon beset with such a host of children, that the floor of their wretched tenement was covered with beds, and their toil had no respite. Then came the small-pox, carrying death and terror among the neighboring Indians. These thronged to Quebec in misery and desperation, begging succor from the French. The labors both of the Ursulines and of the hospital nuns were prodigious. In the infected air of their miserable hovels, where sick and dying savages covered the floor, and were packed one above another in berths,—amid all that is most distressing and most revolting, with little food and less sleep, these women passed the rough beginning of their new life. Several of them fell ill. But the excess of the evil at length brought relief; for so many of the Indians died in these pest-houses that the survivors shunned them in horror.

But how did these women bear themselves amid toils so arduous? A pleasant record has come down to us of one of them,—that fair and delicate girl, Marie de St. Bernard, called, in the convent, Sister St. Joseph, who had been chosen at Tours as the companion of Marie de l'Incarnation. Another Ursuline, writing at a period when the severity of their labors was somewhat relaxed,

---

1   " . . . sans prendre garde si ces petits enfans sauvages estoient sales ou non; . . . la loy d'amour et de charité l'emportoit par dessus toutes les considerations humaines."—Relation, 1639, 26 (Cramoisy).

says, "Her disposition is charming. In our times of recreation, she often makes us cry with laughing: it would be hard to be melancholy when she is near." [Lettre de la Mère Ste Claire à une de ses Sœurs Ursulines de Paris, Québec, 2 Sept., 1640.—See Les Ursulines de Québec, I. 38.]

It was three years later before the Ursulines and their pupils took possession of a massive convent of stone, built for them on the site which they still occupy. Money had failed before the work was done, and the interior was as unfinished as a barn. [The interior was finished after a year or two, with cells as usual. There were four chimneys, with fireplaces burning a hundred and seventy-five cords of wood in a winter; and though the nuns were boxed up in beds which closed like chests, Marie de l'Incarnation complains bitterly of the cold. See her letter of Aug. 26, 1644.] Beside the cloister stood a large ash-tree; and it stands there still. Beneath its shade, says the convent tradition, Marie de l'Incarnation and her nuns instructed the Indian children in the truths of salvation; but it might seem rash to affirm that their teachings were always either wise or useful, since Father Vimont tells us approvingly, that they reared their pupils in so chaste a horror of the other sex, that a little girl, whom a man had playfully taken by the hand, ran crying to a bowl of water to wash off the unhallowed influence. [Vimont, Relation, 1642, 112 (Cramoisy).]

Now and henceforward one figure stands nobly conspicuous in this devoted sisterhood. Marie de l'Incarnation, no longer lost in the vagaries of an insane mysticism, but engaged in the duties of Christian charity and the responsibilities of an arduous post, displays an ability, a fortitude, and an earnestness which command respect and admiration. Her mental intoxication had ceased, or recurred only at intervals; and false excitements no longer sustained her. She was racked with constant anxieties about her son, and was often in a condition described by her biographers as a "deprivation of all spiritual consolations." Her position was a very difficult one. She herself speaks of her life as a succession of crosses and humiliations. Some of these were due to Madame de la Peltrie, who, in a freak of enthusiasm, abandoned her Ursulines for a time, as we shall presently see, leaving them in the utmost destitution. There were dissensions to be healed among them; and money, everything, in short, to be provided. Marie de l'Incarnation, in her saddest moments, neither failed in judgment nor slackened in effort. She carried on a vast correspondence, embracing every one in France who could aid her infant community with money or influence; she harmonized and regulated it with excellent skill; and, in the midst of relentless austerities, she was loved as a mother by her pupils and dependants. Catholic writers extol her as a saint.[1] Protestants may see in her a Christian heroine, admirable, with all her follies and her faults.

The traditions of the Ursulines are full of the virtues of Madame de la Peltrie,—her humility, her charity, her penances, and her acts of mortification. No doubt, with some little allowance, these traditions are true; but there is more of reason than of uncharitableness in the belief, that her zeal would have been less ardent and sustained, if it had had fewer spectators. She was now fairly committed to the conventual life, her enthusiasm was kept within prescribed bounds, and she was no longer mistress of her own movements. On the one hand, she was anxious to accumulate merits against the Day of Judgment; and, on the other, she had a keen appreciation of the applause which the sacrifice of her fortune and her acts of piety had gained for her. Mortal vanity takes many shapes. Sometimes it arrays itself in silk and jewels; sometimes it walks in sackcloth, and speaks the language of self-abasement. In the convent, as in the world, the fair devotee thirsted for admiration. The halo of saintship glittered in her eyes like a diamond crown, and she aspired to outshine her sisters in humility. She was as sincere as Simeon Stylites on his column; and, like him, found encouragement and comfort in the gazing and wondering eyes below. [Madame de la Peltrie died in her convent in 1671. Marie de l'Incarnation died the following year. She had the consolation of knowing that her son had fulfilled her ardent wishes, and become a priest.]

---

1   There is a letter extant from Sister Anne de Ste Claire, an Ursuline who came to Quebec in 1640, written soon after her arrival, and containing curious evidence that a reputation of saintship already attached to Marie de l'Incarnation. "When I spoke to her," writes Sister Anne, speaking of her first interview, "I perceived in the air a certain odor of sanctity, which gave me the sensation of an agreeable perfume." See the letter in a recent Catholic work, Les Ursulines de Québec, I. 38, where the passage is printed in Italics, as worthy the especial attention of the pious reader.

CHAPTER XV.

1636-1642.

VILLEMARIE DE MONTREAL.

DAUVERSIÈRE AND THE VOICE FROM HEAVEN.—
ABBÉ OLIER.—THEIR SCHEMES.—THE SOCIETY OF
NOTRE-DAME DE MONTREAL.—MAISONNEUVE.—
DEVOUT LADIES.—MADEMOISELLE MANCE.—
MARGUERITE BOURGEOIS.—THE MONTREALISTS AT
QUEBEC.—JEALOUSY.—QUARRELS.—ROMANCE AND
DEVOTION.—EMBARKATION.—FOUNDATION OF
MONTREAL.

We come now to an enterprise as singular in its character as it proved important in its results.

At La Flèche, in Anjou, dwelt one Jérôme le Royer de la Dauversière, receiver of taxes. His portrait shows us a round, *bourgeois* face, somewhat heavy perhaps, decorated with a slight moustache, and redeemed by bright and earnest eyes. On his head he wears a black skull-cap; and over his ample shoulders spreads a stiff white collar, of wide expanse and studious plainness. Though he belonged to the *noblesse*, his look is that of a grave burgher, of good renown and sage deportment. Dauversière was, however, an enthusiastic devotee, of mystical tendencies, who whipped himself with a scourge of small chains till his shoulders were one wound, wore a belt with more than twelve hundred sharp points, and invented for himself other torments, which filled his confessor with admiration.

[Fancamp in Faillon, Vie de Mlle Mance, Introduction.] One day, while at his devotions, he heard an inward voice commanding him to become the founder of a new Order of hospital nuns; and he was further ordered to establish, on the island called Montreal, in Canada, a hospital, or Hôtel-Dieu, to be conducted by these nuns. But Montreal was a wilderness, and the hospital would have no patients. Therefore, in order to supply them, the island must first be colonized. Dauversière was greatly perplexed. On the one hand, the voice of Heaven must be obeyed; on the other, he had a wife, six children, and a very moderate fortune. [Faillon, Vie de Mlle Mance, Introduction; Dollier de Casson, Hist. de Montreal, MS.; Les Véritables Motifs des Messieurs et Dames de Montreal, 25; Juchereau, 33.]

Again: there was at Paris a young priest, about twenty-eight years of age,—Jean Jacques Olier, afterwards widely known as founder of the Seminary of St. Sulpice. Judged by his engraved portrait, his countenance, though marked both with energy and intellect, was anything but prepossessing. Every lineament proclaims the priest. Yet the Abbé Olier has high titles to esteem. He signalized his piety, it is true, by the most disgusting exploits of self-mortification; but, at the same time, he was strenuous in his efforts to reform the people and the clergy. So zealous was he for good morals, that he drew upon himself the imputation of a leaning to the heresy of the Jansenists,—a suspicion strengthened by his opposition to certain priests, who, to secure the faithful in their allegiance, justified them in lives of licentiousness. [Faillon, Vie de M. Olier, II. 188.] Yet Olier's catholicity was past attaintment, and in his horror of Jansenists he yielded to the Jesuits alone.

He was praying in the ancient church of St. Germain des Prés, when, like Dauversière, he thought he heard a voice from Heaven, saying that he was destined to be a light to the Gentiles. It is recorded as a mystic coincidence attending this miracle, that the choir was at that very time chanting the words, *Lumen ad revelationem Gentium;*[1] and it seems to have occurred neither to Olier nor to his biographer, that, falling on the ear of the rapt worshipper, they might have unconsciously suggested the supposed revelation. But

---

1   Mémoires Autographes de M. Olier, cited by Faillon, in Histoire de la Colonie Française, I. 384.

there was a further miracle. An inward voice told Olier that he was to form a society of priests, and establish them on the island called Montreal, in Canada, for the propagation of the True Faith; and writers old and recent assert, that, while both he and Dauversière were totally ignorant of Canadian geography, they suddenly found themselves in possession, they knew not how, of the most exact details concerning Montreal, its size, shape, situation, soil, climate, and productions.

The annual volumes of the Jesuit Relations, issuing from the renowned press of Cramoisy, were at this time spread broadcast throughout France; and, in the circles of *haute devotion*, Canada and its missions were everywhere the themes of enthusiastic discussion; while Champlain, in his published works, had long before pointed out Montreal as the proper site for a settlement. But we are entering a region of miracle, and it is superfluous to look far for explanations. The illusion, in these cases, is a part of the history.

Dauversière pondered the revelation he had received; and the more he pondered, the more was he convinced that it came from God. He therefore set out for Paris, to find some means of accomplishing the task assigned him. Here, as he prayed before an image of the Virgin in the church of Notre-Dame, he fell into an ecstasy, and beheld a vision. "I should be false to the integrity of history," writes his biographer, "if I did not relate it here." And he adds, that the reality of this celestial favor is past doubting, inasmuch as Dauversière himself told it to his daughters. Christ, the Virgin, and St. Joseph appeared before him. He saw them distinctly. Then he heard Christ ask three times of his Virgin Mother, Where can I find a faithful servant? On which, the Virgin, taking him (Dauversière) by the hand, replied, See, Lord, here is that faithful servant!—and Christ, with a benignant smile, received him into his service, promising to bestow on him wisdom and strength to do his work. [Faillon, Vie de Mlle Mance, Introduction, xxviii. The Abbé Ferland, in his Histoire du Canada, passes over the miracles in silence.] From Paris he went to the neighboring chateau of Meudon, which overlooks the valley of the Seine, not far from St. Cloud. Entering the gallery of the old castle, he saw a priest approaching him. It was Olier. Now we are told that neither of these men had ever seen or heard of the other; and yet, says the pious historian, "impelled by a kind of inspiration, they knew each other at once, even to the depths of their hearts; saluted each other by name, as we read of St. Paul, the Hermit, and St. Anthony, and of St. Dominic and St. Francis; and ran to embrace each other, like two friends who had met after a long separation." [Ibid., La Colonie Française, I. 390.]

"Monsieur," exclaimed Olier, "I know your design, and I go to commend it to God at the holy altar."

And he went at once to say mass in the chapel. Dauversière received the communion at his hands; and then they walked for three hours in the park, discussing their plans. They were of one mind, in respect both to objects and means; and when they parted, Olier gave Dauversière a hundred louis, saying, "This is to begin the work of God."

They proposed to found at Montreal three religious communities,—three being the mystic number,—one of secular priests to direct the colonists and convert the Indians, one of nuns to nurse the sick, and one of nuns to teach the Faith to the children, white and red. To borrow their own phrases, they would plant the banner of Christ in an abode of desolation and a haunt of demons; and to this end a band of priests and women were to invade the wilderness, and take post between the fangs of the Iroquois. But first they must make a colony, and to do so must raise money. Olier had pious and wealthy penitents; Dauversière had a friend, the Baron de Fancamp, devout as himself and far richer. Anxious for his soul, and satisfied that the enterprise was an inspiration of God, he was eager to bear part in it. Olier soon found three others; and the six together formed the germ of the Society of Notre-Dame de Montreal. Among them they raised the sum of seventy-five thousand livres, equivalent to about as many dollars at the present day.

[Dollier de Casson, Histoire de Montreal, MS.; also Belmont, Histoire du Canada, 2. Juchereau doubles the sum. Faillon agrees with Dollier.

On all that relates to the early annals of Montreal a flood of new light has been thrown by the Abbé Faillon. As a priest of St. Sulpice, he had ready access to the archives of the Seminaries of Montreal and Paris, and to numerous other ecclesiastical depositories, which would have been closed hopelessly against a layman and a heretic. It is impossible to commend too highly the zeal, diligence, exactness, and extent of his conscientious researches. His credulity is enormous, and he is completely in sympathy with the supernaturalists of whom he writes: in other words, he identifies himself with his theme, and is indeed a fragment of the seventeenth century, still extant in the nineteenth. He is minute to prolixity, and abounds in extracts and citations from the ancient manuscripts which his labors have unearthed. In short, the Abbé is a prodigy of patience and industry; and if he taxes the patience of his readers, he also rewards it abundantly. Such of his original authorities as have proved accessible are before me, including a considerable number of manuscripts. Among these, that of Dollier de Casson, Histoire de Montreal, as cited above, is the most important. The copy in my possession was made from the original in the Mazarin Library.]

Now to look for a moment at their plan. Their eulogists say, and with perfect truth, that, from a worldly point of view, it was mere folly. The partners mutually bound themselves to seek no return for the money expended. Their profit was to be reaped in the skies: and, indeed, there was none to be reaped on earth. The feeble settlement at Quebec was at this time in danger of utter ruin; for the Iroquois, enraged at the attacks made on them by Champlain, had begun a fearful course of retaliation, and the very existence of the colony trembled in the balance. But if Quebec was exposed to their ferocious inroads, Montreal was incomparably more so. A settlement here would be a perilous outpost,—a hand thrust into the jaws of the tiger. It would provoke attack, and lie almost in the path of the war-parties. The associates could gain nothing by the fur-trade; for they would not be allowed to share in it. On the other hand, danger apart, the place was an excellent one for a mission; for here met two great rivers: the St. Lawrence, with its countless tributaries, flowed in from the west, while the Ottawa descended from the north; and Montreal, embraced by their uniting waters, was the key to a vast inland navigation. Thither the Indians would naturally resort; and thence the missionaries could make their way into the heart of a boundless heathendom. None of the ordinary motives of colonization had part in this design. It owed its conception and its birth to religious zeal alone.

The island of Montreal belonged to Lauson, former president of the great company of the Hundred Associates; and, as we have seen, his son had a monopoly of fishing in the St. Lawrence.

Dauversière and Fancamp, after much diplomacy, succeeded in persuading the elder Lauson to transfer his title to them; and, as there was a defect in it, they also obtained a grant of the island from the Hundred Associates, its original owners, who, however, reserved to themselves its western extremity as a site for a fort and storehouses.[1] At the same time, the younger Lauson granted them a right of fishery within two leagues of the shores of the island, for which they were to make a yearly acknowledgment of ten pounds of fish. A confirmation of these grants was obtained from the King. Dauversière and his companions were now *seigneurs* of Montreal. They were empowered to appoint a governor, and to establish courts, from which there was to be an appeal to the Supreme Court of Quebec, supposing such to exist. They were excluded from the fur-trade, and forbidden to build castles or forts other than such as were necessary for defence against the Indians.

Their title assured, they matured their plan. First they would send out forty men to take possession of Montreal, intrench themselves, and raise crops. Then they would build a house for the priests, and two convents for the nuns. Meanwhile, Olier was toiling at Vaugirard, on the outskirts of Paris, to inaugurate the seminary of priests, and Dauversière at La Flèche, to form the community of hospital nuns. How the school nuns were provided for we shall see hereafter. The colony, it will be observed, was for the convents, not the convents for the colony.

The Associates needed a soldier-governor to take charge of their forty men; and, directed as they supposed by Providence, they found one wholly to their mind. This was Paul de Chomedey, Sieur de Maisonneuve, a devout and valiant gentleman, who in long service among the heretics of Holland had kept his faith intact, and

---

1   Donation et Transport de la Concession de l'Isle de Montreal par M. Jean de Lauzon aux Sieurs Chevrier de Fouancant (Fancamp) et le Royer de la Doversière, MS.

Concession d'une Partie de l'Isle de Montreal accordée par la Compagnie de la Nouvelle France aux Sieurs Chevrier et le Royer, MS.

Lettres de Ratification, MS.

Acte qui prouve que les Sieurs Chevrier de Fancamps et Royer de la Dauversière n'ont stipulé qu'au nom de la Compagnie de Montreal, MS.

From copies of other documents before me, it appears that in 1659 the reserved portion of the island was also ceded to the Company of Montreal.

See also Edits, Ordonnances Royaux, etc., I. 20-26 (Quebec, 1854).

had held himself resolutely aloof from the license that surrounded him. He loved his profession of arms, and wished to consecrate his sword to the Church. Past all comparison, he is the manliest figure that appears in this group of zealots. The piety of the design, the miracles that inspired it, the adventure and the peril, all combined to charm him; and he eagerly embraced the enterprise. His father opposed his purpose; but he met him with a text of St. Mark, "There is no man that hath left house or brethren or sisters or father for my sake, but he shall receive an hundred-fold." On this the elder Maisonneuve, deceived by his own worldliness, imagined that the plan covered some hidden speculation, from which enormous profits were expected, and therefore withdrew his opposition. [Faillon, La Colonie Française, I. 409.]

Their scheme was ripening fast, when both Olier and Dauversière were assailed by one of those revulsions of spirit, to which saints of the ecstatic school are naturally liable. Dauversière, in particular, was a prey to the extremity of dejection, uncertainty, and misgiving. What had he, a family man, to do with ventures beyond sea? Was it not his first duty to support his wife and children? Could he not fulfil all his obligations as a Christian by reclaiming the wicked and relieving the poor at La Flèche? Plainly, he had doubts that his vocation was genuine. If we could raise the curtain of his domestic life, perhaps we should find him beset by wife and daughters, tearful and wrathful, inveighing against his folly, and imploring him to provide a support for them before squandering his money to plant a convent of nuns in a wilderness. How long his fit of dejection lasted does not appear; but at length[1] he set himself again to his appointed work. Olier, too, emerging from the clouds and darkness, found faith once more, and again placed himself at the head of the great enterprise.[2]

There was imperative need of more money; and Dauversière, under judicious guidance, was active in obtaining it. This miserable victim of illusions had a squat, uncourtly figure, and was no proficient in the graces either of manners or of speech: hence his success in commending his objects to persons of rank and wealth

---

1   Faillon, Vie de Mlle Mance, Introduction, xxxv.
2   Faillon (Vie de M. Olier) devotes twenty-one pages to the history of his fit of nervous depression.

is set down as one of the many miracles which attended the birth of Montreal. But zeal and earnestness are in themselves a power; and the ground had been well marked out and ploughed for him in advance. That attractive, though intricate, subject of study, the female mind, has always engaged the attention of priests, more especially in countries where, as in France, women exert a strong social and political influence. The art of kindling the flames of zeal, and the more difficult art of directing and controlling them, have been themes of reflection the most diligent and profound. Accordingly we find that a large proportion of the money raised for this enterprise was contributed by devout ladies. Many of them became members of the Association of Montreal, which was eventually increased to about forty-five persons, chosen for their devotion and their wealth.

Olier and his associates had resolved, though not from any collapse of zeal, to postpone the establishment of the seminary and the college until after a settlement should be formed. The hospital, however, might, they thought, be begun at once; for blood and blows would be the assured portion of the first settlers. At least, a discreet woman ought to embark with the first colonists as their nurse and housekeeper. Scarcely was the need recognized when it was supplied.

Mademoiselle Jeanne Mance was born of an honorable family of Nogent-le-Roi, and in 1640 was thirty-four years of age. These Canadian heroines began their religious experiences early. Of Marie de l'Incarnation we read, that at the age of seven Christ appeared to her in a vision; [Casgrain, Vie de Marie de l'Incarnation, 78.] and the biographer of Mademoiselle Mance assures us, with admiring gravity, that, at the same tender age, she bound herself to God by a vow of perpetual chastity. [Faillon, Vie de Mlle Mance, I. 3.] This singular infant in due time became a woman, of a delicate constitution, and manners graceful, yet dignified. Though an earnest devotee, she felt no vocation for the cloister; yet, while still "in the world," she led the life of a nun. The Jesuit Relations, and the example of Madame de la Peltrie, of whom she had heard, inoculated her with the Canadian enthusiasm, then so prevalent; and, under the pretence of visiting relatives, she made a journey to Paris, to take counsel of certain priests. Of one thing she was assured: the Divine will called her to Canada, but to what end she neither knew nor asked to know; for she abandoned herself as an atom to be borne to unknown destinies on the breath of God. At Paris, Father St. Jure, a Jesuit, assured her that her vocation to Canada was, past doubt, a call from Heaven; while Father Rapin, a Récollet, spread abroad the fame of her virtues, and introduced her to many ladies of rank, wealth, and zeal. Then, well supplied with money for any pious work to which she might be summoned, she journeyed to Rochelle, whence ships were to sail for New France. Thus far she had been kept in ignorance of the plan with regard to Montreal; but now Father La Place, a Jesuit, revealed it to her. On the day after her arrival at Rochelle, as she entered the Church of the Jesuits, she met Dauversière coming out. "Then," says her biographer, "these two persons, who had never seen nor heard of each other, were enlightened supernaturally, whereby their most hidden thoughts were mutually made known, as had happened already with M. Olier and this same M. de la Dauversière." [Faillon, Vie de Mlle Mance, I. 18. Here again the Abbé Ferland, with his usual good sense, tacitly rejects the supernaturalism.] A long conversation ensued between them; and the delights of this interview were never effaced from the mind of Mademoiselle Mance. "She used to speak of it like a seraph," writes one of her nuns, "and far better than many a learned doctor could have done." [La Sœur Morin, Annales des Hospitalières de Villemarie, MS., cited by Faillon.]

She had found her destiny. The ocean, the wilderness, the solitude, the Iroquois,—nothing daunted her. She would go to Montreal with Maisonneuve and his forty men. Yet, when the vessel was about to sail, a new and sharp misgiving seized her. How could she, a woman, not yet bereft of youth or charms, live alone in the forest, among a troop of soldiers? Her scruples were relieved by two of the men, who, at the last moment, refused to embark without their wives,—and by a young woman, who, impelled by enthusiasm, escaped from her friends, and took passage, in spite of them, in one of the vessels.

All was ready; the ships set sail; but Olier, Dauversière, and Fancamp remained at home, as did also the other Associates, with the exception of Maisonneuve and Mademoiselle Mance. In the following February, an impressive scene took place in the Church of Notre Dame, at Paris. The Associates, at this time numbering about forty-five, [Dollier de Casson, A.D. 1641-42, MS. Vimont says thirty-five.] with Olier at their head, assembled before the altar of the Virgin, and, by a solemn ceremonial, consecrated Montreal to the Holy Family. Henceforth it was to be called Villemarie de Montreal, [Vimont Relation, 1642, 37. Compare Le Clerc, Établissement de la Foy, II. 49.]—a sacred town, reared to the honor and under the patronage of Christ, St. Joseph, and the Virgin, to be typified by three persons on earth, founders respectively of the three destined communities,—Olier, Dauversière, and a maiden of Troyes, Marguerite Bourgeoys: the seminary to be consecrated to Christ, the Hôtel-Dieu to St. Joseph, and the college to the Virgin.

But we are anticipating a little; for it was several years as yet before Marguerite Bourgeoys took an active part in the work of Montreal. She was the daughter of a respectable tradesman, and was now twenty-two years of age. Her portrait has come down to us; and her face is a mirror of frankness, loyalty, and womanly tenderness. Her qualities were those of good sense, conscientiousness, and a warm heart. She had known no miracles, ecstasies, or trances; and though afterwards, when her religious susceptibilities had reached a fuller development, a few such are recorded of her, yet even the Abbé Faillon, with the best intentions, can credit her with but a meagre allowance of these celestial favors. Though in the midst of visionaries, she distrusted the supernatural, and avowed her belief, that, in His government of the world, God does not often set aside its ordinary laws. Her religion was of the affections, and was manifested in an absorbing devotion to duty. She had felt no vocation to the cloister, but had taken the vow of chastity, and was attached, as an externe, to the Sisters of the Congregation of Troyes, who were fevered with eagerness to go to Canada. Marguerite, however, was content to wait until there was a prospect that she could do good by going; and it was not till the year 1653, that renouncing an inheritance, and giving all she had to the poor, she embarked for the savage scene of her labors. To this day, in crowded school-rooms of Montreal and Quebec, fit monuments of her unobtrusive virtue, her successors instruct the children of the poor, and embalm the pleasant memory of Marguerite Bourgeoys. In the martial figure of Maisonneuve, and the fair form of this gentle nun, we find the true heroes of Montreal. [For Marguerite Bourgeoys, see her life by Faillon.]

Maisonneuve, with his forty men and four women, reached Quebec too late to ascend to Montreal that season. They encountered distrust, jealousy, and opposition. The agents of the Company of the Hundred Associates looked on them askance; and the Governor of Quebec, Montmagny, saw a rival governor in Maisonneuve. Every means was used to persuade the adventurers to abandon their project, and settle at Quebec. Montmagny called a council of the principal persons of his colony, who gave it as their opinion that the new-comers had better exchange Montreal for the Island of Orleans, where they would be in a position to give and receive succor; while, by persisting in their first design, they would expose themselves to destruction, and be of use to nobody. [Juchereau, 32; Faillon, Colonie Française, I. 423.] Maisonneuve, who was present, expressed his surprise that they should assume to direct his affairs. "I have not come here," he said, "to deliberate, but to act. It is my duty and my honor to found a colony at Montreal; and I would go, if every tree were an Iroquois!" [La Tour, Mémoire de Laval, Liv. VIII; Belmont, Histoire du Canada, 3.]

At Quebec there was little ability and no inclination to shelter the new colonists for the winter; and they would have fared ill, but for the generosity of M. Puiseaux, who lived not far distant, at a place called St. Michel. This devout and most hospitable person made room for them all in his rough, but capacious dwelling. Their neighbors were the hospital nuns, then living at the mission of Sillery, in a substantial, but comfortless house of stone; where, amidst destitution, sickness, and irrepressible disgust at the filth of the savages whom they had in charge, they were laboring day and night with devoted assiduity. Among the minor ills which beset them were the eccentricities of one of their lay sisters, crazed with religious enthusiasm, who had the care of their poultry and domestic animals, of which she was accustomed to inquire, one by one, if they loved God; when, not receiving an immediate answer in the affirmative, she would instantly put them to death, telling them that their impiety deserved no better fate. [Juchereau, 45. A great mortification to these excellent nuns was the impossibility of keeping their white dresses clean among their Indian patients, so that they were forced to dye them with butternut juice. They were the *Hospitalières* who had come over in 1639.]

At St. Michel, Maisonneuve employed his men in building boats to ascend to Montreal, and in various other labors for the behoof of the future colony. Thus the winter wore away; but, as celestial minds are not exempt from ire, Montmagny and Maisonneuve fell into a quarrel. The twenty-fifth of January was Maisonneuve's *fête* day; and, as he was greatly beloved by his followers, they resolved to celebrate the occasion. Accordingly, an hour and a half before daylight, they made a general discharge of their muskets and cannon. The sound reached Quebec, two or three miles distant, startling the Governor from his morning slumbers; and his indignation was redoubled when he heard it again at night: for Maisonneuve, pleased at the attachment of his men, had feasted them and warmed their hearts with a distribution of wine. Montmagny, jealous of his authority, resented these demonstrations as an infraction of it, affirming that they had no right to fire their pieces without his consent; and, arresting the principal offender, one Jean Gory, he put him in irons. On being released, a few days after, his companions welcomed him with great rejoicing, and Maisonneuve gave them all a feast. He himself came in during the festivity, drank the health of the company, shook hands with the late prisoner, placed him at the head of the table, and addressed him as follows:—

"Jean Gory, you have been put in irons for me: you had the pain, and I the affront. For that, I add ten crowns to your wages." Then, turning to the others: "My boys," he said, "though Jean Gory has been misused, you must not lose heart for that, but drink, all of you, to the health of the man in irons. When we are once at Montreal, we shall be our own masters, and can fire our cannon when we please." [Documents Divers, MSS., now or lately in possession of G. B. Faribault, Esq.; Ferland, Notes sur les Registres de N. D. de Québec, 25; Faillon, La Colonie Française, I. 433.]

Montmagny was wroth when this was reported to him; and, on the ground that what had passed was "contrary to the service of the King and the authority of the Governor," he summoned Gory and six others before him, and put them separately under oath. Their evidence failed to establish a case against their commander; but thenceforth there was great coldness between the powers of Quebec and Montreal.

Early in May, Maisonneuve and his followers embarked. They had gained an unexpected recruit during the winter, in the person of Madame de la Peltrie. The piety, the novelty, and the romance of their enterprise, all had their charms for the fair enthusiast; and an irresistible impulse—imputed by a slandering historian to the levity of her sex [La Tour, Mémoire de Laval, Liv. VIII.]—urged her to share their fortunes. Her zeal was more admired by the Montrealists whom she joined than by the Ursulines whom she abandoned. She carried off all the furniture she had lent them, and left them in the utmost destitution. [Charlevoix, Vie de Marie de l'Incarnation, 279; Casgrain, Vie de Marie de l'Incarnation, 333.] Nor did she remain quiet after reaching Montreal, but was presently seized with a longing to visit the Hurons, and preach the Faith in person to those benighted heathen. It needed all the eloquence of a Jesuit, lately returned from that most arduous mission, to convince her that the attempt would be as useless as rash. [St. Thomas, Life of Madame de la Peltrie, 98.]

It was the eighth of May when Maisonneuve and his followers embarked at St. Michel; and as the boats, deep-laden with men, arms, and stores, moved slowly on their way, the forest, with leaves just opening in the warmth of spring, lay on their right hand and on their left, in a flattering semblance of tranquillity and peace. But behind woody islets, in tangled thickets and damp ravines, and in the shade and stillness of the columned woods, lurked everywhere a danger and a terror.

What shall we say of these adventurers of Montreal,—of these who bestowed their wealth, and, far more, of these who sacrificed their peace and risked their lives, on an enterprise at once so romantic and so devout? Surrounded as they were with illusions, false lights, and false shadows,—breathing an atmosphere of miracle,—compassed about with angels and devils,—urged with stimulants most powerful, though unreal,—their minds drugged, as it were, to preternatural excitement,—it is very difficult to judge of them. High merit, without doubt, there was in some of their number; but one may beg to be spared the attempt to measure or define it. To estimate a virtue involved in conditions so anomalous demands, perhaps, a judgment more than human.

The Roman Church, sunk in disease and corruption when the Reformation began, was roused by that fierce trumpet-blast to purge and brace herself anew. Unable to advance, she drew back to the fresher and comparatively purer life of the past; and the fervors of mediæval Christianity were renewed in the sixteenth century. In many of its aspects, this enterprise of Montreal belonged to the time of the first Crusades. The spirit of Godfrey de Bouillon lived again in Chomedey de Maisonneuve; and in Marguerite Bourgeoys was realized that fair ideal of Christian womanhood, a flower of Earth expanding in the rays of Heaven, which soothed with gentle influence the wildness of a barbarous age.

On the seventeenth of May, 1642, Maisonneuve's little flotilla—a pinnace, a flat-bottomed craft moved by sails, and two row-boats [Dollier de Casson, A.D. 1641-42, MS.]—approached Montreal; and all on board raised in unison a hymn of praise. Montmagny was with them, to deliver the island, in behalf of the Company of the Hundred Associates, to Maisonneuve, representative of the Associates of Montreal. [Le Clerc, II. 50, 51.] And here, too, was Father Vimont, Superior of the missions; for the Jesuits had been prudently invited to accept the spiritual charge of the young colony. On the following day, they glided along the green and solitary shores now thronged with the life of a busy city, and landed on the spot which Champlain, thirty-one years before, had chosen as the fit site of a settlement. ["Pioneers of France," 333. It was the Place Royale of Champlain.] It was a tongue or triangle of land, formed by the junction of a rivulet with the St. Lawrence, and known afterwards as Point Callière. The rivulet was bordered by a meadow, and beyond rose the forest with its vanguard of scattered trees. Early spring flowers were blooming in the young grass, and birds of varied plumage flitted among the boughs. [Dollier de Casson, A.D. 1641-42, MS.]

Maisonneuve sprang ashore, and fell on his knees. His followers imitated his example; and all joined their voices in enthusiastic songs of thanksgiving. Tents, baggage, arms, and stores were landed. An altar was raised on a pleasant spot near at hand; and Mademoiselle Mance, with Madame de la Peltrie, aided by her servant, Charlotte Barré, decorated it with a taste which was the admiration of the beholders. [Morin, Annales, MS., cited by Faillon, La Colonie Française, I. 440; also Dollier de Casson, A.D. 1641-42, MS.] Now all the company gathered before the shrine. Here stood Vimont, in the rich vestments of his office. Here were the two ladies, with their servant; Montmagny, no very willing spectator; and Maisonneuve, a warlike figure, erect and tall, his men clustering around him,—

soldiers, sailors, artisans, and laborers,—all alike soldiers at need. They kneeled in reverent silence as the Host was raised aloft; and when the rite was over, the priest turned and addressed them:—

"You are a grain of mustard-seed, that shall rise and grow till its branches overshadow the earth. You are few, but your work is the work of God. His smile is on you, and your children shall fill the Land." [Dollier de Casson, MS., as above. Vimont, in the Relation of 1642, p. 87, briefly mentions the ceremony.]

The afternoon waned; the sun sank behind the western forest, and twilight came on. Fireflies were twinkling over the darkened meadow. They caught them, tied them with threads into shining festoons, and hung them before the altar, where the Host remained exposed. Then they pitched their tents, lighted their bivouac fires, stationed their guards, and lay down to rest. Such was the birth-night of Montreal.

[The Associates of Montreal published, in 1643, a thick pamphlet in quarto, entitled Les Véritables Motifs de Messieurs et Dames de la Société de Notre-Dame de Montréal, pour la Conversion des Sauvages de la Nouvelle France. It was written as an answer to aspersions cast upon them, apparently by persons attached to the great Company of New France known as the "Hundred Associates," and affords a curious exposition of the spirit of their enterprise. It is excessively rare; but copies of the essential portions are before me. The following is a characteristic extract:—

"Vous dites que l'entreprise de Montréal est d'une dépense infinie, plus convenable à un roi qu'a quelques particuliers, trop faibles pour la soutenir; & vous alléguez encore les périls de la navigation & les naufrages qui peuvent la ruiner. Vous avez mieux rencontré que vous ne pensiez, en disant que c'est une œuvre de roi, puisque le Roi des rois s'en mêle, lui à qui obéissent la mer & les vents. Nous ne craignons donc pas les naufrages; il n'en suscitera que lorsque nous en aurons besoin, & qu'il sera plus expédient pour sa gloire, que nous cherchons uniquement. Comment avez-vous pu mettre dans votre esprit qu'appuyés de nos propres forces, nous eussions présumé de penser à un si glorieux dessein? Si Dieu n'est point dans l'affaire de Montréal, si c'est une invention humaine, ne vous en mettez point en peine, elle ne durera guère. Ce que vous prédisez arrivera, & quelque chose de pire encore; mais si

Dieu l'a ainsi voulu, qui êtes-vous pour lui contredire? C'était la reflexion que le docteur Gamaliel faisait aux Juifs, en faveur des Apôtres; pour vous, qui ne pouvez ni croire, ni faire, laissez les autres en liberté de faire ce qu'ils croient que Dieu demande d'eux. Vous assurez qu'il ne se fait plus de miracles; mais qui vous l'a dit? où cela est-il écrit? Jésus-Christ assure, au contraire, que ceux qui auront autant de Foi qu'un grain de senevé, feront, en son nom, des miracles plus grands que ceux qu'il a faits lui-même. Depuis quand êtes-vous les directeurs des operations divines, pour les réduire à certains temps & dans la conduite ordinaire? Tant de saints mouvements, d'inspirations & de vues intérieures, qu'il lui plait de donner à quelques âmes dont il se sert pour l'avancement de cette œuvre, sont des marques de son bon plaisir. Jusqu'-ici, il a pourvu au nécessaire; nous ne voulons point d'abondance, & nous espérons que sa Providence continuera."]

Is this true history, or a romance of Christian chivalry? It is both.

CHAPTER XVI.

1641-1644.

ISAAC JOGUES.

THE IROQUOIS WAR.—JOGUES.—HIS CAPTURE.—HIS
JOURNEY TO THE MOHAWKS.—LAKE GEORGE.—THE
MOHAWK TOWNS.—THE MISSIONARY TORTURED.—
DEATH OF GOUPIL.—MISERY OF JOGUES.—THE
MOHAWK "BABYLON."—FORT ORANGE.—ESCAPE OF
JOGUES.—MANHATTAN.—THE VOYAGE TO FRANCE.—
JOGUES AMONG HIS BRETHREN.—HE RETURNS TO
CANADA.

The waters of the St. Lawrence rolled through a virgin
wilderness, where, in the vastness of the lonely woodlands, civilized
man found a precarious harborage at three points only,—at Quebec,
at Montreal, and at Three Rivers. Here and in the scattered missions
was the whole of New France,—a population of some three
hundred souls in all. And now, over these miserable settlements,
rose a war-cloud of frightful portent.

It was thirty-two years since Champlain had first attacked
the Iroquois. [See "Pioneers of France," 318.] They had nursed
their wrath for more than a generation, and at length their hour
was come. The Dutch traders at Fort Orange, now Albany, had
supplied them with fire-arms. The Mohawks, the most easterly
of the Iroquois nations, had, among their seven or eight hundred
warriors, no less than three hundred armed with the arquebuse, a

weapon somewhat like the modern carbine.[1] They were masters of the thunderbolts which, in the hands of Champlain, had struck terror into their hearts.

We have surveyed in the introductory chapter the character and organization of this ferocious people; their confederacy of five nations, bound together by a peculiar tie of clanship; their chiefs, half hereditary, half elective; their government, an oligarchy in form and a democracy in spirit; their minds, thoroughly savage, yet marked here and there with traits of a vigorous development. The war which they had long waged with the Hurons was carried on by the Senecas and the other Western nations of their league; while the conduct of hostilities against the French and their Indian allies in Lower Canada was left to the Mohawks. In parties of from ten to a hundred or more, they would leave their towns on the River Mohawk, descend Lake Champlain and the River Richelieu, lie in ambush on the banks of the St. Lawrence, and attack the passing boats or canoes. Sometimes they hovered about the fortifications of Quebec and Three Rivers, killing stragglers, or luring armed parties into ambuscades. They followed like hounds on the trail of travellers and hunters; broke in upon unguarded camps at midnight; and lay in wait, for days and weeks, to intercept the Huron traders on their yearly descent to Quebec. Had they joined to their ferocious courage the discipline and the military knowledge that belong to civilization, they could easily have blotted out New France from the map, and made the banks of the St. Lawrence once more a solitude; but, though the most formidable of savages, they were savages only.

In the early morning of the second of August, 1642, [For the date, see Lalemant, Relation des Hurons, 1647, 18.] twelve Huron canoes were moving slowly along the northern shore of the expansion of the St. Lawrence known as the Lake of St. Peter. There were on board about forty persons, including four Frenchmen, one of them being the Jesuit, Isaac Jogues, whom we have already

---

1   Vimont, Relation, 1643, 62. The Mohawks were the Agniés, or Agneronons, of the old French writers.

      According to the Journal of New Netherland, a contemporary Dutch document, (see Colonial Documents of New York, I. 179,) the Dutch at Fort Orange had supplied the Mohawks with four hundred guns; the profits of the trade, which was free to the settlers, blinding them to the danger.

followed on his missionary journey to the towns of the Tobacco Nation. In the interval he had not been idle. During the last autumn, (1641,) he, with Father Charles Raymbault, had passed along the shore of Lake Huron northward, entered the strait through which Lake Superior discharges itself, pushed on as far as the Sault Sainte Marie, and preached the Faith to two thousand Ojibwas, and other Algonquins there assembled. [Lalemant, Relation des Hurons, 1642, 97.] He was now on his return from a far more perilous errand. The Huron mission was in a state of destitution. There was need of clothing for the priests, of vessels for the altars, of bread and wine for the eucharist, of writing materials,—in short, of everything; and, early in the summer of the present year, Jogues had descended to Three Rivers and Quebec with the Huron traders, to procure the necessary supplies. He had accomplished his task, and was on his way back to the mission. With him were a few Huron converts, and among them a noted Christian chief, Eustache Ahatsistari. Others of the party were in course of instruction for baptism; but the greater part were heathen, whose canoes were deeply laden with the proceeds of their bargains with the French fur-traders.

Jogues sat in one of the leading canoes. He was born at Orleans in 1607, and was thirty-five years of age. His oval face and the delicate mould of his features indicated a modest, thoughtful, and refined nature. He was constitutionally timid, with a sensitive conscience and great religious susceptibilities. He was a finished scholar, and might have gained a literary reputation; but he had chosen another career, and one for which he seemed but ill fitted. Physically, however, he was well matched with his work; for, though his frame was slight, he was so active, that none of the Indians could surpass him in running.

[Buteux, Narré de la Prise du Père Jogues, MS.; Mémoire touchant le Père Jogues, MS.

There is a portrait of him prefixed to Mr. Shea's admirable edition in quarto of Jogues's Novum Belgium.]

With him were two young men, René Goupil and Guillaume Couture, *donnés* of the mission,—that is to say, laymen who, from a religious motive and without pay, had attached themselves to the service of the Jesuits. Goupil had formerly entered upon the Jesuit novitiate at Paris, but failing health had obliged him to leave it. As soon as he was able, he came to Canada, offered his services to the

Superior of the mission, was employed for a time in the humblest offices, and afterwards became an attendant at the hospital. At length, to his delight, he received permission to go up to the Hurons, where the surgical skill which he had acquired was greatly needed; and he was now on his way thither. [Jogues, Notice sur René Goupil.] His companion, Couture, was a man of intelligence and vigor, and of a character equally disinterested. [For an account of him, see Ferland, Notes sur les Registres de N. D. de Québec, 83 (1863).] Both were, like Jogues, in the foremost canoes; while the fourth Frenchman was with the unconverted Hurons, in the rear.

The twelve canoes had reached the western end of the Lake of St. Peter, where it is filled with innumerable islands. [Buteux, Narré de le Prise du Père Jogues, MS. This document leaves no doubt as to the locality.] The forest was close on their right, they kept near the shore to avoid the current, and the shallow water before them was covered with a dense growth of tall bulrushes. Suddenly the silence was frightfully broken. The war-whoop rose from among the rushes, mingled with the reports of guns and the whistling of bullets; and several Iroquois canoes, filled with warriors, pushed out from their concealment, and bore down upon Jogues and his companions. The Hurons in the rear were seized with a shameful panic. They leaped ashore; left canoes, baggage, and weapons; and fled into the woods. The French and the Christian Hurons made fight for a time; but when they saw another fleet of canoes approaching from the opposite shores or islands, they lost heart, and those escaped who could. Goupil was seized amid triumphant yells, as were also several of the Huron converts. Jogues sprang into the bulrushes, and might have escaped; but when he saw Goupil and the neophytes in the clutches of the Iroquois, he had no heart to abandon them, but came out from his hiding-place, and gave himself up to the astonished victors. A few of them had remained to guard the prisoners; the rest were chasing the fugitives. Jogues mastered his agony, and began to baptize those of the captive converts who needed baptism.

Couture had eluded pursuit; but when he thought of Jogues and of what perhaps awaited him, he resolved to share his fate, and, turning, retraced his steps. As he approached, five Iroquois ran forward to meet him; and one of them snapped his gun at his breast, but it missed fire. In his confusion and excitement, Couture fired his own piece, and laid the savage dead. The remaining four sprang upon him, stripped off all his clothing, tore away his finger-nails with their teeth, gnawed his fingers with the fury of famished dogs, and thrust a sword through one of his hands. Jogues broke from his guards, and, rushing to his friend, threw his arms about his neck. The Iroquois dragged him away, beat him with their fists and war-clubs till he was senseless, and, when he revived, lacerated his fingers with their teeth, as they had done those of Couture. Then they turned upon Goupil, and treated him with the same ferocity. The Huron prisoners were left for the present unharmed. More of them were brought in every moment, till at length the number of captives amounted in all to twenty-two, while three Hurons had been killed in the fight and pursuit. The Iroquois, about seventy in number, now embarked with their prey; but not until they had knocked on the head an old Huron, whom Jogues, with his mangled hands, had just baptized, and who refused to leave the place. Then, under a burning sun, they crossed to the spot on which the town of Sorel now stands at the mouth of the river Richelieu, where they encamped.

[The above, with much of what follows, rests on three documents. The first is a long letter, written in Latin, by Jogues, to the Father Provincial at Paris. It is dated at Rensselaerswyck (Albany), Aug. 5, 1643, and is preserved in the Societas Jesu Militans of Tanner, and in the Mortes Illustres et Gesta eorum de Societate Jesu, etc., of Alegambe. There is a French translation in Martin's Bressani, and an English translation, by Mr. Shea, in the New York Hist. Coll. of 1857. The second document is an old manuscript, entitled Narré de la Prise du Père Jogues. It was written by the Jesuit Buteux, from the lips of Jogues. Father Martin, S.J., in whose custody it was, kindly permitted me to have a copy made from it. Besides these, there is a long account in the Relation des Hurons of 1647, and a briefer one in that of 1644. All these narratives show the strongest internal evidence of truth, and are perfectly concurrent. They are also supported by statements of escaped Huron prisoners, and by several letters and memoirs of the Dutch at Rensselaerswyck.]

Their course was southward, up the River Richelieu and Lake Champlain; thence, by way of Lake George, to the Mohawk towns. The pain and fever of their wounds, and the clouds of mosquitoes, which they could not drive off, left the prisoners no peace by day nor sleep by night. On the eighth day, they learned that a large Iroquois war-party, on their way to Canada, were near at hand; and they soon approached their camp, on a small island near the southern end of Lake Champlain. The warriors, two hundred in number, saluted their victorious countrymen with volleys from their guns; then, armed with clubs and thorny sticks, ranged themselves in two lines, between which the captives were compelled to pass up the side of a rocky hill. On the way, they were beaten with such fury, that Jogues, who was last in the line, fell powerless, drenched in blood and half dead. As the chief man among the French captives, he fared the worst. His hands were again mangled, and fire applied to his body; while the Huron chief, Eustache, was subjected to tortures even more atrocious. When, at night, the exhausted sufferers tried to rest, the young warriors came to lacerate their wounds and pull out their hair and beards.

In the morning they resumed their journey. And now the lake narrowed to the semblance of a tranquil river. Before them was a woody mountain, close on their right a rocky promontory, and between these flowed a stream, the outlet of Lake George. On those rocks, more than a hundred years after, rose the ramparts of Ticonderoga. They landed, shouldered their canoes and baggage, took their way through the woods, passed the spot where the fierce Highlanders and the dauntless regiments of England breasted in vain the storm of lead and fire, and soon reached the shore where Abercrombie landed and Lord Howe fell. First of white men, Jogues and his companions gazed on the romantic lake that bears the name, not of its gentle discoverer, but of the dull Hanoverian king. Like a fair Naiad of the wilderness, it slumbered between the guardian mountains that breathe from crag and forest the stern poetry of war. But all then was solitude; and the clang of trumpets, the roar of cannon, and the deadly crack of the rifle had never as yet awakened their angry echoes.

[Lake George, according to Jogues, was called by the Mohawks "Andiatarocte," or Place where the Lake closes. "Andiataraque" is found on a map of Sanson. Spofford, Gazetteer of New York, article "Lake George," says that it was called "Canideri-oit," or Tail of the Lake. Father Martin, in his notes on Bressani, prefixes to this name that of "Horicon," but gives no original authority.

I have seen an old Latin map on which the name "Horiconi" is set down as belonging to a neighboring tribe. This seems to be only a misprint for "Horicoui," that is, "Irocoui," or "Iroquois." In an old English map, prefixed to the rare tract, A Treatise of New England, the "Lake of Hierocoyes" is laid down. The name "Horicon," as used by Cooper in his Last of the Mohicans, seems to have no sufficient historical foundation. In 1646, the lake, as we shall see, was named "Lac St. Sacrement."]

Again the canoes were launched, and the wild flotilla glided on its way,—now in the shadow of the heights, now on the broad expanse, now among the devious channels of the narrows, beset with woody islets, where the hot air was redolent of the pine, the spruce, and the cedar,—till they neared that tragic shore, where, in the following century, New-England rustics baffled the soldiers of Dieskau, where Montcalm planted his batteries, where the red cross waved so long amid the smoke, and where at length the summer night was hideous with carnage, and an honored name was stained with a memory of blood.

[The allusion is, of course, to the siege of Fort William Henry in 1757, and the ensuing massacre by Montcalm's Indians. Charlevoix, with his usual carelessness, says that Jogues's captors took a circuitous route to avoid enemies. In truth, however, they were not in the slightest danger of meeting any; and they followed the route which, before the present century, was the great highway between Canada and New Holland, or New York.]

The Iroquois landed at or near the future site of Fort William Henry, left their canoes, and, with their prisoners, began their march for the nearest Mohawk town. Each bore his share of the plunder. Even Jogues, though his lacerated hands were in a frightful condition and his body covered with bruises, was forced to stagger on with the rest under a heavy load. He with his fellow-prisoners, and indeed the whole party, were half starved, subsisting chiefly on wild berries. They crossed the upper Hudson, and, in thirteen days after leaving the St. Lawrence, neared the wretched goal of their pilgrimage, a palisaded town, standing on a hill by the banks of the River Mohawk.

The whoops of the victors announced their approach, and the savage hive sent forth its swarms. They thronged the side of the hill, the old and the young, each with a stick, or a slender iron rod, bought from the Dutchmen on the Hudson. They ranged themselves in a double line, reaching upward to the entrance of the town; and through this "narrow road of Paradise," as Jogues calls it, the captives were led in single file, Couture in front, after him a half-score of Hurons, then Goupil, then the remaining Hurons, and at last Jogues. As they passed, they were saluted with yells, screeches, and a tempest of blows. One, heavier than the others, knocked Jogues's breath from his body, and stretched him on the ground; but it was death to lie there, and, regaining his feet, he staggered on with the rest. [This practice of forcing prisoners to "run the gauntlet" was by no means peculiar to the Iroquois, but was common to many tribes.] When they reached the town, the blows ceased, and they were all placed on a scaffold, or high platform, in the middle of the place. The three Frenchmen had fared the worst, and were frightfully disfigured. Goupil, especially, was streaming with blood, and livid with bruises from head to foot.

They were allowed a few minutes to recover their breath, undisturbed, except by the hootings and gibes of the mob below. Then a chief called out, "Come, let us caress these Frenchmen!"— and the crowd, knife in hand, began to mount the scaffold. They ordered a Christian Algonquin woman, a prisoner among them, to cut off Jogues's left thumb, which she did; and a thumb of Goupil was also severed, a clam-shell being used as the instrument, in order to increase the pain. It is needless to specify further the tortures to which they were subjected, all designed to cause the greatest possible suffering without endangering life. At night, they were removed from the scaffold, and placed in one of the houses, each stretched on his back, with his limbs extended, and his ankles and wrists bound fast to stakes driven into the earthen floor. The children now profited by the examples of their parents, and amused themselves by placing live coals and red-hot ashes on the naked bodies of the prisoners, who, bound fast, and covered with wounds and bruises which made every movement a torture, were sometimes unable to shake them off.

In the morning, they were again placed on the scaffold, where, during this and the two following days, they remained exposed to the taunts of the crowd. Then they were led in triumph to the second Mohawk town, and afterwards to the third,[1] suffering at each a repetition of cruelties, the detail of which would be as monotonous as revolting.

In a house in the town of Teonontogen, Jogues was hung by the wrists between two of the upright poles which supported the structure, in such a manner that his feet could not touch the ground; and thus he remained for some fifteen minutes, in extreme torture, until, as he was on the point of swooning, an Indian, with an impulse of pity, cut the cords and released him. While they were in this town, four fresh Huron prisoners, just taken, were brought in, and placed on the scaffold with the rest. Jogues, in the midst of his pain and exhaustion, took the opportunity to convert them. An ear of green corn was thrown to him for food, and he discovered a few rain-drops clinging to the husks. With these he baptized two of the Hurons. The remaining two received baptism soon after from a brook which the prisoners crossed on the way to another town.

Couture, though he had incensed the Indians by killing one of their warriors, had gained their admiration by his bravery; and, after torturing him most savagely, they adopted him into one of their families, in place of a dead relative. Thenceforth he was comparatively safe. Jogues and Goupil were less fortunate. Three of the Hurons had been burned to death, and they expected to share their fate. A council was held to pronounce their doom; but dissensions arose, and no result was reached. They were led back to the first village, where they remained, racked with suspense and half dead with exhaustion. Jogues, however, lost no opportunity to baptize dying infants, while Goupil taught children to make the sign of the cross. On one occasion, he made the sign on the forehead of a child, grandson of an Indian in whose lodge they lived. The superstition of the old savage was aroused. Some Dutchmen had told him that the sign of the cross came from the Devil, and would cause mischief. He thought that Goupil was bewitching the child;

---

1   The Mohawks had but three towns. The first, and the lowest on the river, was Osseruenon; the second, two miles above, was Andagaron; and the third, Teonontogen: or, as Megapolensis, in his Sketch of the Mohawks, writes the names, Asserué, Banagiro, and Thenondiogo. They all seem to have been fortified in the Iroquois manner, and their united population was thirty-five hundred, or somewhat more. At a later period, 1720, there were still three towns, named respectively Teahtontaioga, Ganowauga, and Ganeganaga. See the map in Morgan, League of the Iroquois.

and, resolving to rid himself of so dangerous a guest, applied for aid to two young braves. Jogues and Goupil, clad in their squalid garb of tattered skins, were soon after walking together in the forest that adjoined the town, consoling themselves with prayer, and mutually exhorting each other to suffer patiently for the sake of Christ and the Virgin, when, as they were returning, reciting their rosaries, they met the two young Indians, and read in their sullen visages an augury of ill. The Indians joined them, and accompanied them to the entrance of the town, where one of the two, suddenly drawing a hatchet from beneath his blanket, struck it into the head of Goupil, who fell, murmuring the name of Christ. Jogues dropped on his knees, and, bowing his head in prayer, awaited the blow, when the murderer ordered him to get up and go home. He obeyed but not until he had given absolution to his still breathing friend, and presently saw the lifeless body dragged through the town amid hootings and rejoicings.

Jogues passed a night of anguish and desolation, and in the morning, reckless of life, set forth in search of Goupil's remains. "Where are you going so fast?" demanded the old Indian, his master. "Do you not see those fierce young braves, who are watching to kill you?" Jogues persisted, and the old man asked another Indian to go with him as a protector. The corpse had been flung into a neighboring ravine, at the bottom of which ran a torrent; and here, with the Indian's help, Jogues found it, stripped naked, and gnawed by dogs. He dragged it into the water, and covered it with stones to save it from further mutilation, resolving to return alone on the following day and secretly bury it. But with the night there came a storm; and when, in the gray of the morning, Jogues descended to the brink of the stream, he found it a rolling, turbid flood, and the body was nowhere to be seen. Had the Indians or the torrent borne it away? Jogues waded into the cold current; it was the first of October; he sounded it with his feet and with his stick; he searched the rocks, the thicket, the forest; but all in vain. Then, crouched by the pitiless stream, he mingled his tears with its waters, and, in a voice broken with groans, chanted the service of the dead. [Jogues in Tanner, Societas Militans, 519; Bressani, 216; Lalemant, Relation, 1647, 25, 26; Buteux, Narré, MS.; Jogues, Notice sur René Goupil.]

The Indians, it proved, and not the flood, had robbed him of the remains of his friend. Early in the spring, when the snows were melting in the woods, he was told by Mohawk children that the body was lying, where it had been flung, in a lonely spot lower down the stream. He went to seek it; found the scattered bones, stripped by the foxes and the birds; and, tenderly gathering them up, hid them in a hollow tree, hoping that a day might come when he could give them a Christian burial in consecrated ground.

After the murder of Goupil, Jogues's life hung by a hair. He lived in hourly expectation of the tomahawk, and would have welcomed it as a boon. By signs and words, he was warned that his hour was near; but, as he never shunned his fate, it fled from him, and each day, with renewed astonishment, he found himself still among the living.

Late in the autumn, a party of the Indians set forth on their yearly deer-hunt, and Jogues was ordered to go with them. Shivering and half famished, he followed them through the chill November forest, and shared their wild bivouac in the depths of the wintry desolation. The game they took was devoted to Areskoui, their god, and eaten in his honor. Jogues would not taste the meat offered to a demon; and thus he starved in the midst of plenty. At night, when the kettle was slung, and the savage crew made merry around their fire, he crouched in a corner of the hut, gnawed by hunger, and pierced to the bone with cold. They thought his presence unpropitious to their hunting, and the women especially hated him. His demeanor at once astonished and incensed his masters. He brought them fire-wood, like a squaw; he did their bidding without a murmur, and patiently bore their abuse; but when they mocked at his God, and laughed at his devotions, their slave assumed an air and tone of authority, and sternly rebuked them. [Lalemant, Relation, 1647, 41.]

He would sometimes escape from "this Babylon," as he calls the hut, and wander in the forest, telling his beads and repeating passages of Scripture. In a remote and lonely spot, he cut the bark in the form of a cross from the trunk of a great tree; and here he made his prayers. This living martyr, half clad in shaggy furs, kneeling on the snow among the icicled rocks and beneath the gloomy pines, bowing in adoration before the emblem of the faith in which was his only consolation and his only hope, is alike a theme for the pen and a subject for the pencil.

The Indians at last grew tired of him, and sent him back to the village. Here he remained till the middle of March, baptizing infants and trying to convert adults. He told them of the sun, moon, planets, and stars. They listened with interest; but when from astronomy he passed to theology, he spent his breath in vain. In March, the old man with whom he lived set forth for his spring fishing, taking with him his squaw, and several children. Jogues also was of the party. They repaired to a lake, perhaps Lake Saratoga, four days distant. Here they subsisted for some time on frogs, the entrails of fish, and other garbage. Jogues passed his days in the forest, repeating his prayers, and carving the name of Jesus on trees, as a terror to the demons of the wilderness. A messenger at length arrived from the town; and on the following day, under the pretence that signs of an enemy had been seen, the party broke up their camp, and returned home in hot haste. The messenger had brought tidings that a war-party, which had gone out against the French, had been defeated and destroyed, and that the whole population were clamoring to appease their grief by torturing Jogues to death. This was the true cause of the sudden and mysterious return; but when they reached the town, other tidings had arrived. The missing warriors were safe, and on their way home in triumph with a large number of prisoners. Again Jogues's life was spared; but he was forced to witness the torture and butchery of the converts and allies of the French. Existence became unendurable to him, and he longed to die. War-parties were continually going out. Should they be defeated and cut off, he would pay the forfeit at the stake; and if they came back, as they usually did, with booty and prisoners, he was doomed to see his countrymen and their Indian friends mangled, burned, and devoured.

Jogues had shown no disposition to escape, and great liberty was therefore allowed him. He went from town to town, giving absolution to the Christian captives, and converting and baptizing the heathen. On one occasion, he baptized a woman in the midst of the fire, under pretence of lifting a cup of water to her parched lips. There was no lack of objects for his zeal. A single war-party returned from the Huron country with nearly a hundred prisoners, who were distributed among the Iroquois towns, and the greater part burned.[1] Of the children of the Mohawks and their neighbors, he had baptized, before August, about seventy; insomuch that he began to regard his captivity as a Providential interposition for the saving of souls.

At the end of July, he went with a party of Indians to a fishing-place on the Hudson, about twenty miles below Fort Orange. While here, he learned that another war-party had lately returned with prisoners, two of whom had been burned to death at Osseruenon. On this, his conscience smote him that he had not remained in the town to give the sufferers absolution or baptism; and he begged leave of the old woman who had him in charge to return at the first opportunity. A canoe soon after went up the river with some of the Iroquois, and he was allowed to go in it. When they reached Rensselaerswyck, the Indians landed to trade with the Dutch, and took Jogues with them.

The centre of this rude little settlement was Fort Orange, a miserable structure of logs, standing on a spot now within the limits of the city of Albany. [The site of the Phœnix Hotel.—Note by Mr. Shea to Jogues's Novum Belgium.] It contained several houses and other buildings; and behind it was a small church, recently erected, and serving as the abode of the pastor, Dominie Megapolensis, known in our day as the writer of an interesting, though short, account of the Mohawks. Some twenty-five or thirty houses, roughly built of boards and roofed with thatch, were scattered at intervals on or near the borders of the Hudson, above and below the fort. Their inhabitants, about a hundred in number, were for the most part rude Dutch farmers, tenants of Van Rensselaer, the patroon, or lord of the manor. They raised wheat, of which they made beer, and oats, with which they fed their numerous horses. They traded, too, with the Indians, who profited greatly by the competition among them, receiving guns, knives, axes, kettles, cloth, and beads, at moderate rates, in exchange for their furs.[2] The

---

1   The Dutch clergyman, Megapolensis, at this time living at Fort Orange, bears the strongest testimony to the ferocity with which his friends, the Mohawks, treated their prisoners. He mentions the same modes of torture which Jogues describes, and is very explicit as to cannibalism. "The common people," he says, "eat the arms, buttocks, and trunk; but the chiefs eat the head and the heart." (Short Sketch of the Mohawk Indians.) This feast was of a religious character.

2   Jogues, Novum Belgium; Barnes, Settlement of Albany, 50-55; O'Callaghan, New Netherland, Chap. VI.

Dutch were on excellent terms with their red neighbors, met them in the forest without the least fear, and sometimes intermarried with them. They had known of Jogues's captivity, and, to their great honor, had made efforts for his release, offering for that purpose goods to a considerable value, but without effect.[1]

At Fort Orange Jogues heard startling news. The Indians of the village where he lived were, he was told, enraged against him, and determined to burn him. About the first of July, a war-party had set out for Canada, and one of the warriors had offered to Jogues to be the bearer of a letter from him to the French commander at Three Rivers, thinking probably to gain some advantage under cover of a parley. Jogues knew that the French would be on their guard; and he felt it his duty to lose no opportunity of informing them as to the state of affairs among the Iroquois. A Dutchman gave him a piece of paper; and he wrote a letter, in a jargon of Latin, French, and Huron, warning his countrymen to be on their guard, as war-parties were constantly going out, and they could hope for no respite from attack until late in the autumn. [See a French rendering of the letter in Vimont, Relation, 1643, p. 75.] When the Iroquois reached the mouth of the River Richelieu, where a small fort had been built by the French the preceding summer, the messenger asked for a parley, and gave Jogues's letter to the commander of the post, who, after reading it, turned his cannon on the savages. They fled in dismay, leaving behind them their baggage and some of their guns; and, returning home in a fury, charged Jogues with having caused their discomfiture. Jogues had expected this result, and was prepared to meet it; but several of the principal Dutch settlers, and among them Van Curler, who had made the previous attempt to rescue him, urged that his death was certain, if he returned to the Indian town, and advised him to make his escape. In the Hudson, opposite the settlement, lay a small Dutch vessel nearly ready to sail. Van Curler offered him a passage in her

---

On the relations of the Mohawks and Dutch, see Megapolensis, Short Sketch of the Mohawk Indians, and portions of the letter of Jogues to his Superior, dated Rensselaerswyck, Aug. 30, 1643.

1   See a long letter of Arendt Van Curler (Corlaer) to Van Rensselaer, June 16, 1643, in O'Callaghan's New Netherland, Appendix L. "We persuaded them so far," writes Van Curler, "that they promised not to kill them . . . The French captives ran screaming after us, and besought us to do all in our power to release them out of the hands of the barbarians."

to Bordeaux or Rochelle,—representing that the opportunity was too good to be lost, and making light of the prisoner's objection, that a connivance in his escape on the part of the Dutch would excite the resentment of the Indians against them. Jogues thanked him warmly; but, to his amazement, asked for a night to consider the matter, and take counsel of God in prayer.

He spent the night in great agitation, tossed by doubt, and full of anxiety lest his self-love should beguile him from his duty. [Buteux, Narré, MS.] Was it not possible that the Indians might spare his life, and that, by a timely drop of water, he might still rescue souls from torturing devils, and eternal fires of perdition? On the other hand, would he not, by remaining to meet a fate almost inevitable, incur the guilt of suicide? And even should he escape torture and death, could he hope that the Indians would again permit him to instruct and baptize their prisoners? Of his French companions, one, Goupil, was dead; while Couture had urged Jogues to flight, saying that he would then follow his example, but that, so long as the Father remained a prisoner, he, Couture, would share his fate. Before morning, Jogues had made his decision. God, he thought, would be better pleased should he embrace the opportunity given him. He went to find his Dutch friends, and, with a profusion of thanks, accepted their offer. They told him that a boat should be left for him on the shore, and that he must watch his time, and escape in it to the vessel, where he would be safe.

He and his Indian masters were lodged together in a large building, like a barn, belonging to a Dutch farmer. It was a hundred feet long, and had no partition of any kind. At one end the farmer kept his cattle; at the other he slept with his wife, a Mohawk squaw, and his children, while his Indian guests lay on the floor in the middle. [Buteux, Narré, MS.] As he is described as one of the principal persons of the colony, it is clear that the civilization of Rensselaerswyck was not high.

In the evening, Jogues, in such a manner as not to excite the suspicion of the Indians, went out to reconnoitre. There was a fence around the house, and, as he was passing it, a large dog belonging to the farmer flew at him, and bit him very severely in the leg. The Dutchman, hearing the noise, came out with a light, led Jogues back into the building, and bandaged his wound. He seemed to have some suspicion of the prisoner's design; for, fearful perhaps that his escape might exasperate the Indians, he made fast the door in such a manner that it could not readily be opened. Jogues now lay down among the Indians, who, rolled in their blankets, were stretched around him. He was fevered with excitement; and the agitation of his mind, joined to the pain of his wound, kept him awake all night. About dawn, while the Indians were still asleep, a laborer in the employ of the farmer came in with a lantern, and Jogues, who spoke no Dutch, gave him to understand by signs that he needed his help and guidance. The man was disposed to aid him, silently led the way out, quieted the dogs, and showed him the path to the river. It was more than half a mile distant, and the way was rough and broken. Jogues was greatly exhausted, and his wounded limb gave him such pain that he walked with the utmost difficulty. When he reached the shore, the day was breaking, and he found, to his dismay, that the ebb of the tide had left the boat high and dry. He shouted to the vessel, but no one heard him. His desperation gave him strength; and, by working the boat to and fro, he pushed it at length, little by little, into the water, entered it, and rowed to the vessel. The Dutch sailors received him kindly, and hid him in the bottom of the hold, placing a large box over the hatchway.

He remained two days, half stifled, in this foul lurking-place, while the Indians, furious at his escape, ransacked the settlement in vain to find him. They came off to the vessel, and so terrified the officers, that Jogues was sent on shore at night, and led to the fort. Here he was hidden in the garret of a house occupied by a miserly old man, to whose charge he was consigned. Food was sent to him; but, as his host appropriated the larger part to himself, Jogues was nearly starved. There was a compartment of his garret, separated from the rest by a partition of boards. Here the old Dutchman, who, like many others of the settlers, carried on a trade with the Mohawks, kept a quantity of goods for that purpose; and hither he often brought his customers. The boards of the partition had shrunk, leaving wide crevices; and Jogues could plainly see the Indians, as they passed between him and the light. They, on their part, might as easily have seen him, if he had not, when he heard them entering the house, hidden himself behind some barrels in the corner, where he would sometimes remain crouched for hours, in a constrained and painful posture, half suffocated with heat, and afraid to move a limb. His wounded leg began to show dangerous symptoms; but he was relieved by the care of a Dutch surgeon of the fort. The minister, Megapolensis, also visited him, and did all in his power for the comfort of his Catholic brother, with whom he seems to have been well pleased, and whom he calls "a very learned scholar." [Megapolensis, A Short Sketch of the Mohawk Indians.]

When Jogues had remained for six weeks in this hiding-place, his Dutch friends succeeded in satisfying his Indian masters by the payment of a large ransom. [Lettre de Jogues à Lalemant, Rennes, Jan. 6, 1644.—See Relation, 1643, p. 79.—Goods were given the Indians to the value of three hundred livres.] A vessel from Manhattan, now New York, soon after brought up an order from the Director-General, Kieft, that he should be sent to him. Accordingly he was placed in a small vessel, which carried him down the Hudson. The Dutch on board treated him with great kindness; and, to do him honor, named after him one of the islands in the river. At Manhattan he found a dilapidated fort, garrisoned by sixty soldiers, and containing a stone church and the Director-General's house, together with storehouses and barracks. Near it were ranges of small houses, occupied chiefly by mechanics and laborers; while the dwellings of the remaining colonists, numbering in all four or five hundred, were scattered here and there on the island and the neighboring shores. The settlers were of different sects and nations, but chiefly Dutch Calvinists. Kieft told his guest that eighteen different languages were spoken at Manhattan. [Jogues, Novum Belgium.] The colonists were in the midst of a bloody Indian war, brought on by their own besotted cruelty; and while Jogues was at the fort, some forty of the Dutchmen were killed on the neighboring farms, and many barns and houses burned. [This war was with Algonquin tribes of the neighborhood.—See O'Callaghan, New Netherland, I., Chap. III.]

The Director-General, with a humanity that was far from usual with him, exchanged Jogues's squalid and savage dress for a suit of Dutch cloth, and gave him passage in a small vessel which was then about to sail. The voyage was rough and tedious; and the passenger slept on deck or on a coil of ropes, suffering greatly from cold, and often drenched by the waves that broke over the vessel's side. At length she reached Falmouth, on the southern coast of England, when all the crew went ashore for a carouse, leaving Jogues alone on board. A boat presently came alongside with a gang of desperadoes, who boarded her, and rifled her of everything valuable, threatened Jogues with a pistol, and robbed him of his hat and coat. He obtained some assistance from the crew of a French ship in the harbor, and, on the day before Christmas, took passage in a small coal vessel for the neighboring coast of Brittany. In the following afternoon he was set on shore a little to the north of Brest, and, seeing a peasant's cottage not far off, he approached it, and asked the way to the nearest church. The peasant and his wife, as the narrative gravely tells us, mistook him, by reason of his modest deportment, for some poor, but pious Irishman, and asked him to share their supper, after finishing his devotions, an invitation which Jogues, half famished as he was, gladly accepted. He reached the church in time for the evening mass, and with an unutterable joy knelt before the altar, and renewed the communion of which he had been deprived so long. When he returned to the cottage, the attention of his hosts was at once attracted to his mutilated and distorted hands. They asked with amazement how he could have received such injuries; and when they heard the story of his tortures, their surprise and veneration knew no bounds. Two young girls, their daughters, begged him to accept all they had to give,—a handful of sous; while the peasant made known the character of his new guest to his neighbors. A trader from Rennes brought a horse to the door, and offered the use of it to Jogues, to carry him to the Jesuit college in that town. He gratefully accepted it; and, on the morning of the fifth of January, 1644, reached his destination.

He dismounted, and knocked at the door of the college. The porter opened it, and saw a man wearing on his head an old woollen nightcap, and in an attire little better than that of a beggar. Jogues asked to see the Rector; but the porter answered, coldly, that the Rector was busied in the Sacristy. Jogues begged him to say that a man was at the door with news from Canada. The missions of Canada were at this time an object of primal interest to the Jesuits, and above all to the Jesuits of France. A letter from Jogues, written during his captivity, had already reached France, as had also the Jesuit Relation of 1643, which contained a long account of his capture; and he had no doubt been an engrossing theme of conversation in every house of the French Jesuits. The Father Rector was putting on his vestments to say mass; but when he heard that a poor man from Canada had asked for him at the door, he postponed the service, and went to meet him.

Jogues, without discovering himself, gave him a letter from the Dutch Director-General attesting his character. The Rector, without reading it, began to question him as to the affairs of Canada, and at length asked him if he knew Father Jogues.

"I knew him very well," was the reply.

"The Iroquois have taken him," pursued the Rector. "Is he dead? Have they murdered him?"

"No," answered Jogues; "he is alive and at liberty, and I am he." And he fell on his knees to ask his Superior's blessing.

That night was a night of jubilation and thanksgiving in the college of Rennes. [For Jogues's arrival in Brittany, see Lettre de Jogues à Lalemant, Rennes, Jan. 6, 1644; Lettre de Jogues à—, Rennes, Jan. 5, 1644, (in Relation, 1643,) and the long account in the Relation of 1647.]

Jogues became a centre of curiosity and reverence. He was summoned to Paris. The Queen, Anne of Austria, wished to see him; and when the persecuted slave of the Mohawks was conducted into her presence, she kissed his mutilated hands, while the ladies of the Court thronged around to do him homage. We are told, and no doubt with truth, that these honors were unwelcome to the modest and single-hearted missionary, who thought only of returning to his work of converting the Indians. A priest with any deformity of body is debarred from saying mass. The teeth and knives of the Iroquois had inflicted an injury worse than the torturers imagined, for they had robbed Jogues of the privilege which was the chief consolation of his life; but the Pope, by a special dispensation, restored it to him, and with the opening spring he sailed again for Canada.

CHAPTER XVII.

1641-1646.

THE IROQUOIS.—BRESSANI.—DE NOUË.

WAR.—DISTRESS AND TERROR.—RICHELIEU.—
BATTLE.—RUIN OF INDIAN TRIBES.—MUTUAL
DESTRUCTION.—IROQUOIS AND ALGONQUIN.—
ATROCITIES.—FRIGHTFUL POSITION OF THE
FRENCH.—JOSEPH BRESSANI.—HIS CAPTURE.—HIS
TREATMENT.—HIS ESCAPE.—ANNE DE NOUË.—HIS
NOCTURNAL JOURNEY.—HIS DEATH.

Two forces were battling for the mastery of Canada: on the one side, Christ, the Virgin, and the Angels, with their agents, the priests; on the other, the Devil, and his tools, the Iroquois. Such at least was the view of the case held in full faith, not by the Jesuit Fathers alone, but by most of the colonists. Never before had the fiend put forth such rage, and in the Iroquois he found instruments of a nature not uncongenial with his own.

At Quebec, Three Rivers, Montreal, and the little fort of Richelieu, that is to say, in all Canada, no man could hunt, fish, till the fields, or cut a tree in the forest, without peril to his scalp. The Iroquois were everywhere, and nowhere. A yell, a volley of bullets, a rush of screeching savages, and all was over. The soldiers hastened to the spot to find silence, solitude, and a mangled corpse.

"I had as lief," writes Father Vimont, "be beset by goblins as by the Iroquois. The one are about as invisible as the other.

Our people on the Richelieu and at Montreal are kept in a closer confinement than ever were monks or nuns in our smallest convents in France."

The Confederates at this time were in a flush of unparalleled audacity. They despised white men as base poltroons, and esteemed themselves warriors and heroes, destined to conquer all mankind.[1] The fire-arms with which the Dutch had rashly supplied them, joined to their united councils, their courage, and ferocity, gave them an advantage over the surrounding tribes which they fully understood. Their passions rose with their sense of power. They boasted that they would wipe the Hurons, the Algonquins, and the French from the face of the earth, and carry the "white girls," meaning the nuns, to their villages. This last event, indeed, seemed more than probable; and the Hospital nuns left their exposed station at Sillery, and withdrew to the ramparts and palisades of Quebec. The St. Lawrence and the Ottawa were so infested, that communication with the Huron country was cut off; and three times the annual packet of letters sent thither to the missionaries fell into the hands of the Iroquois.

It was towards the close of the year 1640 that the scourge of Iroquois war had begun to fall heavily on the French. At that time, a party of their warriors waylaid and captured Thomas Godefroy and François Marguerie, the latter a young man of great energy and daring, familiar with the woods, a master of the Algonquin language, and a scholar of no mean acquirements. [During his captivity, he wrote, on a beaver-skin, a letter to the Dutch in French, Latin, and English.] To the great joy of the colonists, he and his companion were brought back to Three Rivers by their captors, and given up, in the vain hope that the French would respond with a gift of fire-arms. Their demand for them being declined, they broke off the parley in a rage, fortified themselves, fired on the French, and withdrew under cover of night.

Open war now ensued, and for a time all was bewilderment and terror. How to check the inroads of an enemy so stealthy

---

1   Bressani, when a prisoner among them, writes to this effect in a letter to his Superior.—See Relation Abrégée, 131.

     The anonymous author of the Relation of 1660 says, that, in their belief, if their nation were destroyed, a general confusion and overthrow of mankind must needs be the consequence.—Relation, 1660, 6.

and so keen for blood was the problem that taxed the brain of Montmagny, the Governor. He thought he had found a solution, when he conceived the plan of building a fort at the mouth of the River Richelieu, by which the Iroquois always made their descents to the St. Lawrence. Happily for the perishing colony, the Cardinal de Richelieu, in 1642, sent out thirty or forty soldiers for its defence. [Faillon, Colonie Française, II. 2; Vimont, Relation, 1642, 2, 44.] Ten times the number would have been scarcely sufficient; but even this slight succor was hailed with delight, and Montmagny was enabled to carry into effect his plan of the fort, for which hitherto he had had neither builders nor garrison. He took with him, besides the new-comers, a body of soldiers and armed laborers from Quebec, and, with a force of about a hundred men in all, [Marie de l'Incarnation, Lettre, Sept. 29, 1642.] sailed for the Richelieu, in a brigantine and two or three open boats.

On the thirteenth of August he reached his destination, and landed where the town of Sorel now stands. It was but eleven days before that Jogues and his companions had been captured, and Montmagny's followers found ghastly tokens of the disaster. The heads of the slain were stuck on poles by the side of the river; and several trees, from which portions of the bark had been peeled, were daubed with the rude picture-writing in which the victors recorded their exploit.[1] Among the rest, a representation of Jogues himself was clearly distinguishable. The heads were removed, the trees cut down, and a large cross planted on the spot. An altar was raised, and all heard mass; then a volley of musketry was fired; and then they fell to their work. They hewed an opening into the forest, dug up the roots, cleared the ground, and cut, shaped, and planted palisades. Thus a week passed, and their defences were nearly completed, when suddenly the war-whoop rang in their ears, and two hundred Iroquois rushed upon them from the borders of the clearing. [The Relation of 1642 says three hundred. Jogues who had been among them to his cost, is the better authority.]

---

1   Vimont, Relation, 1642, 52.

        This practice was common to many tribes, and is not yet extinct. The writer has seen similar records, made by recent war-parties of Crows or Blackfeet, in the remote West. In this case, the bark was removed from the trunks of large cotton-wood trees, and the pictures traced with charcoal and vermilion. There were marks for scalps, for prisoners, and for the conquerors themselves.

It was the party of warriors that Jogues had met on an island in Lake Champlain. But for the courage of Du Rocher, a corporal, who was on guard, they would have carried all before them. They were rushing through an opening in the palisade, when he, with a few soldiers, met them with such vigor and resolution, that they were held in check long enough for the rest to snatch their arms. Montmagny, who was on the river in his brigantine, hastened on shore, and the soldiers, encouraged by his arrival, fought with great determination.

The Iroquois, on their part, swarmed up to the palisade, thrust their guns through the loop-holes, and fired on those within; nor was it till several of them had been killed and others wounded that they learned to keep a more prudent distance. A tall savage, wearing a crest of the hair of some animal, dyed scarlet and bound with a fillet of wampum, leaped forward to the attack, and was shot dead. Another shared his fate, with seven buck-shot in his shield, and as many in his body. The French, with shouts, redoubled their fire, and the Indians at length lost heart and fell back. The wounded dropped guns, shields, and war-clubs, and the whole band withdrew to the shelter of a fort which they had built in the forest, three miles above. On the part of the French, one man was killed and four wounded. They had narrowly escaped a disaster which might have proved the ruin of the colony; and they now gained time so far to strengthen their defences as to make them reasonably secure against any attack of savages.[1] The new fort, however, did not effectually answer its purpose of stopping the inroads of the Iroquois. They would land a mile or more above it, carry their canoes through the forest across an intervening tongue of land, and then launch them in the St. Lawrence, while the garrison remained in total ignorance of their movements.

While the French were thus beset, their Indian allies fared still worse. The effect of Iroquois hostilities on all the Algonquin tribes

---

1   Vimont, Relation, 1642, 50, 51.

    Assaults by Indians on fortified places are rare. The Iroquois are known, however, to have made them with success in several cases, some of the most remarkable of which will appear hereafter. The courage of Indians is uncertain and spasmodic. They are capable, at times, of a furious temerity, approaching desperation; but this is liable to sudden and extreme reaction. Their courage, too, is much oftener displayed in covert than in open attacks.

of Canada, from the Saguenay to the Lake of the Nipissings, had become frightfully apparent. Famine and pestilence had aided the ravages of war, till these wretched bands seemed in the course of rapid extermination. Their spirit was broken. They became humble and docile in the hands of the missionaries, ceased their railings against the new doctrine, and leaned on the French as their only hope in this extremity of woe. Sometimes they would appear in troops at Sillery or Three Rivers, scared out of their forests by the sight of an Iroquois footprint; then some new terror would seize them, and drive them back to seek a hiding-place in the deepest thickets of the wilderness. Their best hunting-grounds were beset by the enemy. They starved for weeks together, subsisting on the bark of trees or the thongs of raw hide which formed the net-work of their snow-shoes. The mortality among them was prodigious. "Where, eight years ago," writes Father Vimont, "one would see a hundred wigwams, one now sees scarcely five or six. A chief who once had eight hundred warriors has now but thirty or forty; and in place of fleets of three or four hundred canoes, we see less than a tenth of that number." [Relation, 1644, 8.]

These Canadian tribes were undergoing that process of extermination, absorption, or expatriation, which, as there is reason to believe, had for many generations formed the gloomy and meaningless history of the greater part of this continent. Three or four hundred Dutch guns, in the hands of the conquerors, gave an unwonted quickness and decision to the work, but in no way changed its essential character. The horrible nature of this warfare can be known only through examples; and of these one or two will suffice.

A band of Algonquins, late in the autumn of 1641, set forth from Three Rivers on their winter hunt, and, fearful of the Iroquois, made their way far northward, into the depths of the forests that border the Ottawa. Here they thought themselves safe, built their lodges, and began to hunt the moose and beaver. But a large party of their enemies, with a persistent ferocity that is truly astonishing, had penetrated even here, found the traces of the snow-shoes, followed up their human prey, and hid at nightfall among the rocks and thickets around the encampment. At midnight, their yells and the blows of their war-clubs awakened their sleeping victims. In a few minutes all were in their power. They bound the prisoners hand

and foot, rekindled the fire, slung the kettles, cut the bodies of the slain to pieces, and boiled and devoured them before the eyes of the wretched survivors. "In a word," says the narrator, "they ate men with as much appetite and more pleasure than hunters eat a boar or a stag." [Vimont, Relation, 1642, 46.]

Meanwhile they amused themselves with bantering their prisoners. "Uncle," said one of them to an old Algonquin, "you are a dead man. You are going to the land of souls. Tell them to take heart: they will have good company soon, for we are going to send all the rest of your nation to join them. This will be good news for them." [Vimont, Relation, 1642, 45.]

This old man, who is described as no less malicious than his captors, and even more crafty, soon after escaped, and brought tidings of the disaster to the French. In the following spring, two women of the party also escaped; and, after suffering almost incredible hardships, reached Three Rivers, torn with briers, nearly naked, and in a deplorable state of bodily and mental exhaustion. One of them told her story to Father Buteux, who translated it into French, and gave it to Vimont to be printed in the Relation of 1642. Revolting as it is, it is necessary to recount it. Suffice it to say, that it is sustained by the whole body of contemporary evidence in regard to the practices of the Iroquois and some of the neighboring tribes.

The conquerors feasted in the lodge till nearly daybreak, and then, after a short rest, began their march homeward with their prisoners. Among these were three women, of whom the narrator was one, who had each a child of a few weeks or months old. At the first halt, their captors took the infants from them, tied them to wooden spits, placed them to die slowly before a fire, and feasted on them before the eyes of the agonized mothers, whose shrieks, supplications, and frantic efforts to break the cords that bound them were met with mockery and laughter. "They are not men, they are wolves!" sobbed the wretched woman, as she told what had befallen her to the pitying Jesuit. [Vimont, Relation, 1642, 46.] At the Fall of the Chaudière, another of the women ended her woes by leaping into the cataract. When they approached the first Iroquois town, they were met, at the distance of several leagues, by a crowd of the inhabitants, and among them a troop of women, bringing food to regale the triumphant warriors. Here they halted, and passed the night in songs of victory, mingled with the dismal chant of the prisoners, who were forced to dance for their entertainment.

On the morrow, they entered the town, leading the captive Algonquins, fast bound, and surrounded by a crowd of men, women, and children, all singing at the top of their throats. The largest lodge was ready to receive them; and as they entered, the victims read their doom in the fires that blazed on the earthen floor, and in the aspect of the attendant savages, whom the Jesuit Father calls attendant demons, that waited their coming. The torture which ensued was but preliminary, designed to cause all possible suffering without touching life. It consisted in blows with sticks and cudgels, gashing their limbs with knives, cutting off their fingers with clam-shells, scorching them with firebrands, and other indescribable torments.[1] The women were stripped naked, and forced to dance to the singing of the male prisoners, amid the applause and laughter of the crowd. They then gave them food, to strengthen them for further suffering.

On the following morning, they were placed on a large scaffold, in sight of the whole population. It was a gala-day. Young and old were gathered from far and near. Some mounted the scaffold, and scorched them with torches and firebrands; while the children, standing beneath the bark platform, applied fire to the feet of the prisoners between the crevices. The Algonquin women were told to burn their husbands and companions; and one of them obeyed, vainly thinking to appease her tormentors. The stoicism of one of the warriors enraged his captors beyond measure. "Scream! why don't you scream?" they cried, thrusting their burning brands at his naked body. "Look at me," he answered; "you cannot make me wince. If you were in my place, you would screech like babies." At this they fell upon him with redoubled fury, till their knives and firebrands left in him no semblance of humanity. He was defiant to the last, and when death came to his relief, they tore out his heart and devoured it; then hacked him in pieces, and made their feast of triumph on his mangled limbs.

---

1   "Cette pauure creature qui s'est sauuée, a les deux pouces couppez, ou plus tost hachez. Quand ils me les eurent couppez, disoit-elle, ils me les voulurent faire manger; mais ie les mis sur mon giron, et leur dis qu'ils me tuassent s'ils vouloient, que ie ne leur pouuois obeir."—Buteux in Relation, 1642, 47.

[The diabolical practices described above were not peculiar to the Iroquois. The Neutrals and other kindred tribes were no whit less cruel. It is a remark of Mr. Gallatin, and I think a just one, that the Indians west of the Mississippi are less ferocious than those east of it. The burning of prisoners is rare among the prairie tribes, but is not unknown. An Ogillallah chief, in whose lodge I lived for several weeks in 1846, described to me, with most expressive pantomime, how he had captured and burned a warrior of the Snake Tribe, in a valley of the Medicine Bow Mountains, near which we were then encamped.]

All the men and all the old women of the party were put to death in a similar manner, though but few displayed the same amazing fortitude. The younger women, of whom there were about thirty, after passing their ordeal of torture, were permitted to live; and, disfigured as they were, were distributed among the several villages, as concubines or slaves to the Iroquois warriors. Of this number were the narrator and her companion, who, being ordered to accompany a war-party and carry their provisions, escaped at night into the forest, and reached Three Rivers, as we have seen.

While the Indian allies of the French were wasting away beneath this atrocious warfare, the French themselves, and especially the travelling Jesuits, had their full share of the infliction. In truth, the puny and sickly colony seemed in the gasps of dissolution. The beginning of spring, particularly, was a season of terror and suspense; for with the breaking up of the ice, sure as a destiny, came the Iroquois. As soon as a canoe could float, they were on the war-path; and with the cry of the returning wild-fowl mingled the yell of these human tigers. They did not always wait for the breaking ice, but set forth on foot, and, when they came to open water, made canoes and embarked.

Well might Father Vimont call the Iroquois "the scourge of this infant church." They burned, hacked, and devoured the neophytes; exterminated whole villages at once; destroyed the nations whom the Fathers hoped to convert; and ruined that sure ally of the missions, the fur-trade. Not the most hideous nightmare of a fevered brain could transcend in horror the real and waking perils with which they beset the path of these intrepid priests.

In the spring of 1644, Joseph Bressani, an Italian Jesuit, born in Rome, and now for two years past a missionary in Canada, was ordered by his Superior to go up to the Hurons. It was so early in the season that there seemed hope that he might pass in safety; and as the Fathers in that wild mission had received no succor for three years, Bressani was charged with letters to them, and such necessaries for their use as he was able to carry. With him were six young Hurons, lately converted, and a French boy in his service. The party were in three small canoes. Before setting out they all confessed and prepared for death.

They left Three Rivers on the twenty-seventh of April, and found ice still floating in the river, and patches of snow lying in the naked forests. On the first day, one of the canoes overset, nearly drowning Bressani, who could not swim. On the third day, a snow-storm began, and greatly retarded their progress. The young Indians foolishly fired their guns at the wild-fowl on the river, and the sound reached the ears of a war-party of Iroquois, one of ten that had already set forth for the St. Lawrence, the Ottawa, and the Huron towns. [Vimont, Relation, 1644, 41.] Hence it befell, that, as they crossed the mouth of a small stream entering the St. Lawrence, twenty-seven Iroquois suddenly issued from behind a point, and attacked them in canoes. One of the Hurons was killed, and all the rest of the party captured without resistance.

On the fifteenth of July following, Bressani wrote from the Iroquois country to the General of the Jesuits at Rome—"I do not know if your Paternity will recognize the handwriting of one whom you once knew very well. The letter is soiled and ill-written; because the writer has only one finger of his right hand left entire, and cannot prevent the blood from his wounds, which are still open, from staining the paper. His ink is gunpowder mixed with water, and his table is the earth." [This letter is printed anonymously in the Second Part, Chap. II, of Bressani's Relation Abrégée. A comparison with Vimont's account, in the Relation of 1644, makes its authorship apparent. Vimont's narrative agrees in all essential points. His informant was "vne personne digne de foy, qui a esté tesmoin oculaire de tout ce qu'il a soufiert pendant sa captiuité."— Vimont, Relation, 1644, 43.]

Then follows a modest narrative of what be endured at the hands of his captors. First they thanked the Sun for their victory; then plundered the canoes; then cut up, roasted, and devoured the slain Huron before the eyes of the prisoners. On the next day they crossed to the southern shore, and ascended the River Richelieu as far as the rapids of Chambly, whence they pursued their march on foot among the brambles, rocks, and swamps of the trackless forest. When they reached Lake Champlain, they made new canoes and re-embarked, landed at its southern extremity six days afterwards, and thence made for the Upper Hudson. Here they found a fishing camp of four hundred Iroquois, and now Bressani's torments began in earnest. They split his hand with a knife, between the little finger and the ring finger; then beat him with sticks, till he was covered with blood; and afterwards placed him on one of their torture-scaffolds of bark, as a spectacle to the crowd. Here they stripped him, and while he shivered with cold from head to foot they forced him to sing. After about two hours they gave him up to the children, who ordered him to dance, at the same time thrusting sharpened sticks into his flesh, and pulling out his hair and beard. "Sing!" cried one; "Hold your tongue!" screamed another; and if he obeyed the first, the second burned him. "We will burn you to death; we will eat you." "I will eat one of your hands." "And I will eat one of your feet." ["Ils me répétaient sans cesse: Nous te brûlerons; nous te mangerons;—je te mangerai un pied;—et moi, une main," etc.—Bressani, in Relation Abrégée, 137.] These scenes were renewed every night for a week. Every evening a chief cried aloud through the camp, "Come, my children, come and caress our prisoners!"— and the savage crew thronged jubilant to a large hut, where the captives lay. They stripped off the torn fragment of a cassock, which was the priest's only garment; burned him with live coals and red-hot stones; forced him to walk on hot cinders; burned off now a finger-nail and now the joint of a finger,—rarely more than one at a time, however, for they economized their pleasures, and reserved the rest for another day. This torture was protracted till one or two o'clock, after which they left him on the ground, fast bound to four stakes, and covered only with a scanty fragment of deer-skin.[1] The other prisoners had their share of torture; but

---

1   "Chaque nuit après m'avoir fait chanter, et m'avoir tourmenté comme ie l'ai dit, ils passaient environ un quart d'heure à me brûler un ongle ou un doigt. Il ne m'en reste maintenant qu'un seul entier, et encore ils en ont arraché l'ongle avec les dents. Un soir ils m'enlevaient un ongle, le lendemain la première phalange, le jour suivant la seconde. En six fois, ils en brûlèrent presque six. Aux mains seules, ils m'ont appliqué le feu et le fer plus de 18 fois, et i'étais obligé de chanter

the worst fell upon the Jesuit, as the chief man of the party. The unhappy boy who attended him, though only twelve or thirteen years old, was tormented before his eyes with a pitiless ferocity.

At length they left this encampment, and, after a march of several days,—during which Bressani, in wading a rocky stream, fell from exhaustion and was nearly drowned,—they reached an Iroquois town. It is needless to follow the revolting details of the new torments that succeeded. They hung him by the feet with chains; placed food for their dogs on his naked body, that they might lacerate him as they ate; and at last had reduced his emaciated frame to such a condition, that even they themselves stood in horror of him. "I could not have believed," he writes to his Superior, "that a man was so hard to kill." He found among them those who, from compassion, or from a refinement of cruelty, fed him, for he could not feed himself. They told him jestingly that they wished to fatten him before putting him to death.

The council that was to decide his fate met on the nineteenth of June, when, to the prisoner's amazement, and, as it seemed, to their own surprise, they resolved to spare his life. He was given, with due ceremony, to an old woman, to take the place of a deceased relative; but, since he was as repulsive, in his mangled condition, as, by the Indian standard, he was useless, she sent her son with him to Fort Orange, to sell him to the Dutch. With the same humanity which they had shown in the case of Jogues, they gave a generous ransom for him, supplied him with clothing, kept him till his strength was in some degree recruited, and then placed him on board a vessel bound for Rochelle. Here he arrived on the fifteenth of November; and in the following spring, maimed and disfigured, but with health restored, embarked to dare again the knives and firebrands of the Iroquois.

[Immediately on his return to Canada he was ordered to set out again for the Hurons. More fortunate than on his first attempt, he

---

pendant ce supplice. Ils ne cessaient de me tourmenter qu'à une ou deux heures de la nuit."—Bressani, Relation Abrégée, 122.

Bressani speaks in another passage of tortures of a nature yet more excruciating. They were similar to those alluded to by the anonymous author of the Relation of 1660: "Ie ferois rougir ce papier, et les oreilles frémiroient, si ie rapportois les horribles traitemens que les Agnieronnons" (the Mohawk nation of the Iroquois) "ont faits sur quelques captifs." He adds, that past ages have never heard of such.—Relation, 1660, 7, 8.

arrived safely, early in the autumn of 1645.—Ragueneau, Relation des Hurons, 1646, 73.

On Bressani, besides the authorities cited, see Du Creux, Historia Canadensis, 399-403; Juchereau, Histoire de l'Hôtel-Dieu, 53; and Martin, Biographie du P. François-Joseph Bressani, prefixed to the Relation Abrégée.

He made no converts while a prisoner, but he baptized a Huron catechumen at the stake, to the great fury of the surrounding Iroquois. He has left, besides his letters, some interesting notes on his captivity, preserved in the Relation Abrégée.]

It should be noticed, in justice to the Iroquois, that, ferocious and cruel as past all denial they were, they were not so bereft of the instincts of humanity as at first sight might appear. An inexorable severity towards enemies was a very essential element, in their savage conception, of the character of the warrior. Pity was a cowardly weakness, at which their pride revolted. This, joined to their thirst for applause and their dread of ridicule, made them smother every movement of compassion,[1] and conspired with their native fierceness to form a character of unrelenting cruelty rarely equalled.

The perils which beset the missionaries did not spring from the fury of the Iroquois alone, for Nature herself was armed with terror in this stern wilderness of New France. On the thirtieth of January, 1646, Father Anne de Noüe set out from Three Rivers to go to the fort built by the French at the mouth of the River Richelieu, where he was to say mass and hear confessions. De Noüe was sixty-three years old, and had come to Canada in 1625. [See "Pioneers of France," 393.] As an indifferent memory disabled him from mastering the Indian languages, he devoted himself to the spiritual charge of the French, and of the Indians about the forts, within reach of an interpreter. For the rest, he attended the sick, and, in times of scarcity, fished in the river or dug roots in the woods for the subsistence of his flock. In short, though sprung from a noble family of Champagne, he shrank from no toil, however humble, to which his idea of duty or his vow of obedience

---

1   Thus, when Bressani, tortured by the tightness of the cords that bound him, asked an Indian to loosen them, he would reply by mockery, if others were present; but if no one saw him, he usually complied.

called him. [He was peculiarly sensitive as regarded the cardinal Jesuit virtue of obedience; and both Lalemant and Bressani say, that, at the age of sixty and upwards, he was sometimes seen in tears, when he imagined that he had not fulfilled to the utmost the commands of his Superior.]

The old missionary had for companions two soldiers and a Huron Indian. They were all on snow-shoes, and the soldiers dragged their baggage on small sledges. Their highway was the St. Lawrence, transformed to solid ice, and buried, like all the country, beneath two or three feet of snow, which, far and near, glared dazzling white under the clear winter sun. Before night they had walked eighteen miles, and the soldiers, unused to snow-shoes, were greatly fatigued. They made their camp in the forest, on the shore of the great expansion of the St. Lawrence called the Lake of St. Peter,—dug away the snow, heaped it around the spot as a barrier against the wind, made their fire on the frozen earth in the midst, and lay down to sleep. At two o'clock in the morning De Noüe awoke. The moon shone like daylight over the vast white desert of the frozen lake, with its bordering fir-trees bowed to the ground with snow; and the kindly thought struck the Father, that he might ease his companions by going in advance to Fort Richelieu, and sending back men to aid them in dragging their sledges. He knew the way well. He directed them to follow the tracks of his snow-shoes in the morning; and, not doubting to reach the fort before night, left behind his blanket and his flint and steel. For provisions, he put a morsel of bread and five or six prunes in his pocket, told his rosary, and set forth.

Before dawn the weather changed. The air thickened, clouds hid the moon, and a snow-storm set in. The traveller was in utter darkness. He lost the points of the compass, wandered far out on the lake, and when day appeared could see nothing but the snow beneath his feet, and the myriads of falling flakes that encompassed him like a curtain, impervious to the sight. Still he toiled on, winding hither and thither, and at times unwittingly circling back on his own footsteps. At night he dug a hole in the snow under the shore of an island, and lay down, without fire, food, or blanket.

Meanwhile the two soldiers and the Indian, unable to trace his footprints, which the snow had hidden, pursued their way for the fort; but the Indian was ignorant of the country, and the

Frenchmen were unskilled. They wandered from their course, and at evening encamped on the shore of the island of St. Ignace, at no great distance from De Noüe. Here the Indian, trusting to his instinct, left them and set forth alone in search of their destination, which he soon succeeded in finding. The palisades of the feeble little fort, and the rude buildings within, were whitened with snow, and half buried in it. Here, amid the desolation, a handful of men kept watch and ward against the Iroquois. Seated by the blazing logs, the Indian asked for De Noüe, and, to his astonishment, the soldiers of the garrison told him that he had not been seen. The captain of the post was called; all was anxiety; but nothing could be done that night.

At daybreak parties went out to search. The two soldiers were readily found; but they looked in vain for the missionary. All day they were ranging the ice, firing their guns and shouting; but to no avail, and they returned disconsolate. There was a converted Indian, whom the French called Charles, at the fort, one of four who were spending the winter there. On the next morning, the second of February, he and one of his companions, together with Baron, a French soldier, resumed the search; and, guided by the slight depressions in the snow which had fallen on the wanderer's footprints, the quick-eyed savages traced him through all his windings, found his camp by the shore of the island, and thence followed him beyond the fort. He had passed near without discovering it,—perhaps weakness had dimmed his sight,—stopped to rest at a point a league above, and thence made his way about three leagues farther. Here they found him. He had dug a circular excavation in the snow, and was kneeling in it on the earth. His head was bare, his eyes open and turned upwards, and his hands clasped on his breast. His hat and his snow-shoes lay at his side. The body was leaning slightly forward, resting against the bank of snow before it, and frozen to the hardness of marble.

Thus, in an act of kindness and charity, died the first martyr of the Canadian mission.

[Lalemant, Relation, 1646, 9; Marie de l'Incarnation, Lettre, 10 Sept., 1646; Bressani, Relation Abrégée, 175.

One of the Indians who found the body of De Noüe was killed by the Iroquois at Ossossané, in the Huron country, three years after. He received the death-blow in a posture like that in which he had seen the dead missionary. His body was found with the hands still clasped on the breast.—Lettre de Chaumonot à Lalemant, 1 Juin, 1649.

The next death among the Jesuits was that of Masse, who died at Sillery, on the twelfth of May of this year, 1646, at the age of seventy-two. He had come with Biard to Acadia as early as 1611. (See "Pioneers of France," 262.) Lalemant, in the Relation of 1646, gives an account of him, and speaks of penances which he imposed on himself, some of which are to the last degree disgusting.]

CHAPTER XVIII.

1642-1644.

VILLEMARIE.

INFANCY OF MONTREAL.—THE FLOOD.—VOW OF MAISONNEUVE.—PILGRIMAGE.—D'AILLEBOUST.— THE HÔTEL-DIEU.—PIETY.—PROPAGANDISM.—WAR.— HURONS AND IROQUOIS.—DOGS.—SALLY OF THE FRENCH.—BATTLE.—EXPLOIT OF MAISONNEUVE.

Let us now ascend to the island of Montreal. Here, as we have seen, an association of devout and zealous persons had essayed to found a mission-colony under the protection of the Holy Virgin; and we left the adventurers, after their landing, bivouacked on the shore, on an evening in May. There was an altar in the open air, decorated with a taste that betokened no less of good nurture than of piety; and around it clustered the tents that sheltered the commandant, Maisonneuve, the two ladies, Madame de la Peltrie and Mademoiselle Mance, and the soldiers and laborers of the expedition.

In the morning they all fell to their work, Maisonneuve hewing down the first tree,—and labored with such good-will, that their tents were soon inclosed with a strong palisade, and their altar covered by a provisional chapel, built, in the Huron mode, of bark. Soon afterward, their canvas habitations were supplanted by solid structures of wood, and the feeble germ of a future city began to take root.

The Iroquois had not yet found them out; nor did they discover them till they had had ample time to fortify themselves. Meanwhile, on a Sunday, they would stroll at their leisure over the adjacent meadow and in the shade of the bordering forest, where, as the old chronicler tells us, the grass was gay with wild-flowers, and the branches with the flutter and song of many strange birds. [Dollier de Casson, MS.]

The day of the Assumption of the Virgin was celebrated with befitting solemnity. There was mass in their bark chapel; then a Te Deum; then public instruction of certain Indians who chanced to be at Montreal; then a procession of all the colonists after vespers, to the admiration of the redskinned beholders. Cannon, too, were fired, in honor of their celestial patroness. "Their thunder made all the island echo," writes Father Vimont; "and the demons, though used to thunderbolts, were scared at a noise which told them of the love we bear our great Mistress; and I have scarcely any doubt that the tutelary angels of the savages of New France have marked this day in the calendar of Paradise." [Vimont, Relation, 1642, 38. Compare Le Clerc, Premier Etablissement de la Foy, II. 51.]

The summer passed prosperously, but with the winter their faith was put to a rude test. In December, there was a rise of the St. Lawrence, threatening to sweep away in a night the results of all their labor. They fell to their prayers; and Maisonneuve planted a wooden cross in face of the advancing deluge, first making a vow, that, should the peril be averted, he, Maisonneuve, would bear another cross on his shoulders up the neighboring mountain, and place it on the summit. The vow seemed in vain. The flood still rose, filled the fort ditch, swept the foot of the palisade, and threatened to sap the magazine; but here it stopped, and presently began to recede, till at length it had withdrawn within its lawful channel, and Villemarie was safe.

[A little MS. map in M. Jacques Viger's copy of Le Petit Registre de la Cure de Montreal, lays down the position and shape of the fort at this time, and shows the spot where Maisonneuve planted the cross.]

Now it remained to fulfil the promise from which such happy results had proceeded. Maisonneuve set his men at work to clear a path through the forest to the top of the mountain. A large cross was made, and solemnly blessed by the priest; then, on the sixth of

January, the Jesuit Du Peron led the way, followed in procession by Madame de la Peltrie, the artisans, and soldiers, to the destined spot. The commandant, who with all the ceremonies of the Church had been declared First Soldier of the Cross, walked behind the rest, bearing on his shoulder a cross so heavy that it needed his utmost strength to climb the steep and rugged path. They planted it on the highest crest, and all knelt in adoration before it. Du Peron said mass; and Madame de la Peltrie, always romantic and always devout, received the sacrament on the mountain-top, a spectacle to the virgin world outstretched below. Sundry relics of saints had been set in the wood of the cross, which remained an object of pilgrimage to the pious colonists of Villemarie. [Vimont, Relation, 1643, 52, 53.]

Peace and harmony reigned within the little fort; and so edifying was the demeanor of the colonists, so faithful were they to the confessional, and so constant at mass, that a chronicler of the day exclaims, in a burst of enthusiasm, that the deserts lately a resort of demons were now the abode of angels. [Véritables Motifs, cited by Faillon, I. 453, 454.] The two Jesuits who for the time were their pastors had them well in hand. They dwelt under the same roof with most of their flock, who lived in community, in one large house, and vied with each other in zeal for the honor of the Virgin and the conversion of the Indians.

At the end of August, 1643, a vessel arrived at Villemarie with a reinforcement commanded by Louis d'Ailleboust de Coulonges, a pious gentleman of Champagne, and one of the Associates of Montreal. [Chaulmer, 101; Juchereau, 91.] Some years before, he had asked in wedlock the hand of Barbe de Boulogne; but the young lady had, when a child, in the ardor of her piety, taken a vow of perpetual chastity. By the advice of her Jesuit confessor, she accepted his suit, on condition that she should preserve, to the hour of her death, the state to which Holy Church has always ascribed a peculiar merit.[1] D'Ailleboust married her; and when, soon after, he conceived the purpose of devoting his life to the work of the Faith in Canada, he invited his maiden spouse to go with him. She

---

1   Juchereau, Histoire de l'Hôtel-Dieu de Québec, 276. The confessor told D'Ailleboust, that, if he persuaded his wife to break her vow of continence, "God would chastise him terribly." The nun historian adds, that, undeterred by the menace, he tried and failed.

refused, and forbade him to mention the subject again. Her health was indifferent, and about this time she fell ill. As a last resort, she made a promise to God, that, if He would restore her, she would go to Canada with her husband; and forthwith her maladies ceased. Still her reluctance continued; she hesitated, and then refused again, when an inward light revealed to her that it was her duty to cast her lot in the wilderness. She accordingly embarked with d'Ailleboust, accompanied by her sister, Mademoiselle Philippine de Boulogne, who had caught the contagion of her zeal. The presence of these damsels would, to all appearance, be rather a burden than a profit to the colonists, beset as they then were by Indians, and often in peril of starvation; but the spectacle of their ardor, as disinterested as it was extravagant, would serve to exalt the religious enthusiasm in which alone was the life of Villemarie.

Their vessel passed in safety the Iroquois who watched the St. Lawrence, and its arrival filled the colonists with joy. D'Ailleboust was a skilful soldier, specially versed in the arts of fortification; and, under his direction, the frail palisades which formed their sole defence were replaced by solid ramparts and bastions of earth. He brought news that the "unknown benefactress," as a certain generous member of the Association of Montreal was called, in ignorance of her name, had given funds, to the amount, as afterwards appeared, of forty-two thousand livres, for the building of a hospital at Villemarie. [Archives du Séminaire de Villemarie, cited by Faillon, I. 466. The amount of the gift was not declared until the next year.] The source of the gift was kept secret, from a religious motive; but it soon became known that it proceeded from Madame de Bullion, a lady whose rank and wealth were exceeded only by her devotion. It is true that the hospital was not wanted, as no one was sick at Villemarie and one or two chambers would have sufficed for every prospective necessity; but it will be remembered that the colony had been established in order that a hospital might be built, and Madame de Bullion would not hear to any other application of her money. [Mademoiselle Mance wrote to her, to urge that the money should be devoted to the Huron mission; but she absolutely refused. Dollier de Casson, MS.] Instead, therefore, of tilling the land to supply their own pressing needs, all the laborers of the settlement were set at this pious, though superfluous, task.[1] There was no room in the fort, which, moreover, was in danger of inundation; and the hospital was accordingly built on higher ground adjacent. To leave it unprotected would be to abandon its inmates to the Iroquois; it was therefore surrounded by a strong palisade, and, in time of danger, a part of the garrison was detailed to defend it. Here Mademoiselle Mance took up her abode, and waited the day when wounds or disease should bring patients to her empty wards.

Dauversière, who had first conceived this plan of a hospital in the wilderness, was a senseless enthusiast, who rejected as a sin every protest of reason against the dreams which governed him; yet one rational and practical element entered into the motives of those who carried the plan into execution. The hospital was intended not only to nurse sick Frenchmen, but to nurse and convert sick Indians; in other words, it was an engine of the mission.

From Maisonneuve to the humblest laborer, these zealous colonists were bent on the work of conversion. To that end, the ladies made pilgrimages to the cross on the mountain, sometimes for nine days in succession, to pray God to gather the heathen into His fold. The fatigue was great; nor was the danger less; and armed men always escorted them, as a precaution against the Iroquois. [Morin, Annales de l'Hôtel-Dieu de St. Joseph, MS., cited by Faillon, I. 457.] The male colonists were equally fervent; and sometimes as many as fifteen or sixteen persons would kneel at once before the cross, with the same charitable petition. [Marguerite Bourgeoys, Écrits Autographes, MS., extracts in Faillon, I. 458.] The ardor of their zeal may be inferred from the fact, that these pious expeditions consumed the greater part of the day, when time and labor were of a value past reckoning to the little colony. Besides their pilgrimages, they used other means, and very efficient ones, to attract and gain over the Indians. They housed, fed, and clothed them at every opportunity; and though they were subsisting chiefly

---

1   Journal des Supérieurs des Jésuites, MS.

The hospital was sixty feet long and twenty-four feet wide, with a kitchen, a chamber for Mademoiselle Mance, others for servants, and two large apartments for the patients. It was amply provided with furniture, linen, medicines, and all necessaries; and had also two oxen, three cows, and twenty sheep. A small oratory of stone was built adjoining it. The inclosure was four arpents in extent.—Archives du Séminaire de Villemarie, cited by Faillon.

on provisions brought at great cost from France, there was always a portion for the hungry savages who from time to time encamped near their fort. If they could persuade any of them to be nursed, they were consigned to the tender care of Mademoiselle Mance; and if a party went to war, their women and children were taken in charge till their return. As this attention to their bodies had for its object the profit of their souls, it was accompanied with incessant catechizing. This, with the other influences of the place, had its effect; and some notable conversions were made. Among them was that of the renowned chief, Tessouat, or Le Borgne, as the French called him,—a crafty and intractable savage, whom, to their own surprise, they succeeded in taming and winning to the Faith. [Vimont, Relation, 1643, 54, 55. Tessouat was chief of Allumette Island, in the Ottawa. His predecessor, of the same name, was Champlain's host in 1613.—See "Pioneers of France," Chap. XII.] He was christened with the name of Paul, and his squaw with that of Madeleine. Maisonneuve rewarded him with a gun, and celebrated the day by a feast to all the Indians present.

[It was the usual practice to give guns to converts, "pour attirer leur compatriotes à la Foy." They were never given to heathen Indians. "It seems," observes Vimont, "that our Lord wishes to make use of this method in order that Christianity may become acceptable in this country."—Relation, 1643, 71.]

The French hoped to form an agricultural settlement of Indians in the neighborhood of Villemarie; and they spared no exertion to this end, giving them tools, and aiding them to till the fields. They might have succeeded, but for that pest of the wilderness, the Iroquois, who hovered about them, harassed them with petty attacks, and again and again drove the Algonquins in terror from their camps. Some time had elapsed, as we have seen, before the Iroquois discovered Villemarie; but at length ten fugitive Algonquins, chased by a party of them, made for the friendly settlement as a safe asylum; and thus their astonished pursuers became aware of its existence. They reconnoitred the place, and went back to their towns with the news. [Dollier de Casson, MS.] From that time forth the colonists had no peace; no more excursions for fishing and hunting; no more Sunday strolls in woods and meadows. The men went armed to their work, and returned at the sound of a bell, marching in a compact body, prepared for an attack.

Early in June, 1643, sixty Hurons came down in canoes for traffic, and, on reaching the place now called Lachine, at the head of the rapids of St. Louis, and a few miles above Villemarie, they were amazed at finding a large Iroquois war-party in a fort hastily built of the trunks and boughs of trees. Surprise and fright seem to have infatuated them. They neither fought nor fled, but greeted their inveterate foes as if they were friends and allies, and, to gain their good graces, told them all they knew of the French settlement, urging them to attack it, and promising an easy victory. Accordingly, the Iroquois detached forty of their warriors, who surprised six Frenchmen at work hewing timber within a gunshot of the fort, killed three of them, took the remaining three prisoners, and returned in triumph. The captives were bound with the usual rigor; and the Hurons taunted and insulted them, to please their dangerous companions. Their baseness availed them little; for at night, after a feast of victory, when the Hurons were asleep or off their guard, their entertainers fell upon them, and killed or captured the greater part. The rest ran for Villemarie, where, as their treachery was as yet unknown, they were received with great kindness.

[I have followed Dollier de Casson. Vimont's account is different. He says that the Iroquois fell upon the Hurons at the outset, and took twenty-three prisoners, killing many others; after which they made the attack at Villemarie.—Relation, 1643, 62.

Faillon thinks that Vimont was unwilling to publish the treachery of the Hurons, lest the interests of the Huron mission should suffer in consequence.

Belmont, Histoire du Canada, 1643, confirms the account of the Huron treachery.]

The next morning the Iroquois decamped, carrying with them their prisoners, and the furs plundered from the Huron canoes. They had taken also, and probably destroyed, all the letters from the missionaries in the Huron country, as well as a copy of their Relation of the preceding year. Of the three French prisoners, one escaped and reached Montreal; the remaining two were burned alive.

At Villemarie it was usually dangerous to pass beyond the ditch of the fort or the palisades of the hospital. Sometimes a solitary warrior would lie hidden for days, without sleep and almost without food, behind a log in the forest, or in a dense thicket, watching like a lynx for some rash straggler. Sometimes parties of a hundred or more made ambuscades near by, and sent a few of their number to lure out the soldiers by a petty attack and a flight. The danger was much diminished, however, when the colonists received from France a number of dogs, which proved most efficient sentinels and scouts. Of the instinct of these animals the writers of the time speak with astonishment. Chief among them was a bitch named Pilot, who every morning made the rounds of the forests and fields about the fort, followed by a troop of her offspring. If one of them lagged behind, she hit him to remind him of his duty; and if any skulked and ran home, she punished them severely in the same manner on her return. When she discovered the Iroquois, which she was sure to do by the scents if any were near, she barked furiously, and ran at once straight to the fort, followed by the rest. The Jesuit chronicler adds, with an amusing naïveté, that, while this was her duty, "her natural inclination was for hunting squirrels."

[Lalemant, Relation, 1647, 74, 75. "Son attrait naturel estoit la chasse aux écurieux." Dollier de Casson also speaks admiringly of her and her instinct. Faillon sees in it a manifest proof of the protecting care of God over Villemarie.]

Maisonneuve was as brave a knight of the cross as ever fought in Palestine for the sepulchre of Christ; but he could temper his valor with discretion. He knew that he and his soldiers were but indifferent woodsmen; that their crafty foe had no equal in ambuscades and surprises; and that, while a defeat might ruin the French, it would only exasperate an enemy whose resources in men were incomparably greater. Therefore, when the dogs sounded the alarm, he kept his followers close, and stood patiently on the defensive. They chafed under this Fabian policy, and at length imputed it to cowardice. Their murmurings grew louder, till they reached the ear of Maisonneuve. The religion which animated him had not destroyed the soldierly pride which takes root so readily and so strongly in a manly nature; and an imputation of cowardice from his own soldiers stung him to the quick. He saw, too, that such an opinion of him must needs weaken his authority, and impair the discipline essential to the safety of the colony.

On the morning of the thirtieth of March, Pilot was heard barking with unusual fury in the forest eastward from the fort; and in a few moments they saw her running over the clearing, where the snow was still deep, followed by her brood, all giving tongue together. The excited Frenchmen flocked about their commander.

"Monsieur, les ennemis sont dans le bois; ne les irons-nous jamais voir?" [Dollier de Casson, MS.]

Maisonneuve, habitually composed and calm, answered sharply,—

"Yes, you shall see the enemy. Get yourselves ready at once, and take care that you are as brave as you profess to be. I shall lead you myself."

All was bustle in the fort. Guns were loaded, pouches filled, and snow-shoes tied on by those who had them and knew how to use them. There were not enough, however, and many were forced to go without them. When all was ready, Maisonneuve sallied forth at the head of thirty men, leaving d'Ailleboust, with the remainder, to hold the fort. They crossed the snowy clearing and entered the forest, where all was silent as the grave. They pushed on, wading through the deep snow, with the countless pitfalls hidden beneath it, when suddenly they were greeted with the screeches of eighty Iroquois,[1] who sprang up from their lurking-places, and showered bullets and arrows upon the advancing French. The emergency called, not for chivalry, but for woodcraft; and Maisonneuve ordered his men to take shelter, like their assailants, behind trees. They stood their ground resolutely for a long time; but the Iroquois pressed them close, three of their number were killed, others were wounded, and their ammunition began to fail. Their only alternatives were destruction or retreat; and to retreat was not easy. The order was given. Though steady at first, the men soon became confused, and over-eager to escape the galling fire which the Iroquois sent after them. Maisonneuve directed them towards a sledge-track which had been used in dragging timber for building the hospital, and where the snow was firm beneath the foot. He himself remained to the last, encouraging his followers and aiding the wounded to escape. The French, as they struggled through the snow, faced about from time to time, and fired back to check the pursuit; but no sooner had they reached the sledge-track than they

---

1   Vimont, Relation, 1644, 42. Dollier de Casson says two hundred, but it is usually safe in these cases to accept the smaller number, and Vimont founds his statement on the information of an escaped prisoner.

gave way to their terror, and ran in a body for the fort. Those within, seeing this confused rush of men from the distance, mistook them for the enemy; and an over-zealous soldier touched the match to a cannon which had been pointed to rake the sledge-track. Had not the piece missed fire, from dampness of the priming, he would have done more execution at one shot than the Iroquois in all the fight of that morning.

Maisonneuve was left alone, retreating backwards down the track, and holding his pursuers in check, with a pistol in each hand. They might easily have shot him; but, recognizing him as the commander of the French, they were bent on taking him alive. Their chief coveted this honor for himself, and his followers held aloof to give him the opportunity. He pressed close upon Maisonneuve, who snapped a pistol at him, which missed fire. The Iroquois, who had ducked to avoid the shot, rose erect, and sprang forward to seize him, when Maisonneuve, with his remaining pistol, shot him dead. Then ensued a curious spectacle, not infrequent in Indian battles. The Iroquois seemed to forget their enemy, in their anxiety to secure and carry off the body of their chief; and the French commander continued his retreat unmolested, till he was safe under the cannon of the fort. From that day, he was a hero in the eyes of his men.

[Dollier de Casson, MS. Vimont's mention of the affair is brief. He says that two Frenchmen were made prisoners, and burned. Belmont, Histoire du Canada, 1645, gives a succinct account of the fight, and indicates the scene of it. It seems to have been a little below the site of the Place d'Armes, on which stands the great Parish Church of Villemarie, commonly known to tourists as the "Cathedral." Faillon thinks that Maisonneuve's exploit was achieved on this very spot.

Marguerite Bourgeoys also describes the affair in her unpublished writings.]

Quebec and Montreal are happy in their founders. Samuel de Champlain and Chomedey de Maisonneuve are among the names that shine with a fair and honest lustre on the infancy of nations.

CHAPTER XIX.

1644, 1645.

PEACE.

IROQUOIS PRISONERS.—PISKARET.—HIS EXPLOITS.—
MORE PRISONERS. —IROQUOIS EMBASSY.—THE
ORATOR.—THE GREAT COUNCIL.—SPEECHES
OF KIOTSATON.—MUSTER OF SAVAGES.—PEACE
CONFIRMED.

In the damp and freshness of a midsummer morning, when
the sun had not yet risen, but when the river and the sky were red
with the glory of approaching day, the inmates of the fort at Three
Rivers were roused by a tumult of joyous and exultant voices. They
thronged to the shore,—priests, soldiers, traders, and officers,
mingled with warriors and shrill-voiced squaws from Huron and
Algonquin camps in the neighboring forest. Close at hand they saw
twelve or fifteen canoes slowly drifting down the current of the St.
Lawrence, manned by eighty young Indians, all singing their songs
of victory, and striking their paddles against the edges of their bark
vessels in cadence with their voices. Among them three Iroquois
prisoners stood upright, singing loud and defiantly, as men not
fearing torture or death.

A few days before, these young warriors, in part Huron and
in part Algonquin, had gone out on the war-path to the River
Richelieu, where they had presently found themselves entangled
among several bands of Iroquois. They withdrew in the night, after

a battle in the dark with an Iroquois canoe, and, as they approached Fort Richelieu, had the good fortune to discover ten of their enemy ambuscaded in a clump of bushes and fallen trees, watching to waylay some of the soldiers on their morning visit to the fishing-nets in the river hard by. They captured three of them, and carried them back in triumph.

The victors landed amid screams of exultation. Two of the prisoners were assigned to the Hurons, and the third to the Algonquins, who immediately took him to their lodges near the fort at Three Rivers, and began the usual "caress," by burning his feet with red-hot stones, and cutting off his fingers. Champfleur, the commandant, went out to them with urgent remonstrances, and at length prevailed on them to leave their victim without further injury, until Montmagny, the Governor, should arrive. He came with all dispatch,—not wholly from a motive of humanity, but partly in the hope that the three captives might be made instrumental in concluding a peace with their countrymen.

A council was held in the fort at Three Rivers. Montmagny made valuable presents to the Algonquins and the Hurons, to induce them to place the prisoners in his hands. The Algonquins complied; and the unfortunate Iroquois, gashed, maimed, and scorched, was given up to the French, who treated him with the greatest kindness. But neither the Governor's gifts nor his eloquence could persuade the Hurons to follow the example of their allies; and they departed for their own country with their two captives,—promising, however, not to burn them, but to use them for negotiations of peace. With this pledge, scarcely worth the breath that uttered it, Montmagny was forced to content himself. [Vimont, Relation, 1644, 45-49.]

Thus it appeared that the fortune of war did not always smile even on the Iroquois. Indeed, if there is faith in Indian tradition, there had been a time, scarcely half a century past, when the Mohawks, perhaps the fiercest and haughtiest of the confederate nations, had been nearly destroyed by the Algonquins, whom they now held in contempt.[1] This people, whose inferiority arose chiefly from the

---

1   Relation, 1660, 6 (anonymous).
        Both Parrot and La Potherie recount traditions of the ancient superiority of the Algonquins over the Iroquois, who formerly, it is said, dwelt near Montreal and Three Rivers, whence the Algonquins expelled them. They withdrew, first to the neighborhood of Lake Erie, then to that of Lake Ontario, their historic seat. There

want of that compact organization in which lay the strength of the Iroquois, had not lost their ancient warlike spirit; and they had one champion of whom even the audacious confederates stood in awe. His name was Piskaret; and he dwelt on that great island in the Ottawa of which Le Borgne was chief. He had lately turned Christian, in the hope of French favor and countenance,—always useful to an ambitious Indian,—and perhaps, too, with an eye to the gun and powder-horn which formed the earthly reward of the convert.[1] Tradition tells marvellous stories of his exploits. Once, it is said, he entered an Iroquois town on a dark night. His first care was to seek out a hiding-place, and he soon found one in the midst of a large wood-pile.[2] Next he crept into a lodge, and, finding the inmates asleep, killed them with his war-club, took their scalps, and quietly withdrew to the retreat he had prepared. In the morning a howl of lamentation and fury rose from the astonished villagers. They ranged the fields and forests in vain pursuit of the mysterious enemy, who remained all day in the wood-pile, whence, at midnight, he came forth and repeated his former exploit. On the third night, every family placed its sentinels; and Piskaret, stealthily creeping from lodge to lodge, and reconnoitring each through crevices in the bark, saw watchers everywhere. At length he descried a sentinel who had fallen asleep near the entrance of a lodge, though his companion at the other end was still awake and vigilant. He pushed aside the sheet of bark that served as a door, struck the sleeper a deadly blow, yelled his war-cry, and fled like the wind. All the village swarmed out in furious chase; but Piskaret was the swiftest runner of his time, and easily kept in advance of his pursuers. When daylight came, he showed himself from time to time to lure them on, then yelled defiance, and distanced them again. At night, all but six had given over the chase; and even these, exhausted as they were, had begun to despair. Piskaret, seeing a hollow tree, crept into it like a bear, and hid himself; while the Iroquois, losing his traces

is much to support the conjecture that the Indians found by Cartier at Montreal in 1535 were Iroquois (See "Pioneers of France," 189.) That they belonged to the same family of tribes is certain. For the traditions alluded to, see Perrot, 9, 12, 79, and La Potherie, I. 288-295.

1   "Simon Pieskaret . . . n'estoit Chrestien qu'en apparence et par police."—Lalemant, Relation, 1647, 68.—He afterwards became a convert in earnest.

2   Both the Iroquois and the Hurons collected great quantities of wood in their villages in the autumn.

in the dark, lay down to sleep near by. At midnight he emerged from his retreat, stealthily approached his slumbering enemies, nimbly brained them all with his war-club, and then, burdened with a goodly bundle of scalps, journeyed homeward in triumph.[1]

This is but one of several stories that tradition has preserved of his exploits; and, with all reasonable allowances, it is certain that the crafty and valiant Algonquin was the model of an Indian warrior. That which follows rests on a far safer basis.

Early in the spring of 1645, Piskaret, with six other converted Indians, some of them better Christians than he, set out on a war-party, and, after dragging their canoes over the frozen St. Lawrence, launched them on the open stream of the Richelieu. They ascended to Lake Champlain, and hid themselves in the leafless forests of a large island, watching patiently for their human prey. One day they heard a distant shot. "Come, friends," said Piskaret, "let us get our dinner: perhaps it will be the last, for we must dine before we run." Having dined to their contentment, the philosophic warriors prepared for action. One of them went to reconnoitre, and soon reported that two canoes full of Iroquois were approaching the island. Piskaret and his followers crouched in the bushes at the point for which the canoes were making, and, as the foremost drew near, each chose his mark, and fired with such good effect that, of seven warriors, all but one were killed. The survivor jumped overboard, and swam for the other canoe, where he was taken in. It now contained eight Iroquois, who, far from attempting to escape, paddled in haste for a distant part of the shore, in order to land, give battle, and avenge their slain comrades. But the Algonquins, running through the woods, reached the landing before them, and, as one of them rose to fire, they shot him. In his fall he overset the canoe. The water was shallow, and the submerged warriors, presently finding foothold, waded towards the shore, and made desperate fight. The Algonquins had the advantage of position, and used it so well, that they killed all but three of their enemies, and captured two of the survivors. Next they sought out the bodies, carefully scalped them, and set out in triumph on their return. To

---

1   This story is told by La Potherie, I. 299, and, more briefly, by Perrot, 107. La Potherie, writing more than half a century after the time in question, represents the Iroquois as habitually in awe of the Algonquins. In this all the contemporary writers contradict him.

the credit of their Jesuit teachers, they treated their prisoners with a forbearance hitherto without example. One of them, who was defiant and abusive, received a blow to silence him; but no further indignity was offered to either.

[According to Marie de l'Incarnation, Lettre, 14 Sept., 1645, Piskaret was for torturing the captives; but a convert, named Bernard by the French, protested against it.]

As the successful warriors approached the little mission settlement of Sillery, immediately above Quebec, they raised their song of triumph, and beat time with their paddles on the edges of their canoes; while, from eleven poles raised aloft, eleven fresh scalps fluttered in the wind. The Father Jesuit and all his flock were gathered on the strand to welcome them. The Indians fired their guns, and screeched in jubilation; one Jean Baptiste, a Christian chief of Sillery, made a speech from the shore; Piskaret replied, standing upright in his canoe; and, to crown the occasion, a squad of soldiers, marching in haste from Quebec, fired a salute of musketry, to the boundless delight of the Indians. Much to the surprise of the two captives, there was no running of the gantlet, no gnawing off of finger-nails or cutting off of fingers; but the scalps were hung, like little flags, over the entrances of the lodges, and all Sillery betook itself to feasting and rejoicing. [Vimont, Relation, 1645, 19-21.] One old woman, indeed, came to the Jesuit with a pathetic appeal: "Oh, my Father! let me caress these prisoners a little: they have killed, burned, and eaten my father, my husband, and my children." But the missionary, answered with a lecture on the duty of forgiveness. [Vimont, Relation, 1645, 21, 22.]

On the next day, Montmagny came to Sillery, and there was a grand council in the house of the Jesuits. Piskaret, in a solemn harangue, delivered his captives to the Governor, who replied with a speech of compliment and an ample gift. The two Iroquois were present, seated with a seeming imperturbability, but great anxiety of heart; and when at length they comprehended that their lives were safe, one of them, a man of great size and symmetry, rose and addressed Montmagny:—

"Onontio,[1] I am saved from the fire; my body is delivered from death. Onontio, you have given me my life. I thank you for it. I will never forget it. All my country will be grateful to you. The earth will be bright; the river calm and smooth; there will be peace and friendship between us. The shadow is before my eyes no longer. The spirits of my ancestors slain by the Algonquins have disappeared. Onontio, you are good: we are bad. But our anger is gone; I have no heart but for peace and rejoicing." As he said this, he began to dance, holding his hands upraised, as if apostrophizing the sky. Suddenly he snatched a hatchet, brandished it for a moment like a madman, and then flung it into the fire, saying, as he did so, "Thus I throw down my anger! thus I cast away the weapons of blood! Farewell, war! Now I am your friend forever!"[2]

The two prisoners were allowed to roam at will about the settlement, withheld from escaping by an Indian point of honor. Montmagny soon after sent them to Three Rivers, where the Iroquois taken during the last summer had remained all winter. Champfleur, the commandant, now received orders to clothe, equip, and send him home, with a message to his nation that Onontio made them a present of his life, and that he had still two prisoners in his hands, whom he would also give them, if they saw fit to embrace this opportunity of making peace with the French and their Indian allies.

This was at the end of May. On the fifth of July following, the liberated Iroquois reappeared at Three Rivers, bringing with him two men of renown, ambassadors of the Mohawk nation. There was a fourth man of the party, and, as they approached, the Frenchmen on the shore recognized, to their great delight, Guillaume Couture, the young man captured three years before with Father Jogues, and long since given up as dead. In dress and appearance he was an Iroquois. He had gained a great influence over his captors, and this

---

1   *Onontio, Great Mountain,* a translation of Montmagny's name. It was the Iroquois name ever after for the Governor of Canada. In the same manner, *Onas, Feather* or *Quill,* became the official name of William Penn, and all succeeding Governors of Pennsylvania. We have seen that the Iroquois hereditary chiefs had official names, which are the same to-day that they were at the period of this narrative.

2   Vimont, Relation, 1645, 22, 23. He adds, that, "if these people are barbarous in deed, they have thoughts worthy of Greeks and Romans."

embassy of peace was due in good measure to his persuasions. [Marie de l'Incarnation, Lettre, 14 Sept., 1645.]

The chief of the Iroquois, Kiotsaton, a tall savage, covered from head to foot with belts of wampum, stood erect in the prow of the sail-boat which had brought him and his companions from Richelieu, and in a loud voice announced himself as the accredited envoy of his nation. The boat fired a swivel, the fort replied with a cannon-shot, and the envoys landed in state. Kiotsaton and his colleague were conducted to the room of the commandant, where, seated on the floor, they were regaled sumptuously, and presented in due course with pipes of tobacco. They had never before seen anything so civilized, and were delighted with their entertainment. "We are glad to see you," said Champfleur to Kiotsaton; "you may be sure that you are safe here. It is as if you were among your own people, and in your own house."

"Tell your chief that he lies," replied the honored guest, addressing the interpreter.

Champfleur, though he probably knew that this was but an Indian mode of expressing dissent, showed some little surprise; when Kiotsaton, after tranquilly smoking for a moment, proceeded:—"Your chief says it is as if I were in my own country. This is not true; for there I am not so honored and caressed. He says it is as if I were in my own house; but in my own house I am some times very ill served, and here you feast me with all manner of good cheer." From this and many other replies, the French conceived that they had to do with a man of *esprit*. [Vimont, Relation, 1645, 24.]

He undoubtedly belonged to that class of professed orators who, though rarely or never claiming the honors of hereditary chieftainship, had great influence among the Iroquois, and were employed in all affairs of embassy and negotiation. They had memories trained to an astonishing tenacity, were perfect in all the conventional metaphors in which the language of Indian diplomacy and rhetoric mainly consisted, knew by heart the traditions of the nation, and were adepts in the parliamentary usages, which, among the Iroquois, were held little less than sacred.

The ambassadors were feasted for a week, not only by the French, but also by the Hurons and Algonquins; and then the grand peace council took place. Montmagny had come up from Quebec, and with him the chief men of the colony. It was a bright midsummer day; and the sun beat hot upon the parched area of the fort, where awnings were spread to shelter the assembly. On one side sat Montmagny, with officers and others who attended him. Near him was Vimont, Superior of the Mission, and other Jesuits,— Jogues among the rest. Immediately before them sat the Iroquois, on sheets of spruce-bark spread on the ground like mats: for they had insisted on being near the French, as a sign of the extreme love they had of late conceived towards them. On the opposite side of the area were the Algonquins, in their several divisions of the Algonquins proper, the Montagnais, and the Atticamegues,[1] sitting, lying, or squatting on the ground. On the right hand and on the left were Hurons mingled with Frenchmen. In the midst was a large open space like the arena of a prize-ring; and here were planted two poles with a line stretched from one to the other, on which, in due time, were to be hung the wampum belts that represented the words of the orator. For the present, these belts were in part hung about the persons of the two ambassadors, and in part stored in a bag carried by one of them.

When all was ready, Kiotsaton arose, strode into the open space, and, raising his tall figure erect, stood looking for a moment at the sun. Then he gazed around on the assembly, took a wampum belt in his hand, and began:—

"Onontio, give ear. I am the mouth of all my nation. When you listen to me, you listen to all the Iroquois. There is no evil in my heart. My song is a song of peace. We have many war-songs in our country; but we have thrown them all away, and now we sing of nothing but gladness and rejoicing."

Hereupon he began to sing, his countrymen joining with him. He walked to and fro, gesticulated towards the sky, and seemed to apostrophize the sun; then, turning towards the Governor, resumed his harangue. First he thanked him for the life of the Iroquois prisoner released in the spring, but blamed him for sending him home without company or escort. Then he led forth the young Frenchman, Guillaume Couture, and tied a wampum belt to his arm.

---

1   The Atticamegues, or tribe of the White Fish, dwelt in the forests north of Three Rivers. They much resembled their Montagnais kindred.

"With this," he said, "I give you back this prisoner. I did not say to him, 'Nephew, take a canoe and go home to Quebec.' I should have been without sense, had I done so. I should have been troubled in my heart, lest some evil might befall him. The prisoner whom you sent back to us suffered every kind of danger and hardship on the way." Here he proceeded to represent the difficulties of the journey in pantomime, "so natural," says Father Vimont, "that no actor in France could equal it." He counterfeited the lonely traveller toiling up some rocky portage track, with a load of baggage on his head, now stopping as if half spent, and now tripping against a stone. Next he was in his canoe, vainly trying to urge it against the swift current, looking around in despair on the foaming rapids, then recovering courage, and paddling desperately for his life. "What did you mean," demanded the orator, resuming his harangue, "by sending a man alone among these dangers? I have not done so. 'Come, nephew,' I said to the prisoner there before you,"—pointing to Couture,—"'follow me: I will see you home at the risk of my life.'" And to confirm his words, he hung another belt on the line.

The third belt was to declare that the nation of the speaker had sent presents to the other nations to recall their war-parties, in view of the approaching peace. The fourth was an assurance that the memory of the slain Iroquois no longer stirred the living to vengeance. "I passed near the place where Piskaret and the Algonquins slew our warriors in the spring. I saw the scene of the fight where the two prisoners here were taken. I passed quickly; I would not look on the blood of my people. Their bodies lie there still; I turned away my eyes, that I might not be angry." Then, stooping, he struck the ground and seemed to listen. "I heard the voice of my ancestors, slain by the Algonquins, crying to me in a tone of affection, 'My grandson, my grandson, restrain your anger: think no more of us, for you cannot deliver us from death; think of the living; rescue them from the knife and the fire.' When I heard these voices, I went on my way, and journeyed hither to deliver those whom you still hold in captivity."

The fifth, sixth, and seventh belts were to open the passage by water from the French to the Iroquois, to chase hostile canoes from the river, smooth away the rapids and cataracts, and calm the waves of the lake. The eighth cleared the path by land. "You would have said," writes Vimont, "that he was cutting down trees, hacking off branches, dragging away bushes, and filling up holes."—"Look!" exclaimed the orator, when he had ended this pantomime, "the road is open, smooth, and straight"; and he bent towards the earth, as if to see that no impediment remained. "There is no thorn, or stone, or log in the way. Now you may see the smoke of our villages from Quebec to the heart of our country."

Another belt, of unusual size and beauty, was to bind the Iroquois, the French, and their Indian allies together as one man. As he presented it, the orator led forth a Frenchman and an Algonquin from among his auditors, and, linking his arms with theirs, pressed them closely to his sides, in token of indissoluble union.

The next belt invited the French to feast with the Iroquois. "Our country is full of fish, venison, moose, beaver, and game of every kind. Leave these filthy swine that run about among your houses, feeding on garbage, and come and eat good food with us. The road is open; there is no danger."

There was another belt to scatter the clouds, that the sun might shine on the hearts of the Indians and the French, and reveal their sincerity and truth to all; then others still, to confirm the Hurons in thoughts of peace. By the fifteenth belt, Kiotsaton declared that the Iroquois had always wished to send home Jogues and Bressani to their friends, and had meant to do so; but that Jogues was stolen from them by the Dutch, and they had given Bressani to them because he desired it. "If he had but been patient," added the ambassador, "I would have brought him back myself. Now I know not what has befallen him. Perhaps he is drowned. Perhaps he is dead." Here Jogues said, with a smile, to the Jesuits near him, "They had the pile laid to burn me. They would have killed me a hundred times, if God had not saved my life."

Two or three more belts were hung on the line, each with its appropriate speech; and, then the speaker closed his harangue: "I go to spend what remains of the summer in my own country, in games and dances and rejoicing for the blessing of peace." He had interspersed his discourse throughout with now a song and now a dance; and the council ended in a general dancing, in which Iroquois, Hurons, Algonquins, Montagnais, Atticamegues, and French, all took part, after their respective fashions.

In spite of one or two palpable falsehoods that embellished his oratory, the Jesuits were delighted with him. "Every one admitted," says Vimont, "that he was eloquent and pathetic. In short, he showed himself an excellent actor, for one who has had no instructor but Nature. I gathered only a few fragments of his speech from the mouth of the interpreter, who gave us but broken portions of it, and did not translate consecutively."

[Vimont describes the council at length in the Relation of 1645. Marie de l'Incarnation also describes it in a letter to her son, of Sept. 14, 1645. She evidently gained her information from Vimont and the other Jesuits present.]

Two days after, another council was called, when the Governor gave his answer, accepting the proffered peace, and confirming his acceptance by gifts of considerable value. He demanded as a condition, that the Indian allies of the French should be left unmolested, until their principal chiefs, who were not then present, should make a formal treaty with the Iroquois in behalf of their several nations. Piskaret then made a present to wipe away the remembrance of the Iroquois he had slaughtered, and the assembly was dissolved.

In the evening, Vimont invited the ambassadors to the mission-house, and gave each of them a sack of tobacco and a pipe. In return, Kiotsaton made him a speech: "When I left my country, I gave up my life; I went to meet death, and I owe it to you that I am yet alive. I thank you that I still see the sun; I thank you for all your words and acts of kindness; I thank you for your gifts. You have covered me with them from head to foot. You left nothing free but my mouth; and now you have stopped that with a handsome pipe, and regaled it with the taste of the herb we love. I bid you farewell,—not for a long time, for you will hear from us soon. Even if we should be drowned on our way home, the winds and the waves will bear witness to our countrymen of your favors; and I am sure that some good spirit has gone before us to tell them of the good news that we are about to bring." [Vimont, Relation, 1645, 28.]

On the next day, he and his companion set forth on their return. Kiotsaton, when he saw his party embarked, turned to the French and Indians who lined the shore, and said with a loud voice, "Farewell, brothers! I am one of your relations now." Then turning to the Governor,—"Onontio, your name will be great over all the earth. When I came hither, I never thought to carry back my head, I never thought to come out of your doors alive; and now I return loaded with honors, gifts, and kindness." "Brothers,"—to the Indians,—"obey Onontio and the French. Their hearts and their thoughts are good. Be friends with them, and do as they do. You shall hear from us soon."

The Indians whooped and fired their guns; there was a cannon-shot from the fort; and the sail-boat that bore the distinguished visitors moved on its way towards the Richelieu.

But the work was not done. There must be more councils, speeches, wampum-belts, and gifts of all kinds,—more feasts, dances, songs, and uproar. The Indians gathered at Three Rivers were not sufficient in numbers or in influence to represent their several tribes; and more were on their way. The principal men of the Hurons were to come down this year, with Algonquins of many tribes, from the North and the Northwest; and Kiotsaton had promised that Iroquois ambassadors, duly empowered, should meet them at Three Rivers, and make a solemn peace with them all, under the eye of Onontio. But what hope was there that this swarm of fickle and wayward savages could be gathered together at one time and at one place,—or that, being there, they could be restrained from cutting each other's throats? Yet so it was; and in this happy event the Jesuits saw the interposition of God, wrought upon by the prayers of those pious souls in France who daily and nightly besieged Heaven with supplications for the welfare of the Canadian missions. [Vimont, Relation, 1645, 29.]

First came a band of Montagnais; next followed Nipissings, Atticamegues, and Algonquins of the Ottawa, their canoes deep-laden with furs. Then, on the tenth of September, appeared the great fleet of the Hurons, sixty canoes, bearing a host of warriors, among whom the French recognized the tattered black cassock of Father Jerome Lalemant. There were twenty French soldiers, too, returning from the Huron country, whither they had been sent the year before, to guard the Fathers and their flock.

Three Rivers swarmed like an ant-hill with savages. The shore was lined with canoes; the forests and the fields were alive with busy camps. The trade was brisk; and in its attendant speeches, feasts, and dances, there was no respite.

But where were the Iroquois? Montmagny and the Jesuits grew very anxious. In a few days more the concourse would begin to disperse, and the golden moment be lost. It was a great relief when a canoe appeared with tidings that the promised embassy was on its way; and yet more, when, on the seventeenth, four Iroquois approached the shore, and, in a loud voice, announced themselves as envoys of their nation. The tumult was prodigious. Montmagny's soldiers formed a double rank, and the savage rabble, with wild eyes and faces smeared with grease and paint, stared over the shoulders and between the gun-barrels of the musketeers, as the ambassadors of their deadliest foe stalked, with unmoved visages, towards the fort.

Now council followed council, with an insufferable prolixity of speech-making. There were belts to wipe out the memory of the slain; belts to clear the sky, smooth the rivers, and calm the lakes; a belt to take the hatchet from the hands of the Iroquois; another to take away their guns; another to take away their shields; another to wash the war-paint from their faces; and another to break the kettle in which they boiled their prisoners. [Vimont, Relation, 1645, 34.] In short, there were belts past numbering, each with its meaning, sometimes literal, sometimes figurative, but all bearing upon the great work of peace. At length all was ended. The dances ceased, the songs and the whoops died away, and the great muster dispersed,— some to their smoky lodges on the distant shores of Lake Huron, and some to frozen hunting-grounds in northern forests.

There was peace in this dark and blood-stained wilderness. The lynx, the panther, and the wolf had made a covenant of love; but who should be their surety? A doubt and a fear mingled with the joy of the Jesuit Fathers; and to their thanksgivings to God they joined a prayer, that the hand which had given might still be stretched forth to preserve.

CHAPTER XX.

1645, 1646.

THE PEACE BROKEN.

There is little doubt that the Iroquois negotiators acted, for the moment, in sincerity. Guillaume Couture, who returned with them and spent the winter in their towns, saw sufficient proof that they sincerely desired peace. And yet the treaty had a double defect. First, the wayward, capricious, and ungoverned nature of the Indian parties to it, on both sides, made a speedy rupture more than likely. Secondly, in spite of their own assertion to the contrary, the Iroquois envoys represented, not the confederacy of the five nations, but only one of these nations, the Mohawks: for each of the members of this singular league could, and often did, make peace and war independently of the rest.

It was the Mohawks who had made war on the French and their Indian allies on the lower St. Lawrence. They claimed, as against the other Iroquois, a certain right of domain to all this region; and though the warriors of the four upper nations had sometimes poached on the Mohawk preserve, by murdering both French and Indians at Montreal, they employed their energies for the most part in attacks on the Hurons, the Upper Algonquins, and other tribes of the interior. These attacks still continued, unaffected by the peace with the Mohawks. Imperfect, however, as the treaty was, it was invaluable, could it but be kept inviolate; and to this end Montmagny, the Jesuits, and all the colony, anxiously turned their thoughts.

[The Mohawks were at this time more numerous, as compared with the other four nations of the Iroquois, than they were a few years later. They seem to have suffered more reverses in war than any of the others. At this time they may be reckoned at six or seven hundred warriors. A war with the Mohegans, and another with the Andastes, besides their war with the Algonquins and the French of Canada soon after, told severely on their strength. The following are estimates of the numbers of the Iroquois warriors made in 1660 by the author of the Relation of that year, and by Wentworth Greenhalgh in 1677, from personal inspection:—

	660.	1677.
Mohawks	500	300
Oneidas	100	200
Onondagas	300	350
Cayugas	300	300
Senecas	1,000	1,000
	—	—
	2,200	2,150]

It was to hold the Mohawks to their faith that Couture had bravely gone back to winter among them; but an agent of more acknowledged weight was needed, and Father Isaac Jogues was chosen. No white man, Couture excepted, knew their language and their character so well. His errand was half political, half religious; for not only was he to be the bearer of gifts, wampum-belts, and messages from the Governor, but he was also to found a new mission, christened in advance with a prophetic name,—the Mission of the Martyrs.

For two years past, Jogues had been at Montreal; and it was here that he received the order of his Superior to proceed to the Mohawk towns. At first, nature asserted itself, and he recoiled involuntarily at the thought of the horrors of which his scarred body and his mutilated hands were a living memento. [Lettre du P. Isaac Jogues au B. P. Jérosme L'Allemant. Montreal, 2 Mai, 1646. MS.] It was a transient weakness; and he prepared to depart with more than willingness, giving thanks to Heaven that he had been found worthy to suffer and to die for the saving of souls and the greater glory of God.

He felt a presentiment that his death was near, and wrote to a friend, "I shall go, and shall not return." ["Ibo et non redibo." Lettre du P. Jogues au R. P. No date.] An Algonquin convert gave him sage advice. "Say nothing about the Faith at first, for there is nothing so repulsive, in the beginning, as our doctrine, which seems to destroy everything that men hold dear; and as your long cassock preaches, as well as your lips, you had better put on a short coat." Jogues, therefore, exchanged the uniform of Loyola for a civilian's doublet and hose; "for," observes his Superior, "one should be all things to all men, that he may gain them all to Jesus Christ." [Lalemant, Relation, 1646, 15.] It would be well, if the application of the maxim had always been as harmless.

Jogues left Three Rivers about the middle of May, with the Sieur Bourdon, engineer to the Governor, two Algonquins with gifts to confirm the peace, and four Mohawks as guides and escort. He passed the Richelieu and Lake Champlain, well-remembered scenes of former miseries, and reached the foot of Lake George on the eve of Corpus Christi. Thence he called the lake Lac St. Sacrement; and this name it preserved, until, a century after, an ambitious Irishman, in compliment to the sovereign from whom he sought advancement, gave it the name it bears.

[Mr. Shea very reasonably suggests, that a change from Lake George to Lake Jogues would be equally easy and appropriate.]

From Lake George they crossed on foot to the Hudson, where, being greatly fatigued by their heavy loads of gifts, they borrowed canoes at an Iroquois fishing station, and descended to Fort Orange. Here Jogues met the Dutch friends to whom he owed his life, and who now kindly welcomed and entertained him. After a few days he left them, and ascended the River Mohawk to the first Mohawk town. Crowds gathered from the neighboring towns to gaze on the man whom they had known as a scorned and abused slave, and who now appeared among them as the ambassador of a power which hitherto, indeed, they had despised, but which in their present mood they were willing to propitiate.

There was a council in one of the lodges; and while his crowded auditory smoked their pipes, Jogues stood in the midst, and harangued them. He offered in due form the gifts of the Governor, with the wampum belts and their messages of peace, while at every pause his words were echoed by a unanimous grunt of applause from the attentive concourse. Peace speeches were made in return; and all was harmony. When, however, the Algonquin deputies stood before the council, they and their gifts were coldly received. The old hate, maintained by traditions of mutual atrocity, burned fiercely under a thin semblance of peace; and though no outbreak took place, the prospect of the future was very ominous.

The business of the embassy was scarcely finished, when the Mohawks counselled Jogues and his companions to go home with all despatch, saying, that, if they waited longer, they might meet on the way warriors of the four upper nations, who would inevitably kill the two Algonquin deputies, if not the French also. Jogues, therefore, set out on his return; but not until, despite the advice of the Indian convert, he had made the round of the houses, confessed and instructed a few Christian prisoners still remaining here, and baptized several dying Mohawks. Then he and his party crossed through the forest to the southern extremity of Lake George, made bark canoes, and descended to Fort Richelieu, where they arrived on the twenty seventh of June. [Lalemant, Relation, 1646, 17.]

His political errand was accomplished. Now, should he return to the Mohawks, or should the Mission of the Martyrs be for a time abandoned? Lalemant, who had succeeded Vimont as Superior of the missions, held a council at Quebec with three other Jesuits, of whom Jogues was one, and it was determined, that, unless some new contingency should arise, he should remain for the winter at Montreal. [Journal des Supérieurs des Jésuites. MS.] This was in July. Soon after, the plan was changed, for reasons which do not appear, and Jogues received orders to repair to his dangerous post. He set out on the twenty-fourth of August, accompanied by a young Frenchman named Lalande, and three or four Hurons. [Journal des Supérieurs des Jésuites. MS.] On the way they met Indians who warned them of a change of feeling in the Mohawk towns, and the Hurons, alarmed, refused to go farther. Jogues, naturally perhaps the most timid man of the party, had no thought of drawing back, and pursued his journey with his young companion, who, like other *donnés* of the missions; was scarcely behind the Jesuits themselves in devoted enthusiasm.

The reported change of feeling had indeed taken place; and the occasion of it was characteristic. On his previous visit to the Mohawks, Jogues, meaning to return, had left in their charge a small chest or box. From the first they were distrustful, suspecting that it contained some secret mischief. He therefore opened it, and showed them the contents, which were a few personal necessaries; and having thus, as he thought, reassured them, locked the box, and left it in their keeping. The Huron prisoners in the town attempted to make favor with their Iroquois enemies by abusing their French friends,—declaring them to be sorcerers, who had bewitched, by their charms and mummeries, the whole Huron nation, and caused drought, famine, pestilence, and a host of insupportable miseries. Thereupon, the suspicions of the Mohawks against the box revived with double force, and they were convinced that famine, the pest, or some malignant spirit was shut up in it, waiting the moment to issue forth and destroy them. There was sickness in the town, and caterpillars were eating their corn: this was ascribed to the sorceries of the Jesuit. [Lettre de Marie de l'Incarnation à son Fils. Québec, . . . 1647.] Still they were divided in opinion. Some stood firm for the French; others were furious against them. Among the Mohawks, three clans or families were predominant, if indeed they did not compose the entire nation,—the clans of the Bear, the Tortoise, and the Wolf. [See Introduction.] Though, by the nature of their constitution, it was scarcely possible that these clans should come to blows, so intimately were they bound together by ties of blood, yet they were often divided on points of interest or policy; and on this occasion the Bear raged against the French, and howled for war, while the Tortoise and the Wolf still clung to the treaty. Among savages, with no government except the intermittent one of councils, the party of action and violence must always prevail. The Bear chiefs sang their war-songs, and, followed by the young men of their own clan, and by such others as they had infected with their frenzy, set forth, in two bands, on the war-path.

The warriors of one of these bands were making their way through the forests between the Mohawk and Lake George, when they met Jogues and Lalande. They seized them, stripped them, and led them in triumph to their town. Here a savage crowd surrounded them, beating them with sticks and with their fists. One of them cut thin strips of flesh from the back and arms of Jogues, saying, as he did so, "Let us see if this white flesh is the flesh of an oki."—"I am a man like yourselves," replied Jogues; "but I do not fear death or torture. I do not know why you would kill me. I come here to confirm the peace and show you the way to heaven, and you treat me like a dog."[1]—"You shall die to-morrow," cried the rabble. "Take courage, we shall not burn you. We shall strike you both with a hatchet, and place your heads on the palisade, that your brothers may see you when we take them prisoners."[2] The clans of the Wolf and the Tortoise still raised their voices in behalf of the captive Frenchmen; but the fury of the minority swept all before it.

In the evening,—it was the eighteenth of October,—Jogues, smarting with his wounds and bruises, was sitting in one of the lodges, when an Indian entered, and asked him to a feast. To refuse would have been an offence. He arose and followed the savage, who led him to the lodge of the Bear chief. Jogues bent his head to enter, when another Indian, standing concealed within, at the side of the doorway, struck at him with a hatchet. An Iroquois, called by the French Le Berger,[3] who seems to have followed in order to defend him, bravely held out his arm to ward off the blow; but the hatchet cut through it, and sank into the missionary's brain. He fell at the feet of his murderer, who at once finished the work by hacking off his head. Lalande was left in suspense all night, and in the morning was killed in a similar manner. The bodies of the two Frenchmen were then thrown into the Mohawk, and their heads displayed on the points of the palisade which inclosed the town.[4]

1   Lettre du P. De Quen au R. P. Lallemant; no date. MS.

2   Lettre de J. Labatie à M. La Montagne, Fort d'Orange, 30 Oct. 1646. MS.

3   It has been erroneously stated that this brave attempt to save Jogues was made by the orator Kiotsaton. Le Berger was one of those who had been made prisoners by Piskaret, and treated kindly by the French. In 1648, he voluntarily came to Three Rivers, and gave himself up to a party of Frenchmen. He was converted, baptized, and carried to France, where his behavior is reported to have been very edifying, but where he soon died. "Perhaps he had eaten his share of more than fifty men," is the reflection of Father Ragueneau, after recounting his exemplary conduct.—Relation, 1650, 43-48.

4   In respect to the death of Jogues, the best authority is the letter of Labatie, before cited. He was the French interpreter at Fort Orange, and, being near the scene of

Thus died Isaac Jogues, one of the purest examples of Roman Catholic virtue which this Western continent has seen. The priests, his associates, praise his humility, and tell us that it reached the point of self-contempt,—a crowning virtue in their eyes; that he regarded himself as nothing, and lived solely to do the will of God as uttered by the lips of his Superiors. They add, that, when left to the guidance of his own judgment, his self-distrust made him very slow of decision, but that, when acting under orders, he knew neither hesitation nor fear. With all his gentleness, he had a certain warmth or vivacity of temperament; and we have seen how, during his first captivity, while humbly submitting to every caprice of his tyrants and appearing to rejoice in abasement, a derisive word against his faith would change the lamb into the lion, and the lips that seemed so tame would speak in sharp, bold tones of menace and reproof.

---

the murder, took pains to learn the facts. The letter was inclosed in another written to Montmagny by the Dutch Governor, Kieft, which is also before me, together with a MS. account, written from hearsay, by Father Buteux, and a letter of De Quen, cited above. Compare the Relations of 1647 and 1650.

CHAPTER XXI.

1646, 1647.

ANOTHER WAR.

MOHAWK INROADS.—THE HUNTERS OF MEN.—THE CAPTIVE CONVERTS.—THE ESCAPE OF MARIE.—HER STORY.—THE ALGONQUIN PRISONER'S REVENGE.— HER FLIGHT.—TERROR OF THE COLONISTS.—JESUIT INTREPIDITY.

The peace was broken, and the hounds of war turned loose. The contagion spread through all the Mohawk nation, the war-songs were sung, and the warriors took the path for Canada. The miserable colonists and their more miserable allies woke from their dream of peace to a reality of fear and horror. Again Montreal and Three Rivers were beset with murdering savages, skulking in thickets and prowling under cover of night, yet, when it came to blows, displaying a courage almost equal to the ferocity that inspired it. They plundered and burned Fort Richelieu, which its small garrison had abandoned, thus leaving the colony without even the semblance of protection. Before the spring opened, all the fighting men of the Mohawks took the war-path; but it is clear that many of them still had little heart for their bloody and perfidious work; for, of these hardy and all-enduring warriors, two-thirds gave out on the way, and returned, complaining that the season was too severe. [Lettre du P. Buteux au R. P. Lalemant. MS.] Two hundred or more kept on, divided into several bands.

On Ash-Wednesday, the French at Three Rivers were at mass in the chapel, when the Iroquois, quietly approaching, plundered two houses close to the fort, containing all the property of the neighboring inhabitants, which had been brought hither as to a place of security. They hid their booty, and then went in quest of two large parties of Christian Algonquins engaged in their winter hunt. Two Indians of the same nation, whom they captured, basely set them on the trail; and they took up the chase like hounds on the scent of game. Wrapped in furs or blanket-coats, some with gun in hand, some with bows and quivers, and all with hatchets, war-clubs, knives, or swords,—striding on snow-shoes, with bodies half bent, through the gray forests and the frozen pine-swamps, among wet, black trunks, along dark ravines and under savage hill-sides, their small, fierce eyes darting quick glances that pierced the farthest recesses of the naked woods,—the hunters of men followed the track of their human prey. At length they descried the bark wigwams of the Algonquin camp. The warriors were absent; none were here but women and children. The Iroquois surrounded the huts, and captured all the shrieking inmates. Then ten of them set out to find the traces of the absent hunters. They soon met the renowned Piskaret returning alone. As they recognized him and knew his mettle, they thought treachery better than an open attack. They therefore approached him in the attitude of friends; while he, ignorant of the rupture of the treaty, began to sing his peace-song. Scarcely had they joined him, when one of them ran a sword through his body; and, having scalped him, they returned in triumph to their companions.[1] All the hunters were soon after waylaid, overpowered by numbers, and killed or taken prisoners.

Another band of the Mohawks had meanwhile pursued the other party of Algonquins, and overtaken them on the march, as, incumbered with their sledges and baggage, they were moving from one hunting-camp to another. Though taken by surprise, they made fight, and killed several of their assailants; but in a few moments their resistance was overcome, and those who survived the fray were helpless in the clutches of the enraged victors. Then began

---

1   Lalemant, Relation, 1647, 4. Marie de l'Incarnation, Lettre à son Fils. Québec, . . . 1647. Perrot's account, drawn from tradition, is different, though not essentially so.

a massacre of the old, the disabled, and the infants, with the usual beating, gashing, and severing of fingers to the rest. The next day, the two bands of Mohawks, each with its troop of captives fast bound, met at an appointed spot on the Lake of St. Peter, and greeted each other with yells of exultation, with which mingled a wail of anguish, as the prisoners of either party recognized their companions in misery. They all kneeled in the midst of their savage conquerors, and one of the men, a noted convert, after a few words of exhortation, repeated in a loud voice a prayer, to which the rest responded. Then they sang an Algonquin hymn, while the Iroquois, who at first had stared in wonder, broke into laughter and derision, and at length fell upon them with renewed fury. One was burned alive on the spot. Another tried to escape, and they burned the soles of his feet that he might not repeat the attempt. Many others were maimed and mangled; and some of the women who afterwards escaped affirmed, that, in ridicule of the converts, they crucified a small child by nailing it with wooden spikes against a thick sheet of bark.

The prisoners were led to the Mohawk towns; and it is needless to repeat the monotonous and revolting tale of torture and death. The men, as usual, were burned; but the lives of the women and children were spared, in order to strengthen the conquerors by their adoption,—not, however, until both, but especially the women, had been made to endure the extremes of suffering and indignity. Several of them from time to time escaped, and reached Canada with the story of their woes. Among these was Marie, the wife of Jean Baptiste, one of the principal Algonquin converts, captured and burned with the rest. Early in June, she appeared in a canoe at Montreal, where Madame d'Ailleboust, to whom she was well known, received her with great kindness, and led her to her room in the fort. Here Marie was overcome with emotion. Madame d'Ailleboust spoke Algonquin with ease; and her words of sympathy, joined to the associations of a place where the unhappy fugitive, with her murdered husband and child, had often found a friendly welcome, so wrought upon her, that her voice was smothered with sobs.

She had once before been a prisoner of the Iroquois, at the town of Onondaga. When she and her companions in misfortune had reached the Mohawk towns, she was recognized by several

Onondagas who chanced to be there, and who, partly by threats and partly by promises, induced her to return with them to the scene of her former captivity, where they assured her of good treatment. With their aid, she escaped from the Mohawks, and set out with them for Onondaga. On their way, they passed the great town of the Oneidas; and her conductors, fearing that certain Mohawks who were there would lay claim to her, found a hiding-place for her in the forest, where they gave her food, and told her to wait their return. She lay concealed all day, and at night approached the town, under cover of darkness. A dull red glare of flames rose above the jagged tops of the palisade that encompassed it; and, from the pandemonium within, an uproar of screams, yells, and bursts of laughter told her that they were burning one of her captive countrymen. She gazed and listened, shivering with cold and aghast with horror. The thought possessed her that she would soon share his fate, and she resolved to fly. The ground was still covered with snow, and her footprints would infallibly have betrayed her, if she had not, instead of turning towards home, followed the beaten Indian path westward. She journeyed on, confused and irresolute, and tortured between terror and hunger. At length she approached Onondaga, a few miles from the present city of Syracuse, and hid herself in a dense thicket of spruce or cedar, whence she crept forth at night, to grope in the half-melted snow for a few ears of corn, left from the last year's harvest. She saw many Indians from her lurking-place, and once a tall savage, with an axe on his shoulder, advanced directly towards the spot where she lay: but, in the extremity of her fright, she murmured a prayer, on which he turned and changed his course. The fate that awaited her, if she remained,—for a fugitive could not hope for mercy,—and the scarcely less terrible dangers of the pitiless wilderness between her and Canada, filled her with despair, for she was half dead already with hunger and cold. She tied her girdle to the bough of a tree, and hung herself from it by the neck. The cord broke. She repeated the attempt with the same result, and then the thought came to her that God meant to save her life. The snow by this time had melted in the forests, and she began her journey for home, with a few handfuls of corn as her only provision. She directed her course by the sun, and for food dug roots, peeled the soft inner bark of trees, and sometimes caught tortoises in the muddy brooks. She had the good fortune to find a hatchet in a deserted camp, and with it made one of those wooden implements which the Indians used for kindling fire by friction. This saved her from her worst suffering; for she had no covering but a thin tunic, which left her legs and arms bare, and exposed her at night to tortures of cold. She built her fire in some deep nook of the forest, warmed herself, cooked what food she had found, told her rosary on her fingers, and slept till daylight, when she always threw water on the embers, lest the rising smoke should attract attention. Once she discovered a party of Iroquois hunters; but she lay concealed, and they passed without seeing her. She followed their trail back, and found their bark canoe, which they had hidden near the bank of a river. It was too large for her use; but, as she was a practised canoe-maker, she reduced it to a convenient size, embarked in it, and descended the stream. At length she reached the St. Lawrence, and paddled with the current towards Montreal. On islands and rocky shores she found eggs of water-fowl in abundance; and she speared fish with a sharpened pole, hardened at the point with fire. She even killed deer, by driving them into the water, chasing them in her canoe, and striking them on the head with her hatchet. When she landed at Montreal, her canoe had still a good store of eggs and dried venison.

[This story is taken from the Relation of 1647, and the letter of Marie de l'Incarnation to her son, before cited. The woman must have descended the great rapids of Lachine in her canoe: a feat demanding no ordinary nerve and skill.]

Her journey from Onondaga had occupied about two months, under hardships which no woman but a squaw could have survived. Escapes not less remarkable of several other women are chronicled in the records of this year; and one of them, with a notable feat of arms which attended it, calls for a brief notice.

Eight Algonquins, in one of those fits of desperate valor which sometimes occur in Indians, entered at midnight a camp where thirty or forty Iroquois warriors were buried in sleep, and with quick, sharp blows of their tomahawks began to brain them as they lay. They killed ten of them on the spot, and wounded many more. The rest, panic-stricken and bewildered by the surprise and the thick darkness, fled into the forest, leaving all they had in the hands of the victors, including a number of Algonquin captives, of whom one had been unwittingly killed by his countrymen in the confusion. Another captive, a woman, had escaped on a previous night. They had stretched her on her back, with limbs extended, and bound her wrists and ankles to four stakes firmly driven into the earth,—their ordinary mode of securing prisoners. Then, as usual, they all fell asleep. She presently became aware that the cord that bound one of her wrists was somewhat loose, and, by long and painful efforts, she freed her hand. To release the other hand and her feet was then comparatively easy. She cautiously rose. Around her, breathing in deep sleep, lay stretched the dark forms of the unconscious warriors, scarcely visible in the gloom. She stepped over them to the entrance of the hut; and here, as she was passing out, she descried a hatchet on the ground. The temptation was too strong for her Indian nature. She seized it, and struck again and again, with all her force, on the skull of the Iroquois who lay at the entrance. The sound of the blows, and the convulsive struggles of the victim, roused the sleepers. They sprang up, groping in the dark, and demanding of each other what was the matter. At length they lighted a roll of birch-bark, found their prisoner gone and their comrade dead, and rushed out in a rage in search of the fugitive. She, meanwhile, instead of running away, had hid herself in the hollow of a tree, which she had observed the evening before. Her pursuers ran through the dark woods, shouting and whooping to each other; and when all had passed, she crept from her hiding-place, and fled in an opposite direction. In the morning they found her tracks and followed them. On the second day they had overtaken and surrounded her, when, hearing their cries on all sides, she gave up all hope. But near at hand, in the thickest depths of the forest, the beavers had dammed a brook and formed a pond, full of gnawed stumps, dead fallen trees, rank weeds, and tangled bushes. She plunged in, and, swimming and wading, found a hiding-place, where her body was concealed by the water, and her head by the masses of dead and living vegetation. Her pursuers were at fault, and, after a long search, gave up the chase in despair. Shivering, naked, and half-starved, she crawled out from her wild asylum, and resumed her flight. By day, the briers and bushes tore her unprotected limbs; by night, she shivered with cold, and the mosquitoes and small black gnats of the forest persecuted her with torments which the modern sportsman will appreciate. She subsisted on such roots, bark, reptiles, or other small animals, as her Indian habits enabled her to gather on her way. She crossed streams by swimming, or on rafts of driftwood, lashed together with strips of linden-bark; and at length reached the St. Lawrence, where, with the aid of her hatchet, she made a canoe. Her home was on the Ottawa, and she was ignorant of the great river, or, at least, of this part of it. She had scarcely even seen a Frenchman, but had heard of the French as friends, and knew that their dwellings were on the banks of the St. Lawrence. This was her only guide; and she drifted on her way, doubtful whether the vast current would bear her to the abodes of the living or to the land of souls. She passed the watery wilderness of the Lake of St. Peter, and presently descried a Huron canoe. Fearing that it was an enemy, she hid herself, and resumed her voyage in the evening, when she soon came in sight of the wooden buildings and palisades of Three Rivers. Several Hurons saw her at the same moment, and made towards her; on which she leaped ashore and hid in the bushes, whence, being entirely without clothing, she would not come out till one of them threw her his coat. Having wrapped herself in it, she went with them to the fort and the house of the Jesuits, in a wretched state of emaciation, but in high spirits at the happy issue of her voyage. [Lalemant, Relation, 1647, 15, 16.]

Such stories might be multiplied; but these will suffice. Nor is it necessary to dwell further on the bloody record of inroads, butcheries, and tortures. We have seen enough to show the nature of the scourge that now fell without mercy on the Indians and the French of Canada. There was no safety but in the imprisonment of palisades and ramparts. A deep dejection sank on the white and red men alike; but the Jesuits would not despair.

"Do not imagine," writes the Father Superior, "that the rage of the Iroquois, and the loss of many Christians and many catechumens, can bring to nought the mystery of the cross of Jesus Christ, and the efficacy of his blood. We shall die; we shall be captured, burned, butchered: be it so. Those who die in their beds do not always die the best death. I see none of our company cast down. On the contrary, they ask leave to go up to the Hurons, and some of them protest that the fires of the Iroquois are one of their motives for the journey." [Lalemant, Relation, 1647, 8.]

CHAPTER XXII.

1645-1651.

PRIEST AND PURITAN.

Before passing to the closing scenes of this wilderness drama, we will touch briefly on a few points aside from its main action, yet essential to an understanding of the scope of the mission. Besides their establishments at Quebec, Sillery, Three Rivers, and the neighborhood of Lake Huron, the Jesuits had an outlying post at the island of Miscou, on the Gulf of St. Lawrence, near the entrance of the Bay of Chaleurs, where they instructed the wandering savages of those shores, and confessed the French fishermen. The island was unhealthy in the extreme. Several of the priests sickened and died; and scarcely one convert repaid their toils. There was a more successful mission at Tadoussac, or Sadilege, as the neighboring Indians called it. In winter, this place was a solitude; but in summer, when the Montagnais gathered from their hunting-grounds to meet the French traders, Jesuits came yearly from Quebec to instruct them in the Faith. Some times they followed them northward, into wilds where, at this day, a white man rarely penetrates. Thus, in 1646, De Quen ascended the Saguenay, and, by a series of rivers, torrents, lakes, and rapids, reached a Montagnais horde called the Nation of the Porcupine, where he found that the teachings at Tadoussac had borne fruit, and that the converts had planted a cross on the borders of the savage lake where they dwelt. There was a kindred band, the Nation of the White Fish, among the rocks and forests north of Three Rivers. They proved tractable beyond all others, threw away their "medicines" or fetiches, burned their magic drums, renounced their medicine-songs, and accepted instead rosaries, crucifixes, and versions of Catholic hymns.

In a former chapter, we followed Father Paul Le Jeune on his winter roamings, with a band of Montagnais, among the forests on the northern boundary of Maine. Now Father Gabriel Druilletes sets forth on a similar excursion, but with one essential difference. Le Jeune's companions were heathen, who persecuted him day and night with their gibes and sarcasms. Those of Druilletes were all converts, who looked on him as a friend and a father. There were prayers, confessions, masses, and invocations of St. Joseph. They built their bark chapel at every camp, and no festival of the Church passed unobserved. On Good Friday they laid their best robe of beaver-skin on the snow, placed on it a crucifix, and knelt around it in prayer. What was their prayer? It was a petition for the forgiveness and the conversion of their enemies, the Iroquois. [Vimont, Relation, 1645, 16.] Those who know the intensity and tenacity of an Indian's hatred will see in this something more than a change from one superstition to another. An idea had been presented to the mind of the savage, to which he had previously been an utter stranger. This is the most remarkable record of success in the whole body of the Jesuit Relations; but it is very far from being the only evidence, that, in teaching the dogmas and observances of the Roman Church, the missionaries taught also the morals of Christianity. When we look for the results of these missions, we soon become aware that the influence of the French and the Jesuits extended far beyond the circle of converts. It eventually modified and softened the manners of many unconverted tribes. In the wars of the next century we do not often find those examples of diabolic atrocity with which the earlier annals are crowded. The savage burned his enemies alive, it is true, but he rarely ate them; neither did he torment them with the same deliberation and persistency. He was a savage still, but not so often a devil. The improvement was not great, but it was distinct; and it seems to have taken place wherever Indian tribes were in close relations with any respectable community of white men. Thus Philip's war in New England, cruel as it was, was less ferocious, judging from Canadian experience, than it would have been, if a generation of civilized intercourse had not worn down the sharpest asperities of barbarism. Yet it was to French priests and colonists, mingled as they were soon to be among the tribes of the vast interior, that the change is chiefly to be ascribed. In this softening of manners, such as it was, and in the obedient Catholicity of a few hundred tamed savages gathered at stationary missions in various parts of Canada, we find, after a century had elapsed, all the results of the heroic toil of the Jesuits. The missions had failed, because the Indians had ceased to exist. Of the great tribes on whom rested the hopes of the early Canadian Fathers, nearly all were virtually extinct. The missionaries built laboriously and well, but they were doomed to build on a failing foundation. The Indians melted away, not because civilization destroyed them, but because their own ferocity and intractable indolence made it impossible that they should exist in its presence. Either the plastic energies of a higher race or the servile pliancy of a lower one would, each in its way, have preserved them: as it was, their extinction was a foregone conclusion. As for the religion which the Jesuits taught them, however Protestants may carp at it, it was the only form of Christianity likely to take root in their crude and barbarous nature.

To return to Druilletes. The smoke of the wigwam blinded him; and it is no matter of surprise to hear that he was cured by a miracle. He returned from his winter roving to Quebec in high health, and soon set forth on a new mission. On the River Kennebec, in the present State of Maine, dwelt the Abenaquis, an Algonquin people, destined hereafter to become a thorn in the sides of the New-England colonists. Some of them had visited their friends, the Christian Indians of Sillery. Here they became converted, went home, and preached the Faith to their countrymen, and this to such purpose that the Abenaquis sent to Quebec to ask for a missionary. Apart from the saving of souls, there were solid reasons for acceding to their request. The Abenaquis were near the colonies of New England,—indeed, the Plymouth colony, under its charter, claimed jurisdiction over them; and in case of rupture, they would prove serviceable friends or dangerous enemies to New France. [Charlevoix, I. 280, gives this as a motive of the mission.] Their messengers were favorably received; and Druilletes was ordered to proceed upon the new mission.

He left Sillery, with a party of Indians, on the twenty-ninth of August, 1646, [Lalemant, Relation, 1647, 51.] and following, as it seems, the route by which, a hundred and twenty-nine years later, the soldiers of Arnold made their way to Quebec, he reached the waters of the Kennebec and descended to the Abenaqui villages. Here he nursed the sick, baptized the dying, and gave such instruction as, in his ignorance of the language, he was able. Apparently he had been ordered to reconnoitre; for he presently descended the river from Norridgewock to the first English trading-post, where Augusta now stands. Thence he continued his journey to the sea, and followed the coast in a canoe to the Penobscot, visiting seven or eight English posts on the way, where, to his surprise, he was very well received. At the Penobscot he found several Capuchin friars, under their Superior, Father Ignace, who welcomed him with the utmost cordiality. Returning, he again ascended the Kennebec to the English post at Augusta. At a spot three miles above the Indians had gathered in considerable numbers, and here they built him a chapel after their fashion. He remained till midwinter, catechizing and baptizing, and waging war so successfully against the Indian sorcerers, that medicine-bags were thrown away, and charms and incantations were supplanted by prayers. In January the whole troop set off on their grand hunt, Druilletes following them, "with toil," says the chronicler, "too great to buy the kingdoms of this world, but very small as a price for the Kingdom of Heaven." [Lalemant, Relation, 1647, 54. For an account of this mission, see also Maurault, Histoire des Abenakis, 116-156.] They encamped on Moosehead Lake, where new disputes with the "medicine-men" ensued, and the Father again remained master of the field. When, after a prosperous hunt, the party returned to the English trading-house, John Winslow, the agent in charge again received the missionary with a kindness which showed no trace of jealousy or religious prejudice.

[Winslow would scarcely have recognized his own name in the Jesuit spelling,—"Le Sieur de Houinslaud." In his journal of 1650 Druilletes is more successful in his orthography, and spells it Winslau.]

Early in the summer Druilletes went to Quebec; and during the two following years, the Abenaquis, for reasons which are not clear, were left without a missionary. He spent another winter of extreme hardship with the Algonquins on their winter rovings, and during summer instructed the wandering savages of Tadoussac. It was not until the autumn of 1650 that he again descended the Kennebec. This time he went as an envoy charged with the negotiation of a treaty. His journey is worthy of notice, since, with the unimportant exception of Jogues's embassy to the Mohawks, it is the first occasion on which the Canadian Jesuits appear in a character distinctly political. Afterwards, when the fervor and freshness of the missions had passed away, they frequently did the work of political agents among the Indians: but the Jesuit of the earlier period was, with rare exceptions, a missionary only; and though he was expected to exert a powerful influence in gaining subjects and allies for France, he was to do so by gathering them under the wings of the Church.

The Colony of Massachusetts had applied to the French officials at Quebec, with a view to a reciprocity of trade. The Iroquois had brought Canada to extremity, and the French Governor conceived the hope of gaining the powerful support of New England by granting the desired privileges on condition of military aid. But, as the Puritans would scarcely see it for their interest to provoke a dangerous enemy, who had thus far never molested them, it was resolved to urge the proposed alliance as a point of duty. The Abenaquis had suffered from Mohawk inroads; and the French, assuming for the occasion that they were under the jurisdiction of the English colonies, argued that they were bound to protect them. Druilletes went in a double character,—as an envoy of the government at Quebec, and as an agent of his Abenaqui flock, who had been advised to petition for English assistance. The time seemed inauspicious for a Jesuit visit to Boston; for not only had it been announced as foremost among the objects in colonizing New England, "to raise a bulwark against the kingdom of Antichrist, which the Jesuits labor to rear up in all places of the world,"[1] but, three years before, the Legislature of Massachusetts had enacted, that Jesuits entering the colony should be expelled, and if they returned, hanged.[2]

Nevertheless, on the first of September, Druilletes set forth from Quebec with a Christian chief of Sillery, crossed forests, mountains, and torrents, and reached Norridgewock, the highest Abenaqui settlement on the Kennebec. Thence he descended to the English trading-house at Augusta, where his fast friend, the Puritan Winslow, gave him a warm welcome, entertained him hospitably, and promised to forward the object of his mission. He went with him, at great personal inconvenience, to Merrymeeting Bay, where Druilletes embarked in an English vessel for Boston. The passage was stormy, and the wind ahead. He was forced to land at Cape Ann, or, as he calls it, *Kepane*, whence, partly on foot, partly in boats along the shore, he made his way to Boston. The three-hilled city of the Puritans lay chill and dreary under a December sky, as the priest crossed in a boat from the neighboring peninsula of Charlestown.

Winslow was agent for the merchant, Edward Gibbons, a personage of note, whose life presents curious phases,—a reveller of Merry Mount, a bold sailor, a member of the church, an adventurous trader, an associate of buccaneers, a magistrate of the commonwealth, and a major-general.[3] The Jesuit, with credentials from the Governor of Canada and letters from Winslow, met a reception widely different from that which the law enjoined against persons of his profession.[4] Gibbons welcomed him heartily, prayed him to accept no other lodging than his house while he remained in Boston, and gave him the key of a chamber, in order that he might pray after his own fashion, without fear of disturbance. An accurate Catholic writer thinks it likely that he brought with him the means of celebrating the Mass. [J. G. Shea, in Boston Pilot.] If so, the house of the Puritan was, no doubt, desecrated by that Popish

---

1   Considerations for the Plantation in New England.—See Hutchinson, Collection, 27. Mr. Savage thinks that this paper was by Winthrop. See Savage's Winthrop, I. 360, note.

2   See the Act, in Hazard, 550.

3   An account of him will be found in Palfrey, Hist. of New England, II. 225, note.

4   In the Act, an exception, however, was made in favor of Jesuits coming as ambassadors or envoys from their government, who were declared not liable to the penalty of hanging.

abomination; but be this as it may, Massachusetts, in the person of her magistrate, became the gracious host of one of those whom, next to the Devil and an Anglican bishop, she most abhorred.

On the next day, Gibbons took his guest to Roxbury,—called *Rogsbray* by Druilletes,—to see the Governor, the harsh and narrow Dudley, grown gray in repellent virtue and grim honesty. Some half a century before, he had served in France, under Henry the Fourth; but he had forgotten his French, and called for an interpreter to explain the visitor's credentials. He received Druilletes with courtesy, and promised to call the magistrates together on the following Tuesday to hear his proposals. They met accordingly, and Druilletes was asked to dine with them. The old Governor sat at the head of the table, and after dinner invited the guest to open the business of his embassy. They listened to him, desired him to withdraw, and, after consulting among themselves, sent for him to join them again at supper, when they made him an answer, of which the record is lost, but which evidently was not definitive.

As the Abenaqui Indians were within the jurisdiction of Plymouth,[1] Druilletes proceeded thither in his character of their agent. Here, again, he was received with courtesy and kindness. Governor Bradford invited him to dine, and, as it was Friday, considerately gave him a dinner of fish. Druilletes conceived great hope that the colony could be wrought upon to give the desired assistance; for some of the chief inhabitants had an interest in the trade with the Abenaquis.[2] He came back by land to Boston, stopping again at Roxbury on the way. It was night when he arrived; and, after the usual custom, he took lodging with the minister. Here were several young Indians, pupils of his host: for he was no other than the celebrated Eliot, who, during the past summer, had established his mission at Natick,[3] and was now laboring, in the fulness of his zeal, in the work of civilization and conversion.

---

1   For the documents on the title of Plymouth to lands on the Kennebec, see Drake's additions to Baylies's History of New Plymouth, 36, where they are illustrated by an ancient map. The patent was obtained as early as 1628, and a trading-house soon after established.

2   The Record of the Colony of Plymouth, June 5, 1651, contains, however the entry, "The Court declare themselves not to be willing to aid them (the French) in their design, or to grant them liberty to go through their jurisdiction for the aforesaid purpose" (to attack the Mohawks).

3   See Palfrey, New England, II. 336.

There was great sympathy between the two missionaries; and Eliot prayed his guest to spend the winter with him.

At Salem, which Druilletes also visited, in company with the minister of Marblehead, he had an interview with the stern, but manly, Endicott, who, he says, spoke French, and expressed both interest and good-will towards the objects of the expedition. As the envoy had no money left, Endicott paid his charges, and asked him to dine with the magistrates.

[On Druilletes's visit to New England, see his journal, entitled Narre du Voyage faict pour la Mission des Abenaquois, et des Connoissances tiréz de la Nouvelle Angleterre et des Dispositions des Magistrats de cette Republique pour le Secours contre les Iroquois. See also Druilletes, Rapport sur le Résultat deses Négotiations, in Ferland, Notes sur les Registres, 95.]

Druilletes was evidently struck with the thrift and vigor of these sturdy young colonies, and the strength of their population. He says that Boston, meaning Massachusetts, could alone furnish four thousand fighting men, and that the four united colonies could count forty thousand souls.[1] These numbers may be challenged; but, at all events, the contrast was striking with the attenuated and suffering bands of priests, nuns, and fur-traders on the St. Lawrence. About twenty-one thousand persons had come from Old to New England, with the resolve of making it their home; and though this immigration had virtually ceased, the natural increase had been great. The necessity, or the strong desire, of escaping from persecution had given the impulse to Puritan colonization; while, on the other hand, none but good Catholics, the favored class of France, were tolerated in Canada. These had no motive for exchanging the comforts of home and the smiles of Fortune for a starving wilderness and the scalping-knives of the Iroquois. The Huguenots would have emigrated in swarms; but they were rigidly forbidden. The zeal of propagandism and the fur-trade were, as we have seen, the vital forces of New France. Of her feeble population, the best part was bound to perpetual chastity; while the fur-traders and those in their service rarely brought their wives to the wilderness. The fur-trader, moreover, is always the worst

---

1   Druilletes, Reflexions touchant ce qu'on peut esperer de la Nouvelle Angleterre contre l'Irocquois (sic), appended to his journal.

of colonists; since the increase of population, by diminishing the numbers of the fur-bearing animals, is adverse to his interest. But behind all this there was in the religious ideal of the rival colonies an influence which alone would have gone far to produce the contrast in material growth.

To the mind of the Puritan, heaven was God's throne; but no less was the earth His footstool: and each in its degree and its kind had its demands on man. He held it a duty to labor and to multiply; and, building on the Old Testament quite as much as on the New, thought that a reward on earth as well as in heaven awaited those who were faithful to the law. Doubtless, such a belief is widely open to abuse, and it would be folly to pretend that it escaped abuse in New England; but there was in it an element manly, healthful, and invigorating. On the other hand, those who shaped the character, and in great measure the destiny, of New France had always on their lips the nothingness and the vanity of life. For them, time was nothing but a preparation for eternity, and the highest virtue consisted in a renunciation of all the cares, toils, and interests of earth. That such a doctrine has often been joined to an intense worldliness, all history proclaims; but with this we have at present nothing to do. If all mankind acted on it in good faith, the world would sink into decrepitude. It is the monastic idea carried into the wide field of active life, and is like the error of those who, in their zeal to cultivate their higher nature, suffer the neglected body to dwindle and pine, till body and mind alike lapse into feebleness and disease.

Druilletes returned to the Abenaquis, and thence to Quebec, full of hope that the object of his mission was in a fair way of accomplishment. The Governor, d'Ailleboust,[1] who had succeeded Montmagny, called his council, and Druilletes was again dispatched to New England, together with one of the principal inhabitants of Quebec, Jean Paul Godefroy.[2] They repaired to New Haven, and appeared before the Commissioners of the Four Colonies, then in session there; but their errand proved bootless. The Commissioners refused either to declare war or to permit volunteers to be raised in

---

1   The same who, with his wife, had joined the colonists of Montreal. See ante, chapter 18 (page 264).

2   He was one of the Governor's council.—Ferland, Notes sur les Registres, 67.

New England against the Iroquois. The Puritan, like his descendant, would not fight without a reason. The bait of free-trade with Canada failed to tempt him; and the envoys retraced their steps, with a flat, though courteous refusal.[1]

Now let us stop for a moment at Quebec, and observe some notable changes that had taken place in the affairs of the colony. The Company of the Hundred Associates, whose outlay had been great and their profit small, transferred to the inhabitants of the colony their monopoly of the fur-trade, and with it their debts. The inhabitants also assumed their obligations to furnish arms, munitions, soldiers, and works of defence, to pay the Governor and other officials, introduce emigrants, and contribute to support the missions. The Company was to receive, besides, an annual acknowledgement of a thousand pounds of beaver, and was to retain all seigniorial rights. The inhabitants were to form a corporation, of which any one of them might be a member; and no individual could trade on his own account, except on condition of selling at a fixed price to the magazine of this new company.

[Articles accordés entre les Directeurs et Associés de la Compagnie de la Nelle France et les Députés des Habitans du dit Pays, 6 Mars, 1645. MS.]

This change took place in 1645. It was followed, in 1647, by the establishment of a Council, composed of the Governor-General, the Superior of the Jesuits, and the Governor of Montreal, who were invested with absolute powers, legislative, judicial, and executive. The Governor-General had an appointment of twenty-five thousand livres, besides the privilege of bringing over seventy tons of freight, yearly, in the Company's ships. Out of this he was required to pay the soldiers, repair the forts, and supply arms and munitions. Ten thousand livres and thirty tons of freight, with similar conditions, were assigned to the Governor of Montreal. Under these circumstances, one cannot wonder that

---

1   On Druilletes's second embassy, see Lettre écrite par le Conseil de Quebec aux Commissionaires de la Nouvelle Angleterre, in Charlevoix, I. 287; Extrait des Registres de l'Ancien Conseil de Quebec, Ibid., I. 288; Copy of a Letter from the Commissioners of the United Colonies to the Governor of Canada, in Hazard, II. 183; Answare to the Propositions presented by the honered French Agents, Ibid., II. 184; and Hutchinson, Collection of Papers, 240. Also, Records of the Commissioners of the United Colonies, Sept. 5, 1651; and Commission of Druilletes and Godefroy, in N. Y. Col. Docs., IX. 6.

the colony was but indifferently defended against the Iroquois, and that the King had to send soldiers to save it from destruction. In the next year, at the instance of Maisonneuve, another change was made. A specified sum was set apart for purposes of defence, and the salaries of the Governors were proportionably reduced. The Governor-General, Montmagny, though he seems to have done better than could reasonably have been expected, was removed; and, as Maisonneuve declined the office, d'Ailleboust, another Montrealist, was appointed to it. This movement, indeed, had been accomplished by the interest of the Montreal party; for already there was no slight jealousy between Quebec and her rival.

The Council was reorganized, and now consisted of the Governor, the Superior of the Jesuits, and three of the principal inhabitants. [The Governors of Montreal and Three Rivers, when present had also seats in the Council.] These last were to be chosen every three years by the Council itself, in conjunction with the Syndics of Quebec, Montreal, and Three Rivers. The Syndic was an officer elected by the inhabitants of the community to which he belonged, to manage its affairs. Hence a slight ingredient of liberty was introduced into the new organization.

The colony, since the transfer of the fur-trade, had become a resident corporation of merchants, with the Governor and Council at its head. They were at once the directors of a trading company, a legislative assembly, a court of justice, and an executive body: more even than this, for they regulated the private affairs of families and individuals. The appointment and payment of clerks and the examining of accounts mingled with high functions of government; and the new corporation of the inhabitants seems to have been managed with very little consultation of its members. How the Father Superior acquitted himself in his capacity of director of a fur-company is nowhere recorded.

[Those curious in regard to these new regulations will find an account of them, at greater length, in Ferland and Faillon.]

As for Montreal, though it had given a Governor to the colony, its prospects were far from hopeful. The ridiculous Dauversière, its chief founder, was sick and bankrupt; and the Associates of Montreal, once so full of zeal and so abounding in wealth, were reduced to nine persons. What it had left of vitality was in the enthusiastic Mademoiselle Mance, the earnest and disinterested soldier, Maisonneuve, and the priest, Olier, with his new Seminary of St. Sulpice.

Let us visit Quebec in midwinter. We pass the warehouses and dwellings of the lower town, and as we climb the zigzag way now called Mountain Street, the frozen river, the roofs, the summits of the cliff, and all the broad landscape below and around us glare in the sharp sunlight with a dazzling whiteness. At the top, scarcely a private house is to be seen; but, instead, a fort, a church, a hospital, a cemetery, a house of the Jesuits, and an Ursuline convent. Yet, regardless of the keen air, soldiers, Jesuits, servants, officials, women, all of the little community who are not cloistered, are abroad and astir. Despite the gloom of the times, an unwonted cheer enlivens this rocky perch of France and the Faith; for it is New-Year's Day, and there is an active interchange of greetings and presents. Thanks to the nimble pen of the Father Superior, we know what each gave and what each received. He thus writes in his private journal:—"The soldiers went with their guns to salute Monsieur the Governor; and so did also the inhabitants in a body. He was beforehand with us, and came here at seven o'clock to wish us a happy New-Year, each in turn, one after another. I went to see him after mass. Another time we must be beforehand with him. M. Giffard also came to see us. The Hospital nuns sent us letters of compliment very early in the morning; and the Ursulines sent us some beautiful presents, with candles, rosaries, a crucifix, etc., and, at dinner time, two excellent pies. I sent them two images, in enamel, of St. Ignatius and St. Francis Xavier. We gave to M. Giffard Father Bonnet's book on the life of Our Lord; to M. des Châtelets, a little volume on Eternity; to M. Bourdon, a telescope and compass; and to others, reliquaries, rosaries, medals, images, etc. I went to see M. Giffard, M. Couillard, and Mademoiselle de Repentigny. The Ursulines sent to beg that I would come and see them before the end of the day. I went, and paid my compliments also to Madame de la Peltrie, who sent us some presents. I was near leaving this out, which would have been a sad oversight. We gave a crucifix to the woman who washes the church-linen, a bottle of eau-de-vie to Abraham, four handkerchiefs to his wife, some books of devotion to others, and two handkerchiefs to Robert Hache. He asked for two more, and we gave them to him."

[Journal des Supérieurs des Jésuites, MS. Only fragments of this curious record are extant. It was begun by Lalemant in 1645. For the privilege of having what remains of it copied I am indebted to M. Jacques Viger. The entry translated above is of Jan. 1, 1646. Of the persons named in it, Giffard was seigneur of Beauport, and a member of the Council; Des Châtelets was one of the earliest settlers, and connected by marriage with Giffard; Couillard was son-in-law of the first settler, Hébert; Mademoiselle de Repentigny was daughter of Le Gardeur de Repentigny, commander of the fleet; Madame de la Peltrie has been described already; Bourdon was chief engineer of the colony; Abraham was Abraham Martin, pilot for the King on the St. Lawrence, from whom the historic Plains of Abraham received their name. (See Ferland, Notes sur Registres, 16.) The rest were servants, or persons of humble station.]

CHAPTER XXIII.

1645-1648.

A DOOMED NATION.

INDIAN INFATUATION.—IROQUOIS AND HURON.—
HURON TRIUMPHS.—THE CAPTIVE IROQUOIS.—HIS
FEROCITY AND FORTITUDE.—PARTISAN EXPLOITS.—
DIPLOMACY.—THE ANDASTES.—THE HURON
EMBASSY.—NEW NEGOTIATIONS.—THE IROQUOIS
AMBASSADOR.—HIS SUICIDE.—IROQUOIS HONOR.

It was a strange and miserable spectacle to behold the savages of this continent at the time when the knell of their common ruin had already sounded. Civilization had gained a foothold on their borders. The long and gloomy reign of barbarism was drawing near its close, and their united efforts could scarcely have availed to sustain it. Yet, in this crisis of their destiny, these doomed tribes were tearing each other's throats in a wolfish fury, joined to an intelligence that served little purpose but mutual destruction.

How the quarrel began between the Iroquois and their Huron kindred no man can tell, and it is not worth while to conjecture. At this time, the ruling passion of the savage Confederates was the annihilation of this rival people and of their Algonquin allies,— if the understanding between the Hurons and these incoherent hordes can be called an alliance. United, they far outnumbered the Iroquois. Indeed, the Hurons alone were not much inferior in force; for, by the largest estimates, the strength of the five Iroquois nations must now have been considerably less than three thousand warriors. Their true superiority was a moral one. They were in one of those transports of pride, self-confidence, and rage for ascendency, which, in a savage people, marks an era of conquest. With all the defects of their organization, it was far better than that of their neighbors. There were bickerings, jealousies, plottings, and counter plottings, separate wars and separate treaties, among the five members of the league; yet nothing could sunder them. The bonds that united them were like cords of India-rubber: they would stretch, and the parts would be seemingly disjoined, only to return to their old union with the recoil. Such was the elastic strength of those relations of clanship which were the life of the league. [See ante, Introduction.]

The first meeting of white men with the Hurons found them at blows with the Iroquois; and from that time forward, the war raged with increasing fury. Small scalping-parties infested the Huron forests, killing squaws in the cornfields, or entering villages at midnight to tomahawk their sleeping inhabitants. Often, too, invasions were made in force. Sometimes towns were set upon and burned, and sometimes there were deadly conflicts in the depths of the forests and the passes of the hills. The invaders were not always successful. A bloody rebuff and a sharp retaliation now and then requited them. Thus, in 1638, a war-party of a hundred Iroquois met in the forest a band of three hundred Huron and Algonquin warriors. They might have retreated, and the greater number were for doing so; but Ononkwaya, an Oneida chief, refused. "Look!" he said, "the sky is clear; the Sun beholds us. If there were clouds to hide our shame from his sight, we might fly; but, as it is, we must fight while we can." They stood their ground for a time, but were soon overborne. Four or five escaped; but the rest were surrounded, and killed or taken. This year, Fortune smiled on the Hurons; and they took, in all, more than a hundred prisoners, who were distributed among their various towns, to be burned. These scenes, with them, occurred always in the night; and it was held to be of the last importance that the torture should be protracted from sunset till dawn. The too valiant Ononkwaya was among the victims. Even in death he took his revenge; for it was thought an augury of disaster to the victors, if no cry of pain could be extorted from the sufferer, and, on the present occasion, he displayed an unflinching courage, rare even among Indian warriors. His execution took place at the town of Teanaustayé, called St. Joseph by the Jesuits. The Fathers could not save his life, but, what was more to the purpose, they baptized him. On the scaffold where he was burned, he wrought himself into a fury which seemed to render him insensible to pain. Thinking him nearly spent, his tormentors scalped him, when, to their amazement, he leaped up, snatched the brands that had been the instruments of his torture, drove the screeching crowd from the scaffold, and held them all at bay, while they pelted him from below with sticks, stones, and showers of live coals. At length he made a false step and fell to the ground, when they seized him and threw him into the fire. He instantly leaped out, covered with blood, cinders, and ashes, and rushed upon them, with a blazing brand in each hand. The crowd gave way before him, and he ran towards the town, as if to set it on fire. They threw a pole across his way, which tripped him and flung him headlong to the earth, on which they all fell upon him, cut off his hands and feet, and again threw him into the fire. He rolled himself out, and crawled forward on his elbows and knees, glaring upon them with such unutterable ferocity that they recoiled once more, till, seeing that he was helpless, they threw themselves upon him, and cut off his head.

[Lalemant, Relation des Hurons, 1639, 68. It was this chief whose severed hand was thrown to the Jesuits. See ante, chapter 11 (page 137).]

When the Iroquois could not win by force, they were sometimes more successful with treachery. In the summer of 1645, two war-parties of the hostile nations met in the forest. The Hurons bore themselves so well that they had nearly gained the day, when the Iroquois called for a parley, displayed a great number of wampum-belts, and said that they wished to treat for peace. The Hurons had the folly to consent. The chiefs on both sides sat down to a council, during which the Iroquois, seizing a favorable moment, fell upon their dupes and routed them completely, killing and capturing a considerable number. [Ragueneau, Relation des Hurons, 1646, 55.]

The large frontier town of St. Joseph was well fortified with palisades, on which, at intervals, were wooden watch-towers. On an evening of this same summer of 1645, the Iroquois approached the place in force; and the young Huron warriors, mounting their palisades, sang their war-songs all night, with the utmost power of their lungs, in order that the enemy, knowing them to be on their guard, might be deterred from an attack. The night was dark, and the hideous dissonance resounded far and wide; yet, regardless of the din, two Iroquois crept close to the palisade, where they lay motionless till near dawn. By this time the last song had died away, and the tired singers had left their posts or fallen asleep. One of the Iroquois, with the silence and agility of a wild-cat, climbed to the top of a watch-tower, where he found two slumbering Hurons, brained one of them with his hatchet, and threw the other down to his comrade, who quickly despoiled him of his life and his scalp. Then, with the reeking trophies of their exploit, the adventurers rejoined their countrymen in the forest.

The Hurons planned a counter-stroke; and three of them, after a journey of twenty days, reached the great town of the Senecas. They entered it at midnight, and found, as usual, no guard; but the doors of the houses were made fast. They cut a hole in the bark side of one of them, crept in, stirred the fading embers to give them light, chose each his man, tomahawked him, scalped him, and escaped in the confusion. [Ragueneau, Relation des Hurons, 1646, 55, 56.]

Despite such petty triumphs, the Hurons felt themselves on the verge of ruin. Pestilence and war had wasted them away, and left but a skeleton of their former strength. In their distress, they cast about them for succor, and, remembering an ancient friendship with a kindred nation, the Andastes, they sent an embassy to ask of them aid in war or intervention to obtain peace. This powerful people dwelt, as has been shown, on the River Susquehanna.[1] The way was long, even in a direct line; but the Iroquois lay between, and a wide circuit was necessary to avoid them. A Christian chief, whom the Jesuits had named Charles, together with four Christian and four heathen Hurons, bearing wampum-belts and gifts from

---

1   See Introduction. The Susquehannocks of Smith, clearly the same people, are placed, in his map, on the east side of the Susquehanna, some twenty miles from its mouth. He speaks of them as great enemies of the Massawomekes (Mohawks). No other savage people so boldly resisted the Iroquois; but the story in Hazard's Annals of Pennsylvania, that a hundred of them beat off sixteen hundred Senecas, is disproved by the fact, that the Senecas, in their best estate, never had so many warriors. The miserable remnant of the Andastes, called Conestogas, were massacred by the Paxton Boys, in 1763. See "Conspiracy of Pontiac," 414. Compare Historical Magazine, II. 294.

the council, departed on this embassy on the thirteenth of April, 1647, and reached the great town of the Andastes early in June. It contained, as the Jesuits were told, no less than thirteen hundred warriors. The council assembled, and the chief ambassador addressed them:—

"We come from the Land of Souls, where all is gloom, dismay, and desolation. Our fields are covered with blood; our houses are filled only with the dead; and we ourselves have but life enough to beg our friends to take pity on a people who are drawing near their end."[1] Then he presented the wampum-belts and other gifts, saying that they were the voice of a dying country.

The Andastes, who had a mortal quarrel with the Mohawks, and who had before promised to aid the Hurons in case of need, returned a favorable answer, but were disposed to try the virtue of diplomacy rather than the tomahawk. After a series of councils, they determined to send ambassadors, not to their old enemies, the Mohawks, but to the Onondagas, Oneidas, and Cayugas,[2] who were geographically the central nations of the Iroquois league, while the Mohawks and the Senecas were respectively at its eastern and western extremities. By inducing the three central nations, and, if possible, the Senecas also, to conclude a treaty with the Hurons, these last would be enabled to concentrate their force against the Mohawks, whom the Andastes would attack at the same time, unless they humbled themselves and made peace. This scheme, it will be seen, was based on the assumption, that the dreaded league of the Iroquois was far from being a unit in action or counsel.

Charles, with some of his colleagues, now set out for home, to report the result of their mission; but the Senecas were lying in wait for them, and they were forced to make a wide sweep through the Alleghanies, Western Pennsylvania, and apparently Ohio, to avoid these vigilant foes. It was October before they reached the

---

1   "Il leur dit qu'il venoit du pays des Ames, où la guerre et la terreur des ennemis auoit tout desolé, où les campagnes n'estoient couuertes que de sang, où les cabanes n'estoient remplies que de cadaures, et qu'il ne leur restoit à eux-mesmes de vie, sinon autant qu'ils en auoient eu besoin pour venir dire à leurs amis, qu'ils eussent pitié d'vn pays qui tiroit à sa fin."—Ragueneau, Relation des Hurons, 1648, 58.

2   Examination leaves no doubt that the Ouiouenronnons of Ragueneau (Relation des Hurons, 1648, 46, 59) were the Oiogouins or Goyogouins, that is to say, the Cayugas. They must not be confounded with the Ouenrohronnons, a small tribe hostile to the Iroquois, who took refuge among the Hurons in 1638.

Huron towns, and meanwhile hopes of peace had arisen from another quarter. [On this mission of the Hurons to the Andastes, see Ragueneau, Relation des Hurons, 1648, 58-60.]

Early in the spring, a band of Onondagas had made an inroad, but were roughly handled by the Hurons, who killed several of them, captured others, and put the rest to flight. The prisoners were burned, with the exception of one who committed suicide to escape the torture, and one other, the chief man of the party, whose name was Annenrais. Some of the Hurons were dissatisfied at the mercy shown him, and gave out that they would kill him; on which the chiefs, who never placed themselves in open opposition to the popular will, secretly fitted him out, made him presents, and aided him to escape at night, with an understanding that he should use his influence at Onondaga in favor of peace. After crossing Lake Ontario, he met nearly all the Onondaga warriors on the march to avenge his supposed death; for he was a man of high account. They greeted him as one risen from the grave; and, on his part, he persuaded them to renounce their warlike purpose and return home. On their arrival, the chiefs and old men were called to council, and the matter was debated with the usual deliberation.

About this time the ambassador of the Andastes appeared with his wampum-belts. Both this nation and the Onondagas had secret motives which were perfectly in accordance. The Andastes hated the Mohawks as enemies, and the Onondagas were jealous of them as confederates; for, since they had armed themselves with Dutch guns, their arrogance and boastings had given umbrage to their brethren of the league; and a peace with the Hurons would leave the latter free to turn their undivided strength against the Mohawks, and curb their insolence. The Oneidas and the Cayugas were of one mind with the Onondagas. Three nations of the league, to satisfy their spite against a fourth, would strike hands with the common enemy of all. It was resolved to send an embassy to the Hurons. Yet it may be, that, after all, the Onondagas had but half a mind for peace. At least, they were unfortunate in their choice of an ambassador. He was by birth a Huron, who, having been captured when a boy, adopted and naturalized, had become more an Iroquois than the Iroquois themselves; and scarcely one of the fierce confederates had shed so much Huron blood. When he reached the town of St. Ignace, which he did about midsummer, and delivered his messages and wampum-belts, there was a great division of opinion among the Hurons. The Bear Nation—the member of their confederacy which was farthest from the Iroquois, and least exposed to danger—was for rejecting overtures made by so offensive an agency; but those of the Hurons who had suffered most were eager for peace at any price, and, after solemn deliberation, it was resolved to send an embassy in return. At its head was placed a Christian chief named Jean Baptiste Atironta; and on the first of August he and four others departed for Onondaga, carrying a profusion of presents, and accompanied by the apostate envoy of the Iroquois. As the ambassadors had to hunt on the way for subsistence, besides making canoes to cross Lake Ontario, it was twenty days before they reached their destination. When they arrived, there was great jubilation, and, for a full month, nothing but councils. Having thus sifted the matter to the bottom, the Onondagas determined at last to send another embassy with Jean Baptiste on his return, and with them fifteen Huron prisoners, as an earnest of their good intentions, retaining, on their part, one of Baptiste's colleagues as a hostage. This time they chose for their envoy a chief of their own nation, named Scandawati, a man of renown, sixty years of age, joining with him two colleagues. The old Onondaga entered on his mission with a troubled mind. His anxiety was not so much for his life as for his honor and dignity; for, while the Oneidas and the Cayugas were acting in concurrence with the Onondagas, the Senecas had refused any part in the embassy, and still breathed nothing but war. Would they, or still more the Mohawks, so far forget the consideration due to one whose name had been great in the councils of the League as to assault the Hurons while he was among them in the character of an ambassador of his nation, whereby his honor would be compromised and his life endangered. His mind brooded on this idea, and he told one of his colleagues, that, if such a slight were put upon him, he should die of mortification. "I am not a dead dog," he said, "to be despised and forgotten. I am worthy that all men should turn their eyes on me while I am among enemies, and do nothing that may involve me in danger."

What with hunting, fishing, canoe-making, and bad weather, the progress of the august travellers was so slow, that they did not reach the Huron towns till the twenty-third of October. Scandawati presented seven large belts of wampum, each composed of three or four thousand beads, which the Jesuits call the pearls and diamonds of the country. He delivered, too, the fifteen captives, and promised a hundred more on the final conclusion of peace. The three Onondagas remained, as surety for the good faith of those who sent them, until the beginning of January, when the Hurons on their part sent six ambassadors to conclude the treaty, one of the Onondagas accompanying them. Soon there came dire tidings. The prophetic heart of the old chief had not deceived him. The Senecas and Mohawks, disregarding negotiations in which they had no part, and resolved to bring them to an end, were invading the country in force. It might be thought that the Hurons would take their revenge on the Onondaga envoys, now hostages among them; but they did not do so, for the character of an ambassador was, for the most part, held in respect. One morning, however, Scandawati had disappeared. They were full of excitement; for they thought that he had escaped to the enemy. They ranged the woods in search of him, and at length found him in a thicket near the town. He lay dead, on a bed of spruce-boughs which he had made, his throat deeply gashed with a knife. He had died by his own hand, a victim of mortified pride. "See," writes Father Ragueneau, "how much our Indians stand on the point of honor!" [This remarkable story is told by Ragueneau, Relation des Hurons, 1648, 56-58. He was present at the time, and knew all the circumstances.]

We have seen that one of his two colleagues had set out for Onondaga with a deputation of six Hurons. This party was met by a hundred Mohawks, who captured them all and killed the six Hurons but spared the Onondaga, and compelled him to join them. Soon after, they made a sudden onset on about three hundred Hurons journeying through the forest from the town of St. Ignace; and, as many of them were women, they routed the whole, and took forty prisoners. The Onondaga bore part in the fray, and captured a Christian Huron girl; but the next day he insisted on returning to the Huron town. "Kill me, if you will," he said to the Mohawks, "but I cannot follow you; for then I should be ashamed to appear among my countrymen, who sent me on a message of peace to the Hurons; and I must die with them, sooner than seem to act as their enemy." On this, the Mohawks not only permitted him to go, but gave him the Huron girl whom he had taken; and the Onondaga led her back in safety to her countrymen.[1] Here, then, is a ray of light out of Egyptian darkness. The principle of honor was not extinct in these wild hearts.

We hear no more of the negotiations between the Onondagas and the Hurons. They and their results were swept away in the storm of events soon to be related.

1   "Celuy qui l'auoit prise estoit Onnontaeronnon, qui estant icy en os tage à cause de la paix qui se traite auec les Onnontaeronnons, et s'estant trouué auec nos Hurons à cette chasse, y fut pris tout des premiers par les Sonnontoueronnons (Annieronnons?), qui l'ayans reconnu ne luy firent aucun mal, et mesme l'obligerent de les suiure et prendre part à leur victoire; et ainsi en ce rencontre cét Onnontaeronnon auoit fait sa prise, tellement neantmoins qu'il desira s'en retourner le lendemain, disant aux Sonnontoueronnons qu'ils le tuassent s'ils vouloient, mais qu'il ne pouuoit se resoudre à les suiure, et qu'il auroit honte de reparoistre en son pays, les affaires qui l'auoient amené aux Hurons pour la paix ne permettant pas qu'il fist autre chose que de mourir avec eux plus tost que de paroistre s'estre comporté en ennemy. Ainsi les Sonnontoueronnons luy permirent de s'en retourner et de ramener cette bonne Chrestienne, qui estoit sa captiue, laquelle nous a consolé par le recit des entretiens de ces pauures gens dans leur affliction."—Ragueneau, Relation des Hurons, 1648, 65.

Apparently the word Sonnontoueronnons (Senecas), in the above, should read Annieronnons (Mohawks); for, on pp. 50, 57, the writer twice speaks of the party as Mohawks.

CHAPTER XXIV.

1645-1648.

THE HURON CHURCH.

HOPES OF THE MISSION.—CHRISTIAN AND HEATHEN.—BODY AND SOUL.—POSITION OF PROSELYTES.—THE HURON GIRL'S VISIT TO HEAVEN.—A CRISIS.—HURON JUSTICE.—MURDER AND ATONEMENT.—HOPES AND FEARS.

How did it fare with the missions in these days of woe and terror? They had thriven beyond hope. The Hurons, in their time of trouble, had become tractable. They humbled themselves, and, in their desolation and despair, came for succor to the priests. There was a harvest of converts, not only exceeding in numbers that of all former years, but giving in many cases undeniable proofs of sincerity and fervor. In some towns the Christians outnumbered the heathen, and in nearly all they formed a strong party. The mission of La Conception, or Ossossané, was the most successful. Here there were now a church and one or more resident Jesuits,—as also at St. Joseph, St. Ignace, St. Michel, and St. Jean Baptiste:[1] for we have seen that the Huron towns were christened with names of saints. Each church had its bell, which was sometimes hung in a neighboring tree.[2] Every morning it rang its summons to mass;

---

1   Ragueneau, Relation des Hurons, 1646, 56.

2   A fragment of one of these bells, found on the site of a Huron town, is preserved in the museum of Huron relics at the Laval University, Quebec. The bell was not

and, issuing from their dwellings of bark, the converts gathered within the sacred precinct, where the bare, rude walls, fresh from the axe and saw, contrasted with the sheen of tinsel and gilding, and the hues of gay draperies and gaudy pictures. At evening they met again at prayers; and on Sunday, masses, confession, catechism, sermons, and repeating the rosary consumed the whole day.[1]

These converts rarely took part in the burning of prisoners. On the contrary, they sometimes set their faces against the practice; and on one occasion, a certain Étienne Totiri, while his heathen countrymen were tormenting a captive Iroquois at St. Ignace, boldly denounced them, and promised them an eternity of flames and demons, unless they desisted. Not content with this, he addressed an exhortation to the sufferer in one of the intervals of his torture. The dying wretch demanded baptism, which Étienne took it upon himself to administer, amid the hootings of the crowd, who, as he ran with a cup of water from a neighboring house, pushed him to and fro to make him spill it, crying out, "Let him alone! Let the devils burn him after we have done!"

[Ragueneau, Relation des Hurons, 1646, 58. The Hurons often resisted the baptism of their prisoners, on the ground that Hell, and not Heaven, was the place to which they would have them go.—See Lalemant, Relation des Hurons, 1642, 60, Ragueneau, Ibid., 1648, 53, and several other passages.]

In regard to these atrocious scenes, which formed the favorite Huron recreation of a summer night, the Jesuits, it must be confessed, did not quite come up to the requirements of modern sensibility. They were offended at them, it is true, and prevented them when they could; but they were wholly given to the saving of souls, and held the body in scorn, as the vile source of incalculable mischief, worthy the worst inflictions that could be put upon it. What were a few hours of suffering to an eternity of bliss or woe? If the victim were heathen, these brief pangs were but the faint prelude of an undying flame; and if a Christian, they were the fiery portal of Heaven. They might, indeed, be a blessing; since, accepted in atonement for sin, they would shorten the torments

---

large, but was of very elaborate workmanship. Before 1644 the Jesuits had used old copper kettles as a substitute.—Lettre de Lalemant, 31 March, 1644.

1   Ragueneau, Relation des Hurons, 1646, 56.

of Purgatory. Yet, while schooling themselves to despise the body, and all the pain or pleasure that pertained to it, the Fathers were emphatic on one point. It must not be eaten. In the matter of cannibalism, they were loud and vehement in invective.

[The following curious case of conversion at the stake, gravely related by Lalemant, is worth preserving.

"An Iroquois was to be burned at a town some way off. What consolation to set forth, in the hottest summer weather, to deliver this poor victim from the hell prepared for him! The Father approaches him, and instructs him even in the midst of his torments. Forthwith the Faith finds a place in his heart, he recognizes and adores, as the author of his life, Him whose name he had never heard till the hour of his death. He receives the grace of baptism, and breathes nothing but heaven . . . This newly made, but generous Christian, mounted on the scaffold which is the place of his torture, in the sight of a thousand spectators, who are at once his enemies, his judges, and his executioners, raises his eyes and his voice heavenward, and cries aloud, 'Sun, who art witness of my torments, hear my words! I am about to die; but, after my death, I shall go to dwell in heaven.'"—Relation des Hurons, 1641, 67.

The Sun, it will be remembered, was the god of the heathen Iroquois. The convert appealed to his old deity to rejoice with him in his happy future.]

Undeniably, the Faith was making progress; yet it is not to be supposed that its path was a smooth one. The old opposition and the old calumnies were still alive and active. "It is *la prière* that kills us. Your books and your strings of beads have bewitched the country. Before you came, we were happy and prosperous. You are magicians. Your charms kill our corn, and bring sickness and the Iroquois. Echon (Brébeuf) is a traitor among us, in league with our enemies." Such discourse was still rife, openly and secretly.

The Huron who embraced the Faith renounced thenceforth, as we have seen, the feasts, dances, and games in which was his delight, since all these savored of diabolism. And if, being in health, he could not enjoy himself, so also, being sick, he could not be cured; for his physician was a sorcerer, whose medicines were charms and incantations. If the convert was a chief, his case was far worse; since, writes Father Lalemant, "to be a chief and a Christian is to combine water and fire; for the business of the chiefs is mainly to do the Devil's bidding, preside over ceremonies of hell, and excite the young Indians to dances, feasts, and shameless indecencies."

[Relation des Hurons, 1642, 89. The indecencies alluded to were chiefly naked dances, of a superstitious character, and the mystical cure called Andacwandet, before mentioned.]

It is not surprising, then, that proselytes were difficult to make, or that, being made, they often relapsed. The Jesuits complain that they had no means of controlling their converts, and coercing backsliders to stand fast; and they add, that the Iroquois, by destroying the fur-trade, had broken the principal bond between the Hurons and the French, and greatly weakened the influence of the mission. [Lettre du P. Hierosme Lalemant, appended to the Relation of 1645.]

Among the slanders devised by the heathen party against the teachers of the obnoxious doctrine was one which found wide credence, even among the converts, and produced a great effect. They gave out that a baptized Huron girl, who had lately died, and was buried in the cemetery at Sainte Marie, had returned to life, and given a deplorable account of the heaven of the French. No sooner had she entered,—such was the story,—than they seized her, chained her to a stake, and tormented her all day with inconceivable cruelty. They did the same to all the other converted Hurons; for this was the recreation of the French, and especially of the Jesuits, in their celestial abode. They baptized Indians with no other object than that they might have them to torment in heaven; to which end they were willing to meet hardships and dangers in this life, just as a war-party invades the enemy's country at great risk that it may bring home prisoners to burn. After her painful experience, an unknown friend secretly showed the girl a path down to the earth; and she hastened thither to warn her countrymen against the wiles of the missionaries. [Ragueneau, Relation des Hurons, 1646, 65.]

In the spring of 1648 the excitement of the heathen party reached a crisis. A young Frenchman, named Jacques Douart, in the service of the mission, going out at evening a short distance from the Jesuit house of Sainte Marie, was tomahawked by unknown Indians,[1] who proved to be two brothers, instigated by the heathen

---

1   Ragueneau, Relation des Hurons, 1648, 77. Compare Lettre du P. Jean de Brébeuf au T. R. P. Vincent Carafa, Général de la Compagnie de Jésus, Sainte Marie, 2 Juin,

chiefs. A great commotion followed, and for a few days it seemed that the adverse parties would fall to blows, at a time when the common enemy threatened to destroy them both. But sager counsels prevailed. In view of the manifest strength of the Christians, the pagans lowered their tone; and it soon became apparent that it was the part of the Jesuits to insist boldly on satisfaction for the outrage. They made no demand that the murderers should be punished or surrendered, but, with their usual good sense in such matters, conformed to Indian usage, and required that the nation at large should make atonement for the crime by presents.[1] The number of these, their value, and the mode of delivering them were all fixed by ancient custom; and some of the converts, acting as counsel, advised the Fathers of every step it behooved them to take in a case of such importance. As this is the best illustration of Huron justice on record, it may be well to observe the method of procedure,—recollecting that the public, and not the criminal, was to pay the forfeit of the crime.

First of all, the Huron chiefs summoned the Jesuits to meet them at a grand council of the nation, when an old orator, chosen by the rest, rose and addressed Ragueneau, as chief of the French, in the following harangue. Ragueneau, who reports it, declares that he has added nothing to it, and the translation is as literal as possible.

"My Brother," began the speaker, "behold all the tribes of our league assembled!"—and he named them one by one. "We are but a handful; you are the prop and stay of this nation. A thunderbolt has fallen from the sky, and rent a chasm in the earth. We shall fall into it, if you do not support us. Take pity on us. We are here, not so much to speak as to weep over our loss and yours. Our country is but a skeleton, without flesh, veins, sinews, or arteries; and its bones hang together by a thread. This thread is broken by the blow that has fallen on the head of your nephew,[2] for whom we weep. It was a demon of Hell who placed the hatchet in the murderer's hand. Was it you, Sun, whose beams shine on us, who led him to

---

1648, in Carayon.

1   See Introduction.

2   The usual Indian figure in such cases, and not meant to express an actual relationship;—"Uncle" for a superior, "Brother" for an equal, "Nephew" for an inferior.

do this deed? Why did you not darken your light, that he might be stricken with horror at his crime? Were you his accomplice? No; for he walked in darkness, and did not see where he struck. He thought, this wretched murderer, that he aimed at the head of a young Frenchman; but the blow fell upon his country, and gave it a death-wound. The earth opens to receive the blood of the innocent victim, and we shall be swallowed up in the chasm; for we are all guilty. The Iroquois rejoice at his death, and celebrate it as a triumph; for they see that our weapons are turned against each other, and know well that our nation is near its end.

"Brother, take pity on this nation. You alone can restore it to life. It is for you to gather up all these scattered bones, and close this chasm that opens to ingulf us. Take pity on your country. I call it yours, for you are the master of it; and we came here like criminals to receive your sentence, if you will not show us mercy. Pity those who condemn themselves and come to ask forgiveness. It is you who have given strength to the nation by dwelling with it; and if you leave us, we shall be like a wisp of straw torn from the ground to be the sport of the wind. This country is an island drifting on the waves, for the first storm to overwhelm and sink. Make it fast again to its foundation, and posterity will never forget to praise you. When we first heard of this murder, we could do nothing but weep; and we are ready to receive your orders and comply with your demands. Speak, then, and ask what satisfaction you will, for our lives and our possessions are yours; and even if we rob our children to satisfy you, we will tell them that it is not of you that they have to complain, but of him whose crime has made us all guilty. Our anger is against him; but for you we feel nothing but love. He destroyed our lives; and you will restore them, if you will but speak and tell us what you will have us do."

Ragueneau, who remarks that this harangue is a proof that eloquence is the gift of Nature rather than of Art, made a reply, which he has not recorded, and then gave the speaker a bundle of small sticks, indicating the number of presents which he required in satisfaction for the murder. These sticks were distributed among the various tribes in the council, in order that each might contribute its share towards the indemnity. The council dissolved, and the chiefs went home, each with his allotment of sticks, to collect in his village a corresponding number of presents. There was no constraint;

those gave who chose to do so; but, as all were ambitious to show their public spirit, the contributions were ample. No one thought of molesting the murderers. Their punishment was their shame at the sacrifices which the public were making in their behalf.

The presents being ready, a day was set for the ceremony of their delivery; and crowds gathered from all parts to witness it. The assembly was convened in the open air, in a field beside the mission-house of Sainte Marie; and, in the midst, the chiefs held solemn council. Towards evening, they deputed four of their number, two Christians and two heathen, to carry their address to the Father Superior. They came, loaded with presents; but these were merely preliminary. One was to open the door, another for leave to enter; and as Sainte Marie was a large house, with several interior doors, at each one of which it behooved them to repeat this formality, their stock of gifts became seriously reduced before they reached the room where Father Ragueneau awaited them. On arriving, they made him a speech, every clause of which was confirmed by a present. The first was to wipe away his tears; the second, to restore his voice, which his grief was supposed to have impaired; the third, to calm the agitation of his mind; and the fourth, to allay the just anger of his heart.[1] These gifts consisted of wampum and the large shells of which it was made, together with other articles, worthless in any eyes but those of an Indian. Nine additional presents followed: four for the four posts of the sepulchre or scaffold of the murdered man; four for the cross-pieces which connected the posts; and one for a pillow to support his head. Then came eight more, corresponding to the eight largest bones of the victim's body, and also to the eight clans of the Hurons.[2] Ragueneau, as required by established custom, now made them a present in his turn. It consisted of three thousand beads of wampum, and was designed to soften the earth, in order that they might not be hurt, when falling upon it, overpowered by his reproaches for the enormity of their crime. This closed the interview, and the deputation withdrew.

The grand ceremony took place on the next day. A kind of arena had been prepared, and here were hung the fifty presents in which the atonement essentially consisted,—the rest, amounting

1   Ragueneau himself describes the scene. Relation des Hurons, 1648, 80.
2   Ragueneau says, "les huit nations"; but, as the Hurons consisted of only four, or at most five, nations, he probably means the clans. For the nature of these divisions, see Introduction.

to as many more, being only accessory.[1] The Jesuits had the right of examining them all, rejecting any that did not satisfy them, and demanding others in place of them. The naked crowd sat silent and attentive, while the orator in the midst delivered the fifty presents in a series of harangues, which the tired listener has not thought it necessary to preserve. Then came the minor gifts, each with its signification explained in turn by the speaker. First, as a sepulchre had been provided the day before for the dead man, it was now necessary to clothe and equip him for his journey to the next world; and to this end three presents were made. They represented a hat, a coat, a shirt, breeches, stockings, shoes, a gun, powder, and bullets; but they were in fact something quite different, as wampum, beaver-skins, and the like. Next came several gifts to close up the wounds of the slain. Then followed three more. The first closed the chasm in the earth, which had burst through horror of the crime. The next trod the ground firm, that it might not open again; and here the whole assembly rose and danced, as custom required. The last placed a large stone over the closed gulf; to make it doubly secure.

Now came another series of presents, seven in number,—to restore the voices of all the missionaries,—to invite the men in their service to forget the murder,—to appease the Governor when he should hear of it,—to light the fire at Sainte Marie,—to open the gate,—to launch the ferry boat in which the Huron visitors crossed the river,—and to give back the paddle to the boy who had charge of the boat. The Fathers, it seems, had the right of exacting two more presents, to rebuild their house and church,—supposed to have been shaken to the earth by the late calamity; but they forbore to urge the claim. Last of all were three gifts to confirm all the rest, and to entreat the Jesuits to cherish an undying love for the Hurons.

The priests on their part gave presents, as tokens of good-will; and with that the assembly dispersed. The mission had gained a triumph, and its influence was greatly strengthened. The future would have been full of hope, but for the portentous cloud of war that rose, black and wrathful, from where lay the dens of the Iroquois.

---

1   The number was unusually large,—partly because the affair was thought very important, and partly because the murdered man belonged to another nation. See Introduction.

CHAPTER XXV.

1648, 1649.

SAINTE MARIE.

THE CENTRE OF THE MISSIONS.—FORT.—CONVENT.—
HOSPITAL.—CARAVANSARY.—CHURCH.—THE
INMATES OF SAINTE MARIE.—DOMESTIC ECONOMY.—
MISSIONS.—A MEETING OF JESUITS.—THE DEAD
MISSIONARY.

The River Wye enters the Bay of Glocester, an inlet of the
Bay of Matchedash, itself an inlet of the vast Georgian Bay of Lake
Huron. Retrace the track of two centuries and more, and ascend
this little stream in the summer of the year 1648. Your vessel is
a birch canoe, and your conductor a Huron Indian. On the right
hand and on the left, gloomy and silent, rise the primeval woods;
but you have advanced scarcely half a league when the scene is
changed, and cultivated fields, planted chiefly with maize, extend far
along the bank, and back to the distant verge of the forest. Before
you opens the small lake from which the stream issues; and on
your left, a stone's throw from the shore, rises a range of palisades
and bastioned walls, inclosing a number of buildings. Your canoe
enters a canal or ditch immediately above them, and you land at the
Mission, or Residence, or Fort of Sainte Marie.

Here was the centre and base of the Huron missions; and
now, for once, one must wish that Jesuit pens had been more fluent.
They have told us but little of Sainte Marie, and even this is to

be gathered chiefly from incidental allusions. In the forest, which long since has resumed its reign over this memorable spot, the walls and ditches of the fortifications may still be plainly traced; and the deductions from these remains are in perfect accord with what we can gather from the Relations and letters of the priests. [Before me is an elaborate plan of the remains, taken on the spot.] The fortified work which inclosed the buildings was in the form of a parallelogram, about a hundred and seventy-five feet long, and from eighty to ninety wide. It lay parallel with the river, and somewhat more than a hundred feet distant from it. On two sides it was a continuous wall of masonry,[1] flanked with square bastions, adapted to musketry, and probably used as magazines, storehouses, or lodgings. The sides towards the river and the lake had no other defences than a ditch and palisade, flanked, like the others, by bastions, over each of which was displayed a large cross.[2] The buildings within were, no doubt, of wood; and they included a church, a kitchen, a refectory, places of retreat for religious instruction and meditation,[3] and lodgings for at least sixty persons. Near the church, but outside the fortification, was a cemetery. Beyond the ditch or canal which opened on the river was a large area, still traceable, in the form of an irregular triangle, surrounded by a ditch, and apparently by palisades. It seems to have been meant for the protection of the Indian visitors who came in throngs to Sainte Marie, and who were lodged in a large house of bark, after the Huron manner.[4] Here, perhaps, was also the hospital, which was placed without the walls, in order that Indian women, as well as men, might be admitted into it.[5]

---

1 It seems probable that the walls, of which the remains may still be traced, were foundations supporting a wooden superstructure. Ragueneau, in a letter to the General of the Jesuits, dated March 13, 1650, alludes to the defences of Saint Marie as "une simple palissade."

2 "Quatre grandes Croix qui sont aux quatre coins de nostre enclos."—Ragueneau, Relation des Hurons, 1648, 81.

3 It seems that these places, besides those for the priests, were of two kinds,—"vne retraite pour les pelerins (Indians), enfin vn lieu plus separé, où les infideles, qui n'y sont admis que de iour au passage, y puissent tousiours receuoir quelque bon mot pour leur salut."—Lalemant, Relation des Hurons, 1644, 74.

4 At least it was so in 1642. "Nous leur auons dressé vn Hospice ou Cabane d'écorce."—Ibid., 1642, 57.

5 "Cet hospital est tellement separé de nostre demeure, que non seulement les hommes et enfans, mais les femmes y peuuent estre admises."—Ibid., 1644, 74.

No doubt the buildings of Sainte Marie were of the roughest,—rude walls of boards, windows without glass, vast chimneys of unhewn stone. All its riches were centred in the church, which, as Lalemant tells us, was regarded by the Indians as one of the wonders of the world, but which, he adds, would have made but a beggarly show in France. Yet one wonders, at first thought, how so much labor could have been accomplished here. Of late years, however, the number of men at the command of the mission had been considerable. Soldiers had been sent up from time to time, to escort the Fathers on their way, and defend them on their arrival. Thus, in 1644, Montmagny ordered twenty men of a reinforcement just arrived from France to escort Brébeuf, Garreau, and Chabanel to the Hurons, and remain there during the winter.[1] These soldiers lodged with the Jesuits, and lived at their table.[2] It was not, however, on detachments of troops that they mainly relied for labor or defence. Any inhabitant of Canada who chose to undertake so hard and dangerous a service was allowed to do so, receiving only his maintenance from the mission, without pay. In return, he was allowed to trade with the Indians, and sell the furs thus obtained at the magazine of the Company, at a fixed price. [Registres des Arrêts du Conseil, extract in Faillon, II, 94.] Many availed themselves of this permission; and all whose services were accepted by the Jesuits seem to have been men to whom they had communicated no small portion of their own zeal, and who were enthusiastically attached to their Order and their cause. There is abundant evidence that a large proportion of them acted from motives wholly disinterested. They were, in fact, *donnés* of the mission,[3]—given, heart and hand, to its service. There is probability in the conjecture, that the profits of their trade with the Indians were reaped, not for their own behoof, but for that of the mission.[4]

---

1   Vimont, Relation, 1644, 49. He adds, that some of these soldiers, though they had once been "assez mauvais garçons," had shown great zeal and devotion in behalf of the mission.

2   Journal des Supérieurs des Jésuites, MS. In 1648, a small cannon was sent to Sainte Marie in the Huron canoes.—Ibid.

3   See ante, chapter 16 (page 214), "donnés". Garnier calls them "séculiers d'habit, mais religieux de cœur."—Lettres, MSS.

4   The Jesuits, even at this early period, were often and loudly charged with sharing in the fur-trade. It is certain that this charge was not wholly without foundation. Le Jeune, in the Relation of 1657, speaking of the wampum, guns, powder, lead,

It is difficult otherwise to explain the confidence with which the Father Superior, in a letter to the General of the Jesuits at Rome, speaks of its resources. He says, "Though our number is greatly increased, and though we still hope for more men, and especially for more priests of our Society, it is not necessary to increase the pecuniary aid given us."[1]

Much of this prosperity was no doubt due to the excellent management of their resources, and a very successful agriculture. While the Indians around them were starving, they raised maize in such quantities, that, in the spring of 1649, the Father Superior thought that their stock of provisions might suffice for three years. "Hunting and fishing," he says, "are better than heretofore"; and he adds, that they had fowls, swine, and even cattle.[2] How they could have brought these last to Sainte Marie it is difficult to conceive. The feat, under the circumstances, is truly astonishing. Everything

---

hatchets, kettles, and other articles which the missionaries were obliged to give to the Indians, at councils and elsewhere, says that these must be bought from the traders with beaver-skins, which are the money of the country; and he adds, "Que si vn Iesuite en reçoit ou en recueille quelques-vns pour ayder aux frais immenses qu'il faut faire dans ces Missions si éloignées, et pour gagner ces peuples à Iesus-Christ et les porter à la paix, il seroit à souhaiter que ceux-là mesme qui deuroient faire ces despenses pour la conseruation du pays, ne fussent pas du moins les premiers à condamner le zele de ces Peres, et à les rendre par leurs discours plus noirs que leurs robes."—Relation, 1657, 16.

In the same year, Chaumonot, addressing a council of the Iroquois during a period of truce, said, "Keep your beaver-skins, if you choose, for the Dutch. Even such of them as may fall into our possession will be employed for your service."—Ibid., 17.

In 1636, La Jeune thought it necessary to write a long letter of defence against the charge; and in 1643, a declaration, appended to the Relation of that year, and certifying that the Jesuits took no part in the fur-trade, was drawn up and signed by twelve members of the company of New France. Its only meaning is, that the Jesuits were neither partners nor rivals of the Company's monopoly. They certainly bought supplies from its magazines with furs which they obtained from the Indians.

Their object evidently was to make the mission partially self-supporting. To impute mercenary motives to Garnier, Jogues, and their co-laborers, is manifestly idle; but, even in the highest flights of his enthusiasm, the Jesuit never forgot his worldly wisdom.

1   Lettre du P. Paul Ragueneau au T. R. P. Vincent Carafa, Général de la Compagnie de Jésus à Rome, Sainte Marie aux Hurons, 1 Mars, 1649 (Carayon).

2   Lettre du P. Paul Ragueneau au T. R. P. Vincent Carafa, Général de la Compagnie de Jésus à Rome, Sainte Marie aux Hurons, 1 Mars, 1649 (Carayon).

indicates a fixed resolve on the part of the Fathers to build up a solid and permanent establishment.

It is by no means to be inferred that the household fared sumptuously. Their ordinary food was maize, pounded and boiled, and seasoned, in the absence of salt, which was regarded as a luxury, with morsels of smoked fish. [Ragueneau, Relation des Hurons, 1648, 48.]

In March, 1649, there were in the Huron country and its neighborhood eighteen Jesuit priests, four lay brothers, twenty-three men serving without pay, seven hired men, four boys, and eight soldiers.[1] Of this number, fifteen priests were engaged in the various missions, while all the rest were retained permanently at Sainte Marie. All was method, discipline, and subordination. Some of the men were assigned to household work, and some to the hospital; while the rest labored at the fortifications, tilled the fields, and stood ready, in case of need, to fight the Iroquois. The Father Superior, with two other priests as assistants, controlled and guided all. The remaining Jesuits, undisturbed by temporal cares, were devoted exclusively to the charge of their respective missions. Two or three times in the year, they all, or nearly all, assembled at Sainte Marie, to take counsel together and determine their future action. Hither, also, they came at intervals for a period of meditation and prayer, to nerve themselves and gain new inspiration for their stern task.

Besides being the citadel and the magazine of the mission, Sainte Marie was the scene of a bountiful hospitality. On every alternate Saturday, as well as on feast-days, the converts came in crowds from the farthest villages. They were entertained during Saturday, Sunday, and a part of Monday; and the rites of the Church were celebrated before them with all possible solemnity and pomp. They were welcomed also at other times, and entertained, usually with three meals to each. In these latter years the prevailing famine drove them to Sainte Marie in swarms. In the course of 1647 three thousand were lodged and fed here; and in the following year the number was doubled. [Compare Ragueneau in Relation des Hurons,

---

1   See the report of the Father Superior to the General, above cited. The number was greatly increased within the year. In April, 1648, Ragueneau reports but forty-two French in all, including priests. Before the end of the summer a large reinforcement came up in the Huron canoes.

1648, 48, and in his report to the General in 1649.] Heathen Indians were also received and supplied with food, but were not permitted to remain at night. There was provision for the soul as well as the body; and, Christian or heathen, few left Sainte Marie without a word of instruction or exhortation. Charity was an instrument of conversion.

Such, so far as we can reconstruct it from the scattered hints remaining, was this singular establishment, at once military, monastic, and patriarchal. The missions of which it was the basis were now eleven in number. To those among the Hurons already mentioned another had lately been added,—that of Sainte Madeleine; and two others, called St. Jean and St. Matthias, had been established in the neighboring Tobacco Nation.[1] The three remaining missions were all among tribes speaking the Algonquin languages. Every winter, bands of these savages, driven by famine and fear of the Iroquois, sought harborage in the Huron country, and the mission of Sainte Elisabeth was established for their benefit. The next Algonquin mission was that of Saint Esprit, embracing the Nipissings and other tribes east and north-east of Lake Huron; and, lastly, the mission of St. Pierre included the tribes at the outlet of Lake Superior, and throughout a vast extent of surrounding wilderness.[2]

These missions were more laborious, though not more perilous, than those among the Hurons. The Algonquin hordes were never long at rest; and, summer and winter, the priest must follow them by lake, forest, and stream: in summer plying the paddle all day, or toiling through pathless thickets, bending under the weight of a birch canoe or a load of baggage,—at night, his bed the rugged earth, or some bare rock, lashed by the restless

---

1   The mission of the Neutral Nation had been abandoned for the time, from the want of missionaries. The Jesuits had resolved on concentration, and on the thorough conversion of the Hurons, as a preliminary to more extended efforts.

2   Besides these tribes, the Jesuits had become more or less acquainted with many others, also Algonquin on the west and south of Lake Huron; as well as with the Puans, or Winnebagoes, a Dacotah tribe between Lake Michigan and the Mississippi.

      The Mission of Sault Sainte Marie, at the outlet of Lake Superior, was established at a later period. Modern writers have confounded it with Sainte Marie of the Hurons.

      By the Relation of 1649 it appears that another mission had lately been begun at the Grand Manitoulin Island, which the Jesuits also christened Isle Sainte Marie.

waves of Lake Huron; while famine, the snow-storms, the cold, the treacherous ice of the Great Lakes, smoke, filth, and, not rarely, threats and persecution, were the lot of his winter wanderings. It seemed an earthly paradise, when, at long intervals, he found a respite from his toils among his brother Jesuits under the roof of Sainte Marie.

Hither, while the Fathers are gathered from their scattered stations at one of their periodical meetings,—a little before the season of Lent, 1649, [1]—let us, too, repair, and join them. We enter at the eastern gate of the fortification, midway in the wall between its northern and southern bastions, and pass to the hall, where, at a rude table, spread with ruder fare, all the household are assembled,—laborers, domestics, soldiers, and priests.

It was a scene that might recall a remote half feudal, half patriarchal age, when, under the smoky rafters of his antique hail, some warlike thane sat, with kinsmen and dependants ranged down the long board, each in his degree. Here, doubtless, Ragueneau, the Father Superior, held the place of honor; and, for chieftains scarred with Danish battle-axes, was seen a band of thoughtful men, clad in a threadbare garb of black, their brows swarthy from exposure, yet marked with the lines of intellect and a fixed enthusiasm of purpose. Here was Bressani, scarred with firebrand and knife; Chabanel, once a professor of rhetoric in France, now a missionary, bound by a self-imposed vow to a life from which his nature recoiled; the fanatical Chaumonot, whose character savored of his peasant birth,—for the grossest fungus of superstition that ever grew under the shadow of Rome was not too much for his omnivorous credulity, and miracles and mysteries were his daily food; yet, such as his faith was, he was ready to die for it. Garnier, beardless like a woman, was of a far finer nature. His religion was of the affections and the sentiments; and his imagination, warmed with the ardor of his faith, shaped the ideal forms of his worship into visible realities. Brébeuf sat conspicuous among his brethren, portly and tall, his short moustache and beard grizzled with time,—for he was fifty-six years old. If he seemed impassive, it was because one overmastering principle had merged and absorbed all

---

1   The date of this meeting is a supposition merely. It is adopted with reference to events which preceded and followed.

the impulses of his nature and all the faculties of his mind. The enthusiasm which with many is fitful and spasmodic was with him the current of his life,—solemn and deep as the tide of destiny. The Divine Trinity, the Virgin, the Saints, Heaven and Hell, Angels and Fiends,—to him, these alone were real, and all things else were nought. Gabriel Lalemant, nephew of Jerome Lalemant, Superior at Quebec, was Brébeuf's colleague at the mission of St. Ignace. His slender frame and delicate features gave him an appearance of youth, though he had reached middle life; and, as in the case of Garnier, the fervor of his mind sustained him through exertions of which he seemed physically incapable. Of the rest of that company little has come down to us but the bare record of their missionary toils; and we may ask in vain what youthful enthusiasm, what broken hope or faded dream, turned the current of their lives, and sent them from the heart of civilization to this savage outpost of the world.

No element was wanting in them for the achievement of such a success as that to which they aspired,—neither a transcendent zeal, nor a matchless discipline, nor a practical sagacity very seldom surpassed in the pursuits where men strive for wealth and place; and if they were destined to disappointment, it was the result of external causes, against which no power of theirs could have insured them.

There was a gap in their number. The place of Antoine Daniel was empty, and never more to be filled by him,—never at least in the flesh, for Chaumonot averred, that not long since, when the Fathers were met in council, he had seen their dead companion seated in their midst, as of old, with a countenance radiant and majestic.[1] They believed his story,—no doubt he believed it himself;

---

1   "Ce bon Pere s'apparut après sa mort à vn des nostres par deux diuerses fois. En l'vne il se fit voir en estat de gloire, portant le visage d'vn homme d'enuiron trente ans, quoy qu'il soit mort en l'âge de quarante-huict ... Vne autre fois il fut veu assister à vne assemblée que nous tenions," etc.—Ragueneau, Relation des Hurons, 1649, 5.

"Le P. Chaumonot vit au milieu de l'assemblée le P. Daniel qui aidait les Pères de ses conseils, et les remplissait d'une force surnaturelle; son visage était plein de majesté et d'éclat."—Ibid., Lettre au Général de la Compagnie de Jésus (Carayon, 243).

"Le P. Chaumonot nous a quelque fois raconté, à la gloire de cet illustre confesseur de J. C. (Daniel) qu'il s'étoit fait voir à lui dans la gloire, à l'âge d'environ 30 ans, quoiqu'il en eut près de 50, et avec les autres circonstances qui se trouuent

and they consoled one another with the thought, that, in losing their colleague on earth, they had gained him as a powerful intercessor in heaven. Daniel's station had been at St. Joseph; but the mission and the missionary had alike ceased to exist.

là (in the Historia Canadensis of Du Creux). Il ajoutait seulement qu'à la vue de ce bien-heureux tant de choses lui vinrent à l'esprit pour les lui demander, qu'il ne savoit pas où commencer son entretien avec ce cher défunt. Enfin, lui dit-il: "Apprenez moi, mon Père, ce que ie dois faire pour être bien agréable à Dieu."—"Jamais," répondit le martyr, "ne perdez le souvenir de vos péchés."—Suite de la Vie de Chaumonot, 11.

CHAPTER XXVI.

1648.

ANTOINE DANIEL.

HURON TRADERS.—BATTLE AT THREE RIVERS.—ST. JOSEPH.—ONSET OF THE IROQUOIS.—DEATH OF DANIEL.—THE TOWN DESTROYED.

In the summer of 1647 the Hurons dared not go down to the French settlements, but in the following year they took heart, and resolved at all risks to make the attempt; for the kettles, hatchets, and knives of the traders had become necessaries of life. Two hundred and fifty of their best warriors therefore embarked, under five valiant chiefs. They made the voyage in safety, approached Three Rivers on the seventeenth of July, and, running their canoes ashore among the bulrushes, began to grease their hair, paint their faces, and otherwise adorn themselves, that they might appear after a befitting fashion at the fort. While they were thus engaged, the alarm was sounded. Some of their warriors had discovered a large body of Iroquois, who for several days had been lurking in the forest, unknown to the French garrison, watching their opportunity to strike a blow. The Hurons snatched their arms, and, half-greased and painted, ran to meet them. The Iroquois received them with a volley. They fell flat to avoid the shot, then leaped up with a furious yell, and sent back a shower of arrows and bullets. The Iroquois, who were outnumbered, gave way and fled, excepting a few who for a time made fight with their knives. The Hurons pursued. Many prisoners were taken, and many dead left on the field. [Lalemant, Relation, 1648, 11. The Jesuit Bressani had come down with the Hurons, and was with them in the fight.] The rout of the enemy was complete; and when their trade was ended, the Hurons returned home in triumph, decorated with the laurels and the scalps of victory. As it proved, it would have been well, had they remained there to defend their families and firesides.

The oft-mentioned town of Teanaustayé, or St. Joseph, lay on the south-eastern frontier of the Huron country, near the foot of a range of forest-covered hills, and about fifteen miles from Sainte Marie. It had been the chief town of the nation, and its population, by the Indian standard, was still large; for it had four hundred families, and at least two thousand inhabitants. It was well fortified with palisades, after the Huron manner, and was esteemed the chief bulwark of the country. Here countless Iroquois had been burned and devoured. Its people had been truculent and intractable heathen, but many of them had surrendered to the Faith, and for four years past Father Daniel had preached among them with excellent results.

On the morning of the fourth of July, when the forest around basked lazily in the early sun, you might have mounted the rising ground on which the town stood, and passed unchallenged through the opening in the palisade. Within, you would have seen the crowded dwellings of bark, shaped like the arched coverings of huge baggage-wagons, and decorated with the *totems* or armorial devices of their owners daubed on the outside with paint. Here some squalid wolfish dog lay sleeping in the sun, a group of Huron girls chatted together in the shade, old squaws pounded corn in large wooden mortars, idle youths gambled with cherry stones on a wooden platter, and naked infants crawled in the dust. Scarcely a warrior was to be seen. Some were absent in quest of game or of Iroquois scalps, and some had gone with the trading-party to the French settlements. You followed the foul passage-ways among the houses, and at length came to the church. It was full to the door. Daniel had just finished the mass, and his flock still knelt at their devotions. It was but the day before that he had returned to them, warmed with new fervor, from his meditations in retreat at Sainte Marie. Suddenly an uproar of voices, shrill with terror, burst upon the languid silence of the town. "The Iroquois! the Iroquois!" A crowd of hostile warriors had issued from the forest, and were rushing across the clearing, towards the opening in the palisade. Daniel ran out of the church, and hurried to the point of danger. Some snatched weapons; some rushed to and fro in the madness of a blind panic. The priest rallied the defenders; promised Heaven to those who died for their homes and their faith; then hastened from house to house, calling on unbelievers to repent and receive baptism, to snatch them from the Hell that yawned to ingulf them. They crowded around him, imploring to be saved; and, immersing his handkerchief in a bowl of water, he shook it over them, and baptized them by aspersion. They pursued him, as he ran again to the church, where he found a throng of women, children, and old men, gathered as in a sanctuary. Some cried for baptism, some held out their children to receive it, some begged for absolution, and some wailed in terror and despair. "Brothers," he exclaimed again and again, as he shook the baptismal drops from his handkerchief,—"brothers, to-day we shall be in Heaven."

The fierce yell of the war-whoop now rose close at hand. The palisade was forced, and the enemy was in the town. The air quivered with the infernal din. "Fly!" screamed the priest, driving his flock before him. "I will stay here. We shall meet again in Heaven." Many of them escaped through an opening in the palisade opposite to that by which the Iroquois had entered; but Daniel would not follow, for there still might be souls to rescue from perdition. The hour had come for which he had long prepared himself. In a moment he saw the Iroquois, and came forth from the church to meet them. When they saw him in turn, radiant in the vestments of his office, confronting them with a look kindled with the inspiration of martyrdom, they stopped and stared in amazement; then recovering themselves, bent their bows, and showered him with a volley of arrows, that tore through his robes and his flesh. A gun shot followed; the ball pierced his heart, and he fell dead, gasping the name of Jesus. They rushed upon him with yells of triumph, stripped him naked, gashed and hacked his lifeless body, and, scooping his blood in their hands, bathed their faces in it to make them brave. The town was in a blaze; when the flames reached the church, they flung the priest into it, and both were consumed together.

[Ragueneau, Relation des Hurons, 1649, 3-5; Bressani, Relation Abrégée, 247; Du Creux, Historia Canadensis, 524; Tanner, Societas

Jesu Militans, 531; Marie de l'Incarnation, Lettre aux Ursulines de Tours, Quebec, 1649.

Daniel was born at Dieppe, and was forty-eight years old at the time of his death. He had been a Jesuit from the age of twenty.]

Teanaustayé was a heap of ashes, and the victors took up their march with a train of nearly seven hundred prisoners, many of whom they killed on the way. Many more had been slain in the town and the neighboring forest, where the pursuers hunted them down, and where women, crouching for refuge among thickets, were betrayed by the cries and wailing of their infants.

The triumph of the Iroquois did not end here; for a neighboring fortified town, included within the circle of Daniel's mission, shared the fate of Teanaustayé. Never had the Huron nation received such a blow.

CHAPTER XXVII.

1649.

RUIN OF THE HURONS.

ST. LOUIS ON FIRE.—INVASION.—ST. IGNACE CAPTURED.—BRÉBEUF AND LALEMANT.—BATTLE AT ST. LOUIS.—SAINTE MARIE THREATENED.—RENEWED FIGHTING.—DESPERATE CONFLICT.—A NIGHT OF SUSPENSE.—PANIC AMONG THE VICTORS.—BURNING OF ST. IGNACE.—RETREAT OF THE IROQUOIS.

More than eight months had passed since the catastrophe of St. Joseph. The winter was over, and that dreariest of seasons had come, the churlish forerunner of spring. Around Sainte Marie the forests were gray and bare, and, in the cornfields, the oozy, half-thawed soil, studded with the sodden stalks of the last autumn's harvest, showed itself in patches through the melting snow.

At nine o'clock on the morning of the sixteenth of March, the priests saw a heavy smoke rising over the naked forest towards the south-east, about three miles distant. They looked at each other in dismay. "The Iroquois! They are burning St. Louis!" Flames mingled with the smoke; and, as they stood gazing, two Christian Hurons came, breathless and aghast, from the burning town. Their worst fear was realized. The Iroquois were there; but where were the priests of the mission, Brébeuf and Lalemant?

Late in the autumn, a thousand Iroquois, chiefly Senecas and Mohawks, had taken the war-path for the Hurons. They had been all winter in the forests, hunting for subsistence, and moving at their leisure towards their prey. The destruction of the two towns of the mission of St. Joseph had left a wide gap, and in the middle of March they entered the heart of the Huron country, undiscovered. Common vigilance and common sense would have averted the calamities that followed; but the Hurons were like a doomed people, stupefied, sunk in dejection, fearing everything, yet taking no measures for defence. They could easily have met the invaders with double their force, but the besotted warriors lay idle in their towns, or hunted at leisure in distant forests; nor could the Jesuits, by counsel or exhortation, rouse them to face the danger.

Before daylight of the sixteenth, the invaders approached St. Ignace, which, with St. Louis and three other towns, formed the mission of the same name. They reconnoitred the place in the darkness. It was defended on three sides by a deep ravine, and further strengthened by palisades fifteen or sixteen feet high, planted under the direction of the Jesuits. On the fourth side it was protected by palisades alone; and these were left, as usual, unguarded. This was not from a sense of security; for the greater part of the population had abandoned the town, thinking it too much exposed to the enemy, and there remained only about four hundred, chiefly women, children, and old men, whose infatuated defenders were absent hunting, or on futile scalping-parties against the Iroquois. It was just before dawn, when a yell, as of a legion of devils, startled the wretched inhabitants from their sleep; and the Iroquois, bursting in upon them, cut them down with knives and hatchets, killing many, and reserving the rest for a worse fate. They had entered by the weakest side; on the other sides there was no exit, and only three Hurons escaped. The whole was the work of a few minutes. The Iroquois left a guard to hold the town, and secure the retreat of the main body in case of a reverse; then, smearing their faces with blood, after their ghastly custom, they rushed, in the dim light of the early dawn, towards St. Louis, about a league distant.

The three fugitives had fled, half naked, through the forest, for the same point, which they reached about sunrise, yelling the alarm. The number of inhabitants here was less, at this time, than seven hundred; and, of these, all who had strength to escape, excepting about eighty warriors, made in wild terror for a place of safety.

Many of the old, sick, and decrepit were left perforce in the lodges. The warriors, ignorant of the strength of the assailants, sang their war-songs, and resolved to hold the place to the last. It had not the natural strength of St. Ignace; but, like it, was surrounded by palisades.

Here were the two Jesuits, Brébeuf and Lalemant. Brébeuf's converts entreated him to escape with them; but the Norman zealot, bold scion of a warlike stock, had no thought of flight. His post was in the teeth of danger, to cheer on those who fought, and open Heaven to those who fell. His colleague, slight of frame and frail of constitution, trembled despite himself; but deep enthusiasm mastered the weakness of Nature, and he, too, refused to fly.

Scarcely had the sun risen, and scarcely were the fugitives gone, when, like a troop of tigers, the Iroquois rushed to the assault. Yell echoed yell, and shot answered shot. The Hurons, brought to bay, fought with the utmost desperation, and with arrows, stones, and the few guns they had, killed thirty of their assailants, and wounded many more. Twice the Iroquois recoiled, and twice renewed the attack with unabated ferocity. They swarmed at the foot of the palisades, and hacked at them with their hatchets, till they had cut them through at several different points. For a time there was a deadly fight at these breaches. Here were the two priests, promising Heaven to those who died for their faith,—one giving baptism, and the other absolution. At length the Iroquois broke in, and captured all the surviving defenders, the Jesuits among the rest. They set the town on fire; and the helpless wretches who had remained, unable to fly, were consumed in their burning dwellings. Next they fell upon Brébeuf and Lalemant, stripped them, bound them fast, and led them with the other prisoners back to St. Ignace, where all turned out to wreak their fury on the two priests, beating them savagely with sticks and clubs as they drove them into the town. At present, there was no time for further torture, for there was work in hand.

The victors divided themselves into several bands, to burn the neighboring villages and hunt their flying inhabitants. In the flush of their triumph, they meditated a bolder enterprise; and, in the afternoon, their chiefs sent small parties to reconnoitre Sainte Marie, with a view to attacking it on the next day.

Meanwhile the fugitives of St. Louis, joined by other bands as terrified and as helpless as they, were struggling through the soft snow which clogged the forests towards Lake Huron, where the treacherous ice of spring was still unmelted. One fear expelled another. They ventured upon it, and pushed forward all that day and all the following night, shivering and famished, to find refuge in the towns of the Tobacco Nation. Here, when they arrived, they spread a universal panic.

Ragueneau, Bressani, and their companions waited in suspense at Sainte Marie. On the one hand, they trembled for Brébeuf and Lalemant; on the other, they looked hourly for an attack: and when at evening they saw the Iroquois scouts prowling along the edge of the bordering forest, their fears were confirmed. They had with them about forty Frenchmen, well armed; but their palisades and wooden buildings were not fire-proof, and they had learned from fugitives the number and ferocity of the invaders. They stood guard all night, praying to the Saints, and above all to their great patron, Saint Joseph, whose festival was close at hand.

In the morning they were somewhat relieved by the arrival of about three hundred Huron warriors, chiefly converts from La Conception and Sainte Madeleine, tolerably well armed, and full of fight. They were expecting others to join them; and meanwhile, dividing into several bands, they took post by the passes of the neighboring forest, hoping to waylay parties of the enemy. Their expectation was fulfilled; for, at this time, two hundred of the Iroquois were making their way from St. Ignace, in advance of the main body, to begin the attack on Sainte Marie. They fell in with a band of the Hurons, set upon them, killed many, drove the rest to headlong flight, and, as they plunged in terror through the snow, chased them within sight of Sainte Marie. The other Hurons, hearing the yells and firing, ran to the rescue, and attacked so fiercely, that the Iroquois in turn were routed, and ran for shelter to St. Louis, followed closely by the victors. The houses of the town had been burned, but the palisade around them was still standing, though breached and broken. The Iroquois rushed in; but the Hurons were at their heels. Many of the fugitives were captured, the rest killed or put to utter rout, and the triumphant Hurons remained masters of the place.

The Iroquois who escaped fled to St. Ignace. Here, or on the way thither, they found the main body of the invaders; and when they heard of the disaster, the whole swarm, beside themselves with rage, turned towards St. Louis to take their revenge. Now ensued one of the most furious Indian battles on record. The Hurons within the palisade did not much exceed a hundred and fifty; for many had been killed or disabled, and many, perhaps, had straggled away. Most of their enemies had guns, while they had but few. Their weapons were bows and arrows, war-clubs, hatchets, and knives; and of these they made good use, sallying repeatedly, fighting like devils, and driving back their assailants again and again. There are times when the Indian warrior forgets his cautious maxims, and throws himself into battle with a mad and reckless ferocity. The desperation of one party, and the fierce courage of both, kept up the fight after the day had closed; and the scout from Sainte Marie, as he bent listening under the gloom of the pines, heard, far into the night, the howl of battle rising from the darkened forest. The principal chief of the Iroquois was severely wounded, and nearly a hundred of their warriors were killed on the spot. When, at length, their numbers and persistent fury prevailed, their only prize was some twenty Huron warriors, spent with fatigue and faint with loss of blood. The rest lay dead around the shattered palisades which they had so valiantly defended. Fatuity, not cowardice, was the ruin of the Huron nation.

The lamps burned all night at Sainte Marie, and its defenders stood watching till daylight, musket in hand. The Jesuits prayed without ceasing, and Saint Joseph was besieged with invocations. "Those of us who were priests," writes Ragueneau, "each made a vow to say a mass in his honor every month, for the space of a year; and all the rest bound themselves by vows to divers penances." The expected onslaught did not take place. Not an Iroquois appeared. Their victory had been bought too dear, and they had no stomach for more fighting. All the next day, the eighteenth, a stillness, like the dead lull of a tempest, followed the turmoil of yesterday,—as if, says the Father Superior, "the country were waiting, palsied with fright, for some new disaster."

On the following day,—the journalist fails not to mention that it was the festival of Saint Joseph,—Indians came in with tidings that a panic had seized the Iroquois camp, that the chiefs could not control it, and that the whole body of invaders was retreating in disorder, possessed with a vague terror that the Hurons were upon them in force. They had found time, however, for an act of atrocious cruelty. They planted stakes in the bark houses of St. Ignace, and bound to them those of their prisoners whom they meant to sacrifice, male and female, from old age to infancy, husbands, mothers, and children, side by side. Then, as they retreated, they set the town on fire, and laughed with savage glee at the shrieks of anguish that rose from the blazing dwellings.

[The site of St. Ignace still bears evidence of the catastrophe, in the ashes and charcoal that indicate the position of the houses, and the fragments of broken pottery and half-consumed bone, together with trinkets of stone, metal, or glass, which have survived the lapse of two centuries and more. The place has been minutely examined by Dr. Taché.]

They loaded the rest of their prisoners with their baggage and plunder, and drove them through the forest southward, braining with their hatchets any who gave out on the march. An old woman, who had escaped out of the midst of the flames of St. Ignace, made her way to St. Michel, a large town not far from the desolate site of St. Joseph. Here she found about seven hundred Huron warriors, hastily mustered. She set them on the track of the retreating Iroquois, and they took up the chase,—but evidently with no great eagerness to overtake their dangerous enemy, well armed as he was with Dutch guns, while they had little beside their bows and arrows. They found, as they advanced, the dead bodies of prisoners tomahawked on the march, and others bound fast to trees and half burned by the fagots piled hastily around them. The Iroquois pushed forward with such headlong speed, that the pursuers could not, or would not, overtake them; and, after two days, they gave over the attempt.

CHAPTER XXVIII.

1649.

THE MARTYRS.

THE RUINS OF ST. IGNACE.—THE RELICS FOUND.—
BRÉBEUF AT THE STAKE.—HIS UNCONQUERABLE
FORTITUDE.—LALEMANT.—RENEGADE HURONS.—
IROQUOIS ATROCITIES.—DEATH OF BRÉBEUF.—HIS
CHARACTER.—DEATH OF LALEMANT.

On the morning of the twentieth, the Jesuits at Sainte Marie
received full confirmation of the reported retreat of the invaders;
and one of them, with seven armed Frenchmen, set out for the
scene of havoc. They passed St. Louis, where the bloody ground
was strown thick with corpses, and, two or three miles farther
on, reached St. Ignace. Here they saw a spectacle of horror; for
among the ashes of the burnt town were scattered in profusion the
half-consumed bodies of those who had perished in the flames.
Apart from the rest, they saw a sight that banished all else from
their thoughts; for they found what they had come to seek,—the
scorched and mangled relics of Brébeuf and Lalemant.

["Ils y trouuerent vn spectacle d'horreur, les restes de la
cruauté mesme, ou plus tost les restes de l'amour de Dieu, qui seul
triomphe dans la mort des Martyrs."—Ragueneau, Relation des
Hurons, 1649, 13.]

They had learned their fate already from Huron prisoners,
many of whom had made their escape in the panic and confusion

of the Iroquois retreat. They described what they had seen, and the condition in which the bodies were found confirmed their story.

On the afternoon of the sixteenth,—the day when the two priests were captured,—Brébeuf was led apart, and bound to a stake. He seemed more concerned for his captive converts than for himself, and addressed them in a loud voice, exhorting them to suffer patiently, and promising Heaven as their reward. The Iroquois, incensed, scorched him from head to foot, to silence him; whereupon, in the tone of a master, he threatened them with everlasting flames, for persecuting the worshippers of God. As he continued to speak, with voice and countenance unchanged, they cut away his lower lip and thrust a red-hot iron down his throat. He still held his tall form erect and defiant, with no sign or sound of pain; and they tried another means to overcome him. They led out Lalemant, that Brébeuf might see him tortured. They had tied strips of bark, smeared with pitch, about his naked body. When he saw the condition of his Superior, he could not hide his agitation, and called out to him, with a broken voice, in the words of Saint Paul, "We are made a spectacle to the world, to angels, and to men." Then he threw himself at Brébeuf's feet; upon which the Iroquois seized him, made him fast to a stake, and set fire to the bark that enveloped him. As the flame rose, he threw his arms upward, with a shriek of supplication to Heaven. Next they hung around Brébeuf's neck a collar made of hatchets heated red hot; but the indomitable priest stood like a rock. A Huron in the crowd, who had been a convert of the mission, but was now an Iroquois by adoption, called out, with the malice of a renegade, to pour hot water on their heads, since they had poured so much cold water on those of others. The kettle was accordingly slung, and the water boiled and poured slowly on the heads of the two missionaries. "We baptize you," they cried, "that you may be happy in Heaven; for nobody can be saved without a good baptism." Brébeuf would not flinch; and, in a rage, they cut strips of flesh from his limbs, and devoured them before his eyes. Other renegade Hurons called out to him, "You told us, that, the more one suffers on earth, the happier he is in Heaven. We wish to make you happy; we torment you because we love you; and you ought to thank us for it." After a succession of other revolting tortures, they scalped him; when, seeing him nearly dead, they laid open his breast, and came in a crowd to drink the blood of so valiant an enemy, thinking to imbibe with it some portion of his courage. A chief then tore out his heart, and devoured it.

Thus died Jean de Brébeuf, the founder of the Huron mission, its truest hero, and its greatest martyr. He came of a noble race,—the same, it is said, from which sprang the English Earls of Arundel; but never had the mailed barons of his line confronted a fate so appalling, with so prodigious a constancy. To the last he refused to flinch, and "his death was the astonishment of his murderers." [Charlevoix, I. 204. Alegambe uses a similar expression.] In him an enthusiastic devotion was grafted on an heroic nature. His bodily endowments were as remarkable as the temper of his mind. His manly proportions, his strength, and his endurance, which incessant fasts and penances could not undermine, had always won for him the respect of the Indians, no less than a courage unconscious of fear, and yet redeemed from rashness by a cool and vigorous judgment; for, extravagant as were the chimeras which fed the fires of his zeal, they were consistent with the soberest good sense on matters of practical bearing.

Lalemant, physically weak from childhood, and slender almost to emaciation, was constitutionally unequal to a display of fortitude like that of his colleague. When Brébeuf died, he was led back to the house whence he had been taken, and tortured there all night, until, in the morning, one of the Iroquois, growing tired of the protracted entertainment, killed him with a hatchet.[1] It was said, that, at times, he seemed beside himself; then, rallying, with hands uplifted, he offered his sufferings to Heaven as a sacrifice. His robust companion had lived less than four hours under the torture, while he survived it for nearly seventeen. Perhaps the Titanic effort of will with which Brébeuf repressed all show of suffering conspired with the Iroquois knives and firebrands to exhaust his

---

1   "We saw no part of his body," says Ragueneau, "from head to foot, which was not burned, even to his eyes, in the sockets of which these wretches had placed live coals."—Relation des Hurons, 1649, 15.

   Lalemant was a Parisian, and his family belonged to the class of *gens de robe*, or hereditary practitioners of the law. He was thirty-nine years of age. His physical weakness is spoken of by several of those who knew him. Marie de l'Incarnation says, "C'était l'homme le plus faible et le plus délicat qu'on eût pu voir." Both Bressani and Ragueneau are equally emphatic on this point.

vitality; perhaps his tormentors, enraged at his fortitude, forgot their subtlety, and struck too near the life.

The bodies of the two missionaries were carried to Sainte Marie, and buried in the cemetery there; but the skull of Brébeuf was preserved as a relic. His family sent from France a silver bust of their martyred kinsman, in the base of which was a recess to contain the skull; and, to this day, the bust and the relic within are preserved with pious care by the nuns of the Hôtel-Dieu at Quebec.

[Photographs of the bust are before me. Various relics of the two missionaries were preserved; and some of them may still be seen in Canadian monastic establishments. The following extract from a letter of Marie de l'Incarnation to her son, written from Quebec in October of this year, 1649, is curious.

"Madame our foundress (Madame de la Peltrie) sends you relics of our holy martyrs; but she does it secretly, since the reverend Fathers would not give us any, for fear that we should send them to France: but, as she is not bound by vows, and as the very persons who went for the bodies have given relics of them to her in secret, I begged her to send you some of them, which she has done very gladly, from the respect she has for you." She adds, in the same letter, "Our Lord having revealed to him (Brébeuf) the time of his martyrdom three days before it happened, he went, full of joy, to find the other Fathers; who, seeing him in extraordinary spirits, caused him, by an inspiration of God, to be bled; after which time surgeon dried his blood, through a presentiment of what was to take place, lest he should be treated like Father Daniel, who, eight months before, had been so reduced to ashes that no remains of his body could be found."

Brébeuf had once been ordered by the Father Superior to write down the visions, revelations, and inward experiences with which he was favored,—"at least," says Ragueneau, "those which he could easily remember, for their multitude was too great for the whole to be recalled."—"I find nothing," he adds, "more frequent in this memoir than the expression of his desire to die for Jesus Christ: 'Sentio me vehementer impelli ad moriendum pro Christo.' . . . In fine, wishing to make himself a holocaust and a victim consecrated to death, and holily to anticipate the happiness of martyrdom which awaited him, he bound himself by a vow to Christ, which he conceived in these terms"; and Ragueneau gives the vow in the original Latin. It binds him never to refuse "the grace of martyrdom, if at any day, Thou shouldst, in Thy infinite pity, offer it to me, Thy unworthy servant;" . . . "and when I shall have received the stroke of death, I bind myself to accept it at Thy hand, with all the contentment and joy of my heart."

Some of his innumerable visions have been already mentioned. (See ante, chapter 9 (page 108).) Tanner, Societas Militans, gives various others,—as, for example, that he once beheld a mountain covered thick with saints, but above all with virgins, while the Queen of Virgins sat at the top in a blaze of glory. In 1637, when the whole country was enraged against the Jesuits, and above all against Brébeuf, as sorcerers who had caused the pest, Ragueneau tells us that "a troop of demons appeared before him divers times,— sometimes like men in a fury, sometimes like frightful monsters, bears, lions, or wild horses, trying to rush upon him. These spectres excited in him neither horror nor fear. He said to them, 'Do to me whatever God permits you; for without His will not one hair will fall from my head.' And at these words all the demons vanished in a moment."—Relation des Hurons, 1649, 20. Compare the long notice in Alegambe, Mortes Illustres, 644.

In Ragueneau's notice of Brébeuf, as in all other notices of deceased missionaries in the Relations, the saintly qualities alone are brought forward, as obedience, humility, etc.; but wherever Brébeuf himself appears in the course of those voluminous records, he always brings with him an impression of power.

We are told that, punning on his own name, he used to say that he was an ox, fit only to bear burdens. This sort of humility may pass for what it is worth; but it must be remembered, that there is a kind of acting in which the actor firmly believes in the part he is playing. As for the obedience, it was as genuine as that of a well-disciplined soldier, and incomparably more profound. In the case of the Canadian Jesuits, posterity owes to this, their favorite virtue, the record of numerous visions, inward voices, and the like miracles, which the object of these favors set down on paper, at the command of his Superior; while, otherwise, humility would have concealed them forever. The truth is, that with some of these missionaries, one may throw off trash and nonsense by the cart-load, and find under it all a solid nucleus of saint and hero.]

CHAPTER XXIX.

1649, 1650.

THE SANCTUARY.

DISPERSION OF THE HURONS.—SAINTE MARIE ABANDONED.—ISLE ST. JOSEPH.—REMOVAL OF THE MISSION.—THE NEW FORT.—MISERY OF THE HURONS.—FAMINE.—EPIDEMIC.—EMPLOYMENTS OF THE JESUITS.

All was over with the Hurons. The death-knell of their nation had struck. Without a leader, without organization, without union, crazed with fright and paralyzed with misery, they yielded to their doom without a blow. Their only thought was flight. Within two weeks after the disasters of St. Ignace and St. Louis, fifteen Huron towns were abandoned, and the greater number burned, lest they should give shelter to the Iroquois. The last year's harvest had been scanty; the fugitives had no food, and they left behind them the fields in which was their only hope of obtaining it. In bands, large or small, some roamed northward and eastward, through the half-thawed wilderness; some hid themselves on the rocks or islands of Lake Huron; some sought an asylum among the Tobacco Nation; a few joined the Neutrals on the north of Lake Erie. The Hurons, as a nation, ceased to exist.

[Chaumonot, who was at Ossossané at the time of the Iroquois invasion, gives a vivid picture of the panic and lamentation which followed the news of the destruction of the Huron warriors at St.

Louis, and of the flight of the inhabitants to the country of the Tobacco Nation.—Vie, 62.]

Hitherto Sainte Marie had been covered by large fortified towns which lay between it and the Iroquois; but these were all destroyed, some by the enemy and some by their own people, and the Jesuits were left alone to bear the brunt of the next attack. There was, moreover, no reason for their remaining. Sainte Marie had been built as a basis for the missions; but its occupation was gone: the flock had fled from the shepherds, and its existence had no longer an object. If the priests stayed to be butchered, they would perish, not as martyrs, but as fools. The necessity was as clear as it was bitter. All their toil must come to nought. Sainte Marie must be abandoned. They confess the pang which the resolution cost them; but, pursues the Father Superior, "since the birth of Christianity, the Faith has nowhere been planted except in the midst of sufferings and crosses. Thus this desolation consoles us; and in the midst of persecution, in the extremity of the evils which assail us and the greater evils which threaten us, we are all filled with joy: for our hearts tell us that God has never had a more tender love for us than now." [Ragueneau. Relation des Hurons, 1649, 26.]

Several of the priests set out to follow and console the scattered bands of fugitive Hurons. One embarked in a canoe, and coasted the dreary shores of Lake Huron northward, among the wild labyrinth of rocks and islets, whither his scared flock had fled for refuge; another betook himself to the forest with a band of half-famished proselytes, and shared their miserable rovings through the thickets and among the mountains. Those who remained took counsel together at Sainte Marie. Whither should they go, and where should be the new seat of the mission? They made choice of the Grand Manitoulin Island, called by them Isle Sainte Marie, and by the Hurons Ekaentoton. It lay near the northern shores of Lake Huron, and by its position would give a ready access to numberless Algonquin tribes along the borders of all these inland seas. Moreover, it would bring the priests and their flock nearer to the French settlements, by the route of the Ottawa, whenever the Iroquois should cease to infest that river. The fishing, too, was good; and some of the priests, who knew the island well, made a favorable report of the soil. Thither, therefore, they had resolved to transplant the mission, when twelve Huron chiefs arrived, and

asked for an interview with the Father Superior and his fellow Jesuits. The conference lasted three hours. The deputies declared that many of the scattered Hurons had determined to reunite, and form a settlement on a neighboring island of the lake, called by the Jesuits Isle St. Joseph; that they needed the aid of the Fathers; that without them they were helpless, but with them they could hold their ground and repel the attacks of the Iroquois. They urged their plea in language which Ragueneau describes as pathetic and eloquent; and, to confirm their words, they gave him ten large collars of wampum, saying that these were the voices of their wives and children. They gained their point. The Jesuits abandoned their former plan, and promised to join the Hurons on Isle St. Joseph.

They had built a boat, or small vessel, and in this they embarked such of their stores as it would hold. The greater part were placed on a large raft made for the purpose, like one of the rafts of timber which every summer float down the St. Lawrence and the Ottawa. Here was their stock of corn,—in part the produce of their own fields, and in part bought from the Hurons in former years of plenty,—pictures, vestments, sacred vessels and images, weapons, ammunition, tools, goods for barter with the Indians, cattle, swine, and poultry. [Some of these were killed for food after reaching the island. In March following, they had ten fowls, a pair of swine, two bulls and two cows, kept for breeding.—Lettre de Ragueneau au Général de la Compagnie de Jésus, St. Joseph, 13 Mars, 1650.] Sainte Marie was stripped of everything that could be moved. Then, lest it should harbor the Iroquois, they set it on fire, and saw consumed in an hour the results of nine or ten years of toil. It was near sunset, on the fourteenth of June.[1] The houseless

---

1   Ragueneau, Relation des Hurons, 1650, 3. In the Relation of the preceding year he gives the fifteenth of May as the date,—evidently an error.

    "Nous sortismes de ces terres de Promission qui estoient nostre Paradis, et où la mort nous eust esté mille fois plus douce que ne sera la vie en quelque lieu que nous puissions estre. Mais il faut suiure Dieu, et il faut aimer ses conduites, quelque opposées qu'elles paroissent à nos desirs, à nos plus saintes esperances et aux plus tendres amours de nostre cœur."—Lettre de Ragueneau au P. Provincial à Paris, in Relation des Hurons, 1650, 1.

    "Mais il fallut, à tous tant que nous estions, quitter cette ancienne demeure de saincte Marie; ces edifices, qui quoy que pauures, paroissoient des chefs-d'œuure de l'art aux yeux de nos pauures Sauuages; ces terres cultiuées, qui nous promettoient vne riche moisson. Il nous fallut abandonner ce lieu, que ie puis appeller nostre seconde Patrie et nos delices innocentes, puis qu'il auoit esté le berceau de ce

band descended to the mouth of the Wye, went on board their raft, pushed it from the shore, and, with sweeps and oars, urged it on its way all night. The lake was calm and the weather fair; but it crept so slowly over the water that several days elapsed before they reached their destination, about twenty miles distant.

Near the entrance of Matchedash Bay lie the three islands now known as Faith, Hope, and Charity. Of these, Charity or Christian Island, called Ahoendoé by the Hurons and St. Joseph by the Jesuits, is by far the largest. It is six or eight miles wide; and when the Hurons sought refuge here, it was densely covered with the primeval forest. The priests landed with their men, some forty soldiers, laborers, and others, and found about three hundred Huron families bivouacked in the woods. Here were wigwams and sheds of bark, and smoky kettles slung over fires, each on its tripod of poles, while around lay groups of famished wretches, with dark, haggard visages and uncombed hair, in every posture of despondency and woe. They had not been wholly idle; for they had made some rough clearings, and planted a little corn. The arrival of the Jesuits gave them new hope; and, weakened as they were with famine, they set themselves to the task of hewing and burning down the forest, making bark houses, and planting palisades. The priests, on their part, chose a favorable spot, and began to clear the ground and mark out the lines of a fort. Their men—the greater part serving without pay—labored with admirable spirit, and before winter had built a square, bastioned fort of solid masonry, with a deep ditch, and walls about twelve feet high. Within were a small chapel, houses for lodging, and a well, which, with the ruins of the walls, may still be seen on the south-eastern shore of the island, a hundred feet from the water.[1] Detached redoubts were also built near at hand,

---

Christianisme, qu'il estoit le temple de Dieu et la maison des seruiteurs de Iesus-Christ; et crainte que nos ennemis trop impies, ne profanassent ce lieu de saincteté et n'en prissent leur auantage, nous y mismes le feu nous mesmes, et nous vismes brusler à nos yeux, en moins d'vne heure, nos trauaux de neuf et de dix ans."—Ragueneau, Relation des Hurons, 1650, 2, 3.

1   The measurement between the angles of the two southern bastions is 123 feet, and that of the curtain wall connecting these bastions is 78 feet. Some curious relics have been found in the fort,—among others, a steel mill for making wafers for the Host. It was found in 1848, in a remarkable state of preservation, and is now in an English museum, having been bought on the spot by an amateur. As at Sainte Marie on the Wye, the remains are in perfect conformity with the narratives and letters of the priests.

where French musketeers could aid in defending the adjacent Huron village. [Compare Martin, Introduction to Bressani, Relation Abrégée, 38.] Though the island was called St. Joseph, the fort, like that on the Wye, received the name of Sainte Marie. Jesuit devotion scattered these names broadcast over all the field of their labors.

The island, thanks to the vigilance of the French, escaped attack throughout the summer; but Iroquois scalping-parties ranged the neighboring shores, killing stragglers and keeping the Hurons in perpetual alarm. As winter drew near, great numbers, who, trembling and by stealth, had gathered a miserable subsistence among the northern forests and islands, rejoined their countrymen at St. Joseph, until six or eight thousand expatriated wretches were gathered here under the protection of the French fort. They were housed in a hundred or more bark dwellings, each containing eight or ten families. [Ragueneau, Relation des Hurons, 1650, 3, 4. He reckons eight persons to a family.] Here were widows without children, and children without parents; for famine and the Iroquois had proved more deadly enemies than the pestilence which a few years before had wasted their towns.[1] Of this multitude but few had strength enough to labor, scarcely any had made provision for the winter, and numbers were already perishing from want, dragging themselves from house to house, like living skeletons. The priests had spared no effort to meet the demands upon their charity. They sent men during the autumn to buy smoked fish from the Northern Algonquins, and employed Indians to gather acorns in the woods.

---

[1]   "Ie voudrois pouuoir representer à toutes les personnes affectionnées à nos Hurons, l'état pitoyable auquel ils sont reduits; . . . comment seroit-il possible que ces imitateurs de Iésus Christ ne fussent émeus à pitié à la veuë des centaines et centaines de veuues dont non seulement les enfans, mais quasi les parens ont esté outrageusement ou tuez, ou emmenez captifs, et puis inhumainement bruslez, cuits, déchirez et deuorez des ennemis."—Lettre de Chaumonot à Lalemant, Supérieur à Quebec, Isle de St. Joseph, 1 Juin, 1649.

"Vne mère s'est veuë, n'ayant que ses deux mamelles, mais sans suc et sans laict, qui toutefois estoit l'vnique chose qu'elle eust peu presenter à trois ou quatre enfans qui pleuroient y estans attachez. Elle les voyoit mourir entre ses bras, les vns apres les autres, et n'auoit pas mesme les forces de les pousser dans le tombeau. Elle mouroit sous cette charge, et en mourant elle disoit: Ouy, Mon Dieu, vous estes le maistre de nos vies; nous mourrons puisque vous le voulez; voila qui est bien que nous mourrions Chrestiens. l'estois damnée, et mes enfans auec moy, si nous ne fussions morts miserables; ils ont receu le sainct Baptesme, et ie croy fermement que mourans tous de compagnie, nous ressusciterons tous ensemble."—Ragueneau, Relation des Hurons, 1650, 5.

Of this miserable food they succeeded in collecting five or six hundred bushels. To diminish its bitterness, the Indians boiled it with ashes, or the priests served it out to them pounded, and mixed with corn. [Eight hundred sacks of this mixture were given to the Hurons during the winter.—Bressani, Relation Abrégée, 283.]

As winter advanced, the Huron houses became a frightful spectacle. Their inmates were dying by scores daily. The priests and their men buried the bodies, and the Indians dug them from the earth or the snow and fed on them, sometimes in secret and sometimes openly; although, notwithstanding their superstitious feasts on the bodies of their enemies, their repugnance and horror were extreme at the thought of devouring those of relatives and friends.[1] An epidemic presently appeared, to aid the work of famine. Before spring, about half of their number were dead.

Meanwhile, though the cold was intense and the snow several feet deep, yet not an hour was free from the danger of the Iroquois; and, from sunset to daybreak, under the cold moon or in the driving snow-storm, the French sentries walked their rounds along the ramparts.

The priests rose before dawn, and spent the time till sunrise in their private devotions. Then the bell of their chapel rang, and the Indians came in crowds at the call; for misery had softened their hearts, and nearly all on the island were now Christian. There was a mass, followed by a prayer and a few words of exhortation; then the hearers dispersed to make room for others. Thus the little chapel was filled ten or twelve times, until all had had their turn. Meanwhile other priests were hearing confessions and giving advice and encouragement

---

1   "Ce fut alors que nous fusmes contraints de voir des squeletes mourantes, qui soustenoient vne vie miserable, mangeant iusqu'aux ordures et les rebuts de la nature. Le gland estoit à la pluspart, ce que seroient en France les mets les plus exquis. Les charognes mesme deterrées, les restes des Renards et des Chiens ne faisoient point horreur, et se mangeoient, quoy qu'en cachete: car quoy que les Hurons, auant que la foy leur eust donné plus de lumiere qu'ils n'en auoient dans l'infidelité, ne creussent pas commettre aucun peché de manger leurs ennemis, aussi peu qu'il y en a de les tuer, toutefois ie puis dire auec verité, qu'ils n'ont pas moins d'horreur de manger de leurs compatriotes, qu'on peut auoir en France de manger de la chair humaine. Mais la necessité n'a plus de loy, et des dents fameliques ne discernent plus ce qu'elles mangent. Les mères se sont repeuës de leurs enfans, des freres de leurs freres, et des enfans ne reconnoissoient plus en vn cadaure mort, celuy lequel lors qu'il viuoit, ils appelloient leur Pere."—Ragueneau, Relation des Hurons, 1650, 4. Compare Bressani, Relation Abrégée, 283.

in private, according to the needs of each applicant. This lasted till nine o'clock, when all the Indians returned to their village, and the priests presently followed, to give what assistance they could. Their cassocks were worn out, and they were dressed chiefly in skins. [Lettre de Ragueneau au Général de la Compagnie de Jésus, Isle St. Joseph, 13 Mars, 1650.] They visited the Indian houses, and gave to those whose necessities were most urgent small scraps of hide, severally stamped with a particular mark, and entitling the recipients, on presenting them at the fort, to a few acorns, a small quantity of boiled maize, or a fragment of smoked fish, according to the stamp on the leather ticket of each. Two hours before sunset the bell of the chapel again rang, and the religious exercises of the morning were repeated. [Ragueneau, Relation des Hurons, 1650, 6, 7.]

Thus this miserable winter wore away, till the opening spring brought new fears and new necessities.

[Concerning the retreat of the Hurons to Isle St. Joseph, the principal authorities are the Relations of 1649 and 1650, which are ample in detail, and written with an excellent simplicity and modesty; the Relation Abrégée of Bressani; the reports of the Father Superior to the General of the Jesuits at Rome; the manuscript of 1652, entitled Mémoires touchant la Mort et les Vertus des Pères, etc.; the unpublished letters of Garnier; and a letter of Chaumonot, written on the spot, and preserved in the Relations.]

CHAPTER XXX.

1649.

GARNIER.—CHABANEL.

THE TOBACCO MISSIONS.—ST. JEAN ATTACKED.—
DEATH OF GARNIER.—THE JOURNEY OF CHABANEL.—
HIS DEATH.—GARREAU AND GRELON.

Late in the preceding autumn the Iroquois had taken the war-
path in force. At the end of November, two escaped prisoners came
to Isle St. Joseph with the news that a band of three hundred warriors
was hovering in the Huron forests, doubtful whether to invade the
island or to attack the towns of the Tobacco Nation in the valleys of
the Blue Mountains. The Father Superior, Ragueneau, sent a runner
thither in all haste, to warn the inhabitants of their danger.

There were at this time two missions in the Tobacco Nation,
St. Jean and St. Matthias, [1]—the latter under the charge of the
Jesuits Garreau and Grelon, and the former under that of Garnier
and Chabanel. St. Jean, the principal seat of the mission of the same
name, was a town of five or six hundred families. Its population
was, moreover, greatly augmented by the bands of fugitive Hurons
who had taken refuge there. When the warriors were warned by
Ragueneau's messenger of a probable attack from the Iroquois,
they were far from being daunted, but, confiding in their numbers,
awaited the enemy in one of those fits of valor which characterize

---

1   The Indian name of St. Jean was Etarita; and that of St. Matthias, Ekarenniondi.

the unstable courage of the savage. At St. Jean all was paint, feathers, and uproar,—singing, dancing, howling, and stamping. Quivers were filled, knives whetted, and tomahawks sharpened; but when, after two days of eager expectancy, the enemy did not appear, the warriors lost patience. Thinking, and probably with reason, that the Iroquois were afraid of them, they resolved to sally forth, and take the offensive. With yelps and whoops they defiled into the forest, where the branches were gray and bare, and the ground thickly covered with snow. They pushed on rapidly till the following day, but could not discover their wary enemy, who had made a wide circuit, and was approaching the town from another quarter. By ill luck, the Iroquois captured a Tobacco Indian and his squaw, straggling in the forest not far from St. Jean; and the two prisoners, to propitiate them, told them the defenceless condition of the place, where none remained but women, children, and old men. The delighted Iroquois no longer hesitated, but silently and swiftly pushed on towards the town.

It was two o'clock in the afternoon of the seventh of December. [Bressani, Relation Abrégée, 264.] Chabanel had left the place a day or two before, in obedience to a message from Ragueneau, and Garnier was here alone. He was making his rounds among the houses, visiting the sick and instructing his converts, when the horrible din of the war-whoop rose from the borders of the clearing, and, on the instant, the town was mad with terror. Children and girls rushed to and fro, blind with fright; women snatched their infants, and fled they knew not whither. Garnier ran to his chapel, where a few of his converts had sought asylum. He gave them his benediction, exhorted them to hold fast to the Faith, and bade them fly while there was yet time. For himself, he hastened back to the houses, running from one to another, and giving absolution or baptism to all whom he found. An Iroquois met him, shot him with three balls through the body and thigh, tore off his cassock, and rushed on in pursuit of the fugitives. Garnier lay for a moment on the ground, as if stunned; then, recovering his senses, he was seen to rise into a kneeling posture. At a little distance from him lay a Huron, mortally wounded, but still showing signs of life. With the Heaven that awaited him glowing before his fading vision, the priest dragged himself towards the dying Indian, to give him absolution; but his strength failed, and he fell again to the earth. He rose once more, and again crept forward, when a party of Iroquois rushed upon him, split his head with two blows of a hatchet, stripped him, and left his body on the ground.[1] At this time the whole town was on fire. The invaders, fearing that the absent warriors might return and take their revenge, hastened to finish their work, scattered firebrands every where, and threw children alive into the burning houses. They killed many of the fugitives, captured many more, and then made a hasty retreat through the forest with their prisoners, butchering such of them as lagged on the way. St. Jean lay a waste of smoking ruins thickly strewn with blackened corpses of the slain.

Towards evening, parties of fugitives reached St. Matthias, with tidings of the catastrophe. The town was wild with alarm, and all stood on the watch, in expectation of an attack; but when, in the morning, scouts came in and reported the retreat of the Iroquois, Garreau and Grelon set out with a party of converts to visit the scene of havoc. For a long time they looked in vain for the body of Garnier; but at length they found him lying where he had fallen,—so scorched and disfigured, that he was recognized with difficulty. The two priests wrapped his body in a part of their own clothing; the Indian converts dug a grave on the spot where his church had stood; and here they buried him. Thus, at the age of forty-four, died Charles Garnier, the favorite child of wealthy and noble parents, nursed in Parisian luxury and ease, then living and dying, a more than willing exile, amid the hardships and horrors of the Huron wilderness. His life and his death are his best eulogy. Brébeuf was the lion of the Huron mission, and Garnier was the lamb; but the lamb was as fearless as the lion.

[Garnier's devotion to the mission was absolute. He took little or no interest in the news from France, which, at intervals

---

1   The above particulars of Garnier's death rest on the evidence of a Christian Huron woman, named Marthe, who saw him shot down, and also saw his attempt to reach the dying Indian. She was herself struck down immediately after with a war-club, but remained alive, and escaped in the confusion. She died three months later, at Isle St. Joseph, from the effects of the injuries she had received, after reaffirming the truth of her story to Ragueneau, who was with her, and who questioned her on the subject. (Mémoires touchant la Mort et les Vertus des Pères Garnier, etc., MS.). Ragueneau also speaks of her in Relation des Hurons, 1650, 9.—The priests Grelon and Garreau found the body stripped naked, with three gunshot wounds in the abdomen and thigh, and two deep hatchet wounds in the head.

of from one to three years, found its way to the Huron towns. His companion Bressani says, that he would walk thirty or forty miles in the hottest summer day, to baptize some dying Indian, when the country was infested by the enemy. On similar errands, he would sometimes pass the night alone in the forest in the depth of winter. He was anxious to fall into the hands of the Iroquois, that he might preach the Faith to them even out of the midst of the fire. In one of his unpublished letters he writes, "Praised be our Lord, who punishes me for my sins by depriving me of this crown" (the crown of martyrdom). After the death of Brébeuf and Lalemant, he writes to his brother—

"Hélas! Mon cher frère, si ma conscience ne me convainquait et ne me confondait de mon infidélité au service de notre bon maître, je pourrais espérer quelque faveur approchante de celles qu'il a faites aux bien-heureux martyrs avec qui j'avais le bien de converser souvent, étant dans les mêmes occasions et dangers qu'ils étaient, mais sa justice me fait craindre que je ne demeure toujours indigne d'une telle couronne."

He contented himself with the most wretched fare during the last years of famine, living in good measure on roots and acorns; "although," says Ragueneau, "he had been the cherished son of a rich and noble house, on whom all the affection of his father had centred, and who had been nourished on food very different from that of swine."—Relation des Hurons, 1650, 12.

For his character, see Ragueneau, Bressani, Tanner, and Alegambe, who devotes many pages to the description of his religious traits; but the complexion of his mind is best reflected in his private letters.]

When, on the following morning, the warriors of St. Jean returned from their rash and bootless sally, and saw the ashes of their desolated homes and the ghastly relics of their murdered families, they seated themselves amid the ruin, silent and motionless as statues of bronze, with heads bowed down and eyes fixed on the ground. Thus they remained through half the day. Tears and wailing were for women; this was the mourning of warriors.

Garnier's colleague, Chabanel, had been recalled from St. Jean by an order from the Father Superior, who thought it needless to expose the life of more than one priest in a position of so much danger. He stopped on his way at St. Matthias, and on the morning of the seventh of December, the day of the attack, left that town with seven or eight Christian Hurons. The journey was rough and difficult. They proceeded through the forest about eighteen miles, and then encamped in the snow. The Indians fell asleep; but Chabanel, from an apprehension of danger, or some other cause, remained awake. About midnight he heard a strange sound in the distance,—a confusion of fierce voices, mingled with songs and outcries. It was the Iroquois on their retreat with their prisoners, some of whom were defiantly singing their war-songs, after the Indian custom. Chabanel waked his companions, who instantly took flight. He tried to follow, but could not keep pace with the light-footed savages, who returned to St. Matthias, and told what had occurred. They said, however, that Chabanel had left them and taken an opposite direction, in order to reach Isle St. Joseph. His brother priests were for some time ignorant of what had befallen him. At length a Huron Indian, who had been converted, but afterward apostatized, gave out that he had met him in the forest, and aided him with his canoe to cross a river which lay in his path. Some supposed that he had lost his way, and died of cold and hunger; but others were of a different opinion. Their suspicion was confirmed some time afterwards by the renegade Huron, who confessed that he had killed Chabanel and thrown his body into the river, after robbing him of his clothes, his hat, the blanket or mantle which was strapped to his shoulders, and the bag in which he carried his books and papers. He declared that his motive was hatred of the Faith, which had caused the ruin of the Hurons. [Mémoires touchant la Mort et les Vertus des Pères, etc., MS.] The priest had prepared himself for a worse fate. Before leaving Sainte Marie on the Wye, to go to his post in the Tobacco Nation, he had written to his brother to regard him as a victim destined to the fires of the Iroquois. [Abrégé de la Vie du P. Noël Chabanel, MS.] He added, that, though he was naturally timid, he was now wholly indifferent to danger; and he expressed the belief that only a superhuman power could have wrought such a change in him.

["Ie suis fort apprehensif de mon naturel; toutefois, maintenant que ie vay au plus grand danger et qu'il me semble que la mort n'est pas esloignée, ie ne sens plus de crainte. Cette disposition ne vient pas de moy."—Relation des Hurons, 1650, 18.

The following is the vow made by Chabanel, at a time when his disgust at the Indian mode of life beset him with temptations to ask to be recalled from the mission. It is translated from the Latin original:—

"My Lord Jesus Christ, who, in the admirable disposition of thy paternal providence, hast willed that I, although most unworthy, should be a co-laborer with the holy Apostles in this vineyard of the Hurons,—I, Noël Chabanel, impelled by the desire of fulfilling thy holy will in advancing the conversion of the savages of this land to thy faith, do vow, in the presence of the most holy sacrament of thy precious body and blood, which is God's tabernacle among men, to remain perpetually attached to this mission of the Hurons, understanding all things according to the interpretation and disposal of the Superiors of the Society of Jesus. Therefore I entreat thee to receive me as the perpetual servant of this mission, and to render me worthy of so sublime a ministry. Amen. This twentieth day of June, 1647."]

Garreau and Grelon, in their mission of St. Matthias, were exposed to other dangers than those of the Iroquois. A report was spread, not only that they were magicians, but that they had a secret understanding with the enemy. A nocturnal council was called, and their death was decreed. In the morning, a furious crowd gathered before a lodge which they were about to enter, screeching and yelling after the manner of Indians when they compel a prisoner to run the gantlet. The two priests, giving no sign of fear, passed through the crowd and entered the lodge unharmed. Hatchets were brandished over them, but no one would be the first to strike. Their converts were amazed at their escape, and they themselves ascribed it to the interposition of a protecting Providence. The Huron missionaries were doubly in danger,—not more from the Iroquois than from the blind rage of those who should have been their friends.

[Ragueneau, Relation des Hurons, 1650, 20.

One of these two missionaries, Garreau, was afterwards killed by the Iroquois, who shot him through the spine, in 1656, near Montreal.—De Quen, Relation, 1656, 41.]

CHAPTER XXXI.

1650-1652.

THE HURON MISSION ABANDONED.

FAMINE AND THE TOMAHAWK.—A NEW ASYLUM.—
VOYAGE OF THE REFUGEES TO QUEBEC.—MEETING
WITH BRESSANI.—DESPERATE COURAGE OF THE
IROQUOIS.—INROADS AND BATTLES.—DEATH OF
BUTEUX.

As spring approached, the starving multitude on Isle St.
Joseph grew reckless with hunger. Along the main shore, in spots
where the sun lay warm, the spring fisheries had already begun,
and the melting snow was uncovering the acorns in the woods.
There was danger everywhere, for bands of Iroquois were again
on the track of their prey.[1] The miserable Hurons, gnawed with
inexorable famine, stood in the dilemma of a deadly peril and an
assured death. They chose the former; and, early in March, began
to leave their island and cross to the main-land, to gather what
sustenance they could. The ice was still thick, but the advancing
season had softened it; and, as a body of them were crossing, it

---

1   "Mais le Printemps estant venu, les Iroquois nous furent encore plus cruels;
     et ce sont eux qui vrayement ont ruiné toutes nos esperances, et qui ont fait
     vn lieu d'horreur, vne terre de sang et de carnage, vn theatre de cruauté et vn
     sepulchre de carcasses décharnées par les langueurs d'vne longue famine, d'vn
     païs de benediction, d'vne terre de Saincteté et d'vn lieu qui n'auoit plus rien de
     barbare, depuis que le sang respandu pour son amour auoit rendu tout son peuple
     Chrestien."—Ragueneau, Relation des Hurons, 1650, 23.

broke under their feet. Some were drowned; while others dragged themselves out, drenched and pierced with cold, to die miserably on the frozen lake, before they could reach a shelter. Other parties, more fortunate, gained the shore safely, and began their fishing, divided into companies of from eight or ten to a hundred persons. But the Iroquois were in wait for them. A large band of warriors had already made their way, through ice and snow, from their towns in Central New York. They surprised the Huron fishermen, surrounded them, and cut them in pieces without resistance,— tracking out the various parties of their victims, and hunting down fugitives with such persistency and skill, that, of all who had gone over to the main, the Jesuits knew of but one who escaped.[1]

"My pen," writes Ragueneau, "has no ink black enough to describe the fury of the Iroquois." Still the goadings of famine were relentless and irresistible. "It is said," adds the Father Superior, "that hunger will drive wolves from the forest. So, too, our starving Hurons were driven out of a town which had become an abode of horror. It was the end of Lent. Alas, if these poor Christians could have had but acorns and water to keep their fast upon! On Easter Day we caused them to make a general confession. On the following morning they went away, leaving us all their little possessions; and most of them declared publicly that they made us their heirs, knowing well that they were near their end. And, in fact, only a few days passed before we heard of the disaster which we had foreseen. These poor people fell into ambuscades of our Iroquois enemies. Some were killed on the spot; some were dragged into captivity; women and children were burned. A few made their escape, and spread dismay and panic everywhere. A week after, another band was overtaken by the same fate. Go where they

---

1 "Le iour de l'Annonciation, vingt-cinquiesme de Mars, vne armée d'Iroquois ayans marché prez de deux cents lieuës de païs, à trauers les glaces et les neiges, trauersans les montagnes et les forests pleines d'horreur, surprirent au commencement de la nuit le camp de nos Chrestiens, et en firent vne cruelle boucherie. Il sembloit que le Ciel conduisit toutes leurs demarches et qu'ils eurent vn Ange pour guide: car ils diuiserent leurs troupes auec tant de bon-heur, qu'ils trouuerent en moins de deux iours, toutes les bandes de nos Chrestiens qui estoient dispersées çà et là, esloignées les vnes des autres de six, sept et huit lieuës, cent personnes en vn lieu, en vn autre cinquante; et mesme il y auoit quelques familles solitaires, qui s'estoient escartées en des lieux moins connus et hors de tout chemin. Chose estrange! de tout ce monde dissipé, vn seul homme s'eschappa, qui vint nous en apporter les nouuelles."—Ragueneau, Relation des Hurons, 1650, 23, 24.

would, they met with slaughter on all sides. Famine pursued them, or they encountered an enemy more cruel than cruelty itself; and, to crown their misery, they heard that two great armies of Iroquois were on the way to exterminate them . . . Despair was universal." [Ragueneau, Relation des Hurons, 1650, 24.]

The Jesuits at St. Joseph knew not what course to take. The doom of their flock seemed inevitable. When dismay and despondency were at their height, two of the principal Huron chiefs came to the fort, and asked an interview with Ragueneau and his companions. They told them that the Indians had held a council the night before, and resolved to abandon the island. Some would disperse in the most remote and inaccessible forests; others would take refuge in a distant spot, apparently the Grand Manitoulin Island; others would try to reach the Andastes; and others would seek safety in adoption and incorporation with the Iroquois themselves.

"Take courage, brother," continued one of the chiefs, addressing Ragueneau. "You can save us, if you will but resolve on a bold step. Choose a place where you can gather us together, and prevent this dispersion of our people. Turn your eyes towards Quebec, and transport thither what is left of this ruined country. Do not wait till war and famine have destroyed us to the last man. We are in your hands. Death has taken from you more than ten thousand of us. If you wait longer, not one will remain alive; and then you will be sorry that you did not save those whom you might have snatched from danger, and who showed you the means of doing so. If you do as we wish, we will form a church under the protection of the fort at Quebec. Our faith will not be extinguished. The examples of the French and the Algonquins will encourage us in our duty, and their charity will relieve some of our misery. At least, we shall sometimes find a morsel of bread for our children, who so long have had nothing but bitter roots and acorns to keep them alive."

[Ragueneau, Relation des Hurons, 1650, 25. It appears from the MS. Journal des Supérieurs des Jésuites, that a plan of bringing the remnant of the Hurons to Quebec was discussed and approved by Lalemant and his associates, in a council held by them at that place in April.]

The Jesuits were deeply moved. They consulted together again and again, and prayed in turn during forty hours without ceasing, that their minds might be enlightened. At length they resolved to grant the petition of the two chiefs, and save the poor remnant of the Hurons, by leading them to an asylum where there was at least a hope of safety. Their resolution once taken, they pushed their preparations with all speed, lest the Iroquois might learn their purpose, and lie in wait to cut them off. Canoes were made ready, and on the tenth of June they began the voyage, with all their French followers and about three hundred Hurons. The Huron mission was abandoned.

"It was not without tears," writes the Father Superior, "that we left the country of our hopes and our hearts, where our brethren had gloriously shed their blood." [Compare Bressani, Relation Abrégée, 288.] The fleet of canoes held its melancholy way along the shores where two years before had been the seat of one of the chief savage communities of the continent, and where now all was a waste of death and desolation. Then they steered northward, along the eastern coast of the Georgian Bay, with its countless rocky islets; and everywhere they saw the traces of the Iroquois. When they reached Lake Nipissing, they found it deserted,—nothing remaining of the Algonquins who dwelt on its shore, except the ashes of their burnt wigwams. A little farther on, there was a fort built of trees, where the Iroquois who made this desolation had spent the winter; and a league or two below, there was another similar fort. The River Ottawa was a solitude. The Algonquins of Allumette Island and the shores adjacent had all been killed or driven away, never again to return. "When I came up this great river, only thirteen years ago," writes Ragueneau, "I found it bordered with Algonquin tribes, who knew no God, and, in their infidelity, thought themselves gods on earth; for they had all that they desired, abundance of fish and game, and a prosperous trade with allied nations: besides, they were the terror of their enemies. But since they have embraced the Faith and adored the cross of Christ, He has given them a heavy share in this cross, and made them a prey to misery, torture, and a cruel death. In a word, they are a people swept from the face of the earth. Our only consolation is, that, as they died Christians, they have a part in the inheritance of the true children of God, who scourgeth every one whom He receiveth." [Ragueneau, Relation des Hurons, 1650, 27. These Algonquins of the Ottawa, though broken and dispersed, were not destroyed, as Ragueneau supposes.]

As the voyagers descended the river, they had a serious alarm. Their scouts came in, and reported that they had found fresh footprints of men in the forest. These proved, however, to be the tracks, not of enemies, but of friends. In the preceding autumn Bressani had gone down to the French settlements with about twenty Hurons, and was now returning with them, and twice their number of armed Frenchmen, for the defence of the mission. His scouts had also been alarmed by discovering the footprints of Ragueneau's Indians; and for some time the two parties stood on their guard, each taking the other for an enemy. When at length they discovered their mistake, they met with embraces and rejoicing. Bressani and his Frenchmen had come too late. All was over with the Hurons and the Huron mission; and, as it was useless to go farther, they joined Ragueneau's party, and retraced their course for the settlements.

A day or two before, they had had a sharp taste of the mettle of the enemy. Ten Iroquois warriors had spent the winter in a little fort of felled trees on the borders of the Ottawa, hunting for subsistence, and waiting to waylay some passing canoe of Hurons, Algonquins, or Frenchmen. Bressani's party outnumbered them six to one; but they resolved that it should not pass without a token of their presence. Late on a dark night, the French and Hurons lay encamped in the forest, sleeping about their fires. They had set guards: but these, it seems, were drowsy or negligent; for the ten Iroquois, watching their time, approached with the stealth of lynxes, and glided like shadows into the midst of the camp, where, by the dull glow of the smouldering fires, they could distinguish the recumbent figures of their victims. Suddenly they screeched the war-whoop, and struck like lightning with their hatchets among the sleepers. Seven were killed before the rest could spring to their weapons. Bressani leaped up, and received on the instant three arrow-wounds in the head. The Iroquois were surrounded, and a desperate fight ensued in the dark. Six of them were killed on the spot, and two made prisoners; while the remaining two, breaking through the crowd, bounded out of the camp and escaped in the forest.

The united parties soon after reached Montreal; but the Hurons refused to remain in a spot so exposed to the Iroquois. Accordingly, they all descended the St. Lawrence, and at length, on the twenty-eighth of July, reached Quebec. Here the Ursulines, the hospital nuns, and the inhabitants taxed their resources to the utmost to provide food and shelter for the exiled Hurons. Their good will exceeded their power; for food was scarce at Quebec, and the Jesuits themselves had to bear the chief burden of keeping the sufferers alive. [Compare Juchereau, Histoire de l'Hôtel-Dieu, 79, 80.]

But, if famine was an evil, the Iroquois were a far greater one; for, while the western nations of their confederacy were engrossed with the destruction of the Hurons, the Mohawks kept up incessant attacks on the Algonquins and the French. A party of Christian Indians, chiefly from Sillery, planned a stroke of retaliation, and set out for the Mohawk country, marching cautiously and sending forward scouts to scour the forest. One of these, a Huron, suddenly fell in with a large Iroquois war party, and, seeing that he could not escape, formed on the instant a villanous plan to save himself. He ran towards the enemy, crying out, that he had long been looking for them and was delighted to see them; that his nation, the Hurons, had come to an end; and that henceforth his country was the country of the Iroquois, where so many of his kinsmen and friends had been adopted. He had come, he declared, with no other thought than that of joining them, and turning Iroquois, as they had done. The Iroquois demanded if he had come alone. He answered, "No," and said, that, in order to accomplish his purpose, he had joined an Algonquin war-party who were in the woods not far off. The Iroquois, in great delight, demanded to be shown where they were. This Judas, as the Jesuits call him, at once complied; and the Algonquins were surprised by a sudden onset, and routed with severe loss. The treacherous Huron was well treated by the Iroquois, who adopted him into their nation. Not long after, he came to Canada, and, with a view, as it was thought, to some further treachery, rejoined the French. A sharp cross-questioning put him to confusion, and he presently confessed his guilt. He was sentenced to death; and the sentence was executed by one of his own countrymen, who split his head with a hatchet. [Ragueneau, Relation, 1650, 30.]

In the course of the summer, the French at Three Rivers became aware that a band of Iroquois was prowling in the neighborhood, and sixty men went out to meet them. Far from retreating, the Iroquois, who were about twenty-five in number, got out of their canoes, and took post, waist-deep in mud and water, among the tall rushes at the margin of the river. Here they fought stubbornly, and kept all the Frenchmen at bay. At length, finding themselves hard pressed, they entered their canoes again, and paddled off. The French rowed after them, and soon became separated in the chase; whereupon the Iroquois turned, and made desperate fight with the foremost, retreating again as soon as the others came up. This they repeated several times, and then made their escape, after killing a number of the best French soldiers. Their leader in this affair was a famous half-breed, known as the Flemish Bastard, who is styled by Ragueneau "an abomination of sin, and a monster produced between a heretic Dutch father and a pagan mother."

In the forests far north of Three Rivers dwelt the tribe called the Atticamegues, or Nation of the White Fish. From their remote position, and the difficult nature of the intervening country, they thought themselves safe; but a band of Iroquois, marching on snow-shoes a distance of twenty days' journey northward from the St. Lawrence, fell upon one of their camps in the winter, and made a general butchery of the inmates. The tribe, however, still held its ground for a time, and, being all good Catholics, gave their missionary, Father Buteux, an urgent invitation to visit them in their own country. Buteux, who had long been stationed at Three Rivers, was in ill health, and for years had rarely been free from some form of bodily suffering. Nevertheless, he acceded to their request, and, before the opening of spring, made a remarkable journey on snow-shoes into the depths of this frozen wilderness. [Iournal du Pere Iacques Buteux du Voyage qu'il a fait pour la Mission des Attikamegues. See Relation, 1651, 15.] In the year following, he repeated the undertaking. With him were a large party of Atticamegues, and several Frenchmen. Game was exceedingly scarce, and they were forced by hunger to separate, a Huron convert and a Frenchman named Fontarabie remaining with the missionary. The snows had melted, and all the streams were swollen. The three travellers, in a small birch canoe, pushed their way up a turbulent river, where falls and rapids were so numerous, that many times daily they were forced to carry their bark vessel and their baggage through forests and thickets and over rocks and precipices. On the tenth of May, they made two such portages, and soon after, reaching a third fall, again lifted their canoe from the water. They toiled through the naked forest, among the wet, black trees, over tangled roots, green, spongy mosses, mouldering leaves, and rotten, prostrate trunks, while the cataract foamed amidst the rocks hard by. The Indian led the way with the canoe on his head, while Buteux and the other Frenchman followed with the baggage. Suddenly they were set upon by a troop of Iroquois, who had crouched behind thickets, rocks, and fallen trees, to waylay them. The Huron was captured before he had time to fly. Buteux and the Frenchman tried to escape, but were instantly shot down, the Jesuit receiving two balls in the breast. The Iroquois rushed upon them, mangled their bodies with tomahawks and swords, stripped them, and then flung them into the torrent. [Ragueneau, Relation, 1652, 2, 3.]

CHAPTER XXXII.

1650-1866.

THE LAST OF THE HURONS.

FATE OF THE VANQUISHED.—THE REFUGEES OF ST. JEAN BAPTISTE AND ST. MICHEL.—THE TOBACCO NATION AND ITS WANDERINGS.—THE MODERN WYANDOTS.—THE BITER BIT.—THE HURONS AT QUEBEC.—NOTRE-DAME DE LORETTE.

Iroquois bullets and tomahawks had killed the Hurons by hundreds, but famine and disease had killed incomparably more. The miseries of the starving crowd on Isle St. Joseph had been shared in an equal degree by smaller bands, who had wintered in remote and secret retreats of the wilderness. Of those who survived that season of death, many were so weakened that they could not endure the hardships of a wandering life, which was new to them. The Hurons lived by agriculture; their fields and crops were destroyed, and they were so hunted from place to place that they could rarely till the soil. Game was very scarce; and, without agriculture, the country could support only a scanty and scattered population like that which maintained a struggling existence in the wilderness of the lower St. Lawrence. The mortality among the exiles was prodigious.

It is a matter of some interest to trace the fortunes of the shattered fragments of a nation once prosperous, and, in its own eyes and those of its neighbors, powerful and great. None were left alive within their ancient domain. Some had sought refuge among the Neutrals and the Eries, and shared the disasters which soon overwhelmed those tribes; others succeeded in reaching the Andastes; while the inhabitants of two towns, St. Michel and St. Jean Baptiste, had recourse to an expedient which seems equally strange and desperate, but which was in accordance with Indian practices. They contrived to open a communication with the Seneca Nation of the Iroquois, and promised to change their nationality and turn Senecas as the price of their lives. The victors accepted the proposal; and the inhabitants of these two towns, joined by a few other Hurons, migrated in a body to the Seneca country. They were not distributed among different villages, but were allowed to form a town by themselves, where they were afterwards joined by some prisoners of the Neutral Nation. They identified themselves with the Iroquois in all but religion,—holding so fast to their faith, that, eighteen years after, a Jesuit missionary found that many of them were still good Catholics.

[Compare Relation, 1651, 4; 1660, 14, 28; and 1670, 69. The Huron town among the Senecas was called Gandougaraé. Father Fremin was here in 1668, and gives an account of his visit in the Relation of 1670.]

The division of the Hurons called the Tobacco Nation, favored by their isolated position among mountains, had held their ground longer than the rest; but at length they, too, were compelled to fly, together with such other Hurons as had taken refuge with them. They made their way northward, and settled on the Island of Michilimackinac, where they were joined by the Ottawas, who, with other Algonquins, had been driven by fear of the Iroquois from the western shores of Lake Huron and the banks of the River Ottawa. At Michilimackinac the Hurons and their allies were again attacked by the Iroquois, and, after remaining several years, they made another remove, and took possession of the islands at the mouth of the Green Bay of Lake Michigan. Even here their old enemy did not leave them in peace; whereupon they fortified themselves on the main-land, and afterwards migrated southward and westward. This brought them in contact with the Illinois, an Algonquin people, at that time very numerous, but who, like many other tribes at this epoch, were doomed to a rapid diminution from wars with other savage nations. Continuing their migration westward, the Hurons and Ottawas reached the Mississippi, where they fell in with the Sioux. They soon quarrelled with those fierce children of the prairie, who drove them from their country. They retreated to the south-western extremity of Lake Superior, and settled on Point Saint Esprit, or Shagwamigon Point, near the Islands of the Twelve Apostles. As the Sioux continued to harass them, they left this place about the year 1671, and returned to Michilimackinac, where they settled, not on the island, but on the neighboring Point St. Ignace, now Graham's Point, on the north side of the strait. The greater part of them afterwards removed thence to Detroit and Sandusky, where they lived under the name of Wyandots until within the present century, maintaining a marked influence over the surrounding Algonquins. They bore an active part, on the side of the French, in the war which ended in the reduction of Canada; and they were the most formidable enemies of the English in the Indian war under Pontiac. [See "History of the Conspiracy of Pontiac."] The government of the United States at length removed them to reserves on the western frontier, where a remnant of them may still be found. Thus it appears that the Wyandots, whose name is so conspicuous in the history of our border wars, are descendants of the ancient Hurons, and chiefly of that portion of them called the Tobacco Nation.

[The migrations of this band of the Hurons may be traced by detached passages and incidental remarks in the Relations of 1654, 1660, 1667, 1670, 1671, and 1672. Nicolas Perrot, in his chapter, Deffaitte et Füitte des Hurons chassés de leur Pays, and in the chapter following, gives a long and rather confused account of their movements and adventures. See also La Poterie, Histoire de l'Amérique Septentrionale, II. 51-56. According to the Relation of 1670, the Hurons, when living at Shagwamigon Point, numbered about fifteen hundred souls.]

When Ragueneau and his party left Isle St. Joseph for Quebec, the greater number of the Hurons chose to remain. They took possession of the stone fort which the French had abandoned, and where, with reasonable vigilance, they could maintain themselves against attack. In the succeeding autumn a small Iroquois war-party had the audacity to cross over to the island, and build a fort of felled trees in the woods. The Hurons attacked them; but the invaders made so fierce a defence, that they kept their assailants at bay, and at length retreated with little or no loss. Soon after, a much larger band of Onondaga Iroquois, approaching undiscovered, built a fort on the main-land, opposite the island, but concealed from sight in the forest. Here they waited to waylay any party of Hurons who might venture ashore. A Huron war chief, named Étienne Annaotaha, whose life is described as a succession of conflicts and adventures, and who is said to have been always in luck, landed with a few companions, and fell into an ambuscade of the Iroquois. He prepared to defend himself, when they called out to him, that they came not as enemies, but as friends, and that they brought wampum-belts and presents to persuade the Hurons to forget the past, go back with them to their country, become their adopted countrymen, and live with them as one nation. Étienne suspected treachery, but concealed his distrust, and advanced towards the Iroquois with an air of the utmost confidence. They received him with open arms, and pressed him to accept their invitation; but he replied, that there were older and wiser men among the Hurons, whose counsels all the people followed, and that they ought to lay the proposal before them. He proceeded to advise them to keep him as a hostage, and send over his companions, with some of their chiefs, to open the negotiation. His apparent frankness completely deceived them; and they insisted that he himself should go to the Huron village, while his companions remained as hostages. He set out accordingly with three of the principal Iroquois.

When he reached the village, he gave the whoop of one who brings good tidings, and proclaimed with a loud voice that the hearts of their enemies had changed, that the Iroquois would become their countrymen and brothers, and that they should exchange their miseries for a life of peace and plenty in a fertile and prosperous land. The whole Huron population, full of joyful excitement, crowded about him and the three envoys, who were conducted to the principal lodge, and feasted on the best that the village could supply. Étienne seized the opportunity to take aside four or five of the principal chiefs, and secretly tell them his suspicions that the Iroquois were plotting to compass their destruction under cover of overtures of peace; and he proposed that they should meet treachery with treachery. He then explained his plan, which was highly approved by his auditors, who begged him to charge himself with the execution of it. Étienne now caused criers to proclaim through the village that every one should get ready to emigrate in a few days to the country of their new friends. The squaws began their preparations at once, and all was bustle and alacrity; for the Hurons themselves were no less deceived than were the Iroquois envoys.

During one or two succeeding days, many messages and visits passed between the Hurons and the Iroquois, whose confidence was such, that thirty-seven of their best warriors at length came over in a body to the Huron village. Étienne's time had come. He and the chiefs who were in the secret gave the word to the Huron warriors, who, at a signal, raised the war-whoop, rushed upon their visitors, and cut them to pieces. One of them, who lingered for a time, owned before he died that Étienne's suspicions were just, and that they had designed nothing less than the massacre or capture of all the Hurons. Three of the Iroquois, immediately before the slaughter began, had received from Étienne a warning of their danger in time to make their escape. The year before, he had been captured, with Brébeuf and Lalemant, at the town of St. Louis, and had owed his life to these three warriors, to whom he now paid back the debt of gratitude. They carried tidings of what had befallen to their countrymen on the main-land, who, aghast at the catastrophe, fled homeward in a panic.

[Ragueneau, Relation des Hurons, 1651, 5, 6. Le Mercier, in the Relation of 1654, preserves the speech of a Huron chief, in which he speaks of this affair, and adds some particulars not mentioned by Ragueneau. He gives thirty-four as the number killed.]

Here was a sweet morsel of vengeance. The miseries of the Hurons were lighted up with a brief gleam of joy; but it behooved them to make a timely retreat from their island before the Iroquois came to exact a bloody retribution. Towards spring, while the lake was still frozen, many of them escaped on the ice, while another party afterwards followed in canoes. A few, who had neither strength to walk nor canoes to transport them, perforce remained behind, and were soon massacred by the Iroquois. The fugitives directed their course to the Grand Manitoulin Island, where they remained for a short time, and then, to the number of about four hundred, descended the Ottawa, and rejoined their countrymen who had gone to Quebec the year before.

These united parties, joined from time to time by a few other fugitives, formed a settlement on land belonging to the Jesuits, near the south-western extremity of the Isle of Orleans, immediately below Quebec. Here the Jesuits built a fort, like that on Isle St. Joseph, with a chapel, and a small house for the missionaries, while the bark dwellings of the Hurons were clustered around the protecting ramparts.[1] Tools and seeds were given them, and they were encouraged to cultivate the soil. Gradually they rallied from their dejection, and the mission settlement was beginning to wear an appearance of thrift, when, in 1656, the Iroquois made a descent upon them, and carried off a large number of captives, under the very cannon of Quebec; the French not daring to fire upon the invaders, lest they should take revenge upon the Jesuits who were at that time in their country. This calamity was, four years after, followed by another, when the best of the Huron warriors, including their leader, the crafty and valiant Étienne Annaotaha, were slain, fighting side by side with the French, in the desperate conflict of the Long Sault. [Relation, 1660 (anonymous), 14.]

The attenuated colony, replenished by some straggling bands of the same nation, and still numbering several hundred persons, was removed to Quebec after the inroad in 1656, and lodged in a square inclosure of palisades close to the fort. [In a plan of Quebec of 1660, the "Fort des Hurons" is laid down on a spot adjoining the north side of the present Place d'Armes.] Here they remained about ten years, when, the danger of the times having diminished, they were again removed to a place called Notre-Dame de Foy, now Ste. Foi, three or four miles west of Quebec. Six years after, when the soil was impoverished and the wood in the neighborhood exhausted, they again changed their abode, and, under the auspices of the Jesuits, who owned the land, settled at Old Lorette, nine miles from Quebec.

Chaumonot was at this time their missionary. It may be remembered that he had professed special devotion to Our Lady of Loretto, who, in his boyhood, had cured him, as he believed, of a distressing malady. [See ante, chapter 9 (p. 102).] He had always cherished the idea of building a chapel in honor of her in Canada, after the model of the Holy House of Loretto,—which, as all the world knows, is the house wherein Saint Joseph dwelt with

---

1   The site of the fort was the estate now known as "La Terre du Fort," near the landing of the steam ferry. In 1856, Mr. N. H. Bowen, a resident near the spot, in making some excavations, found a solid stone wall five feet thick, which, there can be little doubt, was that of the work in question. This wall was originally crowned with palisades. See Bowen, Historical Sketch of the Isle of Orleans, 25.

his virgin spouse, and which angels bore through the air from the Holy Land to Italy, where it remains an object of pilgrimage to this day. Chaumonot opened his plan to his brother Jesuits, who were delighted with it, and the chapel was begun at once, not without the intervention of miracle to aid in raising the necessary funds. It was built of brick, like its original, of which it was an exact facsimile; and it stood in the centre of a quadrangle, the four sides of which were formed by the bark dwellings of the Hurons, ranged with perfect order in straight lines. Hither came many pilgrims from Quebec and more distant settlements, and here Our Lady granted to her suppliants, says Chaumonot, many miraculous favors, insomuch that "it would require an entire book to describe them all."

["Les grâces qu'on y obtient par l'entremise de la Mère de Dieu vont jusqu'au miracle. Comme il faudroit composer un livre entier pour décrire toutes ces faveurs extraordinaires, je n'en rapporterai que deux, ayant été témoin oculaire de l'une et propre sujet de l'autre."—Vie, 95.

The removal from Notre-Dame de Foy took place at the end of 1673, and the chapel was finished in the following year. Compare Vie de Chaumonot with Dablon, Relation, 1672-73, p. 21; and Ibid., Relation 1673-79, p. 259.]

But the Hurons were not destined to remain permanently even here; for, before the end of the century, they removed to a place four miles distant, now called New Lorette, or Indian Lorette. It was a wild spot, covered with the primitive forest, and seamed by a deep and tortuous ravine, where the St. Charles foams, white as a snow-drift, over the black ledges, and where the sunlight struggles through matted boughs of the pine and fir, to bask for brief moments on the mossy rocks or flash on the hurrying waters. On a plateau beside the torrent, another chapel was built to Our Lady, and another Huron town sprang up; and here, to this day, the tourist finds the remnant of a lost people, harmless weavers of baskets and sewers of moccasins, the Huron blood fast bleaching out of them, as, with every generation, they mingle and fade away in the French population around.

[An interesting account of a visit to Indian Lorette in 1721 will be found in the Journal Historique of Charlevoix. Kalm, in his Travels in North America, describes its condition in 1749. See also Le Beau, Aventures, I. 103; who, however, can hardly be regarded as an authority.]

CHAPTER XXXIII.

1650-1670.

THE DESTROYERS.

IROQUOIS AMBITION.—ITS VICTIMS.—THE FATE OF THE NEUTRALS.—THE FATE OF THE ERIES.—THE WAR WITH THE ANDASTES.—SUPREMACY OF THE IROQUOIS.

It was well for the European colonies, above all for those of England, that the wisdom of the Iroquois was but the wisdom of savages. Their sagacity is past denying; it showed itself in many ways; but it was not equal to a comprehension of their own situation and that of their race. Could they have read their destiny, and curbed their mad ambition, they might have leagued with themselves four great communities of kindred lineage, to resist the encroachments of civilization, and oppose a barrier of fire to the spread of the young colonies of the East. But their organization and their intelligence were merely the instruments of a blind frenzy, which impelled them to destroy those whom they might have made their allies in a common cause.

Of the four kindred communities, two at least, the Hurons and the Neutrals, were probably superior in numbers to the Iroquois. Either one of these, with union and leadership, could have held its ground against them, and the two united could easily have crippled them beyond the power of doing mischief. But these so-called nations were mere aggregations of villages and families, with nothing that deserved to be called a government. They were very liable to panics, because the part attacked by an enemy could never rely with confidence on prompt succor from the rest; and when once broken, they could not be rallied, because they had no centre around which to gather. The Iroquois, on the other hand, had an organization with which the ideas and habits of several generations were interwoven, and they had also sagacious leaders for peace and war. They discussed all questions of policy with the coolest deliberation, and knew how to turn to profit even imperfections in their plan of government which seemed to promise only weakness and discord. Thus, any nation, or any large town, of their confederacy, could make a separate war or a separate peace with a foreign nation, or any part of it. Some member of the league, as, for example, the Cayugas, would make a covenant of friendship with the enemy, and, while the infatuated victims were thus lulled into a delusive security, the war-parties of the other nations, often joined by the Cayuga warriors, would overwhelm them by a sudden onset. But it was not by their craft, nor by their organization,— which for military purposes was wretchedly feeble,—that this handful of savages gained a bloody supremacy. They carried all before them, because they were animated throughout, as one man, by the same audacious pride and insatiable rage for conquest. Like other Indians, they waged war on a plan altogether democratic,—that is, each man fought or not, as he saw fit; and they owed their unity and vigor of action to the homicidal frenzy that urged them all alike.

The Neutral Nation had taken no part, on either side, in the war of extermination against the Hurons; and their towns were sanctuaries where either of the contending parties might take asylum. On the other hand, they made fierce war on their western neighbors, and, a few years before, destroyed, with atrocious cruelties, a large fortified town of the Nation of Fire.[1] Their turn was now come, and their victims found fit avengers; for no sooner were the Hurons

---

1   "Last summer," writes Lalemant in 1643, "two thousand warriors of the Neutral Nation attacked a town of the Nation of Fire, well fortified with a palisade, and defended by nine hundred warriors. They took it after a siege of ten days; killed many on the spot; and made eight hundred prisoners, men, women, and children. After burning seventy of the best warriors, they put out the eyes of the old men, and cut away their lips, and then left them to drag out a miserable existence. Behold the scourge that is depopulating all this country!"—Relation des Hurons, 1644, 98.

broken up and dispersed, than the Iroquois, without waiting to take breath, turned their fury on the Neutrals. At the end of the autumn of 1650, they assaulted and took one of their chief towns, said to have contained at the time more than sixteen hundred men, besides women and children; and early in the following spring, they took another town. The slaughter was prodigious, and the victors drove back troops of captives for butchery or adoption. It was the death-blow of the Neutrals. They abandoned their corn-fields and villages in the wildest terror, and dispersed themselves abroad in forests, which could not yield sustenance to such a multitude. They perished by thousands, and from that time forth the nation ceased to exist.[1]

During two or three succeeding years, the Iroquois contented themselves with harassing the French and Algonquins; but in 1653 they made treaties of peace, each of the five nations for itself, and the colonists and their red allies had an interval of rest. In the following May, an Onondaga orator, on a peace visit to Montreal, said, in a speech to the Governor, "Our young men will no more fight the French; but they are too warlike to stay at home, and this summer we shall invade the country of the Eries. The earth trembles and quakes in that quarter; but here all remains calm." [Le Mercier, Relation, 1654, 9.] Early in the autumn, Father Le Moyne,

---

The Assistaeronnons, Atsistachonnons, Mascoutins, or Nation of Fire (more correctly, perhaps, Nation of the Prairie), were a very numerous Algonquin people of the West, speaking the same language as the Sacs and Foxes. In the map of Sanson, they are placed in the southern part of Michigan; and according to the Relation of 1658, they had thirty towns. They were a stationary, and in some measure an agricultural people. They fled before their enemies to the neighborhood of Fox River in Wisconsin, where they long remained. Frequent mention of them will be found in the later Relations, and in contemporary documents. They are now extinct as a tribe.

1   Ragueneau, Relation, 1651, 4. In the unpublished journal kept by the Superior of the Jesuits at Quebec, it is said, under date of April, 1651, that news had just come from Montreal, that, in the preceding autumn, fifteen hundred Iroquois had taken a Neutral town; that the Neutrals had afterwards attacked them, and killed two hundred of their warriors; and that twelve hundred Iroquois had again invaded the Neutral country to take their revenge. Lafitau, Mœurs des Sauvaqes, II. 176, gives, on the authority of Father Julien Garnier, a singular and improbable account of the origin of the war.

An old chief, named Kenjockety, who claimed descent from an adopted prisoner of the Neutral Nation, was recently living among the Senecas of Western New York.

who had taken advantage of the peace to go on a mission to the Onondagas, returned with the tidings that the Iroquois were all on fire with this new enterprise, and were about to march against the Eries with eighteen hundred warriors. [Le Mercier, Relation, 1654, 10. Le Moyne, in his interesting journal of his mission, repeatedly alludes to their preparations.]

The occasion of this new war is said to have been as follows. The Eries, who it will be remembered dwelt on the south of the lake named after them, had made a treaty of peace with the Senecas, and in the preceding year had sent a deputation of thirty of their principal men to confirm it. While they were in the great Seneca town, it happened that one of that nation was killed in a casual quarrel with an Erie; whereupon his countrymen rose in a fury, and murdered the thirty deputies. Then ensued a brisk war of reprisals, in which not only the Senecas, but the other Iroquois nations, took part. The Eries captured a famous Onondaga chief, and were about to burn him, when he succeeded in convincing them of the wisdom of a course of conciliation; and they resolved to give him to the sister of one of the murdered deputies, to take the place of her lost brother. The sister, by Indian law, had it in her choice to receive him with a fraternal embrace or to burn him; but, though she was absent at the time, no one doubted that she would choose the gentler alternative. Accordingly, he was clothed in gay attire, and all the town fell to feasting in honor of his adoption. In the midst of the festivity, the sister returned. To the amazement of the Erie chiefs, she rejected with indignation their proffer of a new brother, declared that she would be revenged for her loss, and insisted that the prisoner should forthwith be burned. The chiefs remonstrated in vain, representing the danger in which such a procedure would involve the nation: the female fury was inexorable; and the unfortunate prisoner, stripped of his festal robes, was bound to the stake, and put to death. [De Quen, Relation, 1656, 30.] He warned his tormentors with his last breath, that they were burning not only him, but the whole Erie nation; since his countrymen would take a fiery vengeance for his fate. His words proved true; for no sooner was his story spread abroad among the Iroquois, than the confederacy resounded with war-songs from end to end, and the warriors took the field under their two great war-chiefs. Notwithstanding Le Moyne's report, their number, according to the Iroquois account, did not exceed twelve hundred.

[This was their statement to Chaumonot and Dablon, at Onondaga, in November of this year. They added, that the number of the Eries was between three and four thousand, (Journal des PP. Chaumonot et Dablon, in Relation, 1656, 18.) In the narrative of De Quen (Ibid., 30, 31), based, of course, on Iroquois reports, the Iroquois force is also set down at twelve hundred, but that of the Eries is reduced to between two and three thousand warriors. Even this may safely be taken as an exaggeration.

Though the Eries had no fire-arms, they used poisoned arrows with great effect, discharging them, it is said, with surprising rapidity.]

They embarked in canoes on the lake. At their approach the Eries fell back, withdrawing into the forests towards the west, till they were gathered into one body, when, fortifying themselves with palisades and felled trees, they awaited the approach of the invaders. By the lowest estimate, the Eries numbered two thousand warriors, besides women and children. But this is the report of the Iroquois, who were naturally disposed to exaggerate the force of their enemies.

They approached the Erie fort, and two of their chiefs, dressed like Frenchmen, advanced and called on those within to surrender. One of them had lately been baptized by Le Moyne; and he shouted to the Eries, that, if they did not yield in time, they were all dead men, for the Master of Life was on the side of the Iroquois. The Eries answered with yells of derision. "Who is this master of your lives?" they cried; "our hatchets and our right arms are the masters of ours." The Iroquois rushed to the assault, but were met with a shower of poisoned arrows, which killed and wounded many of them, and drove the rest back. They waited awhile, and then attacked again with unabated mettle. This time, they carried their bark canoes over their heads like huge shields, to protect them from the storm of arrows; then planting them upright, and mounting them by the cross-bars like ladders, scaled the barricade with such impetuous fury that the Eries were thrown into a panic. Those escaped who could; but the butchery was frightful, and from that day the Eries as a nation were no more. The victors paid dear for their conquest. Their losses were so heavy that they were forced to remain for two months in the Erie country, to bury their dead and nurse their wounded.

[De Quen, Relation, 1656, 31. The Iroquois, it seems, afterwards made other expeditions, to finish their work. At least, they told Chaumonot and Dablon, in the autumn of this year, that they meant to do so in the following spring.

It seems, that, before attacking the great fort of the Eries, the Iroquois had made a promise to worship the new God of the French, if He would give them the victory. This promise, and the success which followed, proved of great advantage to the mission.

Various traditions are extant among the modern remnant of the Iroquois concerning the war with the Eries. They agree in little beyond the fact of the existence and destruction of that people. Indeed, Indian traditions are very rarely of any value as historical evidence. One of these stories, told me some years ago by a very intelligent Iroquois of the Cayuga Nation, is a striking illustration of Iroquois ferocity. It represents, that, the night after the great battle, the forest was lighted up with more than a thousand fires, at each of which an Erie was burning alive. It differs from the historical accounts in making the Eries the aggressors.]

One enemy of their own race remained,—the Andastes. This nation appears to have been inferior in numbers to either the Hurons, the Neutrals, or the Eries; but they cost their assailants more trouble than all these united. The Mohawks seem at first to have borne the brunt of the Andaste war; and, between the years 1650 and 1660, they were so roughly handled by these stubborn adversaries, that they were reduced from the height of audacious insolence to the depths of dejection.[1] The remaining four nations of the Iroquois league now took up the quarrel, and fared scarcely better than the Mohawks. In the spring of 1662, eight hundred of their warriors set out for the Andaste country, to strike a decisive blow; but when they reached the great town of their enemies, they saw that they had received both aid and counsel from the neighboring Swedish colonists. The town was fortified by a double palisade, flanked by two bastions, on which, it is said, several small

---

1   Relation, 1660, 6 (anonymous).

      The Mohawks also suffered great reverses about this time at the hands of their Algonquin neighbors, the Mohicans.

pieces of cannon were mounted. Clearly, it was not to be carried by assault, as the invaders had promised themselves. Their only hope was in treachery; and, accordingly, twenty-five of their warriors gained entrance, on pretence of settling the terms of a peace. Here, again, ensued a grievous disappointment; for the Andastes seized them all, built high scaffolds visible from without, and tortured them to death in sight of their countrymen, who thereupon decamped in miserable discomfiture. [Lalemant, Relation, 1663, 10.]

The Senecas, by far the most numerous of the five Iroquois nations, now found themselves attacked in turn,—and this, too, at a time when they were full of despondency at the ravages of the small-pox. The French reaped a profit from their misfortunes; for the disheartened savages made them overtures of peace, and begged that they would settle in their country, teach them to fortify their towns, supply them with arms and ammunition, and bring "black-robes" to show them the road to Heaven. [Lalemant, Relation, 1664, 33.]

The Andaste war became a war of inroads and skirmishes, under which the weaker party gradually wasted away, though it sometimes won laurels at the expense of its adversary. Thus, in 1672, a party of twenty Senecas and forty Cayugas went against the Andastes. They were at a considerable distance the one from the other, the Cayugas being in advance, when the Senecas were set upon by about sixty young Andastes, of the class known as "Burnt-Knives," or "Soft-Metals," because as yet they had taken no scalps. Indeed, they are described as mere boys, fifteen or sixteen years old. They killed one of the Senecas, captured another, and put the rest to flight; after which, flushed with their victory, they attacked the Cayugas with the utmost fury, and routed them completely, killing eight of them, and wounding twice that number, who, as is reported by the Jesuit then in the Cayuga towns, came home half dead with gashes of knives and hatchets. [Dablon, Relation, 1672, 24.] "May God preserve the Andastes," exclaims the Father, "and prosper their arms, that the Iroquois may be humbled, and we and our missions left in peace!" "None but they," he elsewhere adds, "can curb the pride of the Iroquois." The only strength of the Andastes, however, was in their courage: for at this time they were reduced to three hundred fighting men; and about the year 1675 they were finally overborne by the Senecas. [État Présent des Missions, in Relations Inédites, II. 44. Relation, 1676, 2. This is one of the Relations printed by Mr. Lenox.] Yet they were not wholly destroyed; for a remnant of this valiant people continued to subsist, under the name of Conestogas, for nearly a century, until, in 1763, they were butchered, as already mentioned, by the white ruffians known as the "Paxton Boys." ["History of the Conspiracy of Pontiac," Chap. XXIV. Compare Shea, in Historical Magazine, II. 297.]

The bloody triumphs of the Iroquois were complete. They had "made a solitude, and called it peace." All the surrounding nations of their own lineage were conquered and broken up, while neighboring Algonquin tribes were suffered to exist only on condition of paying a yearly tribute of wampum. The confederacy remained a wedge thrust between the growing colonies of France and England.

But what was the state of the conquerors? Their triumphs had cost them dear. As early as the year 1660, a writer, evidently well-informed, reports that their entire force had been reduced to twenty-two hundred warriors, while of these not more than twelve hundred were of the true Iroquois stock. The rest was a medley of adopted prisoners,—Hurons, Neutrals, Eries, and Indians of various Algonquin tribes.[1] Still their aggressive spirit was unsubdued. These incorrigible warriors pushed their murderous raids to Hudson's Bay, Lake Superior, the Mississippi, and the Tennessee; they were the tyrants of all the intervening wilderness; and they remained, for more than half a century, a terror and a scourge to the afflicted colonists of New France.

---

1   Relation, 1660, 6, 7 (anonymous). Le Jeune says, "Their victories have so depopulated their towns, that there are more foreigners in them than natives. At Onondaga there are Indians of seven different nations permanently established; and, among the Senecas, of no less than eleven." (Relation, 1657, 34.) These were either adopted prisoners, or Indians who had voluntarily joined the Iroquois to save themselves from their hostility. They took no part in councils, but were expected to join war-parties, though they were usually excused from fighting against their former countrymen. The condition of female prisoners was little better than that of slaves, and those to whom they were assigned often killed them on the slightest pique.

CHAPTER XXXIV.

THE END.

FAILURE OF THE JESUITS.—WHAT THEIR SUCCESS WOULD HAVE INVOLVED.—FUTURE OF THE MISSION.

With the fall of the Hurons, fell the best hope of the Canadian mission. They, and the stable and populous communities around them, had been the rude material from which the Jesuit would have formed his Christian empire in the wilderness; but, one by one, these kindred peoples were uprooted and swept away, while the neighboring Algonquins, to whom they had been a bulwark, were involved with them in a common ruin. The land of promise was turned to a solitude and a desolation. There was still work in hand, it is true,—vast regions to explore, and countless heathens to snatch from perdition; but these, for the most part, were remote and scattered hordes, from whose conversion it was vain to look for the same solid and decisive results.

In a measure, the occupation of the Jesuits was gone. Some of them went home, "well resolved," writes the Father Superior, "to return to the combat at the first sound of the trumpet;"[1] while of those who remained, about twenty in number, several soon fell victims to famine, hardship, and the Iroquois. A few years more, and Canada ceased to be a mission; political and commercial interests gradually became ascendant, and the story of Jesuit propagandism was interwoven with her civil and military annals.

---

1   Lettre de Lalemant au R. P. Provincial (Relation, 1650, 48).

Here, then, closes this wild and bloody act of the great drama of New France; and now let the curtain fall, while we ponder its meaning.

The cause of the failure of the Jesuits is obvious. The guns and tomahawks of the Iroquois were the ruin of their hopes. Could they have curbed or converted those ferocious bands, it is little less than certain that their dream would have become a reality. Savages tamed—not civilized, for that was scarcely possible—would have been distributed in communities through the valleys of the Great Lakes and the Mississippi, ruled by priests in the interest of Catholicity and of France. Their habits of agriculture would have been developed, and their instincts of mutual slaughter repressed. The swift decline of the Indian population would have been arrested; and it would have been made, through the fur-trade, a source of prosperity to New France. Unmolested by Indian enemies, and fed by a rich commerce, she would have put forth a vigorous growth. True to her far-reaching and adventurous genius, she would have occupied the West with traders, settlers, and garrisons, and cut up the virgin wilderness into fiefs, while as yet the colonies of England were but a weak and broken line along the shore of the Atlantic; and when at last the great conflict came, England and Liberty would have been confronted, not by a depleted antagonist, still feeble from the exhaustion of a starved and persecuted infancy, but by an athletic champion of the principles of Richelieu and of Loyola.

Liberty may thank the Iroquois, that, by their insensate fury, the plans of her adversary were brought to nought, and a peril and a woe averted from her future. They ruined the trade which was the life-blood of New France; they stopped the current of her arteries, and made all her early years a misery and a terror. Not that they changed her destinies. The contest on this continent between Liberty and Absolutism was never doubtful; but the triumph of the one would have been dearly bought, and the downfall of the other incomplete. Populations formed in the ideas and habits of a feudal monarchy, and controlled by a hierarchy profoundly hostile to freedom of thought, would have remained a hindrance and a stumbling-block in the way of that majestic experiment of which America is the field.

The Jesuits saw their hopes struck down; and their faith, though not shaken, was sorely tried. The Providence of God seemed in their eyes dark and inexplicable; but, from the stand-point of Liberty, that Providence is clear as the sun at noon. Meanwhile let those who have prevailed yield due honor to the defeated. Their virtues shine amidst the rubbish of error, like diamonds and gold in the gravel of the torrent.

But now new scenes succeed, and other actors enter on the stage, a hardy and valiant band, moulded to endure and dare,—the Discoverers of the Great West.

BIBLIOBAZAAR

The essential book market!

Did you know that you can get any of our titles in large print?

Did you know that we have an ever-growing collection of books in many languages?

**Order online:
www.bibliobazaar.com**

Find all of your favorite classic books!

Stay up to date with the latest government reports!

At BiblioBazaar, we aim to make knowledge more accessible by making thousands of titles available to you- *quickly and affordably*.

Contact us:
BiblioBazaar
PO Box 21206
Charleston, SC 29413

Printed in the United States
204661BV00001B/18/A

9 781434 668103